SEED

Michael Edelson

Cover by Ksenia Kozhevnikova.

www.michaeledelson.net

Acknowledgements

This book would not have been possible without the help of a whole bunch of people, not all of whom I will remember to mention here. Thank you to my many test readers (Michael Ahrens, Polina Viro, Rebecca Glass, Angela Baker Galindo, Jim Crew, Joseph Michael Card and others) for their wonderful feedback and support. Thank you to Jake Norwood, who all but held me down and forced me to rewrite entire chapters just when I thought the book was finished—it is much improved as a result. Thank you to Betsy Winslow, who found so many typos and missing words that I thought she snuck into my house and put them in there herself. Thank you to Jason Yarn of Paradigm Agency, who believed in this project enough to represent me and thereby give me the confidence I needed to move forward. Thank you to Jennifer Nichols, who contacted me after publication and helped me correct some errors that slipped through. Thank you to my brilliant and talented cover artist, Ksenia Kozhevnikova, for all her hard work and patience. Thank you to my wife Judy, who supported me and believed in me enough to keep asking, "When can I quit my job already?" (Never!)

Most of all, thank you, dear reader, for choosing this book and making the hundreds of hours spent working on it worthwhile.

Chapter 1

Alex was killed at 11:43AM. Not quite lunchtime, but close enough. He was stepping out of his armored personnel carrier when a string of pops erupted from the crest of a nearby hill, accompanied by a cloud of dust raised by muzzle blasts. His MILES gear started to buzz, indicating a hit, and Alex lay down on the ground and waited for the end of the engagement. When it was over, only he and Private Haag were left by the disabled APC while the rest of their squad pursued the fleeing Blue Force soldiers into the nearby town.

"Turkey or Spaghetti and Meatballs?" Haag asked, fishing two MREs out of a box under the bench seat.

Alex frowned as he set his rifle down against the treads of the armored vehicle.

"Seriously?" he said. "That's all those assholes left us?"

"Sorry, Alex," Haag said. "I'll take whichever one you don't want." Alex felt sorry for him. Haag had enlisted at seventeen, and the Army was no place for a kid. Especially OPFOR, which was a shit assignment, usually reserved for misfits and troublemakers. Alex was grateful for the four years he spent in college before enlisting. He hadn't graduated, but at least the experience had given him enough maturity to cope with his misery.

"I hate them both," Alex said, giving the kid a reassuring pat on the shoulder. "You pick."

"Thanks!" Haag said, smiling. He took the turkey and handed him the remaining pouch.

"No problem." They sat against the shadier side of the armored vehicle, where the metal surfaces were not quite hot enough to cook eggs on, and prepared their meals.

"Cherry Kool-Aid!" Alex said, taking the drink pouch out of the bag. "My favorite." He fumbled with the canteen, trying to not get any sand inside the cap. The Mojave desert was one of the dustiest places on earth. Arriving soldiers were told to expect to leave their tour of duty with at least a quarter inch of sand sitting at the base of their lungs. Between that and the unbearable heat, it was just about the most miserable chunk of land Alex had ever laid eyes on.

"How'd you do on the test?" Haag asked, chewing on his turkey breast.

"I didn't have time to get to my name on the damned board," Alex complained. "And I missed breakfast trying. I think I did well though…it was a great test. I can't believe how deep it was. All those puzzles and shit. You?"

Haag was about to answer, but then noticed something and pointed. "What do you think they want?"

A Blue Force humvee was approaching their position slowly. A gunner stared at them from behind a .50 caliber machine gun mounted on the roof. Alex knew it was Blue Force because it wasn't modified to look like an enemy vehicle, which meant it wasn't OPFOR, and it lacked the orange flag of a range controller. Blue Force had no business interacting with Opposing Force casualties, so this could only mean trouble.

"Well…we're about to find out."

The humvee pulled up next to the APC and Alex got a good look at the five men inside. Marines, faces covered in perspiration, caked dust and sour expressions, all glaring at him and Haag with apparent enmity. The gunner, a sergeant, leaned forward over the roof.

"You two rag heads got any chow?" he asked. One of the marines inside the humvee tossed an empty cigarette carton and some crumpled candy wrappers out the window. They landed at Alex's feet.

Alex wanted to stand up before replying, but he couldn't think of a convenient way to set down his canteen and Kool-Aid pouch without spilling some of the precious powder.

"We're eating the last of it," he replied. "Why?"

The sergeant grimaced. "Because we're hungry, and you're dead."

"You're not supposed to be here," Alex said, as sternly as he could manage. As an OPFOR trainer, he was technically in a position of authority, though in practice he was just another rankless grunt in the desert. "You're certainly not allowed to ask us for food, and racial slurs aren't appropriate, even if they don't technically apply."

"What?" The marine seemed confused.

"You called us 'rag heads,'" Alex explained. "We're not real Arabs, but even if we were..."

"Fuck you," the sergeant cursed, his face contorting into a grimace. "Couldn't hack it in the real world so you washed up here, and you think you're big shit? We risk our asses overseas and you sit here in fucking California and shoot blanks all day!" There were chuckles from the other marines, some of them with a nervous undertone. They were anticipating trouble, and that wasn't good.

"We go where we're sent, Sergeant," Alex said. "Just like you. No need to get personal." The man was probably sore about his unit losing an engagement. OPFOR spent more time in the field than any other unit of the military that wasn't deployed overseas, and unlike deployed units, the opposing force was never idle. There was a standing joke in Fort Irwin that if the military wanted Blue Force to have a real chance at winning, they needed to give OPFOR more vacation time.

"You're nothing like us," the Sergeant said.

"Alex did a tour in Afghanistan," Haag said. Alex looked at him and shook his head. There was no point in engaging these men in an argument. They were tired, demoralized and just looking to vent. It was best to just let them.

"A whole tour?" the sergeant said with a sneer. "That's great for your boyfriend, but how 'bout you, Princess? How many tours you got? Or's all you got is war games? War games don't make you a real soldier." Again, chuckles, but the nervous undertone was gone.

"Well," Alex said. "You've shot your load. Now move along before someone sees you." Despite his higher rank, the sergeant appeared to be in his mid twenties, no older than Alex. Hopefully, he was mature enough to realize there were consequences for the actions he was contemplating.

"Go fuck yourself," the sergeant shouted, and kicked the seat in front of him. The humvee lurched forward and sped away, bouncing on the rocky ground.

"Welcome to Opforistan!" Alex shouted after him. "Enjoy your stay! Assholes!" By the time the humvee disappeared behind a nearby hill, the dust from its wake settled, leaving them covered head to foot in a layer of light brown filth.

"Wonderful," Alex said, trying to blow the sand out of his mouth and nose. "Same fucking shit every day." He had managed to cover the canteen, but in doing so he had spilled most of the Kool-Aid mix.

Haag was no better off. He stared at his ruined meal and looked like he wanted to cry.

"It'll be alright," Alex said. "Just scoop out the top layer and eat the clean parts underneath."

The young soldier brightened. "Yeah, that'll work."

After they finished their lunch, Haag went into the APC and emerged with a plastic trash bag.

"Good man," Alex said, tossing his garbage inside.

"I'll get the crap they tossed too." Haag walked over to where the marines had dropped their litter and scooped up the wrappers while Alex started over to the hot side of the APC to relieve his bladder. He turned to look at Haag before rounding the vehicle's corner and noticed that the kid was about to pick up a small white cylinder that had been stirred up out of the sand by the humvee's tires.

"Haag!" he screamed, turning to run towards the young soldier. "No! Don't!" Haag turned to look, holding the cylinder in his left hand.

The flash of bright light made Alex cringe away from the explosion just as the thunderous crack slammed into him, leaving dead silence in its wake. A cloud of white smoke drifted where Haag had stood. As Alex ran towards him, the young man's screams started to edge out the ringing in his ears.

There was blood everywhere, flowing mostly from the ruined mass of cloth and flesh that had once been Haag's left hand. The young soldier was clutching the mangled wrist, thrashing in the sand, his eyes pressed shut. Blood leaked from his left ear and his shirt and pants on the left side where plastic shrapnel had shredded his skin.

"Holy shit!" Alex screamed, fighting down panic. "Hold still!

Hold fucking still!" What was he supposed to do? He wasn't a medic.

"Fucking do something," he muttered, slapping himself on the forehead. He remembered his first aid training. He reached under his shirt and pulled off his belt with trembling hands, then fought with Haag to get a hold of his left arm.

"Dammit, Haag, let it go! You'll bleed to death!" He wasn't sure if the kid could even hear him. Haag had been a lot closer to the blast, and Alex could barely hear himself over the ringing. Managing to get a hold of the wounded arm, he applied the tourniquet, tightening the belt as much as he dared. When he was done, his hands were drenched in warm blood.

"Hang on," he shouted. "I'll be right back."

He ran over to the APC and jumped inside, heading straight for the driver's seat. As his slippery fingers fumbled with the earphones and mic, he realized he barely knew what to say. He had used the radio many times before, but his mind was blank.

"Any call sign," he shouted into the mic as he searched the vehicle's instrument panel for the plugger. "This is two two zero india, I need a medical evac, repeat, medical evac! I have one man down, artillery simulator explosion. Grid coordinates to follow." He knew there was probably more he had to say, but he couldn't think straight.

Almost immediately, a voice replied. "Two two zero india, mike echo five five two, received. Holding for grid."

He found the plugger and the button labeled "Mark" that converted his GPS coordinates into a military map grid number. "Mike echo five five two, two two zero india, grid is as follows…" He read the grid number, then repeated it.

"Two two zero india, mike echo five five, grid received. ETA to your position is ten mikes."

"Mike echo five five, two two zero india, received, standing by."

Dropping the headset, he ran back to Haag, who was still thrashing in the sand and screaming.

"They're on their way, buddy!" Alex shouted. "Hang in there!" Why the hell did Haag pick up the artillery simulator? The base was littered with thousands of them, discarded duds from decades of training exercises. Had the kid fallen asleep during the orientation at OPFOR academy? Alex could still remember the pictures of mutilated limbs and burn scars cycling on the projector screen.

For what seemed like an eternity Alex knelt over his friend, trying to comfort him in any way he could, until at last he heard the thrumming of a helicopter's rotors in the distance.

* * *

Lieutenant Campbell found him in the hospital waiting room a little past midnight.

"Specialist Meyer," he said, smiling. "Just as I thought."

"Bill," Alex said, without looking up. He was exhausted, though he didn't want to leave until he learned about Haag's condition. The kid was still in surgery, where he'd been for the last ten hours. To make matters worse, Alex's head was pounding so bad he was tempted to ask one of the doctors for a morphine shot.

The lieutenant did not take offense at the breach in protocol. He sat down next to Alex and leaned back in his chair with a long sigh. He was a very tall, powerfully built man around Alex's age, the only other person in the platoon with a college education. Though Campbell had actually graduated, and done so with honors. The two got along more than was proper for an officer and an enlisted soldier under his command, and Alex had caught more than a few breaks as a result.

"Man, my head is killing me," Campbell said.

Alex nodded, rubbing his temples. "Mine too. Long day, Bill. Very long day."

"It could have been longer," Campbell said. "Sergeant Medlock had a hissy fit. They weren't supposed to let you on the medevac with Haag. He said you were AWOL."

Alex looked up, alarmed. "AWOL? That's bullshit! Come on, Bill, you know that's a load of—"

The lieutenant waved his hand dismissively. "Don't worry about it. I took care of it. Medlock can be an asshole."

Alex smiled. "Officers aren't supposed to say things like that about their platoon sergeants."

Campbell chuckled. "Yeah, but I won't tell anyone if you

don't. And if you do, I'll send you to Leavenworth."

"It'll be between us. Thanks for fixing things."

"What are friends for? Anyway, how are you holding up?"

"I'm fine, I'm just worried about Haag. Why the hell would he pick up that simulator?"

Campbell shrugged. "Shit happens. People space out, don't pay attention. I saw a guy burn his leg to shit trying to get a missile simulator out of a bent launch tube. This fucking base can be more dangerous than the war."

"I just hope he'll be okay."

"I spoke to a doctor on my way in," Campbell said. "They're trying to reconstruct as much of his hand as they can. Lucky bastard is right handed, did you know that? I don't know why he used his left to pick that damned thing up, but that's at least one thing he can be thankful for. That, and he's going home with disability pay, unless they can somehow fix him up good as new."

Alex nodded. "Thank god for small favors." A part of him was envious, but he shrugged it off. One more year, and he could go home in one piece.

"Listen, Alex, you need to go to the barracks and hit the sack. Medlock isn't going to cut you any slack tomorrow, and we're still in the middle of our rotation. Haag is going to be in surgery all night. They're flying in doctors from San Diego Naval Hospital to take over when these guys have had it. You're not doing him any good here."

"Yeah, I guess. If I can sleep with this fucking headache." He stood up, stretched his tired arms and followed Campbell to the elevator.

"I'll drive you back," the lieutenant said. "And I'll pick you up at 0600 tomorrow. One of the bimps is heading out from the motor pool, we can catch a ride to the camp."

"Thanks, Bill, I don't know what I'd do without you."

Campbell flashed a toothy grin and said, "I do. You'd be rotting in prison."

With the rest of the unit still out in the field, Alex was alone in his room that night, which was just fine with him. He had always been a private person, and having to share his living space with three other people was one of the things he hated the most about

Ft. Irwin. Not that he got to sleep there more than a few nights a month. The rest of the time he was in a sleeping bag in the desert, hoping a coyote would climb in to exchange body heat.

"One more year," he muttered bitterly as he waited for the clanging pipes to bring him his hot water. After a long and relaxing shower and some Tylenol, he set his alarm clock and lay down. He was asleep within seconds.

Chapter 2

As soon as Alex's eyes were open, he started to panic. There was no noise from the alarm clock, which meant he had overslept, a fact confirmed by the bright light shining through the windows. There was no way Campbell could save him from this, not without putting himself in a very awkward position.

Sitting up, he searched for his slippers by the foot of the bed as he rubbed his eyes. He was groggy, a lot more so than he usually was when he woke up late. The floor was cold and smooth, not the cheap abrasive rug his feet had been expecting. Blinking away sleep, he looked around, utterly confused by what he saw.

Alex was not in his barracks.

"What the hell?" he said, eyes darting from one unfamiliar detail to another. His first thought was that they had taken him while he slept and put him in prison for going AWOL. He was in a good sized room, about fifteen by ten feet. The walls were a pleasant off white color and looked like they were made of plastic, with interlocking molded panels like the inside of a commercial jetliner.

He was lying on a small but comfortable bed under a white cotton blanket, directly beneath a large window made nearly opaque by frosted glass. A clear partition towards the far end of the room separated the main chamber from a bathroom compartment complete with shower, sink and toilet. The facilities looked modern and attractive, not at all like he would have expected to see in a prison. There was a flat screen monitor on the wall at the foot of his bed, probably thirty inches or so, and a plastic shelf stuck out from the wall on his left to make a desk. A small leather chair stood nearby.

For a moment, Alex couldn't move as his mind struggled to make sense of what he was seeing.

"Where the hell am I?" he whispered, finding comfort in the sound of his own voice. That, at least, was familiar. He climbed out of the bed and searched the strange plastic floor for his slippers, but they weren't there. Looking down, he noticed he was not wearing the same clothes he had gone to sleep in. Instead of his army issue underwear, he wore clean white cotton boxers and a beige t-shirt, both of which fit perfectly.

Feeling dizzy, Alex sat back down, reaching for the desk to steady himself. He closed his eyes and took several deep breaths, all the while trying to calm his racing mind. How long had he been asleep? He was groggy as hell.

"Okay," he said, raising his hands in a calming gesture. "Okay. This isn't jail. So what is it?" Opening his eyes, he stood up and once more took a good look around the room, picking up several details he had missed the first time around. There was a door with a small handle where the knob should be, with two more semi-opaque windows on either side. Next to the door there was a green pad, rectangular and about the size of a credit card. A small red LED glowed ominously just above it. Walking over to the door, he pushed the pad with his finger. There was a harsh sounding tone, like the sound the computer in Star Trek made when the crew did something they weren't supposed to.

"I guess I can't leave," Alex said. "Maybe this is jail after all." Surprisingly, that made him feel better. He had been more scared than he realized, and the idea of being in a military prison was the devil he knew. Responding to an intense need to relieve himself, he crossed into the smaller compartment and used the toilet. The flushing sound was strange—the whirring of a motor followed by suction, like an airplane toilet.

"Not a bad cell at all," he said. "I even get a TV." He started to accept the idea of his incarceration. Once that happened, he began to get angry.

"Fucking Medlock," he growled. "What a dick." It wasn't fair. His friend was almost killed, he had stayed with him, gone to the hospital. Wasn't that what he was supposed to do? And what about Campbell? He said he had taken care of it, hadn't he?

"Fuck Campbell too," Alex said. "Two-faced jerk off."

Only he knew none of that could be right. Taken to jail? *While he was sleeping?*

He decided to stop trying to figure it out, at least for the moment, and see what else he could find in his strange cell. There was a dresser on the far side of the door just below the window. Opening each of its three drawers in turn, he found an assortment of clothing. There were a lot more t-shirts and boxers, perhaps twenty of each, along with several sets of army combat uniforms in digital pattern camouflage—just like his own, only brand new. Removing one of the shirts, he was surprised to see his name above the right breast pocket. The other pocket had the usual "U.S. ARMY" patch on it, above which were his airborne wings. The patch of velcro on his chest, where his rank insignia should have been, was empty, as was the area on the shoulder were his unit patch belonged. The prison theory was starting to make sense again, despite the bizarre way in which he was brought here. They had obviously stripped him of what little rank he had as part of his punishment.

Only—wasn't he entitled to a hearing first?

Faced with the option to wear clothing, he noticed that the room was a little chilly, so he put on one of the uniforms, which fit him perfectly. He found three pairs of brand new combat boots in the bottom drawer, and these were his size as well. After he was dressed, he noticed a speck of color under the uniform shirts in the second drawer, and rifling through the fatigues he was surprised to find an assortment of civilian clothing underneath. Mostly t-shirts, sweat shirts and jeans.

He frowned, wishing he had seen those first, but didn't bother to change now that he was dressed.

"This is a very strange cell," he mumbled, closing the drawers. Turning to the bed, he noticed that the frame below the mattress was solid, and that there was another green pad near the top. This one also had a red LED next to it. Walking over to the bed, he knelt down and examined it closely. The pad was identical to the one by the door except for a tiny hole in its center. Alex touched the pad with the tip of his finger and heard a milder version of the negative tone the door had made. Why put a locked compartment under his bed?

He was about to turn away when he had an idea, and pushed the pad again, this time placing his finger firmly over the tiny hole. There was a brief mechanical sound and a very mild pricking sensation as something pierced his skin. It didn't hurt at all. He was barely aware of it. Another, more positive tone emanated from the device, and the little LED turned green. A drawer slid out from under the bed. Alex gasped in surprise.

The drawer was almost as big as the bed frame and contained a trio of M4 carbines resting in form fitting foam. Next to the rifles were a large knife and two handguns, along with several loaded magazines for each. On one side of the drawer was a large square pocket filled with tactical gear: vests, holsters and other load bearing devices. The M4s were similar to his own issue rifle, but they were the M4A1 full auto variety, usually reserved for special forces and civilian DOD contractors. They were brand new, with all the latest bells and whistles. Rail covers, holographic sights, foregrips, tactical flashlights, single point slings—his mind reeled as he tried to take it all in. What looked like three fully loaded magazines turned out to be three stacks of seven, layered on top of one another.

"Holy shit," he whispered, taking out one of the rifles. Before he realized what he was doing, he had the upper receiver separated from the lower and the bolt assembly out and on top of the bed. It left black spots from its lubricant on the white sheets.

Everything was as it should be, or at least appeared that way. He looked down the barrel and didn't see any obstructions, then reassembled the weapon and put it on the bed.

"This is no god damned jail," he said, then noticed a small white paper in the corner of the large drawer. He picked it up and turned it over. There was something typed neatly in its center:

`peace7102`

Alex stared at the paper for a while, struggling to make sense of it. He thought about the possibility of being in some bizarre reality show, but quickly dismissed it. Too many legal issues. Then another thought occurred to him—what if he were involved in some sort of military psychological experiment? That certainly made a lot more sense. Most people weren't aware of the extent to which a person signed away his or her civil liberties when joining the military. They could certainly pull off something like this without much risk of repercussions. But why him?

He sat down, leaning against the wall at the foot of the bed and rubbed his face, surprised to find several days worth of stubble. Looking towards the bathroom compartment, he noticed a mirrored medicine cabinet above the sink. He was willing to bet he would find a razor or electric shaver inside, along with other toiletries. As he shook his head in frustration, his eyes wandered to the pad near the door, and he noticed that the adjacent LED was now green.

His eyes widened and his heart began to beat faster. The door was unlocked now, there was no question about that, but what would he find on the other side? Would there be others? Why had it only unlocked after he had accessed the weapons?

Driven by fear, he scrambled to his feet and knelt above the drawer, scooping out a chest rig and holster. The straps on both were perfectly fitted, requiring no adjustment. He filled the rig with six magazines, holstered one of the pistols and sheathed the knife, then slid the drawer closed. The LED turned red again.

Taking the rifle he had previously examined, he inserted a magazine and chambered a round, then clipped it into a sling and approached the door, weapon ready.

When he pushed the button, the door clicked and swung open, momentarily blinding him. He waited until his eyes adjusted, then, trembling with fear and anticipation, he stepped outside, prepared for anything.

Chapter 3

The first thing he noticed were people, lots of people. They were standing around, some talking, some yelling. No one seemed to present an immediate threat. He was the only one armed, at least as far he could see. There were strange little buildings all around him, dozens of them, everywhere he looked. Risking a brief glance back, he saw that the room he had stepped out of was actually a building identical to the others. All seemed to be made of—or covered in—beige plastic.

The humidity took a bit longer to notice, but when he started to sweat, his eyes wandered beyond the houses and he saw trees, some of them palms, and he heard the sound of waves breaking in the distance. An ocean? With the sun high overhead, he immediately realized it was far too cool to be midday in the Mojave desert, and too wet.

Some of the people noticed him. A few stood and stared, others backed away. A woman screamed and ran behind one of the buildings. He lowered his weapon, letting it hang in front of his chest, suspended by the sling.

A young woman was walking towards him, glaring angrily. Despite the overwhelming array of sensory data his mind was struggling with, he noticed how pretty she was and he focused on her face, tuning out all else. Her eyes were best described as feline, set amidst a light spattering of freckles that enhanced her elfin features. Wavy auburn hair with a trace of highlights swayed in a warm breeze as she approached. She wore a dark blue denim skirt and an orange t-shirt, her feet swathed in white tennis shoes and ankle high socks. She appeared to be younger than he was, though it wasn't always easy to tell with women.

"What the hell is going on here?" she demanded, stopping just a few feet away, her hands on her hips. The way she glared at him made it clear she wasn't the least bit afraid.

He opened his mouth. "I…"

Her eyes narrowed, but she said nothing.

"I don't know, I just…"

Now her eyes widened in an angry flash as her foot twitched, almost stomping the ground.

"What the hell do you mean you don't know? You kidnapped me from my home, my family, and you don't know? How dare you! When my father's lawyers—"

"Miss, I have no idea what—" Alex tried to say, but stopped when she raised a hand to strike him.

His muscles tensed and he instinctively reached for his rifle, but she lowered her hand and stepped back with an awkward expression, as though she only then became aware of what she was doing. With a final glare that betrayed the slight sheen of moisture in her eyes, she spun around and stormed off defiantly, disappearing around the corner of a nearby building.

"I see you met Yael the Jewish princess," someone said. Alex turned in the direction of the speaker and saw a pleasant looking older man with a heavily wrinkled forehead and wispy white hair. "I'm Max." He held out his hand.

After a brief hesitation, Alex shook it. "I'm Alex. What did you call her?" His brain hadn't yet caught up with the rest of him. It was a strange sensation, almost like a waking dream.

Max smiled. "Oh, nothing. She's a little more upset than the rest of us. She's been screaming a lot, demanding things. Not the most popular person here."

"Popular?" he said. "What are you talking about? What the hell is going on here?"

"So you really don't know what happened?" Max said, raising an arm to lean against the building Alex had come out of. "You're the only one so far to…well…." He motioned at Alex's rifle.

"I just woke up a few minutes ago," Alex said. "These weapons were under my bunk, in a locked drawer. I didn't know where I was, I thought maybe…is this an army base?"

"Locked?" Max asked. "With a DNA pad?"

Alex frowned. "A what?"

"A DNA pad, it's like the other green pads but it has a little hole and it pricks you."

"Yeah, that was it." Sure, that was it, perfectly normal, not at all as though he were stuck in some bizarre alternate reality.

Max nodded. “A few of us have them, but yours is the only one so far with guns. Come.” He motioned, then started to walk towards a clearing between buildings. “I’ll show you around.”

“How long have you been here?” Alex asked, following behind him. “What is this place?” He glanced around, noticing many people staring at him nervously. Each person he saw was as different as the next, a seemingly random assortment of men and women of all races, though most of those he saw were Caucasian. Their clothing was as random as the people themselves, an eclectic mix of casual and formal attire of varying styles. Alex was the only one in a uniform, at least so far. If there was any sort of pattern, it was that most were young, in their twenties or less. Though he did notice a few older people besides Max.

“This is my second day,” Max said. “But I’ve been here as long as you have, I just woke up earlier. It seems we all got here two nights ago. The last thing I remember was falling asleep in my apartment. As for what this place is, none of us have a clue.”

“Where are you from?” Alex asked. He studied the strange little houses as they walked past, looking for some sort of pattern to their arrangement. He couldn’t find one. It seemed as though they had been dumped haphazardly in the middle of a clearing. There were no foundations. Each building sat right on the grass or the sand, depending on where it had been deposited. They looked like plastic Airstream trailers, except that they weren’t trailers at all. No wheels.

“Los Angeles. I’m a law professor at UCLA. What about you? You’re a marine?”

“A soldier,” Alex explained. “Army, paratrooper. Not a marine.” He remembered the five marines in the humvee and grimaced. If they hadn’t come seeking trouble, Haag would never have found that artillery simulator, and then none of this would have happened.

But then, what did this have to do with Haag? If there was one thing he was certain of, it was that this was no military prison. Still, he couldn’t help but feel that there was a connection to recent events, if not to Haag’s accident, then something else. Or it could just be his mind trying to hold on to his prior notion of reality.

“Ah,” Max said apologetically. “I’m not versed in the nuances." They walked across the clearing, and Alex saw a beach past some of the buildings to his right. Clear blue water lapped the orange sand gently, leaving a residue of froth between waves. A massive building, much wider and longer than any of the others, stood by a patch of trees to their left. Looking around, Alex noticed that the surrounding forest—or more accurately a jungle—was dense enough to make passage through it difficult. A range of craggy mountains rose above the trees beyond the beach, their rough surface furred by a thick cover of vegetation.

"I call this the warehouse," Max said, motioning towards the long building. "It's a storage facility. So far we found food and other supplies, but there are many doors we haven't been able to open yet. I'm hoping you'll get us past one more." It wasn't much taller than the other buildings, which made it hard to gauge its size accurately, but Alex estimated it was at least a hundred feet long.

"Warehouse?" Alex demanded, losing patience. "Doors? What the hell is going on? Why are we here?"

Max smiled. "Son, if I knew that, I'd have told you already."

"Don't you have any ideas? You've been here over 24 hours!" The man's casual attitude towards their predicament was starting to get on Alex's nerves.

"It's too early to start hypothesizing with any degree of certainty, but…"

"Max," someone said from behind them. "Max, another one's awake."

Alex turned and saw a young man walking towards them. His eyes widened as he noticed Alex's rifle.

"What the hell?" the man asked, coming to a stop about ten feet away. He looked a bit older than Alex, pleasant looking in a peculiar Eastern European way, with sandy blond hair and dark stubble with a few specks of premature gray.

"It's okay, Reynard," Max said. "He's okay. Tell me, who is it? Anyone interesting?"

"Yes," Reynard said, moving closer. "A woman in her thirties. Says she's a doctor. A surgeon."

Max brightened. "Excellent. Go talk to her, bring her here, see if one of the pads will pop for her."

Reynard frowned. "Don't you want to do it? I mean you're

better at it, I don't even know what to say."

"Nonsense," Max said, shaking his head. "What is there to say? Tell her about the warehouse. When she's ready, show it to her."

"Okay," Reynard said, started to turn away, then stopped, looking at Alex. "You're a soldier? Don't you know what's going on here?"

Alex shook his head. "Sorry, no. I just woke up."

Reynard nodded, but narrowed his eyes slightly, as though he didn't quite believe him, then walked away, presumably to find the doctor woman.

"You seem awfully calm about all of this," Alex said, turning back to Max. "Aren't you scared? Worried?"

"I was," Max admitted. "Scared, that is. I'm still worried, but whoever brought us here seemed to take great pains to make sure our needs were met. I live alone, so it's not like anyone is going to miss me while I figure this out."

"This is crazy," Alex said, his frustration starting to get the better of him. "I feel like I'm in some ridiculous television show. Doesn't anyone have a cell phone or a radio? Can't we find out where the hell we are and get out of here?"

"No," Max said. "No radios, at least not yet. There is a computer terminal in my quarters. I mean we all have computers in our cottages, but those are self contained. Mine looks like a communications terminal, webcam and all, but it's not active, and no one can figure out how to turn it on."

"Cottages?"

Max shrugged. "What would you call them? They're obviously domiciles, and each of us has one."

"Yeah, I guess, but…"

"Come," Max said, placing a gentle hand on Alex's elbow. "Let's go see the warehouse."

They walked around to the forest side of the building, where large double doors swung open as Max pushed through them.

"No pads on the outside," Max explained.

Inside the warehouse was a long corridor, lined on each side with five doors. Each door had a green pad next to it, complete with glowing LEDs, most red, some green. At the far end of the corridor was a single door, and Alex realized that the chamber beyond had to be at least a quarter of the building, judging by its exterior dimensions. There were eleven doors in all, including the one on the end.

"We've opened three so far," Max explained.

"What is in them?" Alex asked.

"Two of them have food. One has nutrient powder canisters. Two table spoons makes enough for a filling meal when mixed with water—there were instructions. We haven't had time to do an accurate count, but I'd estimate that with proper rationing there's enough to keep fifty people alive for several years, if they can stomach it. It's not very appetizing. There's a dispenser in your cottage. You can come here to get more powder when it runs out."

"Fifty people? Is that how many there are here?"

Max nodded. "That's how many cottages there are. Forty one...sorry, forty two, have come out thus far. Hopefully the rest are just sleeping off whatever drugs were used to knock us out."

"What about the other rooms?"

"Dehydrated food in the second, enough for a year, if rationed, and tools in the third. Wrenches, screwdrivers, that sort of thing. It's almost like the tool section in one of those big hardware stores."

"How big are these rooms?" Alex asked.

"Here, I'll show you," Max said, walking up to a marked door. "So far, once the doors are unlocked, they stay that way unless the one who opened them in the first place locks them again." He pushed the pad, and the door slid open, disappearing into the wall. Once again, Alex was reminded of Star Trek. The open doorway revealed a room stocked with large plastic drums. It was a little bigger than the room he woke up in, and the drums took up all available space.

"That's the powder?" Each drum was labeled with the words "Nutrient Powder" and a date, presumably the powder's expiration. If the dates could be trusted, they had well over twenty years to use the stuff. His mind rebelled, not able to accept that he would be here for another day, let alone twenty years.

"Hold on," Alex said. "Why are we messing around with this warehouse when we should be getting the hell out of here? Is this an island? Have you looked around?"

Max shook his head. "If it is an island, it's very big. But we can't leave. That was one of the first things I tried. There's a barrier."

"A barrier? But I didn't see any walls or fences."

"It's not a wall. It's..." Max hesitated, licking his lips as though trying to figure out how to best phrase it. "You'll see soon enough. It's hard to explain. I'll show you when we're done here, if you want."

"Fine," he said, grudgingly. "So what do you want me to do?" He had not given up on leaving, but there didn't seem to be a reason to hurry. It wasn't reasonable to assume that someone would go to all this trouble to bring them here if they could just walk away. Unless that was the purpose of the experiment...to see if they would just accept their fate or try to fight it. Even the experiment theory was starting to wear thin, though. The army could get away with experimenting on soldiers, but so far, he was the only one in uniform.

"Just go to every door and use the pad. Avoid the green lit ones."

"Okay." He walked past each of the doors marked by a red LED, touching its pad. Some of the pads had tiny holes like the one below his bed, but most did not. Each buzzed negatively as he tried it, until he got to the door on the end. Its pad had a hole, and when he touched it, he felt that slight pricking sensation and heard a positive chime. The LED turned green and the door slid open. Behind it was a short corridor, less than five feet long, and another pad-protected door.

"Impressive," Max said, nodding appreciatively. "The big one. Let's see if you can open the inner door as well."

They stepped into the corridor, and Alex touched the pad. Once again, there was a pricking sensation, followed by a positive tone, followed immediately by another tone. This one wasn't harsh, but still sounded negative. Whoever had chosen these tones knew what they were doing. The meaning of each sound was easily understood.

"That's odd," Max said, rubbing his chin. "I've never heard that sound before."

"Oh well," Alex said, mildly disappointed. Despite his confusion and frustration, he was curious to see what was in the big room.

"Maybe it takes two people," Max said. "One to open the outer door, and another to open the inner one."

"Maybe," Alex said. "But I want to try something else first." It was all the Star Trek references going through his mind that triggered the idea. "Go back to the hallway for a minute."

"Why?" Max looked confused.

"Maybe it works like an airlock." There were pads on both sides of the outer door, which made sense if someone was meant to close it while inside the corridor.

The older man brightened. "Yes! That's an excellent idea!" He backed into the main hallway. As soon as he was out, the outer door slid closed. Alex touched the inner door pad again, and this time a positive tone sounded and the LED turned green.

As the door slid open, Alex's eyes widened. Stepping into the room beyond, he let out a deep breath.

"Holy shit…"

It was a large room, over thirty feet on each side, filled with weapons, ammunition and other military equipment. He quickly counted thirty M4 carbines before he lost track, each as well equipped as the one he was carrying. There were also pistols, machine guns, belt fed grenade launchers, even a rack of anti-tank rockets. Ammunition cans were stacked almost to the ceiling. Along a far wall was a shelf unit filled with black plastic boxes marked "NVD," which stood for "night vision device." Behind a rack of pistols, he saw the distinctive barrels of .50 caliber Barrett anti-material rifles. Unable to fully process what he was seeing, he grew faint and grabbed a nearby wall for support.

Whoever brought him here had given him an arsenal, and for reasons he could not yet understand, that scared the shit out of him.

Chapter 4

Alex backed out of the arms room and turned around as the door slid closed behind him. The outer door opened with a touch of the pad, and he walked out into the main hallway, almost knocking Max over as he marched past him.

"What was inside—hey! Where are you going?" Max said. The outer door to the arms room slid closed as soon as he cleared it.

"Guns," Alex said. "Lots of guns." He kept walking, heading for the double doors. "I need to be alone. Need to think."

Max didn't say anything, for which Alex was grateful, and he left the warehouse and retraced his steps back to his own cabin. It was crazy to think of it as his, or even a cabin, but for some reason it was his center in all this madness. He needed to be there, to lock the door behind him and think.

"Excuse me..." a woman started to say, but he ignored her and walked steadily back the way he had come. There was no one by the cottage when he got there, and the door was still open. He noticed another green pad on the outer wall. Apparently the door would lock if he closed it, presumably opening only for him. Stepping inside, he pulled the door shut, saw the LED turn red and went straight for the bed.

Before sitting down, he removed the rifle, chest rig and pistol holster and tossed them onto the mattress, then sat on the floor at the foot of the bed, facing the wall. Taking a deep breath, he closed his eyes. A slight hum emanated from the ceiling as a wash of cool, dry air flowed over his exposed neck and head.

"Air conditioning," he muttered. "Fucking air conditioning."

Opening his eyes, he stared at the corner, focusing on the wall's uniform texture. Reaching out, he ran his finger along its surface, trying to clear his mind of all but the sensation of the cool plastic under his fingertips.

Cool? He rapped at it with his knuckles. It wasn't plastic after all, but some sort of metal, probably aluminum. He got to his feet and walked around the room, knocking on all the various surfaces. The entire structure, except for the plexiglass windows and bathroom panel, was made of the same metal. Even the desk surface and the locked drawer that held his weapons. During his examination, he found the powder dispenser Max had mentioned. It was mounted on the wall near the transparent divider, just to the right of the desk.

Holding his hand below the dispenser's spigot, he pushed down on the lever just enough to release a single puff of white paste onto the palm of his left hand. Apparently the dispenser premixed the powder, which was convenient. Taking some on his finger, he brought it to his mouth and tasted it with the tip of his tongue.

It was mildly sweet with a heavy texture, not unlike the grits that they served in the chow hall on those few days a month he actually got to eat there. After Max's comment, he had expected something foul, and was pleasantly surprised. Realizing he was famished, he finished off what little he had in his hand, then started looking for a plate. Below the dispenser was another green pad, and looking at that section of the wall, Alex noticed the outline of a panel. This particular pad was just a simple spring loaded button, and the panel popped open as soon as he pushed it. Inside was an assortment of miscellaneous trinkets, including cups, plates, tableware and other knick knacks.

He removed a plate, spoon and cup, then dispensed a sizeable quantity of white goo and sat down at his desk. There was a laptop computer there, just as Max had said there would be. It was folded closed and extremely thin, which was why he hadn't noticed it before. He put the plate on top of it.

The sweet goop was surprisingly filling, and though he would have preferred a burger or a steak, it wasn't a bad meal. Filling his cup with water from the bathroom sink, he paused momentarily, wondering if it was safe to drink, then shrugged and took a sip. It was clean and refreshing, like bottled spring water.

Leaning back in the leather chair, he patted his belly and smiled, satisfied. It wasn't all bad, wherever this was. For starters, there was no one to tell him what to do. When he was hungry, he could eat, when he was tired, he could take a nap. There was even a beach. He could go swimming, if he could find a pair of shorts.

He realized what was happening. It was a familiar pattern of ups and downs as his brain struggled to come to terms with a new situation. He remembered feeling much the same way during his first day of basic training, where he had gone from depressed to elated and back to depressed within minutes. Ultimately a mild depression had won out and continued throughout his military career. This place, though, was different. His down period included confusion, fear and frustration, but not depression. In a strange way, being here was somewhat liberating, though he doubted any of the others felt the same way. Unless of course some were also soldiers—or prisoners.

He stood up and slapped his thighs. "I'm going to go to the beach!" he said excitedly, deciding to enjoy the up period while it lasted. He put on his pistol belt, but decided to put the rifle and chest rig back in the compartment under the bed. He also removed his ACU blouse and tossed it onto the chair. A t-shirt would be much more comfortable, considering the humidity.

This time he closed the door behind him when he left his cottage and tested the handle to make sure that it was locked. It was. There were more people up and about than he had seen last time, and most of them still stared at him. He ignored them, though now that he was feeling good he enjoyed the attention.

The beach was easy to find, all he had to do was follow the sound of the waves. He squinted as he looked across the expanse of sparkling blue water, and almost laughed when he found himself wondering why sunglasses had not been included in his supplies. The beach wasn't very big, perhaps a hundred meters across. To the left, the surrounding mountains sloped gently down into the water, forming a natural barrier. A single tree, it's limbs twisted and almost bare, stood alone just past the edge of the jungle that carpeted the mountains. The tree had a stately aspect, like something out of a vacation brochure for a Caribbean island, though Alex had been to the Caribbean and it hadn't looked anything like this. Tall palms leaned over the water on the opposite end of the beach where a patch of forest intruded to the ocean's edge.

"It's a fucking tropical resort," he muttered, sitting down by a fallen tree trunk. "All I need now are some lounge chairs and mai tais." He looked around, noticing that he was alone, and added, "And some girls in bikinis wouldn't hurt either."

He had been there less than a minute when he heard someone walking up behind him, turned, and saw the pretty Jewish girl that had yelled at him earlier. She approached tentatively this time, staring at him with a mix of distaste and curiosity.

"Hi," he said, deciding to remain seated. She stopped a few feet away, then realizing he wasn't going to stand, walked around to face him.

"Hi," she said hesitantly, her lips still pursed in an expression of dissatisfaction.

"Are you going to yell at me again?" he asked, then contorted his mouth into a deliberately obnoxious grin. The noon sun set her hair aglow as it cast shadows that accentuated the lines of her face. She squinted against its brightness, her pale skin betraying her indoor lifestyle in whatever past she had been torn from. The faint freckles on her face extended to her arms, and though Alex did not usually like freckles on a girl, he found himself liking them on her.

"No," she said flatly. "The others, they…well, they made me come and talk to you. They said…they said that since I've been so vocal about my complaints, I should be the one. Of course those weren't the words they used, they probably don't even know how to spell 'vocal.'" Alex looked over her shoulder and noticed a small crowd of people staring at him apprehensively.

"Sit down then," he said, patting the sand next to him, leaning over so as not to make it too close. He didn't want to discourage her. She frowned, but then rolled her eyes in resignation and lowered herself carefully to the sand, taking great pains to make sure her knee length skirt did not ride up too high.

"Okay," he said. "Now tell me what they want."

She brushed a lock of hair out of her eyes. "They think you know something. I know you said you didn't, but if I don't believe you, you can bet they don't either."

"What's your name?" he said, ignoring the question. If he confirmed he knew nothing, she would leave, and he didn't want that, not yet. She wasn't wearing a bikini or holding a tropical drink, but she wasn't bad to look at.

"Yael."

"Yah-ehl," he said, pronouncing each part carefully. "Like gazelle. That's kind of a mouthful. Do you have a nickname or something?"

She glared at him. "It's two syllables."

He shrugged. "I mean I like it. It's cool, but kinda hard to say."

"Can we get on with it, please? Do you know something or not?"

"Why would you think I know something?" Despite having spoken to her less than a minute, he knew that asking her this obvious question would set her off, and that was precisely why he did it. There was something about the intensity of her outbursts that he enjoyed.

Sure enough, her eyes flared. "You're kidding, right? You can't be that dense."

He smiled. "Is it the uniform?"

"You mean that glorified leaf print you're wearing? Yeah, that's part of it. How about the guns, genius? You're the only one with guns."

"Wow," he said, laughing and shaking his head. "You've got a bug up your pretty little ass, alright." Her mouth fell open, and she looked like she was about to start shouting again. "But I like it. I think it works for you. My name is Alex."

He held out his hand, and she seemed taken aback. She hesitated for a moment, not sure what to do, but eventually decided to shake it, however briefly.

"I'm sorry," he said. "I don't know any more than you do. The uniform, the guns, they were in my room…I mean my cottage, or cabin, whatever. I *am* a soldier, it is my uniform, except that it isn't, you know what I mean?"

"Yes," she said, her shoulders slumping slightly. "These clothes, they're just like what I'd wear, but…" She stopped, as though she realized she was talking to him like a normal person. "So you're basically as useless as the rest of them."

"The rest of us, you mean, right?"

She raised an eyebrow, then nodded. "Yeah, I guess it is the rest of *us*." She looked away, and he thought she might start crying.

"Hey," he said, reaching out to put a hand on her shoulder.

"It'll be alright. We're alive, we've got everything we need, and the beach…"

She pulled away and glared at him, again. "Everything we need? You may have everything *you* need, but I need my family. Excuse me." She got up and dusted herself off.

"Wait," he said, also climbing to his feet. "Where are you going?"

"Why the fuck do you care?" She walked towards the village, but away from the crowd. The waiting people shifted their gazes between her and Alex until she announced, "He doesn't know anything!" Then she disappeared around a corner and was gone, leaving him staring after her.

"She's right," he yelled at the crowd. "I don't know anything." That seemed to satisfy them, or more accurately *dis*satisfy them, and they began to disperse, walking in every direction but towards him. For a moment, Alex wondered why he wasn't actively trying to figure out what was going on like the others were, or like he'd wanted to do when he met Max. He did care, but perhaps not as much as they did. As a soldier, he was used to being in a situation completely out of his control, so perhaps he was better adjusted. Still, now that he thought about it, he supposed it might be a good idea to do a bit of investigating of his own.

"Right," he said to himself when the crowd had mostly dispersed. "Time to check out this barrier then." Looking around, he realized that if it were a proper barrier it shouldn't matter which direction he walked in—he would eventually find it. He decided that he would walk along the beach, towards the patch of forest to his right.

As he walked, he noticed people in the complex watching him. A lot of them seemed to hover near their cabins, either standing in the open doorways or leaning on the walls just outside. Scared faces turned away as soon as he looked at them, only to stare at him again when they thought he wasn't looking anymore. Most were alone, though some clustered together in small groups, talking quietly as nervous eyes shifted between each other, their surroundings and him.

An idea occurred to him. Maybe the people who had put them in this place were watching them, like characters in a movie. He supposed they would expect him to get to know the other prisoners, identify the key players and learn their life stories, maybe stir up some drama. Unfortunately for these imaginary spectators, he couldn't care less about getting to know any of his fellow inmates—well, not most of them, anyway. Used to life in the barracks, he had acquired the habit of ignoring people he didn't need to notice. Perhaps it would be better for him to change that habit. He decided to do so—later. He had other things on his mind at the moment. For the time being, at least, most of these people were nothing more than scenery.

The patch of jungle was not as dense as it had looked from a distance, and he was able to walk through it easily. The beach continued on the other side for about three or four hundred meters before disappearing behind more jungle. He rubbed his stomach as he walked, noticing a bit of indigestion. The nutrient powder didn't seem to agree with him. Perhaps that was what Max had meant about being able to stomach it.

The jungle that ran along the beach to his right was very thick, sometimes to the point where he would not be able to get through without a machete. His stomach began to bother him more and more, until finally he didn't feel like walking anymore.

"What the hell did they put in that crap!" he asked himself, his hand on his stomach. It was full blown nausea now, accompanied by the sinking realization that vomiting was becoming inevitable. He decided to look for the barrier later, turned around and started walking back toward his cabin to have a glass of water and lie down. The nausea turned out to be a passing phenomenon. It left him as quickly as it had come. His stomach was still a bit unsettled, but it wasn't so bad that he needed to call off his search.

"So much for that," he said, turning around once more. He resumed his walk down the beach, but within moments the nausea returned. He narrowed his eyes suspiciously and turned around, walking back quickly. Sure enough, the nausea passed.

"Motherfucker!" he said excitedly. This *was* the barrier. He looked around, trying to spot its source, but didn't see anything out of the ordinary. Of course it made sense that whatever caused it would be well hidden. If they put it out in the open, he could just get one of the anti-tank rockets from the arms room and blow it to hell. But that wasn't right either, because he would eventually find it, and they'd given him the means to destroy it—to destroy just about anything, really. Why would they do that? Unless—

Suddenly, a disturbing thought occurred to him. What if the barrier wasn't there to keep them *in*, but to keep something else *out*?

It didn't make sense that they were prisoners, because prisoners weren't typically given enough firepower to take over a small country. And if they were not prisoners, then the barrier made more sense as a defensive fortification than a prison wall. But a fortification against what?

"Fuck this," he said angrily, and started to walk forward, into the field. "It's going to take more than an upset stomach to keep me here." The nausea grew worse, but he ignored it, determined to get to the other side. How big could this field be? If he managed to keep walking forward, no matter how uncomfortable he felt, he would eventually get across. Then he could get to the bottom of this, figure out what was going on and who was behind it. He thought about going back for a rifle, but decided against it. Wherever he emerged, a concealable weapon would probably be best.

The nausea became almost unbearable, but he fought it as hard as he could. The army had taught him to force his body to go on when it was already far past its limits, and he used that ability to fight the effects of the barrier. About twenty meters past the first sign of nausea he couldn't stand it anymore and hastily bent over so that his vomit would not spray all over his uniform. Moments later he was on his hands and knees, too weak to stand. It was worse than anything he had ever felt before. His stomach muscles contracted again and again as they struggled to expel their contents onto the orange sand, and after each spasm another wave of nausea hit him, then another, and another. Specks of blood sprayed into the frothy puddle of bile and partially digested nutrient paste.

He knew he had to get out of there, but he couldn't stand. He didn't have the strength. Suddenly realizing he had made a terrible mistake trying this alone, he began to panic. He could die, and all he had to do was nothing.

Summoning the last of his strength, he fell over backwards, rolled over onto his stomach and began to crawl. Each agonizing tug brought slight relief and gave him strength, until at last he was able to get up on his hands and knees, then finally to stand up and run.

He collapsed when he made it to the patch of jungle that separated the beaches, panting, enjoying the sudden relief from the crippling nausea. Aside from the taste of vomit in his mouth, a slight burning in his throat and a mildly sore stomach, it was almost as though it had never happened. He was exhausted from his struggle though, and that was a feeling that would not dissipate as readily as the nausea. Adjusting his position on the warm sand, he closed his eyes and tried to get his breathing under control. That barrier might as well be a titanium wall a hundred feet tall and fifty feet thick. There was no way through.

Chapter 5

It was dark by the time he woke up. His mouth was sore and he had a headache, almost like a hangover. Whatever the barrier did, it affected more than just his digestive system. In the distance he heard the crackling of a fire, and when he sat up and looked around he saw waves of orange light crawling along the tree trunks.

He spotted the bonfire almost immediately, down by the beach on the village side of the jungle patch. Patting the butt of the pistol to make sure it was still there, he got to his feet and walked towards the light. A large group of people were gathered within the fire's ambiance, listening to someone talk. As he got closer, he saw that it was Max—big surprise there. Alex had known people like Max, they liked to be in charge, or more accurately, they believed they should be in charge by account of some god given virtue. That type usually made the worst officers. Campbell was the opposite, he didn't think it was right that a guy with no experience be put in charge of a platoon, but he did the best he could and didn't let Medlock push him around. The men respected him, and so did Alex. Thinking about those two almost made him miss being back at Ft. Irwin. Almost.

"Alex," Max said, spotting him. "We were wondering where you were." He turned back to the others momentarily and said, "I'll see you all tomorrow then. Please spread the word."

"Max," Alex said, nodding a lazy greeting. "I saw your barrier. Nice. Thanks for the heads up." He looked for Yael among those gathered, but didn't see her. As he got near the fire and felt it's warmth, he realized it was actually cold out, probably in the mid sixties, though a strong breeze from the ocean made it feel colder. The wind carried a salty tang that he enjoyed. It helped clear the foul taste from his mouth.

"Yes," Max agreed, missing or ignoring the sarcasm. "It is quite formidable. Alex, there's someone I'd like you to meet." He ushered a blond woman towards him. She was older, in her late twenties or early thirties, but still very attractive and youthful in appearance. The only thing that gave away her age were faint lines around her eyes and on her neck. Her hair, blond to the roots, was tied back in a pony tail whose floating ends glowed like bulb filaments against the fire's light.

"This is Barbara," Max continued. "She's a doctor. A trauma surgeon, to be exact."

"Hi," Alex said, trying not to stare. Instead, he turned to look at the others, who were standing in clumps and talking, almost casually. Were they having a beach party?

"Alex is our soldier," Max said. "Or perhaps sheriff, since he's the only one that can get to the weapons."

"Another cog in the machine, eh?" Barbara asked rhetorically. Her voice was pleasant, high pitched yet smooth. "If only we knew what the darn thing did. Nice to meet you, Alex."

"Me too," he said, then realized his reply didn't make sense. If Barbara noticed, she didn't acknowledge his verbal clumsiness in any way he could see.

"So, Max," he said, eager to get past his blunder. "Did you get any more of your doors open?"

"Indeed," Max said, his eyes lighting up. "I discovered that I can open them all, from the terminal in my cottage."

"Really?" Alex said, a bit alarmed at the thought of Max getting into the arms room. He had no idea why he should react this way, but he had, for some reason, come to think of it as *his* arms room, and no one else had any business messing around with his stuff. Strange, yet there it was.

"Well," Max admitted. "Every door except yours."

"Oh," Alex said, hiding his relief. "That's odd."

"Yes it is, but it's just another indication that you're someone important."

"Important?" Alex found it hard to pay attention to Max, mostly because he was still groggy from his impromptu nap, but also because he wanted to stare at Barbara's cleavage through her low cut shirt. Fort Irwin was not exactly a target rich environment when it came to dating, and being suddenly surrounded by so many attractive women was not easy to adjust to.

"Max believes that whoever brought us here intended us to fill certain roles," Barbara said. "Not only do some of us have very specialized skills, but we were provided with the tools of our trade."

"So it's like we're some kind of colony," Alex suggested. "Each member chosen to fill a niche."

"Yes," Max agreed. "That is what I believe."

"Okay, so I'm the soldier, Barbara is the doctor, what are you?"

"I believe I'm supposed to be the mayor, or governor or whatever you want to call it," Max said matter-of-factly. Alex almost sneered—he had called that one correctly.

"What makes you think so?" he asked, trying not to sound antagonistic.

"Well," Max began, not in the least bit displeased by the question. "For starters, I am a law professor at a major university as well as a former superior court judge, which I believe is why they chose me. But that aside, my cottage is twice the size of the others and—"

"Really?" Alex interrupted. "Twice?" For some reason that both interested and bothered him. It didn't seem fair, which was an odd reaction for a person in his situation. He should be thinking of how to escape, not how big his cabin was.

"Yes," Max said. "Twice, or roughly so. And I'm the only one with a terminal with universal access to every pad in the colony."

"Except mine," Alex said, narrowing his eyes slightly. The more of this he heard, the less he liked it.

"Except yours," Max agreed. "I can't even open your cabin door, let alone the arms room." Alex hadn't realized he had included cabin doors when he said every pad in the colony. This scared him, despite the fact that his privacy was apparently secure. What else did that terminal do? Were there cameras in the cabins? He thought about asking, but decided against it. Better to do some investigating later on.

"So maybe *I'm* the governor," Alex said, finally failing to hide his contentiousness. "Sword mightier than the pen and all that."

Max smiled patiently, which pissed Alex off even more. "It's a theory, but I don't think so. For one, if you were supposed to be in charge, you would have the terminal, not I."

"Maybe you're my secretary."

Now he saw a slight strain in Max's friendly façade.

"Then why the bigger house?"

"Boys!" Barbara cut in, chuckling. "We can whip them out later. I agree with Max, assuming the theory holds water. We're not sure that it does yet, let's not forget that."

"Right," Max said. "Of course."

"I guess I do too," Alex grudgingly admitted, not wanting to cause any more trouble. He had no desire to be in charge himself, and he knew that the less he argued the faster he could excuse himself. He didn't like Max and saw no reason to be around him any more than he had to.

"I'm pleased to hear that, Alex," Max said. "I've called for a meeting tomorrow afternoon. To get everyone together, talk about our situation, maybe figure out what's going on and how to get out of here."

"So everyone is out now?" Alex asked. "The ones that were sleeping?"

"Yes," Max said. "Every one. The last one came out about an hour ago. You can meet him if you want, he is a scientist, a biochemist, though I'll be darned if I know why we need one."

"Maybe later," Alex said. "I'm gonna take off, go for a walk. Barbara, it was a pleasure to meet you. See you guys later."

"Later," Barbara said, smiling warmly. *Her* he liked.

"We'll see you at the meeting tomorrow?" Max called after him as he turned to walk away. "At around midday?"

"Yeah," Alex said. "I think I can clear my schedule." He walked towards the water, leaving the murmur of voices behind him. The rhythmic rushing of the ocean lapping the sand was a much more pleasing melody.

He waited a few minutes before letting his eyes adjust to the darkness, then started to move towards the cliff, scanning the beach as he walked. The night was strangely familiar, almost completely devoid of the signs of civilization he had once been accustomed to. Besides the glow of the fire and the distant ship lights on the horizon, it was not unlike night in the Mojave desert—

Ship lights? His head snapped in the direction of the ocean as he peered into the darkness. Sure enough, there were lights from at least three vessels. Relief and disappointment flooded through him, and the source of each was the same. Wherever they were, it was nothing fantastical or extraordinary, just a tropical coast or island in some remote part of the world. His heart began to thump loudly and he realized with some surprise that he was afraid. He liked it here. Or at least part of him did, and now, having seen the ships, he realized that whatever this was, it would not last. He wasn't sure how he felt about that, but he did know that he had been in a better place a few seconds ago, before he noticed those damned lights.

He thought about not saying anything, but he couldn't bring himself to do it. These people were not like him, what waited for them at home was more than being stuck in some god forsaken dust bowl with gang bangers, hillbillies and sociopaths. He thought of Yael, and what she had said about her family.

"What the fuck was I thinking?" he asked himself, shaking his head. He turned back to the gathering and shouted, "Max! Get over here! I see lights!"

Within seconds, the entire campfire brigade was charging towards him, shouting excitedly. He realized he should have handled that more discretely, but what was done, was done.

"Where?" Max demanded, breathing heavily from the brief run. Medlock would have loved to get his hands on him. He'd run him across the entire desert until he lost half his body weight in sweat.

"Give it a sec," Alex said. "Give your eyes time to adjust, then look where I'm pointing."

A little while later, a chorus of affirmations declared that people's night vision was finally up to the task.

"We need some way to try to contact them," a young man with shaggy hair shouted. "Does anyone have a radio?"

Alex rolled his eyes, and then smiled, realizing that's exactly what Yael would have done.

"The campfire!" someone else said excitedly. "We can make it bigger! Maybe spell out 'help' or 'SOS' or something!" Alex turned to the speaker and saw a pretty girl about his own age, another blond, but this one with a round face and dimples.

Others agreed, then a murmur broke out as they tried to decide what to do.

"Wait here," Alex said to Max. "I'll be right back."

"Where are you going?"

"To get something."

He ran towards the warehouse and wondered how he would find it until he saw that each cabin had a light mounted near the roof, illuminating his path. He found the warehouse quickly and made his way inside.

The arms room "airlock" worked exactly as before. Once inside, he grabbed one of the NVD boxes and then looked around, searching for flashlights. He spotted a rack of high end combat lights and took one out. Pointing it at a dark corner, he hit the rubber button on the tail cap and was impressed by the intensity of the beam it projected.

"This will do!" he said, taking two more and tucking them into the cargo pockets of his ACU pants. It was uncomfortable, the flashlights dug into his thighs, but it would only be for a little while.

When he was half way down the corridor he realized he had forgotten to lock the outer arms room door, but as he turned back it hissed closed and the LED turned red.

"That's convenient," he said, then resumed a brisk run back. A few people startled as he ran past them.

When he made it to the beach, he ran up to Max and handed him a flashlight.

"Do you know Morse code?" Alex asked, proud to be breathing normally despite having run quite a distance. A silly thing to feel, but he liked anything that distinguished him from the others, especially Max.

The older man hesitated, examining the light. "Um, no, I don't."

"SOS," Alex said patiently. "Three dots, three dashes, three dots. Very simple."

"How…"

"The tail cap of the flashlight has a button. Don't point these things at anyone, they are very powerful and will blind someone for a little while, especially if their eyes are adjusted to the dark. Tap the button for a dot, hold it down for a second for a dash. Got it?"

Max hesitated, considering it, then nodded. "I believe so." He pointed the light towards the ships and hit the button briefly. A powerful beam lanced into the night.

"Holy crap!" someone in the crowd said. "That's the brightest flashlight I've ever seen!"

"Good," Alex said. "Three dots, three dashes, three dots. Got it?"

Max nodded, and Alex handed him the two remaining flashlights.

"Give these to people with more than two brain cells to rub together. Have them spread out along the beach and flash that signal at those ships. Aim carefully for maximum effectiveness."

"Will do. What about you?"

"I'm going away from the lights and the fire, and see what I can see with these." He held up the plastic NVD box. Max looked perplexed.

"Night vision," Alex explained.

"Ah."

Alex turned and ran towards the patch of jungle he had napped in, then looked back towards the others. He didn't see any lights. Max must still be passing along his instructions. Deciding to play it safe, he crossed over to the barrier side of the trees. That was still quite a way from the nausea effect.

Kneeling in the sand, he opened the NVD box and took out a binocular optic with variable magnification mounted on a head harness. Before strapping it on, he examined the device to locate its controls. Once it was on his head, he moved it into position over his eyes and turned it on.

"Wow," he said, instantly impressed by the clarity with which he saw his surroundings. He had thought the goggles he used in Ft. Irwin were the latest and greatest, but these were noticeably superior. They seemed to use a combination of light amplification and thermal imaging technology. Scanning the horizon, he quickly located the ship lights and adjusted the magnification to six, the maximum setting. It was hard to keep the ships in his field of view, but he quickly learned to steady his head and was able to make out the blurry shapes of cargo ships behind the glaring torches of their marker lights.

After staring at the ships for a while, he realized they were moving towards each other, or perhaps passing one another. Suddenly bright pulses of light glowed at the periphery of his vision as Max and the others began to signal with their flashlights. Counting the dots and dashes, he was relieved to find that they weren't bungling the code.

He turned the goggles off, removed them from his head and put them back in the plastic case. He was about to start signaling the ships with his weapon light when he heard something to his right, from the direction of the barrier. It sounded almost like a whimper.

As odd as it was for a soldier to be afraid of the dark, Alex had always had an irrational fear of the night, or more accurately of being alone outside at night. He had gotten used to dealing with it, and having a weapon made it easier. He left the box on the sand, drew his sidearm and held it ready. It had a tiny little optic mounted in a cutout on the rear of the slide. The red dot was just bright enough to see clearly. There was also a weapon light mounted under the slide just forward of the trigger guard. The slide had slots cut into it to reduce weight and the barrel and chamber were coated in a gold colored low friction coating. All of the gear his abductors had given him was very high end stuff.

Scanning the beach as he walked towards the sound, he was able to make out the silhouette of a person almost immediately, and as he got closer, he saw that it was a woman. She was standing at what he assumed was the edge of the barrier effect, looking across to the other side.

Relaxing, he lowered the pistol and approached less stealthily. The closer he got, the better he could see her. She jumped, inhaling sharply, and spun to face him.

"You!" she cried, and Alex recognized her immediately. It was Yael. A louder whimper accompanied the sound of her voice, and at this range Alex was able to determine that it was coming from the other side of the barrier.

Chapter 6

"Why did you sneak up on me?" Yael demanded. Her eyes widened as she saw his pistol, or more accurately how he was holding it. She took a step back. "Don't!"

"Don't what?" Alex asked, perplexed by her reaction. He holstered the pistol and stood staring at her with a raised eyebrow.

She paused, considering the situation. "Never mind. I thought…never mind."

"What are you doing out here?" he asked, looking around. He didn't see anything out of the ordinary.

"What are *you* doing out here?"

"You don't give anything up easily, do you?"

"What the hell is that supposed to mean?" She put her hands on her hips and took a slight step forward. If she were a man, he would have prepared himself for a fight.

"Why can't you just give me a break?" he asked, suddenly overcome with frustration and anger, though he had no idea where it was coming from. "I've tried to be nice to you since we met, and all you do is give me shit!"

She opened her mouth, an angry retort chambered and ready to fire, but then stopped herself, looking at him with uncertainty. After a moment, she crossed her arms in front of her chest and seemed to relax.

"Fine, I'm sorry," she said, looking away. "I'm just… being here, I…"

"I know, I know, I'm sorry too." He felt bad about yelling at her, for all he knew this was her first time away from home, like poor Private Haag. "What are you doing out here alone, though? It's not safe." He wondered what Haag was doing at the moment, and whether they'd managed to save his hand. He hoped the kid was okay.

She turned back towards the field and pointed. "Look."

He followed her finger and tried to see what she was looking at and caught a hint of movement, though he couldn't quite make out what it was. He drew his pistol and pointed it at the source.

"No!" she shouted, making a grab for the gun. "Don't shoot it! It's just a dog!"

"Relax," he said, jerking the weapon away before she could get it. "I'm not going to shoot it. What kind of an asshole do you think I am?" He activated the weapon light and saw the dog in the stark white beam, tail wagging, eyes glowing, about fifty meters away. It was a small dog, mostly white, though with some black patches. Probably a mutt. It paced back and forth along the edge of the nausea field, whimpering. So that's how wide the barrier was: fifty meters.

"Awww," Yael cooed, seeing it clearly in the light. "I wish we could get to it. Poor thing."

"I'll try, if you want," Alex said. "I might be able to meet it close enough in the middle for me to grab it, if it can get as far as I can."

"No," she said quickly. "It's too dangerous. There were some dead animals in the jungle, caught in this thing, where it circles the village. They looked like they puked their guts out. It was horrible."

"I tried it earlier. I made it almost halfway. I didn't realize that before, but now that I see where the dog is…that's my puke there. See it?"

"You could have died!" she cried. "What were you thinking?"

He shrugged. "Do you want me to try or not?"

She thought about it, then shook her head. "I can't ask you to."

"I'll take that as a yes. Hold this." He held his pistol out to her, grip first.

She took a step back. "You would trust me with it?" She looked at him with a peculiar expression.

He smiled. "Promise not to shoot me, okay?" He had meant it as a joke, but she took it seriously.

"I promise," she said as she stepped back towards him.

"The switch to turn the light on and off is right in front of the trigger guard. Keep it pointed at the dog, and keep your finger off the trigger." He handed her the pistol, then turned towards the dog. The light went out for a couple of seconds and then came back on, guiding his way. The dog, seeing him move towards it, yapped and started to move closer, but then stopped and whined again.

"Here boy!" Alex called out. "Come here! Good dog! Good dog!" As he got closer to the animal he started to feel sick, just like before. It was mild at first, but each step made it worse.

"Here boy!" he shouted, trying to keep the pain from his voice. "Good dog! Come here!" When he was twenty meters in, a bit more than a third of the way to the dog, he paused, momentarily overcome by a terrible wave of nausea he could barely contain. If there was a worse feeling in the world, he didn't know what it was. Why was he doing this? For the dog, or for her?

"Please boy," he cried out. "Please come here!" His voice cracked, and he had to take several deep breaths to avoid vomiting. A few steps later, he couldn't contain it, and puked into the sand at his feet, managing to turn his head in time to avoid soiling himself. The dog started barking, then took a tentative step forward, then another, and suddenly bolted towards him. It ran most of the way to him, then started to yelp loudly and run in circles, gagging and coughing.

Alex looked up at the sky and inhaled deeply, trying to forget where he was. He was angry. Angry at the dog, angry at himself for being so stupid as to walk into this deathtrap again, and angry at Yael for being pretty.

"Fuck this shit," he said. Without looking down, he started to run towards the dog. The feeling of intensifying nausea became unbearable, a solid wall that he couldn't push through. He looked down and saw the dog just a few feet away, lying on its side, its whole body convulsing like a grotesque snake trying to swallow something too large for its throat.

No longer able to stand, he collapsed to his knees and clutched his stomach, whimpering from the pain. He would have screamed, but he couldn't suck in enough air.

"Alex!" Yael shouted, running towards him.

"Stay back!" he cried as loud as he could, hoping she would hear him. She did. He thought about going back, but he couldn't stand seeing the dog that way. The expression "a dog's death" didn't do this experience justice. He dropped down and pushed forward on hands and knees, clenching his stomach to stave off what little of the convulsions he could. It helped a little bit, but every foot he moved forward was another notch on the pain scale until he was sure it would drive him mad. The dog saw him and rolled onto its belly, crawling towards him feebly. Just as he thought he would pass out, it came within reach. Grabbing it by the scruff of its neck, he found some reserve of strength he wouldn't have imagined he had and got to his feet. He half leapt and half ran out of the field, unable to contain the foamy bile that spewed out of his mouth and all over his shirt. Yael ran to him, grabbed his arm and pulled him forward.

When he was out of the field he dropped the dog, collapsed onto his back, and tried his best not to pass out.

"I will never fucking do that again!" he managed between gasps. "Holy fuck that was the worst thing I've ever felt in my life!" The dog didn't look much better. It lay on its side, panting, its brown eyes fixed on Alex, tail twitching slightly.

"You did it!" Yael cried excitedly. "I can't believe you did it! That was the bravest thing I've ever seen!" She held the pistol by the slide in her left hand, casually and expertly. Perhaps she had handled a similar weapon in one of those Israeli kids' camps where they live in the desert, plant crops and learn to shoot. That would explain a lot about her.

He looked up at her, and despite the persistent pain in his throat, stomach and head, he smiled.

"Did you just say something nice to me?" he croaked.

She smiled back. "Stranger things have happened."

"Not to me."

"Oh shut up. Are you okay? You look like crap!"

"Yeah," he said, and his smile turned into a grin. "You were worried about me. I saw you run towards me."

"I was worried about the dog."

"The dog's name is Alex?"

"Don't flatter yourself," she said, shaking her head. "I didn't want you to die, at least not then. I didn't want to have to feel guilty."

"Whatever you say."

The dog rolled onto its belly and inched over to him. It sniffed the air next to his head, then moved closer and licked his face.

"It likes you!" Yael said.

Sitting up, Alex picked up the dog and put it on his lap, stroking it gently. In the process, he noticed it was female.

"Yes she does. Now let's see what we can see. Shine that light over here, will you? But not right at me." Yael pointed the pistol at the dog. It was blindingly bright, but his eyes adjusted quickly. It was adjusting back that would be the problem.

He searched the dog's neck and found a collar with two tags, a plastic one shaped like a bone and a portion of a metal one. The metal tag, red or purple aluminum, looked like it had been broken off near the base where it attached to the collar. He could only see the tops of letters—it was impossible to know what it may have said. The plastic tag was in once piece, but there was nothing on it. It's surface was rough, as though someone sanded off the dog's name and whatever goofy picture this type of tag usually came with.

"That's odd," he said. "It looks like someone went out of their way to make sure we couldn't get anything off of these."

"Let me see," she said, leaning forward. "That *is* odd." She reached for the tags, and the dog sniffed her and licked her hand.

"She likes you too," Alex said. "Imagine that. Dogs must be able to sense something people can't."

Yael pulled back, and the light died. He couldn't see her face, but he knew he had gone too far and hurt her.

"I'm sorry," he said quickly. "I didn't mean that, I was just teasing."

"Fine," she said tersely. Then, after a moment of silence, added, "What are you going to do with it?"

"The dog?"

"Yes."

"Don't you mean what are *we* going to do with it?"

She shrugged. "You went and got it. Are you going to keep it?"

"We don't exactly have much choice. Somehow I don't think anyone is going to come through that barrier with 'lost dog' flyers." Feeling better—he recovered much faster this time, maybe he was building up a tolerance—he set the dog down, then climbed to his feet and reached for his pistol. She handed it to him, and he put it back in its holster. The dog, apparently having regained much of its strength, stood next to him, tail wagging.

"Can it be both of ours?" she said, the tension in her voice betraying how difficult it was for her to ask.

He leaned down, picked up the dog and handed it to her. "Of course it can, and mostly yours if you want." The dog was light, maybe fifteen pounds, and did not seem to mind being handled. His eyes still hadn't adjusted back to the darkness, but he thought he saw her smile.

"Thank you." She stroked the dog's head as she held it, and he heard the animal sigh contentedly.

"We should get back to the fire," he said. "I saw ship lights on the horizon, the others were flashing SOS at them."

"Seriously?" He could hear the sudden excitement in her voice. "And you waited until now to tell me? Let's go!"

"Hang on a sec." He took off his shirt and rubbed it in the sand, then shook it out. "Not clean, but it will do."

"There is a laundry machine in your cottage, you know," she said as she watched him.

"Are you sure? I didn't see one. There's not much room, I can't image where it would be."

"It's in the floor," she explained. "I'm not surprised you missed it." She hesitated, frowning slightly. "I didn't mean that as an insult. I meant because it's in the floor, easy to miss."

He smiled. "We're making progress then. That's encouraging."

They set off at a brisk march toward the campfire. On the way, Alex recovered the night vision box where he had left it in the sand.

"It works with some sort of enzyme," she continued as she walked. "There's a powder you sprinkle on your clothes and you leave them overnight. In the morning they're clean and smell fresh. There's no water or anything."

"That's interesting. How'd you figure out how to use it? I also don't mean to insult you. It just doesn't sound very intuitive." It was both funny and a little sad that they had to qualify their statements in this manner.

"I didn't. There were instructions on the powder box."

"Well," he said. "At least something in this god forsaken place comes with instructions."

They approached the fire, where Max and the others were still flashing SOS at the ships. Alex looked out at the horizon, but didn't see the lights anymore.

"What happened?" he asked Max as they got close enough to hear. "Did they sail away?"

"No, the lights just went out—" He saw the dog and pointed. "Where did you get that?" He raised the flashlight to point at Yael, about to push the button.

"Don't!" Alex barked. "I told you not to shine that in people's faces."

"Right, of course," Max said quickly, not at all pleased to be reprimanded. "Hand that animal over. Does it have tags?" He stepped toward Yael and reached for the dog.

"No!" she said, pulling away.

"Give me the dog," Max commanded, inching closer. Alex stepped in front of him.

"She said no, Max."

The older man glared at him a moment, then his expression softened. "Alex, I need to examine that dog, see if it has tags. We can learn—"

"We did that already," Alex said. "There's an aluminum tag broken off at the base, and a plastic one sanded clean."

Max raised an eyebrow. "Indeed? Sanded? That's odd. I'd like to see the tags…Barbara has a microscope in her warehouse room, among other things. She can examine them a lot closer than we can."

Alex nodded, then turned to Yael and reached for the dog. She hesitated, but then held it out to him. Instead of taking it from her, Alex fished around its neck with his fingers and tried to unclasp the collar. The buckle broke as soon as he tugged on it, but that would do just as well. He handed it to Max.

The older man took it and nodded. "Thank you. Please bring the dog to Barbara tomorrow as well. She can take some blood and run some tests. Maybe we can learn something useful…and of course you can see if it's in good health."

"Will do," Alex agreed. "Now what do you mean those lights just went out?"

"They blinked out," Barbara said, walking up from the beach, where a group of people was still signaling for help with Alex's flashlights. "One by one."

"They could be anchored," Alex suggested. "Maybe we can't see their anchor lights from this far away." He wanted to try the night vision device and see if maybe he could spot them, but he was too tired—he hadn't recovered as much as he'd thought. Maybe tomorrow. "It could mean we're near a major harbor. But that would be nuts, wouldn't it? I mean how can this crazy place be near a major city? There would be boats, you know, little ones, pleasure boats. And...wait a minute. You've been here a few days, right? Have you seen any airplanes? Wherever we are, if it isn't the poles, there should be airplanes."

Max blinked, taken aback by the question. "Come to think of it, no, I haven't seen any airplanes. No lights in the sky at night either, except the stars. Where the hell are we?"

"Hey!" Barbara said excitedly, noticing the animal. "You guys found a doggy! Can I pet him?"

"It's a girl," Yael said defensively, but offered the dog to Barbara. The older woman stroked it affectionately, and the dog lapped her hand when it could reach it.

"It's adorable!" she said. "A little scruffy, but nothing a bath can't fix. Where did you guys find it?"

"On the other side of the barrier," Yael said. "Alex went across for it."

"You crossed the barrier?" Max and Barbara said at almost the same time.

"No," Alex said, raising his hands. "No, of course not. I got halfway through, and the dog came to me."

"Was it affected?"

"It nearly died, so yes. But it got a lot farther from its starting point than I did, so maybe it was affected less. Or maybe it has more balls than I do, even though it's a girl."

"Interesting," Barbara said, rubbing her chin. "That you were able to get so far in. How was it? I mean how do you feel?"

"I wouldn't recommend it," Alex said, smiling. "I have a high tolerance for things like that, I was able to stay in the gas room the longest in basic training. That's when they put you in a room with CS riot gas and make you take your mask off. But if you're wondering if someone can just run through, no. If I'd tried to go any further I wouldn't have been able to get back out. I barely managed as is."

"Interesting," she repeated.

"Listen," Alex said. "I'm exhausted, so if it's all the same to you guys, I'm going to hit the sack. Just drop those flashlights off in the morning, okay?"

Max nodded.

Alex turned to go, then glanced at Yael. Still holding the dog, she followed. He waited until they were far from the others, then said, "Can you take care of it tonight? Going into that barrier twice in one day took more out of me than I thought. I'm beat."

She nodded. "Of course. What should I feed it? Do you think it will eat the nutrient paste?"

"It's a dog," Alex said, smiling. "Dogs eat cat shit. It will eat the nutrient paste."

She pursed her lips. "That's disgusting."

"Maybe you can get it a dehydrated steak from the warehouse," he suggested.

She brightened. "Yes, I'll do that."

"Goodnight, Yael," he said as they neared his cottage. "It was a pleasure not being yelled at by you today."

"You're such a…" she started. After a brief pause, she said, "Goodnight, Alex, and thank you, for getting the dog, and for…thank you." She turned away and walked towards the warehouse.

As she disappeared into the night, he felt strangely alone.

Chapter 7

He woke to the sound of music, and for a moment, forgot where he was. How many days did he have left in this motel before his monthly four day leave was over? Was this his first morning? That made him happy, until he started to remember, but what replaced the happiness was not entirely dissimilar—a peculiar satisfaction. The bottom line was still the same. He didn't have to go back to Ft. Irwin, back to the desert. At least not yet.

Sitting up, he noticed the laptop he had left on, the source of the music. He had spent a few minutes last night picking out a playlist before going to bed. He had also turned on the monitor and found a healthy selection of movies to choose from, presumably stored on some central server. Too tired to even think about watching anything, he had settled for the music, though he only got through one or two songs before falling asleep.

"Not a bad place to be trapped," he said, rubbing his eyes. He made his way over to the bathroom compartment and relieved himself, then opened the mirror cabinet. Sure enough, it was full of toiletries: an electric shaver, deodorant, aftershave, toothpaste, toothbrushes, dental floss and more.

Once he had attended to his morning hygiene, he pushed the green pad on the floor, right where Yael had said it would be, and checked on his uniform. It was done: clean and fresh as if it had come from the dry cleaner, though it was not pressed. The box of enzymatic cleaner, or whatever it was, was in the floor compartment next to the "laundry machine." There was a logo on the box, the letter F in a circle. Alex wondered if there was some significance to that, but he was too groggy to focus.

Retrieving the uniform, he considered putting on civilian clothes, perhaps a t-shirt and some shorts, but decided against it, at least for now. This was a complicated situation, and with Max running around playing king, he needed to display a symbol of his own authority.

"Authority," he grumbled. "Might makes right, eh?" He shook

his head, wondering what the architects of this strange prison had been thinking when they set all of this up. Especially when they decided to leave him in charge of an arsenal. They were lucky he wasn't blowing stuff up for shits and giggles. At least not yet. The day was young.

He enjoyed a plate of nutrient paste and a cup of water, though he wondered how long he would be able to eat the stuff before he got sick of it. After donning his uniform, he found a concealed carry holster and a couple of magazine pouches in the gear compartment under the bed. With the pistol out of sight under his shirt, he stepped out into a brightening day and locked the door behind him. The sun rose over the mountains, its beams creating irregular patches of daylight amidst the lingering gray of dawn.

There were lots of people up and about, though the layout of the complex was such that he could only spot a few at any given moment unless they were clustered as they had been at the camp fire. There were several things he knew he should do, such as familiarize himself with the place, inventory the equipment in the arms room and try to see what else he could discover. Not just in the complex itself, but in the warehouse and maybe even his own cabin. Yet he couldn't quite get himself to consider any of those things with any enthusiasm. The army had taught him to never volunteer, to stay out of sight and enjoy what free time he had until someone ordered him to do something. There was no one here to give him orders, and it was proving hard to do anything productive.

"I'll find Yael," he muttered to himself. "She'll have no problem bossing me around." Satisfied with that decision, he started walking, then realized he had no idea which cabin was hers.

"Balls," he cursed, looking around stupidly, hoping to spot her. He noticed a man, probably in his thirties, leaning against the side of a cabin, and started towards him.

"Hi," he said, trying his best to look friendly.

"Hello," the man said, eyeing him cautiously as he noticed his uniform. "You're a soldier?" He was just a bit shorter than Alex, which made him five eight or five nine, and on the thin side. He had a goatee surrounded by stubble that flowed almost seamlessly into short spiky hair.

"Yes," Alex said. "You're not going to ask me if I know anything, are you?" The process of explaining himself was growing tiresome.

"Didn't plan on it. But I guess you must get that a lot." He had a face that was at home wearing a smile, with well worn lines around the eyes and mouth as a result of wearing it often.

Alex nodded, satisfied. "Yeah, that's all anyone seems to want from me. Anyway, I'm looking for Yael, have you seen her?"

"Don't know who that is, sorry," he said, shrugging apologetically. "Maybe if you describe her?"

"Sure. She's about yay high," Alex said, holding his hand up to the base of his nose. "She's wearing…crap I don't know what she's wearing today, but probably a long skirt and white sneakers. She's cute, with freckles and brown hair. Late teens, maybe early twenties. Seen her?"

"Sorry," he said. "I just woke up yesterday afternoon, apparently I'm the last one. Don't know what they drugged me with, but I'm guessing I don't need to sleep for a year."

"Are you the biochemist?"

"The…?" He seemed confused. " Oh, yes. Sorry, I don't really refer to myself as the biochemist, so…"

"What do you call yourself then?"

"Tom," he said, smiling and extending his hand, which Alex took. "And you?"

"Alex."

Tom laughed. "Look at us, exchanging pleasantries! We've been kidnapped, drugged and put on a bad reality show. We should be freaking out."

"Some of us are," Alex said, thinking of Yael. "But I kinda like it here." As soon as he said it, he realized it was true, no longer just an idea to kick around in his head.

"Really? You *like* it here?" The question was accompanied by an incredulous but amused grin.

Alex shrugged. "Why not? It's a tropical resort, for fuck's sake. We've got food, luxury suites and a nice beach. No one tells us what to do, and there are girls." And weapons, he added silently. He wouldn't have liked being a prisoner, but as well armed as he was, it was hard to feel like one.

"How can you be so relaxed? Don't you want to know who put us here? Why?" Tom seemed amused by Alex's attitude, which Alex liked. A good sense of humor said a lot about a person.

"Sure," he admitted. "I care as much as anyone, but until we figure it out there's no sense in stressing over it. I'd much rather kick back and enjoy the break."

"That's one way of looking at it," Tom admitted. "I suppose you're no crazier than the ones locked in their rooms crying. But as for not being ordered around, you must be the only one so lucky. You're the guy with the guns, right? Max mentioned you."

"Max," Alex grumbled. "He can't seem to get over the fact that there's something here he's not in control of. Whoever brought us here picked a real gem of a leader."

"So you believe him?" Tom asked, raising an eyebrow. "About being governor?"

Alex shrugged. "I dunno, I guess. He's got that terminal thing that can open most of the doors, or so he says."

Tom flashed him a strange grin. "I don't see that as a problem."

Alex was about to ask what he meant when he spotted Yael. She was following the dog, who was running around, sniffing things and peeing.

"That," he said, pointing to her. "Is Yael, for future reference."

"Gorgeous," Tom said, nodding appreciatively. "You two an item?"

Alex felt a sudden pang of jealousy. "No, but..."

Tom turned to him and raised his hands defensively. "Hey man, it's cool, don't worry. You've staked your claim, I get it. Hasn't been much time for that sort of thing, I guess."

"It's not like that," Alex said. "I mean I haven't really thought about it…"

"It's cool, man. No need to explain."

Alex smiled and shook his head. "You don't sound much like a biochemist." This was another person here he was starting to like, which made three so far.

Tom laughed. "Oh yeah? How many biochemists have you known?"

"None," Alex admitted, chuckling in agreement. "Well, one

now, I suppose."

"Yeah. But I gotta tell you man, you're in for a world of hurt with that one." He nodded towards Yael. "If you do decide to go after her, that is."

"Why do you say that?"

"The way she's dressed, her name, put those together and it sounds like she's an orthodox Jew. Or maybe conservative, which would make it somewhat easier."

"So what?" Alex didn't know there were different kinds of Jews, except of course for their version of the Amish with the black coats and weird hats, but then he had never cared much for religion or any of its particulars.

"So what? Are you kidding? Those people have more rules than the federal government. If you're not Jewish, you're lucky she even talks to you, except to exchange pleasantries. Though the fact that you're even thinking about it impresses the hell out of me. Considering where we are and all."

Alex was not convinced. Yael was a raging harpy, but other than that she seemed perfectly reasonable.

"We'll see, I guess. Anyway, see you later, Tom. It was nice meeting you."

"Same here, and good luck."

"Thanks."

Alex started walking towards Yael just as she turned a corner and disappeared behind one of the cabins. Deep in thought, he slowed his pace. His conversation with Tom had raised a lot of questions that he found both exciting and disturbing. For starters, why had he gotten so possessive? She hadn't given him an indication that she was interested, and he hadn't even considered the possibility that he was. Yet when Tom had evinced interest…

He almost bumped into her when he turned the corner.

"Hey!" she cried out, taking a step back. "Watch where you're going, you clod!" Yep, a raging harpy alright.

"Morning, sunshine," he said with a wide grin. She was wearing the same denim skirt and tennis shoes as the day before but with a white t-shirt. Her hair was tied back in a pony tail that exposed her slender neck and small ears that stood slightly too far forward. He found himself staring at her well defined collarbone.

"Morning," she said, without much enthusiasm. "Blasted dog kept me up most of the night. Every time I moved it got up and whined." The dog spotted him and came running, tail wagging excitedly. It reared up on his legs and he reached down and picked it up. Bringing it close to his face, he allowed the animal to lick him.

"Buyer's remorse?" he asked, hoping she would say no. He would be disappointed if so small a thing would cause her to cast the dog out after the fuss she made.

"What?" she asked, momentarily confused. "Oh. No, of course not. She's a great dog, very attentive. I'm just cranky."

"You? Cranky? No!" He set the squirming canine on the ground and it ran several circles around him, yipped twice then ran off to find a spot to urinate.

"Stop being so sarcastic," she said. "You don't need to spend time with me if you don't want to. You're the one that keeps coming to find me, remember?"

He flinched, surprised at how much her words bothered him. Was Tom right about her?

"Fine," he said, tight lipped. "I'll leave you alone then, if that's what you want." He turned and started back towards his cabin, feeling a lump forming in his throat.

"No, wait," she said, her voice softening. "I'm sorry. It's not what I want."

He turned back, relieved and excited. So she did want him around after all!

"I'm just not feeling well," she continued. "I haven't eaten since we got here, and with the dog keeping me up…"

"Wait a sec," he demanded, taking a step towards her. "You haven't eaten? Why not? Don't you know about the nutrient paste?"

She looked away, embarrassed. "Yes, but…it's not…it's not kosher. Or at least I don't know if it is."

He blinked. "You're kidding, right?" Tom's warning suddenly didn't seem so farfetched.

"No," she said, her voice uncharacteristically soft. "Why would I be? You…you know I'm Jewish, right?" She looked up at him again, uncertain, as though she wasn't sure how he would react.

"Of course I know, but…I mean it's crazy! Are you going to starve to death to be kosher?"

"No, of course I won't starve, but…" She stomped her foot in frustration. "I don't know how long we'll be here, and I…" Her eyes started to tear up. "What if it's some kind of test? What if we're all…I'm just so scared." Her body shook, and she raised her hands to her face and started to cry. "I just want to go home."

He moved towards her hesitantly, but she didn't push him away. Wrapping his arms around her, he put a hand on the back of her head and pressed it gently to his shoulder. She sobbed, her body shuddering against his, and he held her tightly, stroking her back.

"I'll get you out of this, Yael," he whispered. "All of you. I promise." Even overcome by emotion as he was, he instantly regretted his words. He wanted to help her, but the relaxed innocence with which he had accepted this situation would not survive this. He had come to her looking for motivation, and he found it, though not in the way he had expected.

She pushed away and looked up at him with bloodshot eyes that still managed to look beautiful.

"Do you mean that?" she asked softly.

"I do."

"Why would you say that? I mean…I know you said all of us, but you said it to me. Why? We hardly know each other, and I've been nothing but a bitch to you." Her expression was almost pleading. She was pushing at the foundations of his promise, testing its strength.

He shrugged. "It's the kind of thing I do, I guess. Plus, you're not so bad. I kinda like you. You know…as a person I mean." He grinned at her.

She started to say something, then broke free of his embrace and began to smooth her t-shirt, though it wasn't wrinkled.

"Well thank you," she said in her normal voice. "For the promise, I mean. But I won't hold you to it. It's too much to ask from someone I hardly know." Once she was done with her shirt, she started to rub her eyes, making them even redder than before.

He'd said too much, and she was retreating.

"Anyway," he said, hoping to change the subject before she

managed to pull even further away. "You have to eat something. Does that wacky religion of yours have a provision for situations in which no kosher food is available?"

"Of course it does!" she said. "Survival is more important, but I'm not dying. And it's not wacky, your religion is based on it. Jesus was a Jew, in case you've forgotten."

"My religion?"

"Aren't you a Christian? I just thought…"

He enjoyed seeing her confused. "Nope. I don't believe in religion, but I do think there's something out there. Especially when bad shit happens to me. There are no atheists in the trenches, or so they say."

"Oh," she said, frowning. "Sorry. Anyway, it's not wacky. And please don't start a debate about religion, I'm not interested."

"Fair enough," he said. "But we have more important matters to think about right now, like getting some food in you."

She sighed. "I *am* very hungry."

"Good. Let's get you some nutrient paste."

"No," she said sternly. "I won't eat it until I know what's in it, or until I'm dying of hunger."

He nodded. "Stubborn. I like that. How about beef? Is beef kosher?"

"Only if it's killed a certain way."

"Jesus Christ!" This was harder than he thought, but then that should not have surprised him. If there were a simple solution, she would have found it.

"That wouldn't do it," she said with a crooked smile. "Wrong religion."

He laughed. "You actually made a joke! That's awesome. But I see this isn't going to be easy. How do you eat back in the world? Must be a bitch to go grocery shopping."

"No, it's not hard at all. Normally we know food is kosher if it has a kosher mark on it, which means a rabbi examined it, or the way it was killed or whatever, but a rabbi doesn't need to be involved if something is obviously kosher, like fruits and vegetables."

"Fruits, good. We're in the tropics, so that shouldn't be a problem. Have you looked?"

"Of course I looked. There are some coconuts, but they're on the other side of the barrier."

"Okay, at least we're getting somewhere. What about fish? Can you eat fish? Crabs?"

"Fish yes, crabs no."

He nodded. "Fish then. Has anyone found fishing poles yet?"

She shrugged. "Not that I know of, or I would be using one."

"Okay then," he said excitedly as an idea dawned. "Let's go to the warehouse."

"What for?" she asked, looking at him suspiciously, but when he started walking, she followed.

"Several things," he explained, then turned to the dog and shouted, "Come on, mutt!" The little animal looked up, saw them leaving and ran after them, yipping excitedly.

"You were saying?" Yael asked.

"Right. First, we're going to see if there's an ingredient list in the nutrient powder storage room. Maybe it's on the barrels. If it's all kosher stuff, you can eat it, right? Without a kosher mark or anything like that?"

She nodded. "Yes, I'm not a fascist about it."

"Good! Who knows? Maybe it'll be okay."

"What else?" she asked.

"We're also going to see if there is any kosher meat in the dehydrated storage, and we'll see if there are fishing poles."

"I was there this morning," she said. "I got a piece of beef for the dog. I didn't see any kosher marks on anything, but most of the rooms were locked and I couldn't find anyone to open them." She sounded doubtful, but he saw hope in her eyes.

"No harm in looking again," he said. "Besides, I'm sure we'll find fishing poles. If the people that dumped us here gave us anti-tank rockets, why not fishing poles?"

"Anti tank rockets?" she asked, her eyes widening.

"You don't know about the arms room? I'll explain on the way. But yeah, with all the stuff they gave me, there should be fishing poles."

"Sounds reasonable. But how will we get into the locked rooms?"

"Easy. Either Max opens them for us, or I open them with

breaching charges." He smiled.

"If you say so."

He stopped, reached out and touched her arm, right below the shoulder.

"Yael," he said. "We'll get you something to eat. Even if I have to go fishing with hand grenades like some crazy Russian, okay?"

She nodded, and almost looked like she would cry again. She pulled away, but not until several seconds had passed.

"Come on!" he said. "Let's go. We have work to do." The dog yipped its acknowledgement, and they continued to the warehouse.

There was a man there, about Alex's age, though a bit shorter, wider and more muscular.

"Hey," Alex said. "I'm Alex, this is Yael."

"Bob," the man said. He had a big round head that terminated in a narrow chin that looked out of place. His short brown hair was the same color as his eyes, but his brows had a hint of red to them, as though they had previously been dyed. After three years of military service, Alex had gotten good at judging people by their faces, and he knew instantly that he wasn't going to like Bob.

"What are you doing standing around?" Alex asked. "It almost looks like you're guarding the place."

"I am," he said with no trace of humor.

"Really?" Alex asked, bewildered. "I was just joking. How did Max con you into doing that?"

"No one conned me into anything," Bob said, giving Alex a disapproving look. "We don't know how long we're going to be here, and we all need to pitch in to make this work. My job is to keep people from taking too much food, and to make sure people put back what they borrow."

"Sounds reasonable," Alex said. "How much is too much? I'm talking about the dehydrated meat."

"One person, one item every two days."

Alex nodded. "That's not bad, I would have gone with half that. Okay then, we're going to get two items, since we're two people."

The man nodded. "You can, she can't. She already took something earlier today."

"That was for the dog," Alex explained. He knew rationing was important, but this was getting on his nerves. Right or not, he felt like the rules did not apply to him. It wasn't fair, and he was aware of that, but the way he saw it, he could easily take over the colony and kill anyone who stood in his way if he wanted to. He didn't have the slightest desire to do so, but he figured he was owed a little leeway nonetheless.

"It doesn't matter what she did with it, she took one. She can come back tomorrow."

"Alex," Yael said. "He's right, I did take it, so…"

"Look, Bob," Alex said, not bothering to hide his irritation. "She can only eat kosher food, and she hasn't eaten anything since she got here. We're going to go in there, and look for some kosher stuff. Is that okay with you?"

He nodded. "She can go in, of course. She just can't take any more of the meat, kosher or not."

Alex took a step forward. "If we find kosher meat, she's going to take it."

"I'm sorry, I can't let you do that."

Alex was about to say something, then shook his head and laughed. "Right, sure." He turned to Yael. "Come on, let's go." He started forward, but Bob put a firm hand on his left shoulder. The dog growled. Alex acted without thinking.

He grabbed Bob's wrist with his left hand and struck him in the shoulder joint with the blade of his right. Bob flinched, raising his hands to ward off the strike, but Alex had moved too fast and without warning. Pushing hard into Bob's shoulder, Alex pulled up on his arm, twisting his spine slightly and forcing him off balance. Thus weakened, he wasn't able to resist the torquing of the hips that sent him sailing over Alex's leg.

The dog started to bark and ran at Bob.

"Alex!" Yael shouted. "No!"

Bob went down hard and rolled away. The dog continued to bark, coming closer, but stayed just out of reach, afraid to get too close.

"I'm sorry," Alex said calmly. "You grabbed me and I just reacted." He didn't like acting like a thug, but it had felt good to toss Bob on his ass.

The big man was panting heavily, his eyes shifting between Alex and the barking dog.

"Shut up, mutt!" Alex commanded, and the dog obeyed, though it couldn't entirely contain its ire and growled.

"We can chalk this up to a friendly misunderstanding," Alex continued. "I'm sure Max wouldn't mind if Yael took some food for herself. Hell, there might not even be any kosher meat in there, probably isn't, in fact. We didn't know about the dog, that it would count, and we'll feed it nutrient paste from now on, okay?"

Bob seemed confused, but he nodded. Alex walked up to him and offered him his hand. Bob took it and allowed Alex to pull him to his feet.

"Sorry," Alex said again. "We'll go in now, okay?"

"Yeah," Bob said in a shaky voice. "Go ahead."

Alex smiled and nodded. "Thanks."

He turned around and put a hand under Yael's elbow, moving her forward. She was staring at him with a mixture of wonder and horror, but she allowed him to usher her inside.

Chapter 8

"I'm an idiot," he said, as soon as he closed the doors behind him and realized he had missed the obvious.

"Huh?" she asked, still staring at him.

"I should have just told him I'd give you mine." He smacked himself on the forehead. "Stupid, stupid, stupid."

"Where did you learn to do that?" she asked. "The army?"

"What, the throw?"

She nodded. The dog circled a few times near the door, then lay down and closed its eyes with a satisfied sigh.

"No. They teach it, but they don't have time to go into enough depth. I've been doing it since I was a kid. My dad thought it was important. I can teach you, if you want. It's not hard, just a few basic principles."

She brightened. "Really? You think I can throw someone like that?"

"Sure, one of Britain's top jujitsu masters in the 1920s or 30s was a woman smaller than you."

"I'd love to be able to do that, but…"

Looking down the length of the hall, he noticed that all the door LEDs were green, except of course for the arms room.

"Look," he said. "All the doors are unlocked. Looks like I don't have to blow them after all." He made his way to the nutrient paste storage room and pushed the pad. The door slid open as before.

"That's fancy," Yael commented. "You'd think we were on the Enterprise."

"That's what I thought too. Pretty cool, right?"

They couldn't enter the room as it was stacked floor to ceiling with powder canisters, so Alex pulled one out and set it down on the floor. It was very heavy. He let it rest on its edge as he spun it around to check for markings.

The first thing he noticed was a logo: the letter F, in a circle. The name "Fonseca" was written next to it.

"Looks familiar," Alex said, then realized it was the same logo he had seen on the laundry enzyme in his cabin.

"It's a biotech firm," Yael said. "They make GMO corn and stuff. That's not a good sign."

"GMO food isn't kosher?"

She shrugged. "Depends who you ask, I guess. The big certification groups say no. There were some articles on it recently. That's how I know the company."

Alex frowned. "Are GMOs the only shit Fonseca makes?"

"Well, no, but—"

"Good! Let's judge it based on the ingredients then. You can't just assume it's not kosher because it's made by a company that also makes GMOs, right?"

"I suppose," she said, but she didn't sound convinced.

Alex turned his attention back to the canister. A little past the brand name was a list of ingredients.

"What the hell is Pantothenic Acid?" he asked. "Or Pyridoxine?"

"I'm pretty sure those are vitamins," she said, kneeling down next to him. Her knee brushed his left thigh and he felt a tingle of excitement. "I'm more concerned with calcium propionate. I think that's a preservative."

"What's wrong with preservatives?"

Yael frowned. "Most aren't kosher."

"Balls," Alex swore. "It's gotta have preservatives. But…" He noticed something on the base of the canister. "Well I'll be damned!"

"What is it?" she asked, then saw the word "KOSHER" printed on the canister. "Oh. That's…that's too convenient."

"I kinda know what you mean," he said. "But isn't your obligation fulfilled? How is this any different than buying kosher food at the supermarket?"

She nodded. "Yeah, it's just that I'd feel better if there was some way to confirm it, you know? Considering where we are…it would be easier to just print the word kosher than to actually make it kosher."

"I have an idea," he said excitedly. "We can ask Tom!"

"Tom? Who's Tom?"

"He's the scientist Max was babbling about. A biochemist. He'll know what the ingredients are."

She brightened. "That would be perfect. If he can't say that it's not kosher, I'll be happy to eat it."

"Good! Let's write this stuff down and find him."

She tilted her head slightly and frowned. "Write?"

"Yeah…oh. No pen. Well, let's check the other rooms."

Walking down the hall, they checked each room in turn. There was an amazing assortment of supplies, though he was in no mood to pay too much attention. He noticed tools, farming implements, what looked like spare parts—though he wasn't sure for what—and more. They checked the dehydrated meat storage, but there was nothing there marked kosher. The room just before the arms room on the right looked like a miniature hospital, and the one across held a huge assortment of nets, poles and other fishing implements.

"Bingo," he said before the door slid all the way open.

Yael gasped and clapped her hands over her mouth. "Oh, Alex!"

"One way or another," he said happily. "You get to eat today."

"I don't know what to say," she said, her eyes tearing up once more. "You've been so supportive..."

"My pleasure."

"I don't know why you're doing this for me, but I'm grateful. I want you to know that."

He was about to tell her why, but he saw where that conversation would go. She wouldn't brush it off, not in the mood she was in, but she was likely to use her religion as an excuse to shoot him down. He wasn't sure if Tom was right about that, but he didn't want to take the chance. This would be a conversation they would have eventually, assuming she was interested in him in that way, but now was not the time for it.

"Think nothing of it, what are friends for, right?"

She nodded, wiping her eyes.

"Hang out here a bit," he said. "I'll go look in the arms room, maybe they left me a pen there. If not, I'll get a bullet. You can actually write on dark surfaces with a bullet, the copper jacket rubs off."

"Good to know," she said, smiling. "Why can't I come with you?"

"There's an inner door, and it works like an airlock. No one but me can be in the corridor."

She nodded. "I'll wait here, maybe pick out a pole."

Seconds later, he was standing in the arms room, once again awestruck at the destructive potential of the equipment they had given him. There was so much that he hadn't noticed before, a lot more than just weapons. Fatigues, boots, explosives, even a workbench with tools next to a full length mirror in which he could check his gear.

A desk with a computer monitor caught his eye before he could process most of what he was looking at. There was a leather chair, identical to the one in his cabin, and he pulled it from under the desk and sat down. He wiggled the mouse and the monitor came to life. Like the laptop in his cabin, it had a Microsoft operating system, though besides the host of useless standard applications, the only thing on this particular machine was a database—presumably for keeping track of the arms room inventory—and some sort of communications program called "NTCN." At least he assumed it was a communications program by its satellite dish icon.

He double clicked it and a black window came up, like a command prompt, only without the usual DOS garbage. There was a blinking cursor. After a second, a password prompt appeared.

He stared at it, wondering why his captors would be so annoying as to put an application on his computer that needed a password he couldn't possibly know.

"Bastards," he mumbled and closed the window. Following a sudden flash of inspiration, he immediately opened it again.

As soon as the password prompt came back, he reached into his pocket and produced the piece of paper he had found in the locker under his bed. He typed the string written on it, "peace7102," then hit the Enter key.

Text began to scroll on the screen.

```
Password accepted.

Subject: Alex Meyer, SPC, E-4, United States
```

Army, 11B1P-rifle infantryman, airborne

Current Assignment: NTF103-B

No actions available at this time. Please review general orders.

GENERAL ORDERS
----

1) Do not tamper with the barrier. It is for your own protection. You will be given control of the barrier shortly.

2) Do not tamper with the facility or any part thereof. Do not permit others to do so.

3) You are to support the governor so long as he or she does not endanger the welfare of the colony. The governor can be identified by a larger domicile and a universal access terminal.

4) Maintain order among the residents.

5) Use of deadly force is hereby authorized.

6) Do not distribute the weapons in the arms room except to those you enlist to aid you in performing your duties. Use your best judgment. Always maintain control of the inventory.

7) These orders are subject to change. Check them frequently.

MISCELLANEOUS INSTRUCTIONS

Your situation will be explained to you shortly. Until that time, follow your general orders.

You are hereby promoted to Captain, 0-3, effective immediately. Rank insignia can be located in computer desk. Your residence in this facility is permanent, conduct yourself accordingly.

Alex stared at the monitor for a long time. His heart raced, his hands shook and a feeling of absolute dread momentarily overcame him. He did not understand why, but the words on the screen scared him. They scared him a lot.

Hands still shaking, he pulled open a drawer. It contained paper and several boxes of pens. He took one of each, then opened another drawer. As promised, there was an assortment of rank insignia, both Velcro for his current uniform and metal insignia for his greens and dress blues, which as far he knew he no longer had. They were not all O-3 insignia. He identified several officer's ranks, up to and including colonel. The drawer also contained an assortment of medals, few of which he had any right to wear. He took out the appropriate cloth patch with a Velcro back and stared at it. Two thick vertical bars, parallel, connected at two points. A captain's rank. His rank.

Your residence in this facility is permanent.

Without thinking, he placed the velcro backed insignia in position on his chest and patted it down.

"Still following orders, huh?" he asked himself, his voice shaky.

Use of deadly force is hereby authorized.

"Holy shit," he whispered, then shut down the program. His mind was racing, and he found it difficult to pin down a concrete thought. Standing up, he grabbed the pen and paper and went back out into the hallway.

"You took your time—" Yael started to say. "Hey, what's the matter? You look like you've seen a ghost!"

"I have pen and paper," he muttered without making eye contact. "Here." He held them out to her, but she didn't take them.

"Alex, what is it?" She stood up and faced him. She reached out to him, but held back at the last moment.

"We're not going anywhere," he said stiffly. "Ever. This is it for us."

She blinked. "What are you saying? What did you see? What's in there?"

"Just general orders."

"What the hell is that?"

He shook his head. "It's my orders, from whoever put us here. I'm a captain now, for whatever the hell that's worth."

"Alex," she said firmly. "Slow down. I don't understand what you're saying."

"Your residence in this facility," he repeated the words from the program, trying to make it obvious that he was quoting something. "Is permanent. Conduct yourself accordingly."

She stared at him for a moment without saying anything.

"I'm sorry, Yael," he said, his voice on the verge of cracking. "Something must have happened…something terrible. I might not be able to keep that promise after all."

"No…" she whispered. "Please, god, no."

He realized what he had just done to her and cringed. "No, wait," he said, trying to fix it, his own pain momentarily forgotten. "I'm an idiot…it could just be part of the game. You know, like a psychological experiment."

She turned away and started walking down the hall.

"Yael!"

"Leave me alone!" she snapped, then turned back briefly and said, in a much softer tone, "I just need to be alone for a while, okay?"

He nodded, then watched her walk out of the warehouse. The dog perked up, saw her leaving and followed her out after a long look at Alex.

"Nice going," he muttered to himself.

* * *

He had tried to look for Tom, but everyone he ran into was on their way to Max's meeting. He eventually decided to follow some of them to the gathering, which was taking place by the clearing near the beach. Tom was there as well, hanging towards the back, watching as Max stood talking quietly to Reynard and Bob while the crowd gathered around him.

"Probably ratting me out," Alex muttered, looking at Bob. "The bastard."

"Hi Alex," Tom said when he spotted him. "Here for the show?"

"Yeah, I guess. I hate to sound like a broken record, but have you seen Yael?"

"Nope," Tom said, smiling. "But at least this time I can be sure."

Alex nodded. "Can you do me a quick favor while we wait for

this circus?"

"Sure can," Tom said jovially. "Whatcha need?"

Alex held out the piece of paper he had copied the canister's ingredients onto. "I have this list of ingredients from a nutrient powder keg. It's marked kosher, but Yael wants to be sure. Can you identify these for me? Being a chemist and all?"

Tom nodded. "After the meeting, okay?"

"Can you do it now? She hasn't eaten since she got here. It's kinda urgent."

He frowned, but took the list and looked at it.

"Well?" Alex said.

"They're kosher."

"Are you sure?"

Tom nodded. "Positive. My aunt married a Jewish dude, so I learned which was which."

"So what is Pantothenic Acid, anyway?"

Tom shrugged. "It's a kosher preservative."

"Really?" Yael wasn't a chemist, but she had seemed pretty certain.

"Yep." Tom smiled, but his eyes were cautious, which told Alex what he needed to know.

"It's a vitamin, Tom," Alex said, deciding to play his hunch. He grabbed the paper out of Tom's hands. "What's going on?"

Tom looked around. There was no one near to them, most people were trying to get closer to Max, who looked like he was about to start speaking.

Tom sighed and raised his hands. "You got me."

"What the hell do you mean, I got you?" Alex was confused, and more than a little annoyed. This was serious, Yael needed to eat. In the background, he heard Max talking.

"I'm not a biochemist," Tom explained, and smiled. "Please don't tell anyone."

Alex frowned. "What the fuck do you mean you're not a biochemist? Why would you lie about being a biochemist?"

Before Tom had a chance to say anything, Alex heard Barbara calling his name from the other side of the gathering. She was waving at him as she made her way through the crowd, holding the dog collar in front of her.

“Okay, look,” Alex said, pointing a stern finger at Tom. “I’ll keep your secret for now, but you’re going to tell me what you’re up to later.”

“Yes, I will. It’s nothing sinister, and I don’t think I’m in the wrong here. I was kidnapped and brought here against my will, remember?”

Alex nodded reluctantly. “You have a point. But as far as the others and especially Yael is concerned, you’re a biochemist and these are kosher ingredients, got it?”

“Got it, Chief.”

“Actually, it’s ‘captain.’” Alex muttered. He sort of liked that. It would be great fun to lord his new rank over Medlock, and to have some fun teasing Campbell. But he wished he’d never found that terminal. Permanent? No, that part he didn’t like. Not one bit.

“Right,” Tom said. “Captain.”

“Alex,” Barbara said, finally coming into ear shot. “I examined this collar…oh, hello Tom. Nice to see you again.” She was wearing khaki shorts and a blue tank top with the straps of a white bra showing on her shoulders. She had very nice tanned legs with healthy muscle definition. A runner’s legs.

“Hi Barbara,” Tom said, grinning sheepishly. In the background, Max started droning on about how they had to work together to make the most of their situation.

“So,” Barbara said. “I examined this collar, and it’s not what you thought.”

“How so?” Alex asked.

“For starters, it wasn’t broken off, or sanded off.”

“What do you mean?”

“I examined them under a microscope earlier this morning. They were dissolved.”

Alex raised an eyebrow. What she was saying didn’t make much sense. “Dissolved? You mean like with acid? Why would someone partially dissolve dog tags?”

“Yes,” she said, nodding. “Like with acid, only the patterns don’t match any acid I’ve ever seen.”

“That’s odd,” Tom said.

Barbara turned to him and pointed. “Say, you’re a chemist! Maybe you can take a look!”

Tom swallowed. "Um, yeah, sure, I'd be happy to." He gave Alex a pleading look, and he couldn't help but smile in return. For whatever reason, Tom had made his bed.

"So it is decided then," Alex heard Max say. "We shall vote to see if you will accept me as the temporary leader of the group, until we figure out a way out of here." The noises from the crowd did not sound positive, and Alex knew things would probably not go Max's way. The man thought he was being clever by legitimizing his position with a vote, but his plan would backfire. Most of these people just wanted to go home and likely considered the notion of a leader as ridiculous as Alex himself did.

"Fuck," Alex swore. He was conflicted, but he knew what he had to do. He didn't like Max, but whoever had sent him his orders had made the situation quite clear, leaving him little choice. He was a soldier, and soldiers followed orders. At least for now.

"What is it?" Barbara said, but he ignored her and made his way to where Max and a few of his flunkies were standing.

"Hold on," he said, in as loud and authoritative voice as he could muster. "There isn't going to be a vote."

Max glared at him. "Alex, I don't know what you're up to, but—"

"In the arms room," Alex continued, turning to the crowd. "There is a terminal. On that terminal, I found a copy of my general orders." He turned to Max. "Are you telling the truth about your larger cabin and access terminal?"

"Of course, but—"

"Then you are the governor, as soon as I verify it with my own eyes. I have my orders, and I will obey them. There will be no voting." He turned to the crowd. "Whoever put us here is firmly in control of our destiny, at least until we figure out where we are and how to get the hell out. And until that happens, we do things their way."

There were murmurs from the crowd, but no one looked overly displeased. People generally didn't think they wanted to be bossed around, but most did, at least subconsciously. It was the nature of the human animal.

"Have you found anything else out?" a woman in the crowd asked. "About why we're here?"

Alex turned to Max with a questioning look. The older man stared at him a moment, then nodded. Alex wondered if he received the same information on his terminal, and decided that he must have.

"I don't know how much we can trust what those assholes tell us," Alex said. "But according to them, the barrier is here for our own protection, and it will be turned off shortly. Or rather, we will be given control over it, and will be able to turn it off."

Alex spotted Yael towards the back of the crowd. She was standing near one of the cabins, arms crossed in front of her chest, face red from crying.

"What else?" someone asked. Alex didn't notice who it was, nor did he care to.

"Well," Alex said, looking at her, wishing she wasn't there to hear him say it again. "According to our captors, we're going to be here…permanently. It was just text on a screen, I don't know anything more."

The crowd erupted, screaming in outrage. Alex nodded to Max, as if to say "this is your problem now, not mine," and headed over to Yael. She saw him and turned away, disappearing behind the cluster of cabins.

He stared at the place where she had been and wished, once again, that he'd never set foot in the arms room.

Chapter 9

Alex was sure he had the right cabin when he noticed the small pile of dog droppings at the base of a nearby tree. When he got close, he heard the little animal yip and scratch at the door, announcing his presence. He knocked anyway, and waited for the door to pop open. Yael stood in the doorway, blocking his access as the dog ran out and jumped up on his legs.

"Good dog," he said, and reached down to pat its head.

"What do you want?" she asked. Her eyes were still red, but then not much time had passed since the gathering. "I want to be alone."

"If you really want to be alone," he said. "I'll leave. But I came here to tell you what Tom said about the powder, and to make sure you got something to eat. And…maybe you could use some company. I know I can."

She looked at him, about to say something, then rolled her eyes, stood aside and let him enter.

Her cabin was just like his own, except that it had a smaller wall mounted monitor and no DNA pad under the bed. She had taken some time to decorate. There were flowers in a plastic cup, some sea shells on the computer desk and colorful dresses hanging off of the plexiglass divider.

"Nice place," Alex said. "Is it rent controlled?"

She frowned. "I'm not in the mood for jokes, Alex. I shouldn't even be letting you in here."

"If it helps," he suggested. "You can think of it as an official visit from the town brass." Seeing her like this—defeated, sullen—bothered him. He wanted to help her.

"But it's not, and pretending doesn't make it right."

"Oh but it is," he insisted. "It seems I'm the law in these parts, and I say it's my duty to make sure you're feeling okay. If it helps I'll write it down and make it official. I'll even get Max to publicly proclaim it."

She smiled briefly. "Why are you so nice to me? If it's because you think I'll…sleep with you or something, think again."

"I do not wish to discuss my intentions at this time, but suffice it to say they are honorable."

"You're strange, you know that?" she said, still smiling. This was good, at least he had cheered her up a bit.

"How so?"

"Sometimes you talk like a puerile teenager, other times like an educated adult. I don't get you."

"I almost graduated college," he said, grinning.

"Why almost?"

He shrugged. "I got fed up with the basic requirements. You know, music, philosophy, the crap they make you take. I decided to put it off and join the army." Which had turned out to be a big mistake, but he didn't feel like dredging that up right now. Besides, if he hadn't joined the army, he wouldn't have ended up in the compound and he wouldn't have met her.

She sat down on her bed and pushed the chair towards him. Nodding appreciatively, he rolled it behind him and sat down. The dog jumped up on the bed and lay down next to her, its head on her lap.

"You're still an oddball," she said. "But I guess that's okay."

"How about you?" he asked. "High school senior?"

She frowned. "Um, no. What makes you think I'm that young? Is it how I look, or how I act?" She was sitting with her legs crossed, hands on her knees. Her back was straight and she looked as stiff as a board. He laughed.

"Yael, if I had to go by how you acted I'd ask you where the fountain of youth was. It's how you look."

"That's good, I guess."

"So you're in college?" he asked. "I mean…were you?"

She nodded. "Stern College. It's part of Yeshiva University in New York City."

"You're from the city, huh? I've been there a few times. Crazy place."

"I lived in Queens, we couldn't afford Manhattan."

"So your father doesn't really have any lawyers, does he?"

"No," she said, smiling. "He's never needed any. It's just something I say because I know it gets people's attention."

"Good. It's such a bad Jewish stereotype."

"I'll be sure to bring it up at the next Zionist world domination meeting, right after the media control seminar and the baby tasting." Her expression was blank, but her eyes were smiling.

He laughed and shook his head. "Another joke. This could start to be a habit."

"I'm glad you think it's funny, not everyone would. What about you? Where are you from?"

"What you would call 'Upstate New York.' Though I've lived in California for more than a year now, near Death Valley. It's where I was stationed."

"Wait," she said, looking at his rank insignia. "You're an officer. I thought you had to finish college to be an officer."

He frowned. "I was a specialist, an enlisted man. I just got promoted, remember?"

"I wasn't clear on that," she said. "That's a big promotion then."

"Yea, and if I'm going to be honest, it scares the shit out of me. The fact that they would make me a captain just like that…and why even bother? What difference does it make what rank I am?"

"Well," she said in an even tone. "At least we know who is responsible for this."

"Who?" He stared at her stupidly, then it dawned on him. For the second time today, he smacked himself in the forehead. "Oh my god I'm such a moron! I didn't even think…"

"No, there's a lot going on, and you're used to following orders."

He smiled. "Thank you. You can make fun of me for it later, of course."

"Count on it," she said with a grin. "Now the only question is why the military, or the government, would do this to us."

He looked away. "I can only think of one thing, and I don't want to say it."

"Is it because of me?"

He nodded.

"I appreciate that, Alex, I really do. But I'd like to hear it."

"Well," he began, looking down at the ground. "The only reason that makes sense is that something really bad happened, like an asteroid or something. And they knew it was going to happen, so they grabbed whoever they could and put them in colonies like this one. I think there are many of them, ours is number 103, if I'm right about the designation." Hearing his own words surprised him. He had purposely kept himself busy to avoid over speculation, but apparently his mind had been working when he wasn't paying attention. He had definitely enjoyed being here more when he didn't have a clue what was going on.

She wiped her eyes again. "No, that doesn't make sense, the 'grabbed whoever they could' part I mean. This is too organized. Our clothes, how they are right for us, the DNA pads, how everyone is perfect for their job, except me of course." He sensed some bitterness.

"You don't have any stuff in here? I mean stuff that tells you what you're supposed to do?"

She shook her head.

"Don't feel bad," he said. "I only know of a few people with clear roles. You're right, though, it was very organized. Whoever drugged us and brought us here did it in one day. Where were you when it happened?"

"I was visiting my cousins in Los Angeles."

"Really," he said. "Now that's interesting. Fort Irwin…that's where I'm stationed…is pretty close to Los Angeles. And Max was a professor at UCLA. I bet everyone here is either from California or was in California when this happened. That might also explain why you don't have a job. Maybe you weren't where they expected you to be."

She shrugged. "Maybe."

"Anyway," he said, getting to his feet. "It's time to eat." He took a couple of plates and spoons from her tableware cabinet and dispensed two sizeable puffs of nutrient paste. He set one down on the desk near her. The dog picked its head up and stared at the plate intently.

"Hope you don't mind sharing…I'd be happy to return the favor later."

She stared at the plate. "What did Tom say?"

"He said it was kosher." That wasn't a lie, he had said exactly that. "Eat. That's an order."

She took the plate and spoon, scooped some up and put it in her mouth.

"It's really good!" she said, smiling. She ate heartily, and he joined her. In seconds, her plate was empty.

"Let me get you more," he said, taking it from her. She nodded. She had accepted that she could eat it, but willfully procuring it seemed just a bit beyond her at the moment.

She ate three helpings before deciding she'd had enough.

"Alex, thank you." She reached out to him again, and again pulled back.

"It won't burn you," he said.

"What?"

"Touching me."

She looked away.

"Look," he continued. "I don't care, it doesn't matter. I just like your company. Okay?"

She nodded, then furrowed her brow, as though something had occurred to her.

"Do you think," she said, swallowing. "Do you think they're dead?"

"Your family?"

She nodded again, and he saw a tear roll down her cheek.

"No. I can't imagine it. It's too much."

"I know what you mean," she said, wiping her face. "I had another idea, though. Maybe this is a quarantine."

"Like a medical quarantine?"

"That's the idea, yeah. Maybe there was some kind of outbreak."

"Hey yeah!" he said excitedly. "That would explain a lot!"

"Really?" she said, looking up at him hopefully. "How so?"

He stood up and began to pace. "It makes perfect sense! Let's say something got loose…some really nasty bug. Fast acting, got us in our sleep, maybe lots died, but we're immune!"

"We're carriers!" she exclaimed, also standing. "We survived, and they put us here to quarantine and study us!"

"Exactly! That would explain why everyone is from California! I mean assuming I'm right about that."

She was about to say something when her laptop screen came

to life, displaying a picture of Max's face.

"This is a general announcement," Max said though the computer's little speakers. "Captain Alex Meyer, please come to my cabin immediately."

"I didn't know he could do that," Alex said as he felt his mood deflate. They had been sharing an exciting moment when that air bag interrupted. "That's creepy, I wonder if he can see us."

"Doesn't look like it," Yael said. "I guess you have to go?" she asked, and as he recognized the disappointment in her voice he felt a rush of excitement.

"I guess so," he said. "We'll pick this up later?"

"Okay," she said.

Patting the dog on the head, he gave her a long look and walked outside, closing the door behind him.

When he had walked quite a way from her cabin, he realized he had no idea where he was going. The complex wasn't that big, though, and within a few minutes of walking in random directions he spotted a cabin that was considerably larger than the others. He doubted it was twice the size, but then again which definition of "twice" had Max used? Twice the volume? Double the exterior dimensions? He realized how much importance he was placing on such a meaningless detail and chuckled under his breath.

"At least they gave me a big TV."

The door was open and Max was inside, along with Reynard.

"Max," Alex said, nodding a greeting. "Reynard."

"Alex, good," Max said. He looked pleased to see him. There was an excitement about the two men, and both were fixated on the terminal. "Come look at this."

Alex walked up to the monitor and looked at the screen. It was the same NTCN program that he had on his arms room terminal.

```
    Perimeter Defense Main Menu
    -----------------------------------------


    Barrier Status: Active
    Barrier Grid Status(by zone):   (1)98   (2)85
(3)87   (4)91   (5)77   (6)91   (7)85   (8)92   (9)84
(10)89   (11)93   (12)91
```

```
Actions:

1. Barrier Controls
2. Access Grid Controls
3. Access Fusion Generator Controls
4. Help
5. Return to Main Menu
```

"Fusion generator?" Alex said. "Holy crap! There's a fusion generator here? Does such a thing even exist?"

"It would appear so," Max said. "I have access to some of its parameters, but I have no idea where it is. But Alex, forget about that for a second. Look at the menu."

"Yeah," he said. "I saw. We can turn it off."

"Not quite," Max said excitedly. "It won't let us shut it off completely, but we can drop it down to twenty percent intensity. According to the program, that will make passage through it possible, but I'm guessing quite a bit uncomfortable."

"That's weird," Alex said. "If they want to let us pass through it, why not just let us shut it off completely?"

"I don't know. This menu became active just a few minutes ago. I don't know what most of the settings are, but I'd be willing to bet there's someone among the other residents that can figure it out."

"Did you try option four?" Alex asked.

"Yes. It's just technical information about the settings. I can't make heads or tails of it. Do you want to take a look?"

He shook his head. "No, stuff like that is above my pay grade. But on to more important matters. I want to get a group together and go out there. I've been thinking about that ever since I read my general orders. They mentioned that we would get control of the barrier."

"Do you think that's wise?" Max asked, looking annoyingly concerned.

"Yes," Alex said. "I do. If there's one thing we all have in common, it's that we all want to know what the hell is going on here. And we're not going to learn that sitting here."

"We have some theories," Max said.

"We do too, Yael and I."

Max raised an eyebrow. "Really? I'd love to hear them." Reynard was keeping silent, though Alex didn't like the way he was looking at him. Did he resent his position?

"We have two," he said, though he almost didn't want to tell Max Yael's quarantine theory. He didn't want to share with anyone else what he'd shared with her. "The first is the obvious one…there was some sort of disaster, like an asteroid strike, and the government had lots of time to prepare. They couldn't save everyone, so they saved a random group of people, or maybe we're all special, though I can't see how I am."

"And the second?"

"Quarantine," he continued. "Yael came up with that one." He turned to Reynard. "You're from California, right? Or you were in California when this happened?"

Reynard nodded, then glanced nervously at Max. "How did you know?"

"I think we all are," Alex said. "It makes sense if you go with the quarantine theory. Outbreak, millions die, we get infected without realizing it, but survive. So we're carriers, but we're immune. They grab us all, bring us here. Who knows how long we were actually out?"

Max nodded and rubbed his chin. "That was one we had not considered. The only problem with that one is why did they give us so many weapons?"

Alex shrugged. "Maybe the virus, or whatever it is, turns people into zombies."

Max chuckled, but it was an annoying patronizing chuckle. "I don't think that's very likely."

"I was joking," Alex said. "But if it is some sort of deadly outbreak, maybe there's widespread chaos, rioting, that sort of thing. The point is we have no idea what's going on out there, and we won't until we go have a look. You're the governor, so I need your permission."

Max considered it. "Alright, put a small team together. No more than six or seven people. Go out for one day, then come back and report on what you find. At the first sign of trouble…"

"Got it," Alex said. "We'll come right back. But one day might not be enough. Let's make it three."

Max rubbed his chin. "Fine, three it is, but if you find something, come back sooner."

"Will do."

"You'll need to leave us some guns," Max said. "We need to be able to protect ourselves if something should happen."

Alex was about to protest, but then thought better of it. He didn't like the idea, but if he had been in Max's shoes he would have felt the same way.

"Fine. I'll give you some pistols. Three enough?"

"Let's make it five. When will you leave?"

"First thing tomorrow morning," Alex said. "I'm going to put the team together right now though. Expect gun fire."

"We'll keep the barrier at full strength until you go."

"And after we leave," Alex said. "Until we know what's out there, it's only prudent. I have short range radios in the arms room, I'll give you one and we'll contact you when we're nearby so you can shut it down again."

"Good luck, Alex," Max said, and offered a hand. Alex shook it.

"Do me a favor," Alex said. "Get on that broadcast thing of yours and tell anyone interested in going with me to head down to the beach."

"Good idea, I'll do it right now."

"Be sure to let people know I'm going to set a fast pace, and it's not going to be easy or comfortable."

Alex turned and walked out of Max's cabin, headed towards the warehouse. He was excited at the prospect of finally getting to find out where they were and what was going on out there, but he was also feeling let down. The vacation was over. Whatever happened next, things would never be the same again.

Chapter 10

There was a large group waiting for him by the time he made it down to the beach. Neither Bob nor Reynard were there, which did not surprise him, but Barbara and Tom were, as was Yael. A quick tally indicated about fifteen people in all, along with a couple of spectators— two girls in shorts and tank tops stood off to the side and stared, whispering to each other. They looked like typical college girls on spring break, tanned and healthy. And cute.

"Hello," Alex said as he set down the duffle bag he had brought from the arms room. "Let me save you all some time. If you don't know how to handle a military rifle without me showing you, I can't use you, not for this one. I appreciate the offer of help, but I don't have time to train you. Maybe when we come back, if we don't find a way out of here, but not now."

"No way," a man said. He was tall, with long hair and dark stubble. "Who do you think you are? I'm going." Some of the others shuffled nervously, expecting trouble.

"You can do whatever you want," Alex said calmly. "But you're not going with me." He turned to the others. "When we lower the barrier, no one is going to stop any of you from leaving, but I wouldn't recommend it, not until we know what's out there and why the barrier was up in the first place. To do otherwise would be stupid."

The long haired man scowled. "Who the hell needs you anyway?" He turned and walked away, and several others followed him.

"I repeat," Alex said to those who remained. "Thank you for being willing to help, but if you can't operate an M4 carbine, by which I mean load, chamber, fire, clear and reload, I can't use you. And if you have no idea what I just said, I definitely can't use you."

Most of them started to leave amidst assorted murmurs and grumbles. Barbara was one of them.

"Except you," he said to her. "We may need a doctor."

"Okay," she said, her expression transforming from a frown into a warm smile. "I'm your man then." She turned and walked back to stand with those that remained: Tom, Yael, two men Alex didn't know and the round faced blond from the beach, the one who wanted to use the fire to signal the ships.

"Now then," Alex said. "You need to be in good shape. I'm going to set a brisk pace, and we're not going to stop because you're tired. You're also going to be carrying about thirty pounds of gear. If you can't handle that, or if you've never carried that much weight for extended periods of time, do everyone a favor and walk away now."

He looked at the assembled faces, except for Yael. He couldn't quite meet her gaze. It didn't seem right to him to be including her in this impersonal selection process. No one left.

"Finally," he said. "And this one's a doozy. Assuming we don't walk out of here and find a strip mall and a movie theater, things may get ugly. If you go, you will follow my orders without question. If you disobey me, I may have to shoot you."

There were murmurs, and people exchanged glances. One of the college girls whistled to the other.

"Are you serious?" Tom asked with a bewildered expression. "Shoot us?"

"Yes," Alex said. "But you would only have yourself to blame. Disobeying orders puts everyone in danger."

"How do we know," one of the men asked. "That you won't order us to do something crazy?" He was about Alex's height but a bit heavier, and not from muscle. A bit of fat didn't mean he was out of shape, so Alex wasn't concerned.

"What's your name?" he asked him.

"Ryan."

"Ryan, what's stopping me from shooting you right now?"

The man blanched. "I didn't mean…"

"I'm trying to make a point," Alex explained. "You trust me enough to want to go out there with me, presumably based on the way I've acted in the short time I've been here. I haven't shot anyone, or harassed anyone, otherwise you wouldn't be here, right?"

He nodded.

"Trust is important, and if you don't trust me, don't go. When I give an order, it will be a very specific thing, and you'll know you are being given an order. It won't be arbitrary, and it will be something important. Is that okay with everyone?"

There were nods and other affirmations. This was strange for Alex, being in a position of authority. He thought he sounded like Campbell, which wasn't altogether a bad thing. If he had to emulate someone, Bill was probably his best bet.

"Good." He reached down into the duffle bag and unzipped it, taking out three tactical vests. He set the vests down about ten feet apart, then pulled out three M4s. He set these down, one on each vest. He then placed an empty magazine and three rounds of 5.56mm next to each carbine. Reaching into the bag one last time, he pulled out three empty metal ammo cans, walked them down the beach about forty meters from the vests, and set them down as far apart from each other as the vests were. The ocean would serve as a backstop.

He walked back to where the others were standing, turned to the two college girls and said, "Ladies, this is going to be very loud, so you may want to step back a bit."

"Okay," they both said, almost in unison, and smiled at him. He knew flirting when he saw it, and before he could stop himself, smiled back. He watched them walk away and had to force himself to avert his gaze. He noticed Yael staring at him with a blank expression.

"So here's the deal," he said to the others. "This is a very easy test, and unless you lied about being able to use a rifle you should all pass. There are six of you, and you'll take turns, three at a time. You will have thirty seconds to load those bullets into the magazine, insert the magazine and chamber a round. After that, wait for my signal, then you will have another thirty seconds to activate the Aimpoint sight, take aim at the can that corresponds to your position, and fire, three times. If you take longer than thirty seconds, either time, you fail. If you miss the can more than once, you fail. If you've never used a red dot sight, I'll help you take it off before you begin and you can flip up the irons instead. Everyone got it?"

They nodded.

"Good. Who wants to go first?"

Yael stepped forward, as did Barbara and the guy whose name

Alex still didn't know, a skinny black guy with short hair and fuzzy stubble.

"You can screw it up," he said to Barbara. "It's okay. But try to do your best. Have you ever fired a gun before?"

"Just a pistol," she said. "At a range."

"Good," he said. "It's the same thing, just bigger." He grinned at her, and she smiled back.

"Here, take these ear plugs and put them in." He handed each of them a pair of foam plugs and waited while they stuck them in their ears. "I don't have a stop watch, so I'm going to count out loud. Ready? Go."

As soon as he started counting, he watched Yael, curious to see how she would do.

She immediately dropped to her knees, picked up the rifle and pulled back on the charging handle while activating the bolt catch with her other hand. Leaving the weapon on her lap, she scooped up the empty magazine and popped the bullets in without hesitation. She wasn't especially quick, but she moved with precision. The guy next to her dropped his bullets more than once in his haste. Yael slid the magazine into the well, tapped it to make sure it was seated, then smacked the bolt release with her palm.

When he reached thirty, she had been ready for at least ten seconds. Barbara was still fumbling with getting the bullets into the magazine, and the skinny guy just barely made it.

"Yael," Alex said. "Help Barbara out if you don't mind." She nodded, and picked up Barbara's rifle, locked the bolt back and handed it to her when she was ready. Barbara fumbled the magazine in the well and Yael showed her the bolt release.

"Good," he said. "Now for the next part. Ready…go."

He started counting again. Yael picked up her rifle and examined the Aimpoint sight. She found its control knob almost instantly and looked into the tube as she began to turn it. After a few clicks, she shouldered the weapon, took it off safety, pointed it at the can and fired. The can spun, a large hole clearly visible near its edge.

Barbara jumped at the noise despite her ear plugs and dropped her rifle. Fortunately it fell onto the vest butt first and didn't get sand in the barrel. The college girls weren't too happy and moved back even further, holding their ears.

Yael fired twice more, and hit the can each time. The skinny black guy started shooting just as she fired her last round, and he hit the can two out of three times. Barbara was still fumbling with the sight, cringing at each deafening blast.

"Here we go," she said, getting it to work. She fired three times, but missed the can. Two of her shots came reasonably close. "I'm sorry," she said. "I'm just not very good at this."

"It's okay," he said. "You're not terrible at it either." He turned to the others. "Okay, you two are in."

The black guy walked up to him and extended his hand. "I'm Patrick." Alex shook it.

"Welcome aboard, Patrick."

"Thank you."

"Okay," Alex said. "Time to set up for the other three." As he approached the three stations, Yael put her rifle down and started to walk away. He held up a hand to stop her.

"That was awesome," he said softly so that the others wouldn't hear. "Where did you learn to do that?"

She frowned at him, glancing over to the two spectators. "I spent three summers in a kibbutz."

"That's one of those Israeli farming and shooting camps, right?"

She shook her head, but managed to smile. "That's a narrow way of looking at it, but yes. I learned to farm, and to shoot."

"I knew it," he said, grinning.

"So," she said, tilting her head. "You'll shoot me if I don't obey you?"

He looked around, making sure no one else was close enough to hear. "Of course not, don't be ridiculous."

"So you were lying? Just making sure people would listen?"

"No. I meant it, just not for you."

"Oh, so what I'm special somehow?"

"You are to me," he said, then turned away before he could see her reaction. "Okay. Next three."

Tom, Ryan and the blond stepped forward.

"I'm Sandi," she said. "Thank you for letting me try out. My father had an AR-15 and taught me how to use it. And I'm on the track team."

Alex grinned. "I never looked at it that way, but I guess these *are* try outs, aren't they? I feel like one of those ridiculous bald football coaches."

She laughed. "You don't look like one."

As he cleared the rifles and put fresh bullets onto each vest, he couldn't help but shake his head. There were three, maybe four, very attractive women within a hundred feet of him that he could have had very simple and pleasant relations with, but instead he had to pick a temperamental and emotionally unstable vixen with an incurable case of religion.

"Forbidden fruit," he muttered under his breath, but he knew there was much more to it than that. If only he understood what it was.

Alex repeated the first part of the test. Tom fumbled around when loading bullets into the magazine but finally managed it. Then his rifle failed to go into battery as he attempted to chamber the first round.

"You're not supposed to ride the charging handle," Alex explained between counts. "You're supposed to lock the bolt and release it, or at the very least pull the charging handle all the way back and let it go completely." He felt like he was cheating a bit by helping him, but he liked Tom and wanted him along. He knew it should bother him that Tom had lied about who he was, though the whole situation was so ridiculous he couldn't get himself to take it seriously. Posing as a biochemist? He wanted to hear the story, but only for the sake of a few good laughs.

"Am I hosed?" Tom asked, looking glum.

"Use the forward assist," Alex said, not expecting him to know what it was. Tom looked down at the rifle, hesitated for a second, then tapped the assist. The bullet chambered just as Alex reached thirty.

Looking around, he saw that both Ryan and Sandi had loaded their weapons successfully.

The second part of the test went smoothly, though only Sandi hit the can more than twice.

"Okay then," Alex said. "We have our team. We leave tomorrow morning. I want everyone by Max's cabin, the big one, at sunrise. I have fatigues for everyone in the arms room, so don't worry about what to wear. Find me later today to get your stuff."

They exchanged nervous glances, and started to drift off towards the village. The two college girls lost interest and walked closer to the water. Only Yael stayed behind.

"Why do you want to go?" he asked her. "It could be very dangerous. I could certainly use someone that knows what they're doing, but I'd feel better knowing you were here and safe."

"I need to know what's out there," she said. "Don't ask me to stay behind. I passed your tests."

"I wouldn't," he said. "I know how important it is to you."

"Thank you," she said.

"Who's going to watch the dog? We can't take it with us."

She shrugged. "I'll find someone. I'll let them know it's yours so they don't get any funny ideas."

"Good plan," he said, smiling.

"Everything's settled then. I'll see you tomorrow."

"What's the rush?" he asked. "Just let me put these guns away and we can take a walk on the beach. Maybe check out that cool looking tree over there by the rocks. I think its within the barrier."

She hesitated. "Okay, I guess."

"Good."

He packed the bag and took it back to the arms room. He would have a lot of work to do later tonight setting up everyone's kit, but that could wait. He found Yael where he had left her, though she had gone back to her cabin for the dog.

They walked slowly along the beach until they got to the tree, where they decided to sit and talk. The sky blazed red as the sun set, silhouetting the twisted limbs of the tree against its brightness. He felt something on his hand and looked down in surprise. The tips of Yael's fingers were barely touching him, but she didn't seem to be aware of it. He sighed contentedly, and watched the sun set over a land that would not be a mystery for much longer.

Chapter 11

"Alex to Max," he said into the radio. "Shut it down...or lower it, whatever." He waited for some visible or audible signal that the barrier was passable, but there was nothing. The others exchanged nervous glances, and no one seemed too eager to walk into it.

He looked at them, barely able to contain a wry smile. They looked out of place, uncomfortable. They held their weapons awkwardly, hands shifting, pulling on straps, fidgeting. Only Yael looked remotely at ease, but he would never get used to seeing her in camouflage. The smallest size was a bit large on her, but the uniforms offered sufficient adjustment to make it work. Overall, his team looked like Hollywood soldiers. Their equipment was correct, but everything else about them was wrong.

"It's lowered, Alex," Max's voice said through the little radio. "Let me know when you're across."

"Received...wilco," Alex said. They stood near the spot where Alex had first tried to cross the barrier and later found the dog. He had decided it would be easiest to travel along the coast as far as they could before heading inland. The beach also allowed for a hasty retreat, either back to the complex or into the jungle to their right. He had no idea what was waiting for them on the other side of the barrier, and didn't want to take chances.

"What?" the radio crackled.

Alex rolled his eyes. "I got it, Max, will do." He turned to the group. "Okay, move out. Stay on my six." He paused and sighed. "Six means rear, like six o'clock on a watch. Stay behind me."

"Got it Chief," Tom said. The others murmured or nodded their assent.

"Remember, it's not completely down, so it's going to get uncomfortable." Alex walked briskly across the barrier, and felt nausea, brief but intense, as though he had shoved his fingers down his throat but quickly pulled them out. They really did have control! When they were all well past the place he suspected was its outer limit, he radioed Max to turn it back on.

“The barrier is up, Alex,” Max said. “Good luck out there.”

“Thank you,” he said into the radio, then turned to the others. “Okay, spread out, keep about ten meters apart…that’s about thirty feet. Very important…do not shoot at anything or anyone unless I give the order, unless you’re being shot at. Got it?”

They all nodded.

“Good. Let’s move out. Yael, take up the rear.”

“Got it,” she said, and stood still until the others passed her, then took her place in the back, glancing behind her every few seconds. Of all of those with him, she was the only one he trusted to be remotely effective if something should go wrong, and though he hated to endanger her, he had to put her where she would count the most.

They walked for several minutes before the jungle started encroaching onto the beach to the point where they were running out of sand. He slowed his pace, motioning for Tom to take the lead, then walked next to Barbara, who looked more uncomfortable than the others.

“How are you doing?” he asked, giving her a reassuring smile. She returned the gesture, and he felt a brief twinge of excitement. She was the older woman, not so much that she wasn’t still very attractive, but enough so that she intrigued him with the promise of things he had not yet discovered. She was sweating, breathing deeply, and beads of glistening sweat adorned her tan skin.

“I’m okay,” she said. “I’m a runner, but I’m not used to this heat. I only moved to LA a few months ago. I lived in Portland.”

“Heat?” Alex said, grinning. “Compared to where I’ve been, it’s freezing. A bit on the muggy side, though.” He didn’t feel guilty for his reaction, as he had no intention of acting on it. He was a healthy young male in his early twenties, at the peak of his sex drive, and he had long since given up trying to fight his urges. Far easier to accept and ignore them.

“Don’t worry about me,” she said. “I’ll get used to it.”

“If you’re carrying too much weight…” She had a backpack full of medical supplies along with a hydration pack, rifle and load bearing vest. Alex had only given her four spare magazines, though it would have been smarter to arm her with a pistol instead. He wasn’t used to being in charge and he was making mistakes.

Nothing to do about it now, except learn from it.

"No," she said, shaking her head. "The weight doesn't bother me. Just the heat."

"Okay," he said, nodding. "Let me know if you have any problems."

Taking the lead once more, he took them as far along the beach as he could, then stepped into the jungle, brushing away the foliage. He saw the trail almost immediately, and stopped. It was a well worn dirt road, sprinkled over with a light covering of dead leaves and small rocks.

"How about that," he said. "Wherever this is, it's not uninhabited."

"Or it wasn't," Tom said. "At some point."

"Thank you Mr. Positive," Alex chided, looking back at Yael, who was staring at the trail, furrowing her brows, probably worried about what they would find and what it meant to her family's well being. He realized that he had hardly thought of his own parents, and suddenly felt a wave of dread wash over him. Were they dead? If the asteroid theory was correct…

"Well," he said. "This is a perfectly good trail, and it seems to be going in the same direction we are. We're going to use it."

The trail was made of hard packed dirt, much easier to walk on than sand, and the shade afforded by the jungle canopy allowed the cool ocean breeze to drive away much of the heat. The relief didn't last long. The canopy thinned out gradually, until the sun returned in full force.

"Look!" Ryan said, pointing straight ahead. Alex had already noticed, but was too busy frowning at it to say anything. It was a utility pole, though it was bare, no cross members or wires. He looked around and saw another pole in the distance over the tree tops, just as bare as the first. Whatever small amount of mystery was left in their predicament, it was slowly being eroded by the all too familiar signs of modern civilization. He had entertained more notions than he had shared with Yael, some of them quite fantastical. Perhaps they were on an alien planet, unwitting pawns of humanity's expansion into the cosmos via interstellar teleportation, or perhaps they had been transported back in time, and the weapons and the barrier were there to protect them against Velociraptors and T-Rexes. Of course these were just fanciful flights of the imagination, but living in a fully explored world was dull, and these indulgences had given him a sense of mystery that he had enjoyed. Until now.

Yael walked up to him. "Alex," she said, her voice neutral, flat. "I'm scared."

"Why? I thought you'd be pleased. Signs of civilization and all that. I'm actually getting nervous about being so heavily armed. What if we walk out of the jungle in the middle of a town in Mexico?"

"I've been to a few places in Mexico," Sandi said softly. "This doesn't look like Mexico."

"I don't like it," Yael said. "We just spent days in a futuristic pod colony surrounded by an energy barrier, and we're next to a place with power lines?"

Alex rubbed his chin. "Well, there are no actual lines…the poles are bare. Maybe whatever is around here is deserted. A ghost town or something."

"I guess," she said, though her expression did not change.

They kept walking and soon Alex spotted a clearing up ahead. When they emerged from the jungle, he was even more confused than before. They were standing on a mowed lawn. On one side were three backless park benches, on the other a row of trimmed hedges. Before them was a series of low walls made from piles of dark round stones, each about the size of a man's head. They reminded Alex of the field stone walls that surrounded many farms on the outskirts of his home town. Conical mountains with pointy narrow peaks rose up around the bizarre gardens, their emerald green foliage complimented by the sapphire blue water of the ocean to their left. It would have been a beautiful place, if their presence here were not so utterly incomprehensible.

"This is a garden," Barbara said, looking around. "But I don't see any signs, or people. Where are we?"

"This looks familiar," Tom muttered. "I think I've seen this place before. In pictures or on TV or something."

Alex walked up to one of the benches and kicked it. He wasn't sure why, probably to reassure himself that it was there. The bench fell apart. There was nothing holding it together.

Alex blinked. "What the fuck?"

Tom knelt over the pile of planks and examined them. "This is odd. No nails. Someone just stood this up like a house of cards." He held his rifle awkwardly, but managed to keep the muzzle out of the dirt.

"Why would someone do that?" Barbara asked.

Alex picked up one of the boards that had made up the seat. It was bare wood, rich in color as though new but deeply cracked and pitted. There were holes where nails should have been and he noticed indentations where the nail heads would have been hammered into the wood.

"Someone took the nails," he said. "There used to be nails." Though there were no marks of the kind that would have been left by pry tools.

"Why would someone take the nails then go through the trouble of putting the benches up without them?" Yael asked. "That makes no sense at all."

"No, it doesn't," Barbara agreed. "This is getting spooky."

"Alex!" Patrick shouted. "Look over here!"

Looking where he pointed, Alex noticed some color through the well manicured trees near the shore. As they approached, they saw a pile of rubble in a clearing past the trees. It looked like the remains of a house, or perhaps the supplies to build one. Cracked slate roof tiles were scattered over two-by-fours and other building lumber. Assorted paper trash littered the site, flapping in the wind. Everything was covered in a thin layer of dust that extended well past the house.

"Looks like someone was going to build a house," Tom said. "But decided to dump the materials in a pile instead." Alex frowned. It was another disappointment. Not only was this place inhabited and utterly mundane save for a few oddities, it seemed that it was also affected by the ever deepening economic recession. Abandoned building projects were all too common in Barstow, the town in which he had sought refuge from the dreariness of life in Fort Irwin.

"Hard times," Barbara commented, echoing his thoughts. "Maybe they stole the nails to save on construction costs before abandoning it."

"Hello," Alex said, noticing some familiar patterns on a flap of paper lodged under a piece of lumber. "What's this?" He walked over to the pile and extracted the torn half of a map.

Yael was next to him in an instant. "What is it?"

"Part of a map," he said, turning it right side up.

"A map of what?"

"Kauai," he said, reading the legend. "Hawaii. I guess it's one of the islands."

"That's it!" Tom said excitedly. "That's where I saw this place before! On a travel channel show about Hawaii!"

"So we're in Hawaii?" Barbara asked. "Where is everyone?"

"Hang on," Alex said. "Just because this is a map of Hawaii doesn't mean we're in Hawaii. Tom, are you certain that this is the place you saw, exactly this place?"

"Well," Tom said, scratching his head. "Not like *sure* sure. It just looks very familiar."

"Let's see then," Alex said as he studied the map. The topography matched, at least superficially, as did the ocean, considering the fact that Kauai was an island. It was impossible to judge the contours of the coast, but considering where the sun had set and risen, if they were on Kauai then they would be on the north coast. There was a road that circled half the island, and if this was that island, then heading south would take them to that road very quickly. According to the map, the entire island was just over twenty miles in diameter.

"We can find out," he said. "By heading inland. If we're on the eastern half of the island, then there should be a highway less than a mile south of here. If it's the western half, then there should be some sort of road just through those trees. Let's move out."

"There are lots of trails here," Yael said. "We should be able to follow one of them to the road, if it's there."

"Let's do that," he said, and walked to the nearest southward trail. It led out of the garden and into the jungle, and in about a minute of walking emerged onto a narrow asphalt road barely big enough for two cars to pass each other. A double yellow line separated the lanes, though tire tracks indicated that the boundary was not routinely acknowledged.

"I'll be damned," Alex said. "This could be route 560. We

should look for a sign or something." Suddenly he felt very nervous about their weapons, as though a police car would drive by any second. Of course they wouldn't get in any real trouble considering their circumstances, but he had gotten used to a certain degree of freedom, and the very thought of police showing up disturbed him. He hoped, though, for Yael's sake, that they would come. For his parents' sake too.

"Which way do we go?" Yael asked him, looking over his shoulder.

"Good question," he said. "According to this map, there should be a town of some sort less than two miles east of here, and that would be left." He noticed something on the map, an asterisk hastily scribbled with a red marker. At the base of the map, also in red marker, were the words "Lanakila Gardens building site."

"Lanakila Gardens," he said. "Weird name."

"What?" Barbara said and walked up to look at the map. "Did you say Lanakila Gardens?"

"Yeah, why?"

"I read about that," she said. "Or maybe saw it on TV. Can't remember where."

"Travel channel," Tom said. "Same show. It was some controversial development, condominiums and such. They based the design on those self contained communities they're building for the middle class in India. Like a miniature luxury city. Locals couldn't stand it, fought it in the courts and all. I think they finished it late last year."

"Okay then," he said. "That settles it. We head east until we get to where the map says this thing is. Should be pretty big, right? Hard to miss?"

"Totally," Tom said. "We should see it long before we're anywhere near it. Some of the condos were ten stories or more."

"Perfect. Let's go."

They started walking east, the ocean still to their left, though they could no longer see it through the trees. Although the turns the road took seemed to match the map, there were no signs of any kind, and they didn't see or hear any cars.

"Really, really spooky," Barbara muttered.

"Yeah," Sandi agreed.

"How are you holding up?" Alex asked Yael as he adjusted his pace to match hers.

She shrugged. "Okay, I guess. I'm more scared than ever, but I'm not going to fall apart if that's what you mean." She grinned at him. "Wouldn't want to get shot."

"Har har," he said. "So…why scared?"

"You ever watch the Twilight Zone? Or Outer Limits?"

"Of course. I love those shows. Old and new."

"Me too," she said, and smiled briefly. "People are always giving me grief for liking the new ones. But anyway, there are a few episodes, I think mostly the old shows, where people wake up and find they're all alone in the world. There's also the one where they land on an alien planet but it looks like a town in the middle of America, except there's no one there."

"Yeah," he said. "I feel like that too. I don't know much about Kauai, but it's too small to be this deserted. We should have seen at least one car by now. And I don't think there are any empty beaches when the weather is this nice."

"Well there is the dog," she said.

"Yeah, there is. But that just means there are some people here, not that this is Hawaii."

"Or were."

"What?"

"*Were* people here," she explained glumly.

He didn't say anything, but he continued to walk next to her as he eyed their surroundings warily. They passed a few more abandoned construction sites like the one they had found at the first clearing, but there was no sign of Lanakila Gardens.

"Hold up," Alex said. "We should be there by now."

"If so," Yael said. "We should have been able to see it for quite a while now."

"So this isn't Hawaii?" Tom said, sounding disappointed.

Alex looked at the map. "Route 560 isn't very big. The part before the town is only a mile long, and we've walked at least that far. It may be Hawaii, but maybe not Kauai."

"What the hell do we do now?" Tom asked, sounding irritated.

"We keep going," Alex said. "Until we find something."

"I think we just did," Yael said, pointing south towards the jungle. Alex looked where she indicated.

"Holy shit."

They had found Lanakila Gardens, at least what was left of it.

Chapter 12

The debris was just visible around a bend in the road up ahead. Everyone started to run until Alex ordered them to slow down and spread out. He approached with his rifle at the ready, sweeping the area with the muzzle. He wasn't sure what he was looking for, but he didn't want to get caught with his pants down.

As soon as they cleared the bend it came into full view, a massive pile of concrete rubble that stretched for several hundred meters off the right side of the road. More debris littered the left side all the way to the edge of the beach, though not nearly as much as the main pile. The outlines of the foundations were vaguely visible, though the buildings had collapsed in a haphazard pattern, spreading rubble all around the site. Definitely not the work of a demolition crew.

"Wow," Tom said. "Guess the locals got really pissed off." It was an awe inspiring sight. So much destruction, yet the trees and bushes that surrounded it weren't affected except where a few were struck by falling debris. It was a surreal vista, a juxtaposition of disparate realities—urban disaster meets tropical paradise.

Alex relaxed and lowered his weapon. "Let's spread out in groups of two or three, see what we can find. Don't climb too much, I don't want anyone breaking a leg. And keep those weapons handy."

Yael followed Tom towards the smaller pile by the water while Sandi, Patrick and Ryan headed to the main area. That left Barbara with Alex.

"So what do you think?" he asked.

Barbara shrugged. "Earthquake? I saw a show on demolitions and they always get the buildings to collapse straight down, so the damage doesn't spread. This doesn't look like that."

"Yeah," Alex agreed. "I was thinking the same thing. Maybe the aborted house sites we passed weren't aborted."

"What do you mean?"

"You build the foundation, then the wooden frame, then put a roof on it. It looks like maybe they got to the roof part and then boom. Earthquake or something."

"So you think they were all new developments?" she asked, looking around uncertainly.

"I guess. Then again, Kauai is a small island, maybe the government just took it over and demolished everything."

"Hey Alex," Tom called from the ocean side of the road. "Take a look at this."

"Come on," Alex said to Barbara. "Let's go see what he found."

Tom was standing on the edge of the debris, holding a chunk of concrete. Yael stood next to him. Her hands were dusty and she was holding two smaller fragments.

"What's up?" Alex asked. He didn't see anything unusual about the concrete.

"Watch this," Yael said, motioning with her hand. At her signal, Tom dug his fingers into the concrete, trying to break it. It crumbled easily, disintegrating into dozens of small chunks and dust that fell at Tom's feet.

"So much for building codes," Alex said. "Either that or I want to know what you've been eating."

"Yeah," Tom agreed. "I wonder what made it like this. It couldn't have been built out of this crap or they couldn't have stacked it more than a single story before it collapsed. It feels like dried up packing foam, but it's obviously concrete."

"I dunno," Alex said. "If it had a good steel frame they could have built it out of Play-Doh. This stuff might just be insulation or exterior décor, like stucco or something."

"I guess," Tom agreed, though he didn't sound convinced.

"We're thinking earthquake," Barbara said. "Though who knows what could have caused it."

"Yeah," Alex agreed, then noticed something in the distance. "Check that out," he said, pointing. There were three boats about fifty meters off the beach, moored to floating balls. One was a ratty sailboat, mastless and with a patchwork hull and boarded cabin windows. A bit further out was a big motor boat, probably an old cruising vessel. It was about fifty feet long, run down and in desperate need of a paint job. Closest to shore was a power boat with two outboard motors, apparently new and draped in a canvas boat cover. It floated on some sort of inflated cushion that kept the hull dry.

"Those are the first normal things we've seen," Barbara said, staring at the boats.

"What are those balls they're tied to?" Alex asked.

"Mooring buoys," Barbara explained. "They're attached to anchors on the bottom. Boats tie up to them. It's a cheaper way to store your boat, safer too. See those pylons?"

Alex looked and saw wooden pillars sticking out of the ocean. They started near the edge of the rubble and extended about thirty feet into the water.

"Yeah, I see them."

"They're what's left of a marina. There were probably floating docks attached to them. Whatever it was that destroyed the condominiums got that too."

"There are a lot more balls," Alex said. "They look ratty though." The three buoys with the boats tied to them looked new, while all the others were so frayed they were barely visible above the water's surface.

"I guess those didn't make it," Tom said.

"Can an earthquake do that?" Alex asked. "Destroy floating docks?"

"I haven't the slightest idea," Barbara admitted. "I don't know anything about earthquakes. Anyone else maybe?"

"Not me," Tom said.

Yael shook her head.

"So much for that," Alex said. "You think that little one will run?" he asked Barbara, pointing to the twin engine power boat. "It looks new."

"Yeah," she said. "I see no reason why not, as long as it has gas. Why, do you want to go somewhere?"

Alex nodded. "Now that I'm pretty sure this is indeed Kauai, I wanna go to Honolulu. I'm not sure which island it's on, though. Maybe one of those boats will have a map or something."

"Why Honolulu?" Yael asked. Alex heard the hope in her voice. If they were going to find people anywhere, it would be Hawaii's biggest city.

"You know why," he said. "I don't even want to speculate about anything until we see what's going on over there. There are like a million people living in Honolulu, it's not some remote ass island like this one."

"Alex, what if…" Yael started.

"Don't," Alex said. "No point. If that boat runs, we're going there, and we'll see soon enough." He turned to Tom and Barbara. "Now then, let's see what the other group found, shall we?"

They made their way back to the road, where the others were standing together, looking at something one of them was holding.

"Whatcha got?" Alex asked. Sandi turned and handed him a dress, red flowers on white. It was torn, dirty and blood stained. The blood was dark brown, turning gray in places.

"We found this in the rubble," she said.

"Fuck," Alex said. "Now we know there were people in these buildings." He looked around, a bit less comfortable than he was a moment ago.

"The dress isn't damaged," Barbara said. "We don't even know if that's human blood. Or even blood at all. Though from what I can tell, it is. Blood that is. I can't tell from what."

"Good point," Alex said. "Maybe you can run some tests once we get back. In the mean time, I don't want to stay here any longer than we have to. Who wants to go for a swim?"

"What?" Patrick asked. "A swim?"

"Those boats," Barbara explained. "We're going to take one to Honolulu."

"No time to babble about it," Alex said, eager to leave this place and what he now knew to be buried in the rubble. "Someone needs to swim out there and get that boat to shore. Any takers? I'd go, but the only thing I know about boats is that they are wet on the bottom."

"I'll go," Barbara said quickly. "I'm good with boats. If it runs, I can get it started and off that float."

"Good."

They went down to the debris littered beach and waited while Barbara stripped down to her underwear. Alex tried not to stare, but it wasn't easy. She was in very good shape. As she walked into the water, he hefted his rifle and scanned the ocean nervously, looking for sharks. Alex loved to swim, but growing up in Upstate New York he didn't get to spend a lot of time at the beach. He was a lake and river man, and salt water and its accompanying vastness made him nervous. Objectively he knew it wasn't very deep where she was, but with the ocean one never knew for certain.

She made it to the boat quickly and climbed onto the flotation cushion. Seeing her next to it put the boat's size into perspective, and it was bigger than it looked from shore, maybe thirty feet. Alex watched her unzip the tarp and climb inside, where she spent several minutes looking around and checking things. There was no cabin, but the open deck surrounding the enclosed central console was quite big, more than enough for all of them. She lowered both outboard motors into the water with the push of a button. Alex heard the whine of hydraulic motors over the gentle lapping of the waves. The ocean was calm and the sky a clear blue with a few white clouds rolling lazily southward.

Barbara let loose some lines and did something to the float that deflated it half way, then stood behind the control console. Alex heard the twin Yamaha motors turn over, hesitate a bit, then finally start. White smoke drifted on the breeze, accompanied by a noxious smell. The motors gurgled and grumbled noisily, stirring up the water. After waiting a few minutes, Barbara pulled back on the throttle and the boat shuddered and started to move backwards, and within seconds it slid off the float and was drifting on the water, rocking gently.

"I forgot about the rocking," Alex said glumly, putting a hand on his stomach. "I hate boats." Rowboats on placid lakes were about the extent of his experience, and his tolerance.

Barbara pointed the boat at the beach and approached slowly. As the hull touched the sandy bottom, she cut the engines and raised them out of the water.

"All aboard!" she shouted.

Alex sighed. "Let's go. Take off your boots and socks and roll up your pants...keep your footwear dry." There was no way into the boat without walking into the water, but at least she had gotten it close enough to the shore that nothing above their knees would get wet, unless a large wave managed to make it to the beach.

Once they were all on board and drying their feet, Alex walked up to the control console and looked at the gas gauge.

"That doesn't look like much," he said, pointing at the gauge. There appeared to be less than a half a tank.

"Check out the other one," she said, pointing to another gauge near the first one. It was full.

"Two tanks? Cool. How much gas is that?"

"Not sure," she admitted. "But this is an offshore fishing boat, and they usually have very big tanks. Looks like this boat has been sitting here a while, maybe a long while. The owner had a small solar panel, which explains why the batteries aren't dead. The gas should still be good, but there might be some water in it. Shouldn't be a problem, though."

"Let's pull up to that big one," Alex pointed to the dilapidated cruising boat. "Maybe we can find more gas on board."

"I doubt it," Barbara said. "Boats like that don't use gasoline engines, they're usually diesel."

"Well maybe we can find something else." He noticed one of the instruments, a color screen that was showing what appeared to be a map with numbers all over the blue part.

"What is that?" he asked, pointing. "What are those numbers?"

"It's a chartplotter and those numbers represent depth, so you know where it's too shallow for your boat. Like…right here." She smiled. "It's like the GPS navigation in your car, works off the same satellites."

Alex grinned. "My car never had GPS navigation, that's what phones are for. You're such a doctor."

She laughed. "Yeah, I guess I am."

"So what does the thing say, we're in Kauai?"

"Yep," she said. "Just as we thought. Anyway, I'll look around, maybe I can find an owner's manual or something. Tell us how much gas we have."

"Okay," he said. "I'll mess around with this thing in the mean time." He pointed to the chart plotter. "Figure out where Honolulu is."

"Sounds like a plan," she said, and started rummaging around the numerous cockpit lockers.

Alex used the device's controls to zoom out, then move the display around to the other islands. He assumed that Honolulu would be on what Hawaiians called the "Big Island," but he found it on the much smaller island of Oahu. Fortunately, it was the next isle in the chain, though it was still quite a way off. According to the display, it was ninety miles to Oahu's western shore, and Honolulu was on the east side of the island.

"Found it," Barbara said, holding up a booklet. "Two hundred and forty gallons total. So that means we have…um…"

"One eighty," Yael said. She was sitting on one of the cushioned benches near the front of the boat.

"Right," Barbara said, smiling. "I was never good at math." She turned to the booklet. "According to this, this boat can cruise at thirty miles per hour burning fourteen gallons an hour. That gives us a range of…" she turned to Yael.

"Three hundred and eighty four miles," Yael said.

"Hey!" Alex said. "You're like a walking calculator!"

She shrugged. "I like math. That's why I majored in it."

"Factoring in currents, extra weight and rough water," Barbara continued. "We should probably assume it's less, maybe three thirty, three forty."

"That's plenty," Alex said, looking at the chartplotter. "If we circle the south side of Oahu it's a hundred and twenty miles to Honolulu, two forty round trip. Let's search that big boat anyway, though. Who knows what we'll find."

"Someone should check the radio while we do that," Yael said. "We may be able to raise someone, or at least overhear something."

"What?"

"The radio. This thing has a radio, right?"

Alex turned to Barbara, who cringed and shook her head. "That's right! I'm such a twit!" She walked over to the console and found the marine VHF. She turned it on, and started flipping through channels. Alex smiled. He'd thought he was the only one who suffered from such failings.

"Let's wait until we're next to the other boat," he said. "You can try to find something while we search it."

"Okay. I'll need someone to push off."

Alex looked at his dry feet, then turned to Ryan and Patrick. "You guys. Get in the water and give us a shove." Rank had its privileges.

Launching the boat was easy, and within seconds they were floating, motors running, while the two men helped each other back into the boat. Barbara guided them expertly alongside the big cruiser, then lowered some cylindrical plastic bumpers over the side to keep the two boats from rubbing together. After tying the small craft to the larger cruiser with dock lines, she started to mess with the radio again.

"Radio check," she said. "Can anyone hear me?" After waiting a while, she switched channels and tried again.

"Okay," Alex said. "Tom, Yael, you're with me. Patrick and Ryan, you two go onboard and wait on deck, keep an eye out. Everyone get your boots back on first. I don't want anyone stepping on something and injuring their feet."

The boat was just as rundown on the inside as it was on the outside. There was water damage everywhere, along with garbage, broken furnishings and a very unpleasant moldy smell that, combined with the movement of the boat, threatened to dislodge his stomach. They found the fuel tank cap in the rear cockpit and Alex unscrewed it and took a sniff—definitely diesel. He was very familiar with the smell. Army vehicles generally ran on diesel.

"Well at least we know where we can find diesel if we need it," he said, disappointed. There was nothing else of value on board and he decided to scrub the search.

"Anything?" he asked Barbara while he helped Yael down off the deck of the larger vessel.

"Not a thing," she said. "And that's not normal. Hawaii should be crawling with VHF traffic."

"Not if the government bought out this island," he said. "With the next one ninety miles away…what's the range on those things anyway?"

"Theoretically twenty five miles," she said. "But this boat is small and it's antenna is low in the water, so less."

"Okay. Let's um…what do you call it? Cast off?"

Barbara grinned. "Aye aye, skipper."

"Oh no," he said, holding up his hands. "You're the skipper. I'm just along for the ride."

They picked up the docking lines and bumpers, then Barbara

took her position at the console, cranked the engines and moved the boat slowly away from the floating junk pile. Once clear, she pointed the boat's nose out to sea and gunned the throttle. The motors roared and the vessel lurched forward, but didn't move as fast as Alex expected. After a few seconds, though, the boat's nose rose up in the air and then the entire thing seemed to pop out of the water and run on top of the waves, bouncing off each crest as it sped along at a very respectable speed. Barbara noticed his confusion.

"It's called 'planing'," she explained, speaking loudly to be heard above the roar of the motors and the slapping of the hull. "Like hydroplaning. A boat's speed in the water is limited by the length of its hull, this one would be something like seven or eight miles per hour. As a boat moves it creates waves, and the waves move farther apart the faster it goes. Eventually it reaches the speed where it rides in the trough between two wave crests…like the valley between two mountains. To go faster, it has to climb up the face of the wave in front of it. It takes a lot of power to do that, but once most of the hull is above the water, the speed limit goes away. That's called planing."

"You know a lot about boats," he shouted, impressed. "Do they teach that at medical school?"

She laughed. "They might as well, especially in California. It's going to take us about four hours to get to Honolulu. We should be at the west coast of Oahu in three, though."

"I'll be up front," he said. "Trying not to hurl."

"Good plan! It's called a bow."

"What?"

"The front of the boat, it's called a bow. The rear is called the stern."

"Good to know!" he yelled. Taking advantage of the numerous handholds scattered throughout the cockpit, he walked around the center console and made his way to the front—the bow—and sat down next to Yael. It was a little bit quieter here away from the engines, though every now and then a light spray of cold salty water cleared the hull and chilled his face and neck. The sun was bright in the sky, and the salty air and sparkling water reminded him of the tropical vacations his parents used to take him on.

"You don't look so good," Yael said, noticing his discomfort.

"Are you seasick?" She didn't quite have to yell to be heard, but she did have to speak loudly.

"Yeah," he admitted. "Aren't you?"

She shrugged. "Mind over matter. Looking at the horizon helps. This isn't the best place to be, there's more movement here than elsewhere, but I can't stand to be back there, the smell of the engines is too much for me."

"I know what you mean." Tom was on one side of the console watching Barbara work the controls, but the other three were in the back—the stern—where the cockpit was widest and most spacious.

He started to say something, but his stomach rebelled and he managed to stick his head over the side just in time to avoid throwing up onto the deck.

Chapter 13

Alex's nausea persisted for about an hour, but after being subjected to the barrier it was nothing more than a mild annoyance. After that, it began to slowly subside until by the end of the second hour it was completely gone.

"I think I have my sea legs," he said to Yael. "How about you?" He had kept quiet most of that time, as the boat was not an environment particularly conducive to conversation. Between the roar of the engines, the whistling of the wind and constant slapping of the hull crashing through the waves, it was hard both to hear someone talking and to focus on what he wanted to say.

"I'm feeling better," she said, almost shouting. "I don't get why people think this is fun."

"What is?"

"Boating."

"Oh. You don't like the ocean?" He looked around as he asked her, captivated by its beauty. Sparkling blue water in every direction—vast, empty and so utterly in control of their fate that it was magnificently frightening. The slightest change in weather could destroy them, and it wasn't hard to appreciate just how vulnerable they were, tossed around by what appeared from a distance to be minor undulations in a mostly smooth surface.

"No," she said. "I love the ocean. It's just this boat, so noisy, so bouncy. What's the point?"

"Yeah," he said. "I guess I could see that. Maybe a sailboat would be better."

"Probably, but something like this comes in handy when you need to be somewhere in a hurry."

"Yeah it does."

"Captain Alex," Patrick said, moving forward. "Is it okay if we switch places for a few minutes? I can't take the smell of the engines anymore."

"Sure thing," Alex said, and carefully walked back towards the boat's stern.

As they sped along at an even thirty miles per hour, Alex kept glancing nervously at the twin two hundred fifty horsepower Yamahas, wondering what would happen if they were to fail.

"It's good we have two," Barbara said, noticing his concern. "Odds of both failing are slim to none."

"Don't say that," Alex chided playfully. "You'll anger the sea gods."

"You mean Poseidon?"

"I was thinking more of Murphy."

Towards the end of the third hour, a landmass became visible on the horizon. Despite their speed, it did not grow noticeably larger for quite a while.

"That's Oahu," Barbara said. "Our course is going to take us around the southern side. Do you want to pass closer to land, maybe see something? Or shoot straight for Honolulu?"

"What would be the downside of coming close to land?"

"It's a less efficient course," she explained. "It would cost us extra fuel. I have no idea how much, but you could ask your girlfriend. She has a way with numbers."

Alex blushed. "She's not my girlfriend."

"Oh?" Barbara asked, and there was something to that "oh" that momentarily excited him. Had it been his imagination?

"Not yet, anyway," he explained with a sheepish grin. "I'm working on it." He was fully aware of the potential consequences of his words, but he felt a deep and powerful satisfaction in having spoken them.

"Oh," she said again. "Best of luck. She seems like a nice girl. Let me know if you need any help."

"Help?"

"I could put in a good word for you."

"Thanks, it couldn't hurt. Anyway, let's just shoot for Honolulu, forget about getting close to land. Shouldn't we be seeing other boats right about now?"

She nodded, frowning. "Yeah. We should."

Deciding Patrick had had enough relief, he returned to the bow. In a few minutes they were passing the south side of Oahu, too far from shore to make out any details. Yael scanned the ocean in all directions. There wasn't a single boat in sight. After a while she reached out and put her hand over his, squeezing tightly. He tensed, afraid to move lest she realize what she was doing and take it away. Unfortunately, he saw something in the distance and had to speak up.

"There!" He pointed with his free hand. "What is that?" It was a red metal object floating in the water a bit over a kilometer ahead and off their left side. He was used to thinking in yards and feet, but the army taught him to judge distance in meters. It was often difficult to keep the two systems straight.

"Off the port bow?" Barbara asked. "The red thing? It's a navigation buoy."

"Port bow," Alex said. "Have to learn that cool boat jargon. Well, it's a good sign, isn't it? I mean we didn't see any road signs back on Kauai, but this is like a sea going version of a sign, right?"

"Yeah," Barbara said. "You could look at it that way."

"See?" Alex said to Yael. "Maybe things are okay after all. We're still far from shore, and if there was a hurricane or something a few days ago maybe no one would be boating."

"You don't have to keep doing that," she said, and took her hand away.

"Doing what?"

"Babying me. I'm not a delicate flower, I can handle the truth."

"I didn't mean…"

"No, I appreciate it," she said, giving him a quick smile. "It's just not necessary."

He nodded. "Got it. No more babying."

She resumed her search for signs of life. He watched her for a moment, the way her hair danced in the wind, the way her eyes narrowed to allow her long eyelashes to shield her eyes from the sun. There was such beauty and grace in everything she did, even the way she used a casual smile or a tilt of the head to mask her pain and uncertainty. He wished there was something he could do, but he was just a grunt, doing his best to keep them alive while they poked around a mystery that was far too big for him to handle.

The better part of an hour passed before Barbara started taking the boat closer to shore, and everyone was starting to show signs of fatigue. Alex was worn out, even though all he'd done was sit still and watch the water roll by. The constant motion of the boat and the glaring of the sun, combined with the stress of constant fear and uncertainty, took almost as much out of him as an all day march in full kit through the Mojave desert.

"What's that?" Yael asked, pointing off to port and slightly ahead. Alex looked and saw an area of frothy water. In fact all of the water past a certain point was white with froth. Or was it froth?

"What the hell?" he asked, squinting to make out whatever details he could.

"I have no idea," Barbara said. "I've never seen anything like that before."

As the boat raced closer, Alex saw that the water wasn't frothy at all, just white. Barbara throttled back the motors and the boat fell off plane as they coasted towards the strange border between white and blue. Side to side rocking increased but didn't bother him, while the reduced noise from the engines was a welcome relief.

"It's dust!" Patrick said, and reached over the side. When he brought his hand up, it was covered in a whitish residue. Alex looked around, trying to see how far the white water extended.

"That's a lot of fucking dust!" he said. The white water hugged the coast as far as he could see in both directions. The boundary between clean and dirty water was not as immediate as it had seemed from a distance. Looking over the side, Alex could see the water gradually changing until it was almost completely light gray. That same color looked white when seen from afar under the bright sunlight.

"Why are we still coasting?" Alex asked Barbara. "It's just dirty water."

"It may gunk up the motors. They are raw water cooled…that means sea water is pumped through them as they run."

"They're getting dust in them anyway," he said. "You want that water running through at high pressure, or your chances of clogging the passages are much higher."

"Good point!" Barbara admitted. "I thought you didn't know anything about boats!" She pushed the throttle and the motors roared as the boat climbed back onto plane.

"I don't," he shouted. "Neighbors used to have a spring fed

pond. The pipe that fed it would get clogged whenever there was a drought and water pressure was low, unless they shut the valve in time."

"Makes perfect sense," Barbara said. Alex noticed Yael looking at him, but she turned away as soon as he saw her. The others were all watching the approaching shore, waiting to spot any sign of the biggest city in Hawaii, but Alex knew with a dreadful certainty that such a search would be unnecessary if something were not terribly wrong.

"This isn't right," he muttered, though no one heard him. As they got close enough to make out details, he saw no signs of a city, though the area between the tall inland mountains and the beach was mostly flat, and the trees along the coast were tall enough to conceal residential properties. There was a fair amount of debris littering the beach every so often in scattered piles, but as time went on the piles became denser until they were almost one continuous mass along the shore.

"Is it around that bend, maybe?" Alex asked Barbara. "The one with the mountain right by the water?"

"I don't think that's a mountain," Tom said. "I think that's Diamond Head."

"What's Diamond Head?" Alex asked.

"No," Barbara said. "This is it…the map says we're here." She pulled back on the throttle and the boat sank into the water and slowed.

"Diamond Head is a crater," Tom explained. "Or at least it looks like a crater, it's actually a volcanic cone. It's right on the eastern edge of Honolulu. I, um, watch a lot of travel channel."

"But if that's Diamond Head," Alex asked. "Then where's the city? Are you sure it's not on the western tip? Maybe around that bend…"

"Alex," Barbara said. "Look at the map. It's a GPS for crying out loud. We're here. This is Honolulu." Alex looked, and the map showed their position just off the shore of the city. He looked at Yael, who was staring out at the volcanic cone, her fists clenched and knuckles white.

"So…" Alex started to say, but wasn't sure how to phrase it. "I mean what we're saying then is…Honolulu is gone? The whole city? I mean let's think about that for a second. It's fucking nuts." He knew it was true, knew it deep in the pit of his stomach, but he wanted to argue that knowing away, wanted someone to agree that it was crazy.

"I don't know what to tell you," Barbara said, refusing to take her eyes off the chartplotter. "I've been watching this map for three hours, I've based our course on it. Every feature of the shore was correct. Every depth reading was confirmed by the sounder. If this map were wrong god knows where we would be right now. There's no two ways about it. That…" She pointed towards shore. "Is Honolulu."

"I don't understand," Sandi said, then turned away and started to cry, cupping her face in her hands.

"Come on now," Ryan said, reaching out to her. She pulled away and went to the bow, away from the others.

"This is bullshit," Alex said. "We're going ashore, and we're gonna find out what the hell is going on here. A major US city can't just be gone. For all we know someone reprogrammed this GPS to fuck with us. Barbara, take us in. It was a little too convenient finding this boat."

She nodded, and pushed the throttle slightly. They started to move faster, though not fast enough for the boat to climb out of the water. The rubble strewn beach approached ominously.

"What could wipe out a city?" Yael asked, still staring at the shoreline. "I mean completely." She was eerily calm, so much so it frightened him a bit.

"Tsunami?" Alex ventured. "Earthquake of unprecedented strength? But we can't really be sure this is Honolulu…"

"And the trees? Do you see a single overturned tree? I don't. It's as if God reached down and scooped up all the buildings and left everything else alone."

"Oh no," he said, shaking his head. "Don't go there, come on."

She turned to him. "You have a better idea?"

"No," he admitted. "But that doesn't mean we should start making things up."

"That doesn't stop you from denying it's Honolulu."

He glared at her a moment. "Touché," he said finally. "But whatever happened here, there's a perfectly reasonable explanation. And however bizarre it may seem, when we figure it out, it will be rooted in logic and reality."

She sighed, and seemed to deflate. "Funny thing is, I know that, though maybe I shouldn't. It's just so tempting to believe that this is the work of God, at least that way it's all part of his plan."

"I know what you mean," he said. "And for what it's worth, I'm glad you're not getting too religious on me, especially now." She looked at him with an expression he couldn't read, then turned away.

"I don't know why I'm not," she said softly, and he wasn't sure if he was meant to hear it.

As they neared the beach, the boat slowed and started to zig-zag. Barbara looked from one instrument to another as she turned the wheel back and forth and adjusted the throttle.

"What is it?" Alex asked. "Something wrong?"

"A lot of rocks here," she said. "Just under the surface. I wish I knew how current this map was, or what the tide level is right now. A lot of floating debris too. There!" She pointed to two smaller buoys, one green and one red. "Those are channel markers. This close to shore they usually lead to a marina."

She guided the boat towards the floating cans and when they were roughly between them she turned sharply towards the shore and took them straight in and around a bunch of barnacle encrusted poles that stuck out of the water. They touched bottom on a rubble strewn beach at the base of some tall trees. Alex decided to leave Sandi and Ryan on the boat.

"Take it out," he said, after having Barbara show them how to work the controls. "Far enough that you can't see us on the beach. Keep your radio on."

"Sure thing," Ryan said. Tom and Alex pushed the boat back into the water and watched as Ryan reversed the motors, got the boat turned about and sped away between the two buoys, straight out to sea. A sense of morbidity made Alex wonder if he would ever see them again.

The tree line wasn't very thick, and when they crossed onto a flat open plane, they stood in silence, awed by what they saw.

"God in heaven," Barbara said, crossing herself.

"Barukh ata Adonai," Yael whispered. "Eloheinu melekh

ha'olam, dayan ha-emet."

"What does that mean?" Alex asked without taking his eyes off the scene before him.

"It's the opening verse of a prayer for the dead," she said softly.

"I think you should finish it."

Chapter 14

Honolulu was gone—not demolished, not burned, just gone. Asphalt streets crisscrossed like ribbons across an empty canvas where a great painting once cast its reflected colors onto the sparkling waters of Mamala Bay. Concrete fragments littered the empty lots, not quite filling the naked holes left by foundations that used to hold up massive towers whose shadows reached the ocean. Everything was caked in dust that blew from mounds scattered across the ruins in places where the tallest buildings had once stood.

Alex started to walk along the nearest street, its yellow divider barely visible above a layer of dust and garbage. The stench was everywhere, but it was not the smell of death he had expected. It reeked like a trash can left too long in the sun, of rotting food and decomposing feces.

A mirage glimmered ahead, then another. Buildings? He squinted, but they didn't vanish. There were a few, five or six that he could see, though perhaps there were more behind the dust mounds. His eyes fixed on one in the distance and he started towards it. He picked it for no specific reason, perhaps because it was closest to the street he was walking on. None of the buildings were particularly tall, or large, and all looked as though they were of another age, a style far older than the monotonous rectangles of modern architecture. The one he was heading towards was a cathedral. The others followed in silence.

By far the most noticeable type of garbage was clothing, some of it dusty, some bloody or otherwise soiled. Sometimes there were pieces of something in a shirt, or a dress. He knew Barbara would want to examine them, but he couldn't bring himself to stop. Something about that cathedral was calling him. Not god, but a sense of order, of normality. Something he needed to overcome the desperate instability that was crawling up from the depths to take the reins of his consciousness.

The passage of time became a blur, a repetition of a melancholy song fragment, like an exaggerated rendition of Adagio for Strings where the ascending melody was the buildup of grief at the sight of every infant sized shirt or dress. Blue ducks on yellow or pink daffodils on white. Just like the music it teased with a crescendo of anguish that dropped off in a balancing wave of numbness, then resumed its climb towards an intensifying rage that Alex knew he had to get under control before he lost himself to it.

Through it all there was an undeniable truth laying its foundations in the dust caked holes between the desolate streets. This was no act of nature. *Someone did this*.

The cathedral was not as intact as he had thought when viewing it from a distance. Neatly trimmed hedges surrounded a shell of stone walls, roofless and with holes where beautiful stained glass windows once glowed with all the hues of the rainbow, an infusion of metallic oxides into molten silica by the hands of an artist creating something greater than the sum of its parts. When he was sixteen his parents had taken him to see the cathedral at Wells in the UK, and he remembered staring up into the vaulted ceilings with undisguised awe, wondering what a thirteenth century peasant must have felt when he saw the same thing over seven hundred years before. He wondered if that cathedral was also like this one, an empty shell of lost history and culture. Surely not, but, what if it was? How could such a thing happen?

"What do we do?" he asked, not sure who would hear him.

There was silence, save for the shuffling of feet. He turned, and saw the pain in their faces, but also the need. They were looking to him for strength, but he had none to give.

"I'm just a soldier," he said, apologizing. "This is…this is too much. I don't know what to do." His voice trembled, but he managed to contain tears that were all too ready to flow as he looked into the faces of his friends. Were they his friends? He decided that they had to be, for he had no one else. Perhaps there *was* no one else, anywhere.

"I think we all need some time," Barbara said. He nodded, and turned away. He heard Yael sobbing. He looked at her, but she had her back to him and was staring across the wasteland. He wanted to comfort her, but how? He had no words that could soothe her pain, no profound insights that would give her reason to cast aside her grief. Only her god could help her now, and wasn't that the point of believing?

He found a smooth spot of grass, freshly cut, and sat cross legged, staring at the rifle that he laid across his lap. Safe, semi, auto—glyphs of sanity in a disordered reality. The lever pointed to semi, and he moved it to safe, wishing that was all it took to make his pain go away. He ran his fingers along the coated aluminum receiver, gliding gently over the bumps and ridges. He resisted thinking about his parents as long as he could, until his father's spectacled face stared at him from the patterns in the textured pistol grip, his mother's eyes glimmered in the red glass of the holographic sight.

"I love you," she had said on the parade field at Ft. Benning after they pinned the jump wings to his chest. "And we're both so proud."

"Even dad?" His father had never liked the idea of him giving his life in service of a country he thought had turned its back on its people. He had called the army a tool of the wealthy elite, enforcing their financial agendas at the expense of young lives.

"Even me," the old man had said. "It's not about politics, son, it's about you. I don't agree with your decision, but you made it, and you're sticking to it, doing the best you can. I'm proud of you."

His body trembled as he fought to hold back tears. It wasn't just grief that threatened to overwhelm him, but also an overpowering urge to hit something, to break it, destroy it. His hands itched at the thought of unleashing his carbine on the stones of the ruined cathedral, or pulling the pin on his fragmentation grenades, all at once, tossing them into the shell of god's house to punish the negligent deity for the evil he had by his absence permitted.

One of the others sat next to him, reached out for him, and he flinched away, furious that someone dared to intrude on his solitude. He turned, his face a snarl, and saw Yael. She put a hand behind his head and pulled him to her. All the anger flowed out of him, leaving only anguish, and something else. Gratitude. He allowed her to guide his face to her shoulder and he wrapped his arms around her, letting his weapon slide onto the grass. He was silent, he was still, and he wept. He wasn't sure how long she held him, but her shirt was soaked all the way through at the shoulder when he finally lifted his head.

He looked into her eyes, and she into his, and in that moment, something changed between them.

* * *

"Let's go," Alex said, climbing to his feet. He held out his hand and helped Yael up.

"Where?" Barbara asked. She had done her share of crying. They all had.

"We have a lot of work to do," he explained. "We can't count on finding more gas, so we only get to make this trip once. I told Max we would be gone three days, and I plan to use them all."

"But what do you hope to find?" Tom asked. He looked upbeat, perhaps because Alex was back on his game. Campbell had shared some of the finer points of leadership he had been taught at officer candidate school, and while some of it had sounded ridiculous, there was a lot that made sense. What had interested Alex the most were the psychological aspects, which essentially held that the average human being was most content when being controlled and guided by others, and that the absence of such control often resulted in depression and aberrant behavior. His own experiences seemed to support the idea.

"Maybe nothing," Alex continued, trying to sound as confident as he could. "Maybe some clues, maybe even some answers." He saw them all perk up. These people were his friends and he didn't like to manipulate them, but they needed him, and they had a job to do.

"Where do we start?" Yael asked.

"In this cathedral. Then the other buildings that are standing."

"First question is," Tom said. "Why are they standing?"

"Indeed. But there will be plenty of time for thinking when we get back," Alex said. "Right now let's focus on gathering as much information as we can. Barbara, did you bring sample bags?"

"Got 'em," she said, patting her backpack. "I'm going to take samples of everything. Rocks, concrete, clothing…" She trailed off, but he knew what she had been about to say. Bodies, or more accurately, small pieces of people. "Tom, I have plenty for you too. I'm sure you'll want to take your own samples, I have only the faintest idea of what kind of tests you'll be running."

"Um, yeah," Tom said, nervously. "Right. I'll take some." Alex gave him a look, but didn't say anything. Tom mouthed a silent "thank you" when no one else was looking.

"I'll go in and clear the building," Alex said. "Wait for me before going inside."

"Got it," Tom said.

Alex entered the cathedral, rifle at the ready. Wooden pews stood in even rows amidst thick stone columns that divided the knave into a main hall and two aisles. Arches rose from the top of the columns and ascended to what had once been the ceiling, now a gaping wound in a once beautiful edifice.

There were some clothes and footwear scattered among the pews and in the walkway between them. He wondered if whatever caused the destruction of the city had somehow killed all the people where they stood in an instant, leaving nothing but clothes. He imagined them fleeing to the cathedral to seek shelter from whatever horror was waging its war against the city beyond the sheltering stone walls. Had they cried out to god, begging him to spare their lives? Had they promised to be better people, to believe more, to sin less? Fat lot of good it did them.

Banishing the fantasy, he decided it was far more likely that the clothes had been blown inside by the wind. That didn't explain where the bodies were, though perhaps there were no bodies, perhaps the people had been evacuated. Most of them, anyway. There had been some remains after all.

He realized that they had thus far failed to search the highlands, sticking only to the coastal areas that were at or near sea level. If the source of the destruction was a tsunami or related to the sea in some other way, and if people had any sort of advance warning, then they would have fled to higher elevations. They had two more days, and that gave them plenty of time to go up to one of the mountains and look for survivors and get back to the landing point in time to make the four hour trip back home, assuming they didn't find anything.

Home? Had he really come to think of the complex as home?

He wasn't sure, but he did look forward to getting back, relaxing on the beach or in his bed, munching on a rehydrated steak while sipping cool water from a cup. If only the government had left them some beer, assuming of course it was the government that had kidnapped them—or perhaps saved them?

He was about to call the others when he thought he caught some movement out of the corner of his eye. He lifted his rifle and walked forward warily. He saw it again, between the pews towards the front of the cathedral. Circling around, he positioned himself so that he could identify its source. Perhaps it was a dog or other animal, maybe even a rat. As he turned the corner of that row of pews, he stopped and blinked in surprise.

It was a woman. She was sitting on the floor at the foot of the bench, rocking slightly back and forth. His heart began to pound and he stared for a couple of seconds, unable to react.

"I found someone!" he finally shouted. "Barbara, get your gear!" The pounding of boots on stone signaled the approach of the others, though he dared not take his eyes off of the woman, afraid that she would disappear. It wasn't a rational thought, but after searching for people so long in vain he couldn't be sure that she wasn't a figment of his imagination.

"Oh my god!" Barbara shouted as she flung her pack off her shoulders and held it up with her left hand as she navigated between the pews.

"Wait!" Alex ordered, circling around the front to get to the other side.

"She could be hurt!" Barbara shouted, slowing down just a bit.

"She could be dangerous!" he said.

Through all this shouting, the woman did not speak, or even look up. Perhaps she was in shock, or maybe deaf, but her lack of reaction made Alex very nervous. Barbara ran up to her just as he closed from the other side.

"Miss," Barbara said calmly but firmly, her voice radiating authority. "Miss are you alright?" The woman, probably in her twenties, didn't look up. She continued to rock back and forth, staring at the floor. Her brown curls were dirty and matted, and there was blood on her arms and hands. This close to her, his nose recoiled at the smell, though it was not unfamiliar. Soldiers living in the field often smelled like this, though they themselves got used to it gradually to the point where it only bothered someone who was exposed to it without being given time to acclimate. The woman wore a long green skirt and white t-shirt, both filthy. A silver pendant glittered just below the base of her neck, distracting Alex for the briefest of moments, but it was enough.

Without warning the woman's head snapped up and glared at Barbara with eyes so full of hatred and rage that Alex recoiled. He had never seen such ferocity. Her hands flew up and she grasped Barbara's shirt, pulling her down as her lips pulled back to reveal bloodstained teeth. Her mouth opened as her head came up, her teeth closing around Barbara's cheek.

Alex's rifle snapped out in a blur of motion. The hard edge of its stock smashed into the woman's temple and her head rocked back, striking the edge of the pew with the sound of cracking bone. The woman went limp and crashed to the floor as Barbara fell back, tripping over something in the aisle. She kicked out with her feet, pushing away from her collapsing assailant. She screamed, though her kicking slowed when she saw that the woman wasn't moving. She clutched at her cheek, but when she took her hand away Alex saw only a faint red outline—he had acted in time. He hadn't known he could move that fast.

"What the fuck was that?" Tom shouted hysterically. Patrick was shaking his head, mouthing something Alex couldn't make out. Both were clutching their rifles, barrels swinging wildly.

"Get those weapons under control!" Alex ordered sternly. Both men looked down as though they only then realized what they were doing and lowered their carbines. Yael held hers in the low ready position. Her eyes were wide, but she was slightly crouched, ready, and most importantly, not panicking. He knew he could count on her, and that gratified him.

Alex pointed his rifle at the woman and poked her with the muzzle. She didn't move.

"Barbara," he said. "Please examine her. If she…attacks again, I'll shoot." Barbara hesitated, looking at the body uncertainly, but then got to her feet and approached slowly.

"What the fuck, man," Tom was muttering. "This is some night of the living dead bullshit!"

"She's not breathing," Barbara said, kneeling over her. "No pulse." She reached into her backpack and pulled out a clear plastic mask with a tube sticking out of it. Cupping the mask to the woman's face, she adjusted the position of her head, hesitated, then lowered her face over the mask and began to breath into it. After a few breaths she lifted her head and began to push down on the woman's chest. "I doubt this will work. She's most likely dead."

"Oh man," Tom whimpered. "Oh man."

"Not like *that*," Barbara said as she switched from pumping the woman's chest back to breathing into the mask. "The blow to the head killed her." She turned to Tom, who was breathing heavily and staring at the dead woman. "She was very much alive a few seconds ago, so cut that bullshit out."

Tom nodded. "Sorry. It just freaked me out, the way she attacked like that."

"She's gone," Barbara said after about a minute of breathing and pumping. She was feeling around the bloody mess of matted hair where Alex's rifle had struck. "Her skull is cracked. I could keep trying, but there's not much point, this is a bad fracture."

"Do you think she was…" Alex hesitated, not sure how to phrase his question. "Crazy?" She was dead. He had killed her. He couldn't take his eyes off her.

Barbara shrugged. "I have no idea, but I suppose that's the only reasonable explanation. Why else would she try to bite me?" Her hand touched her cheek momentarily, then fell away. The bite mark was fading, but the skin around it was red. "I want to examine her, as thoroughly as I can." She turned to Alex. "I'd like your permission to do an autopsy."

"You mean cut her open?" She had been lovely, with big green eyes below delicate brows, a slight hook to her nose, just enough to accentuate her long face and prominent cheeks. He had broken her, forever. He hadn't meant to, he only meant to stop her. He had never killed anyone up close before. In Afghanistan he had fired at distant targets. He had seen bodies, but he wasn't sure which were the ones he had shot, or if he had even hit anyone at all. But there was no avoiding it this time. He had killed this woman.

"Yes. I can't learn much, but I want to find out whatever I can."

Alex nodded. "Go ahead. We're going to search the rest of this building while you do that. Patrick, you and Tom stay with the doc, Yael, you're with me. After we clear this place we're going to wait outside." He heard the crack again in his mind, felt her head recoil beneath the rifle's stock. All the king's horses.

It didn't take long to clear the cathedral, most of which was roofless and open to the elements. There was a basement with storage rooms, almost completely empty except for religious paraphernalia and other useless junk. After a few minutes of searching, the two of them returned to the lawn beyond the walls and waited.

"Are you alright?" Yael asked.

He shook his head. "Not even a little bit."

"I can't even begin to imagine what you're going through."

He looked at her. "I killed that woman. The only survivor we found, and I killed her."

Yael reached out to him, hesitated, then put her hand on his arm. "You had no choice."

"I did. I could have hit her a lot less hard."

"Maybe that wouldn't have stopped her. Maybe Barbara would be missing a chunk of her face, and the woman would still be dead."

"She had a name," Alex said. "We shouldn't call her 'the woman.' We should go there and get her wallet. We have to find out her name." He turned towards the cathedral, but she grabbed his collar with both hands and shook him.

"Stop it," she said sternly. "Stop it right now. If you need to let it out again, I'm here for you, but pull yourself together."

He stared at her, blinking, confused. "I'm sorry," he said. "You're right. I'll pull it together. For the others. They need me.""I don't care about the others," she said. "I care about..." she stopped, dropped her hands and turned away, unable to finish her sentence. He stared at the back of her head, riding a maelstrom of conflicting emotions. His eyes caught movement, and he turned to look. Patrick ran from behind a wall, his face pale. He stopped just past the edge of the lawn, bent over and vomited.

"Oh man," he said between gasps. "She's cutting her head open!"

Chapter 15

The sun was near the horizon by the time Barbara came out of the cathedral. Tom had replaced Patrick as her guard and walked behind her, his face pale.

"There was significant brain damage," Barbara said. She was wiping her hands on a piece of cloth. No, not cloth. A shirt, someone's shirt. It was a white shirt, but her hands turned it red. "I don't mean from the crack to the head. Areas of her brain were…well, deteriorated. I've never seen anything like it before, but that's not saying much, it's not my specialty."

Alex frowned. "Do you think that's what happened here? Some kind of biological weapon that makes people crazy? Could we be…contaminated? Exposed?"

She shrugged. "There's always that danger, but I don't think so."

"Why not?"

"Because there are no biological containment suits in my lab back at the warehouse."

"That's…so simple. Come to think of it, I didn't see any NBC gear in the arms room either. So what happened to her?"

"The damage is physical, and apparently random, though most affect behavior centers. I'm not a neurosurgeon, but I know the basics. I took some tissue samples, I can check it out when we're back at the colony."

"But we found a survivor," Tom said. "That means there could be others, and maybe not all of them are crazy. Maybe someone could tell us what happened here."

"If I don't kill them first," Alex muttered under his breath, then felt Yael's boot hit his calf. He turned to glare at her, but she smiled at him and shrugged.

"So what do we do now?" Tom asked.

"It's going to be dark soon," Alex said. "We're going to spend the night on the beach." He picked up the radio. "Ryan, Sandi, this is Alex." He waited for several seconds.

"This is Ryan, did you find anything?"

"Ryan, give me your sitrep."

"What?"

Alex sighed. "How are you doing? What's going on?"

"Oh. We're fine, a little sea sick, just sitting here, lots of rocking."

"Good. Wait ten mikes then return to the beach. Copy?"

"What?"

"Jesus fucking Christ!" he said, then into the radio, "Wait ten minutes, then return to the beach. Did you get that?"

"Yes, got it. See you soon."

They made it back to the beach in just a few minutes. There were no obstacles in their way save for the foundation holes, and visibility was excellent in all directions. The boat was on its way in when they passed through the trees and it touched sand just as they picked a site above the tide line and dumped their gear. The sun started to set and the sky blossomed with pink and lavender clouds.

"I'm going to post a watch," Alex said after everyone settled down. "Everyone is going to stand guard for two hours, that should take us till first light." He paused, making sure he made eye contact with everyone. "If you fall asleep on guard duty, you put all our lives in danger. That will not be acceptable." He knew he had probably lost some of his authority when he had broken down by the cathedral, and then some more after killing the woman, but he also knew he had enough left to get them to do what he needed.

"Danger?" Ryan asked. "Why? What did you find?" Tom had taken Ryan and Sandi through the tree line to see what was left of Honolulu, but apparently hadn't told them about the survivor. Sandi was sitting with her hands around her knees, rifle leaned up against a piece of driftwood. She was rocking back and forth, just like the green eyed woman with the slight hook in her nose. Alex turned away. He couldn't stand to look at her.

"Tom can fill you in," he said. "Okay then. Barbara, you're up first, then Tom, then Yael, then me, then Ryan, and finally Sandi will take morning watch."

"Do we make a fire?" Tom asked. Alex considered it.

"Yes," he said finally. "If there are survivors, a fire might draw them here."

"Is that such a good idea?" Tom asked.

"I think it's worth the risk," Alex said.

"I agree," Barbara said, then turned to Tom. "No more zombie crap, okay?"

"I know, I know," Tom said. "I'm sorry."

Alex hadn't wanted to burden them with unnecessary weight and so hadn't brought sleeping bags, though being on the beach in Hawaii made such things largely unnecessary. While Barbara and Ryan helped Yael gather wood and start a fire—another thing she apparently learned to do in the kibbutz—Alex took an entrenching tool from his backpack and dug a latrine pit as far from the camp as he dared. No one seemed in any hurry to go to sleep, but there was no avoiding that. They needed time to wind down, process what they had seen. It was almost completely dark now. The last of the brilliant colors had drained from the sky, replaced by somber grays and dark blues.

"Too bad we can't barbeque nutrient paste," Tom said after the fire was lit and going strong. He mixed his powder in a canteen cup and started to drink it like a milkshake. His face had an ominous glow that scintillated in rhythm with the dancing flames.

Alex looked around nervously, waiting for hundreds of shuffling forms to creep out of the darkness and try to eat their brains, but all he saw were birds. Giving up his pointless vigil, he found Yael standing away from the others, watching the waves roll across the sand.

"I brought you something," he said, and handed her a block of foam.

"What is it?" She had taken off her vest, but still wore her rifle on her shoulder.

"A piece of packing foam. You can use it as a pillow."

She brightened. "Hey, thanks. That's a good idea."

"I um," he began, suddenly too choked up to speak. "I wanted to say…"

"Don't worry about it," she said. "After all you've done for me, it was the least I could do. Besides, it's a mitzvah."

"A what?"

"A mitzvah," she explained. "It's what we call good deeds. Helping others, that sort of thing."

"Oh," he said, and for some reason felt slightly disappointed. "I get it. Keep in God's good graces and all that."

She shrugged. "Fringe benefit, I suppose. Are you feeling better?"

"Yeah, I guess. I'm not going to run off to find that woman's wallet in the middle of the night, if that's what you mean."

She almost laughed. "Good. Wouldn't want that."

"Look," he said and kicked the sand in front of him. "I have to say this, so be quiet and let me talk. Maybe you just did it as a mitzvah or whatever, but what you did, and the way you had my back, no one's ever done that for me before. I mean except my family. I just want you to know it means a lot to me."

"It wasn't just a mitzvah," she said, then before he could say anything, "Goodnight, Alex."

"Goodnight, Yael." He stared after her as she walked away, wishing he could figure her out. His own feelings were slowly becoming clear, but she was still a mystery.

After making sure Barbara was up and about, he settled down on the sand with another foam block and tried to sleep. He couldn't help hearing the others talking, which he supposed was a form of snooping, but as their commander he felt entitled. He made a morbid game of counting the number of times someone said "I can't believe this is happening" or mentioned God in connection with the ravaged city. Sandi cried for a while, but then composed herself long enough to say goodnight and settled down within a few feet of Alex, probably because she felt safe next to him. He wondered if she would still have felt that way if she'd seen him cry on Yael's shoulder.

Tom apologized to Barbara for how he had acted, and she shrugged it off, saying she couldn't blame him. Patrick and Ryan made some pretty wild speculations about what could have caused Honolulu's destruction, but none of them were ridiculous or completely impossible, given the circumstances. All of the colonists so far seemed at least above average intelligence, and while that may have been a coincidence, Alex didn't think so. That fact alone had implications he was too tired to consider.

After a while, conversations died down or veered off topic. Tom told Barbara he wasn't a real chemist, and she claimed that she wasn't surprised. She asked for his reasons, and he told her it was a long story and that he would tell her and Alex when they got back to the colony. Patrick and Ryan's conversation drifted from comparing IQ scores to arguing over Sandi as they tried to figure out which of the two she preferred.

Alex smiled when he heard that, and wondered if Sandi was awake and listening. He decided that she probably was. Here they were, in the devastated city of Honolulu, the midst of the greatest mystery and tragedy in the history of mankind, and in the end it always came back to the simple basics. That gave Alex enough comfort that he was finally able to let go and drift off into sleep.

* * *

Yael woke him when her watch was up, and he in turn woke Ryan. Morning came without incident, and before Alex was fully awake they were back across the tree line. This time they left the boat on the beach, and Alex glanced back nervously as they started walking towards another of the old standing structures. This was more of a small complex than a building, and unlike the cathedral it still had its roof and some of its windows.

They saw the man before they got within fifty yards of the main entrance: middle aged, balding, wearing a white smock and sweat pants. He was sitting under an overhang next to a thick square pillar, completely unaware of their approach. Either he was just like the woman, or he hadn't spotted them yet.

"Weapons ready," Alex said. "But don't shoot until I say so. Got it?"

"Got it," a few of them said simultaneously.

When they got to within twenty meters of the man he looked up at them, but didn't seem to react in any significant way. He studied them for a few seconds, then looked away. There was no blood on him at all, but the closer they got the worse the smell of excrement became. There were stains on both sides of his pants.

"Fuck," Alex swore. "This guy's shit himself!"

"All part of the job," Barbara said cheerfully as she approached the disheveled survivor. "Cover me, will ya?"

Alex nodded. His weapon had never veered from the man's center mass.

Barbara held her backpack in both hands before her like a shield as she walked. Alex's finger tensed on the trigger as his targeting reticle moved from the man's chest to the top of his head. At this range the bullet would hit a few inches below the point of aim, and he wanted to nail him in the brain at the slightest provocation. If he so much as flinched, Alex was prepared to put him down. In hindsight the decision to kill was always clouded in uncertainty, but in the moment, he had a friend to protect and all was clear.

The man looked up and smiled. "Wawa," he said, and pointed to his pants. "Wawa." He had friendly eyes and was otherwise unimposing, but then the woman in the cathedral hadn't looked particularly frightening either until she'd leaped at Barbara's face.

"Yes," Barbara said in a friendly voice. "Wawa." She knelt by him and set her pack down, then fished inside and came out with an ear thermometer. "Temperature?" she asked, holding it up before him. "Can I take your temperature? I have to touch your ear."

"Wawa," the man said, and smiled again. He leaned forward, but slowly, not aggressively. Alex's finger tightened up on the trigger slightly.

Barbara reached out to him and put the thermometer into his ear. He turned his head to follow it with his eyes, and Alex cringed at how close his mouth was to her forearm. How close his *teeth* were. Alex was so tense he could barely stand it.

Barbara turned the man's head with her free hand and inserted the thermometer in his ear. After a few seconds, there was a beep.

"Ninety nine point one," she said, looking at the display. "Slight fever."

"Wawa," the man said, still smiling.

"I'm not going to cut open his head to confirm it," Barbara said as she took some more things out of her pack. "But I'd bet he has the same type of random brain damage the woman had, though obviously it's not so much his behavior as his mental acuity that is affected."

"What do we do with him?" Alex asked. "You're the doctor, it's your call."

Barbara didn't answer right away. She pulled down on his jaw and looked inside his mouth with a type of instrument Alex remembered from hospital exam rooms, a magnifying scope with a built in flashlight.

"We take him with us," she said. "What else can we do? We can't leave him here. He'll die on his own."

"You don't think he could be dangerous?"

Barbara shook her head. "I mean…anything is possible, but I see nothing to indicate any aggression on his part."

"Fine, but you'll have to clean him up. Tom, you and Barbara stay here and watch our new buddy 'Wawa.' The rest of you, follow me, we're going to look inside."

The complex turned out to be some kind of art school, and much of that art was spared the destruction that claimed almost everything else. Finding nothing of interest, they regrouped and headed back to the beach, where Barbara stripped down and took Wawa into the water to clean him. He had proven extremely cooperative, doing everything she wanted him to do, as long as she gestured and shoved him along. He didn't seem to be able to understand anything she said to him but he did comprehend basic hand gestures.

When she pulled down his pants Alex almost lost his breakfast. Turning away, he tried to think about anything other than what he had just seen.

"Oh man," Tom said, cringing. "That's nasty!"

The sun was already well above the horizon. They had lost a couple of hours of daylight and he had no idea how long it would take Barbara to finish her business. On top of that, having Wawa with them would slow them down considerably.

"This is costing us too much time," Alex said. "I'm going to split us up. Barbara, you stay here with Patrick and Yael. Guys, I'm counting on you to keep the doc safe. Yael, you're the closest thing I have to a soldier, so you're in command. Don't let anyone do anything stupid, and at the first sign of trouble, get on the boat and head out to sea."

"I will," she said. He couldn't read the look she gave him, but he thought it might be surprise.

"Tom, Ryan, Sandi," he said. "You're with me. We're going to forget about the buildings and head up into the mountain." He turned to Yael. "We should be back by sundown. If not, get on the boat. Give us a couple of hours, then head back home. Got it?"

"You want me to just leave you?" She didn't look happy. "I can't do that."

"If we're able, we'll be back. If we're not, it means we're dead. Okay?"

She frowned, but nodded. "Okay."

Alex and his group set off across the ruins of the city and were at the base of the nearest mountain in just over half an hour. The boundary between the mostly open clearing left by the city's destruction and the surrounding jungle was strangely abrupt, as though whatever force annihilated Honolulu had not existed beyond the city's borders. Trees and bushes stood completely unharmed, though all those on the outskirts of the jungle were covered by a thick layer of dust. He could hear bird songs and other jungle sounds. Apparently the island's animal life had been similarly spared the fate of its humans.

"Let's move along the perimeter," he said. "Look for a trail or something, a way for people to get up and out of the city."

"What about that over there?" Tom said and pointed. A dirt road split the tree line not far to their right, close to what used to be a cul-de-sac of upscale homes, now reduced to a pile of roof tiles and timbers.

"That'll do."

They started along the road, walking in a staggered single file formation and looking out for signs of human passage. Ryan took point and Alex covered the rear, keeping an eye out in all directions. The absence of buildings opened a wide path for the wind, which had carried assorted detritus and rubbish well into the path's first few hundred yards. After that, Alex kept a close eye out for telltale signs that a large number of people had passed this way. One of the types of training conducted by the OPFOR was how to deal with indigenous populations, and because of the constant political and religious turmoil in the current conflict regions, part of that training covered refugees. People tended to take more than they needed when they first set out, then, burdened by unnecessary weight, discarded much of it along the way in predictable patterns.

Alex saw no sign of that. What little garbage remained seemed to be random.

The road ended abruptly at another destroyed house. The jungle wasn't particularly thick, but making progress would be a lot tougher now. Alex looked around, trying to figure out which was the best route to higher elevations. Then Ryan's shoulder exploded.

Blood sprayed on Alex's face and neck and he felt its warmth as it oozed down his shirt. The crack of the gunshot came an instant later. Another crack sounded, then another.

Chapter 16

Alex was moving before he realized what he was doing. He headed for the pile of lumber and roofing tiles. The others stood frozen, staring at Ryan.

"Take cover!" he shouted. "Move!" Tom was the first to react, following Alex, then Sandi ran into the trees in the direction from which they came. Ryan was lying on the road, kicking his feet.

"What the fuck!" Tom shouted, holding his rifle awkwardly. Alex scanned the trees up ahead, but saw nothing. He calculated where the shot had come from based on where Ryan had been standing, then flicked his rifle's selector switch to auto and fired a long burst into the trees. The familiar sound of his weapon cleared his head even as its roar clogged his ears, and he pushed Tom's head down behind the pile of roof tiles as he continued to look for signs of their attackers. From the corner of his eye, he noticed Sandi taking cover behind a tree. She wasn't shooting, but she didn't seem to be panicking either.

"Sandi, get Ryan!" he shouted. "Drag him behind cover! Do it now!" He turned back to the tree line just in time to see them.

Movement. In the trees, just past a large gray boulder. There were two of them, and they were moving to the rock for cover. Alex switched his rifle to semi, aimed, and fired a string of shots at one of the moving targets, leading him just a little. One of the attackers dropped. The other one paused, but moved behind the rock before Alex had a chance to take him down. Tom was clutching his ears, his rifle discarded on the ground by his side.

Alex dropped his magazine, probably less than half full, then pulled a fresh one from his chest rig and slammed it into place. He grabbed a hand grenade with his left hand and pulled the pin without taking his right off the weapon.

He fired a few rounds then got to his feet. The hand holding the grenade supported the front of the weapon as he fired again and again at the boulder, forcing the man behind it to stay down. Advancing to the edge of the debris, he took cover behind a tree and tossed the grenade over the rock. The safety lever popped off with a click and he watched the grenade tumble through the air and disappear behind the edge of the boulder.

A white flash and thunderous crack happened almost simultaneously, followed by a puff of white smoke that drifted further into the jungle, pushed by what little of the ocean's wind survived this far past the trees.

He waited, looking around for movement, but didn't see anything. He got up and started moving towards the boulder, weapon ready. Circling around the left side, he saw the man who had made it to cover. His body was a shredded mess, but Alex could tell by his clothing that he wasn't a soldier. Blue jeans, dark button shirt. His weapon was an old military rifle, probably a Garand. The other man, lying just past the boulder, had been hit twice, once in the head. He also wore jeans, but with a black t-shirt. A scoped bolt action rifle lay a few feet away from him.

There was no sign of anyone else, so Alex ran back to Ryan. The kid was lying on his back, still kicking. Sandi was on her knees by his side, hovering over him uncertainly. Alex reached under Ryan and pulled him behind the debris pile, then knelt over him, looking at his shoulder. Tom retrieved his rifle and ran over, staring at Ryan's shoulder, his face pale.

"Stay low!" Alex shouted.

Ryan was alive and conscious. His eyes were wild, shifting back and forth. His hands and feet were twitching, kicking, shaking. Thick blood welled from the hole in his left shoulder, but it flowed slowly, which meant the artery had been spared. Alex took his knife and cut away at the chest rig and shirt near the wound on both sides. He then took his first aid kit, tore open the QuickClot pouch and stuffed the gauze into the wound.

"Sandi," Alex shouted. "Help me." Her eyes widened, but she moved closer.

"Hold this in place," Alex said. Sandi put a hand over the bunched up QuickClot while Alex turned Ryan on his side and tied it in place with a field dressing, looping it around his neck and armpit. Using the contents of Ryan's first aid kit, he secured the exit wound on his back in the same manner. Some dirt had gotten into the wound, but there wasn't time to try and clean it. Barbara would have to take care of it later.

"Let's move!" Alex shouted, then dropped his backpack, picked Ryan up and slung him over his shoulder. "Grab my pack, and get his weapon!" he said to Tom. "And get that spare magazine I dropped."

Tom did as he was told and Alex began to run down the road back towards the city. "Sandi, let's go!" She got up and followed him. "Keep an eye out behind us."

In what seemed like seconds they were running across the open field of ruins. Ryan's weight began to take its toll. Alex's legs and back burned with the strain and his shoulder ached where some of Ryan's gear was pressing into it painfully.

"Thank you, fucking Medlock," Alex muttered as he ran. If it were not for the platoon sergeant's nearly religious devotion to physical training, Alex would not have been able to move this fast or for this long carrying a 200lb load. He almost laughed. The idea of thanking Sergeant Medlock for anything was almost ludicrous, and yet there he was doing it.

He couldn't risk looking over his shoulder, but if someone had been following them they would have opened fire by now. They were pretty much sitting ducks for anyone who wanted to shoot them from the other side of the city.

After a few minutes of running, Alex called a halt behind a pile of rubble. They found a pair of two-by-fours and tied them together to form a makeshift stretcher. Alex grabbed one end and Tom grabbed the other. Their pace was slow but steady, and before long they crossed the ruined city.

As they neared the beach Alex saw riflemen positioned in the trees and almost dropped Ryan before he realized they were his people. Yael must have heard the shooting and was covering their retreat. Good girl!

"Stay in position!" he shouted as he ran past. He saw Yael to his right, her weapon pointing straight out.

Barbara was on the beach with Wawa, and as soon as she saw them she ran to Alex and grabbed Ryan. Together they laid him on the sand.

"What happened?" she shouted, going for her backpack.

"No time," Alex said. "Tom, help Barbara get Ryan in the

boat." He turned to those in the trees. "Fall back! Fall back to the boat. We're getting out of here."

Yael ran out onto the beach, Patrick just behind her. Ryan screamed as Barbara and Tom all but tossed him over the side of the boat. Tom jumped in with him, but Barbara went back for Wawa, who was looking around, confused and scared. Despite his near panicked state, the man allowed himself to be hustled towards the boat.

When they were all on board, Alex pushed it into the water and jumped in, heedless of wet boots. Barbara started the motors, then got it turned around and jerked the throttle hard. The boat lurched and climbed up on plane, speeding away from the beach. Alex watched for signs of pursuit, but saw nothing. Questions flooded his mind, but he knew he would probably never have answers.

* * *

The ride back to the colony was long and difficult. Alex had to pilot the boat while Barbara tended to Ryan and the others looked after Wawa and kept him from trying to climb over the side. Ocean conditions were significantly worse than the day before and maintaining thirty miles per hour was brutal. The boat hammered into each wave, hard enough to make Alex wonder how much pounding the hull could take.

After cleaning Ryan's wound and applying a new dressing, Barbara announced that he needed surgery if he wanted to keep the use of his right arm. Alex decided to use some of their extra fuel by increasing speed to get him back to the colony as fast as possible, but the waves kept getting bigger and eventually he had to slow down to twenty miles per hour just to keep from breaking his teeth with every impact. Barbara assured him he was doing fine, but piloting the boat was one of the most stressful things he had ever done. All of their lives depended on that glorified fiberglass tub, and one mistake at the helm could break it in half. That was a lot of pressure to put on someone behind the controls for the first time in his life.

One hour into the ride, just as they were leaving sight of Oahu's coast, it started to rain. There was a roof over the center console, but it was small and could only fit two of them comfortably with two more pressed up behind them and partially exposed. However miserable everyone was before the rain, they were now that much more so.

No one was particularly talkative, though Alex could hardly blame them. Between the devastation of the city, the brain damaged survivors and getting shot at, there was a lot to think about. For Alex, the most pressing questions were related to the attack. Who were those people? How did they survive the destruction? Most importantly, why had they opened fire without provocation?

He thought about the fact that he had killed yet again, but surprisingly he had no regrets, not about killing those men. They attacked, they were the enemy, he had destroyed the enemy. It was all rather simple and impersonal, just like the few times he had done it in Afghanistan. He still couldn't think about the insane woman without a pang of guilt and a sense of loss, but he had no such feelings for the two in the woods.

A sense of duality of time that had been plaguing him for the last few days followed him home to the colony. It seemed as though the trip took forever, and also that they were pulling up to the beach just moments after leaving Honolulu. The rain let up just as they approached the island and the sky cleared. The sun was shining and the waves died down to gentle swells.

"Max, this is Alex," he said into the radio, and waited. There was nothing. "Alex to Max," he said again.

"Yes Alex," Max's voice crackled through the radio's tiny speaker. "Good to hear from you!"

"Lower the barrier, Max," Alex said. "We're coming in by boat, and we have wounded. Meet us on the beach."

"Got it, Alex, the barrier is down." At least that was what Alex thought he said—Max had released the talk button a bit too early.

"Say again? Confirm 'barrier is down'?"

"Yes, Alex, it's down, or as close as we can get it."

"Understood." He turned to Barbara and said, "You'd better take the helm for this."

She nodded and took the wheel, guiding the boat onto the beach. For a moment, Alex worried that Max had lied about the barrier in an attempt to murder him and gain control of the arms room, but he dismissed it as paranoia.

There were more than a dozen people on the beach, standing and staring at the boat with hands over their eyes to shield them from the afternoon sun. More people were coming in from the colony. Alex saw something strange just past the patch of jungle that separated the main beach from the bit near the edge of the barrier—a pole with something tied to it.

"What the hell is that?" he asked. "Barbara, steer the boat that way a little, if you can. I want to check it out."

"There are a lot of reefs here…ah, shit." She swallowed hard as they passed through the barrier. The expected surge of nausea passed quickly. Alex once again wondered why they were not able to shut the barrier off completely. It seemed an unnecessary annoyance.

Barbara cleared her throat. "We might hit bottom. Even if I go straight in we might hit, but going along the beach is a bad idea."

"Okay, never mind then," he said. Although they wouldn't really be able to use the boat much after this, he supposed it could come in handy and he should at least try to keep it in one piece. They had enough gas for some quick runs along the coast, and maybe enough to get to one of the closer islands and back.

The boat scraped something coming onto the sand, but it didn't sound bad, and by that time Barbara had already cut and raised the outboards. Max was waiting for them, along with Reynard and Bob, who it seemed were his permanent entourage now. Alex frowned when he saw that they were wearing the pistols he had given them. He agreed it was necessary, but for some reason he didn't like it. A large crowd was gathering behind Max, including the long haired loud mouth who hadn't wanted to take no for an answer when Alex asked for volunteers.

"We need some help!" Alex shouted. "We have to get Ryan to Barbara's operating room."

Max motioned to Reynard and Bob, who ran to the side of the boat to assist. Between the two of them and Patrick and Barbara, they easily lowered Ryan out of the boat and carried him off at a brisk pace.

"What happened to him?" Max asked. "And who is that?" He

motioned to Wawa. "You found a survivor?" Alex noticed that many of the others were staring at their mentally defective new friend. Now that there was no one stopping him, Wawa climbed over the side and jumped down onto the sand. He hadn't soiled himself since Barbara cleaned him, for which Alex was immensely grateful.

"Ryan got shot," Alex explained. "And yes, Wawa is a survivor, but he's got brain damage. I have a lot to tell you, Max, and we should do it somewhere quiet." It was only then that he realized Max had used the word "survivor." Was it simply a matter of word choice, or did he know something he wasn't sharing?

"We all want to hear it," the loudmouth said. "We have a right to know." The crowd announced its assent.

Alex opened his mouth for an angry retort, but then reconsidered. "Yeah, you're right. Let's all meet in front of Max's house in an hour and I'll tell everyone what we found. It's um…it's a lot to take in, so prepare yourselves, okay?"

Many people in the crowd exchanged nervous glances, and the loudmouth seemed taken aback. He had been expecting a different answer.

"Yeah, okay," he said.

"Good idea," Max said. "I have some things to tell you too, though, so be there a bit early."

"Will do," Alex said, then turned to Yael. "Can I trouble you to help me police up the gear and get it back in the arms room?"

"Yes sir," she said, without a trace of sarcasm. Alex furrowed his brow, not sure how to take that, but decided she was too tired to be toying with him.

"Sandi," he said. "Please keep an eye on Wawa. I'll take your rifle and vest, so you can relax, but he shouldn't be left alone until Barbara figures out what to do with him, okay?" Max was staring at Wawa and he did not look pleased. Alex supposed he wouldn't be happy either if he'd sent a team out and the only survivor they brought back was a mental defective.

Sandi nodded. "Yes sir."

Everyone had left their rifles in the boat, so that part was easy. He took three others besides his own, leaving the rest for Yael, and they set off to the arms room.

"You were great out there," he said to her. "If you're up for it, I'd like to make our relationship official." He smiled in anticipation, as he knew his particular choice of words would throw her.

"What?" she asked, just as confused as he had expected. "What exactly are you proposing? What relationship?"

He chuckled. "Relax, killer, I'm talking about our professional relationship. A good captain needs a good lieutenant. I can give you a field commission, if you're interested."

"Oh, that. I guess, but I just can't think about that right now. I mean there's so much…the city…"

"No, I get it," he said. "I should have waited to ask you. I get distracted too easily, there's a lot we all need to think about."

They got the rifles back in the armory and Alex decided it would be okay to wait until later to get the rest of the gear. He dumped his pack and the few chest rigs he had with him on the floor and set the rifles on a metal table towards the back of the room next to a cabinet full of solvents and other cleaning supplies. Those parts of the weapons susceptible to corrosion were treated with high tech coatings, so the cleaning could also wait.

"I'll see you later then," Yael said once he was back out in the hallway. "If you're done with me."

"Not by a long shot," he said, and just before she could protest he added, "But yeah, go ahead. I'll meet you by Max's in a little bit."

They left the warehouse together, but then Alex veered off towards his own cabin. Just as he was about to pass out of sight, he looked back and caught her staring at him. Turning away, he smiled and resumed his walk.

The sight of his cabin made him strangely happy, and when he was inside, he sighed contentedly and collapsed into his chair. He popped open his laptop just like he used to do in his barracks, and before that his dorm, and before that his room in his parents' house. This was home, he realized, for better or worse. When the screen lit up, he decided that there was nothing he wanted to do with the computer, he had just turned it on out of habit. It wasn't like he could surf the internet.

He looked at his bed with genuine longing, but settled for a quick meal and some water, then forced himself out of his chair and back outside. He wasn't sure how much time he had, but he wanted to check out that strange pole on the beach before going over to Max's.

People stared at him as he walked, but he ignored them, as usual, though this time with a slight grin on his face. Despite everything that had happened, he was happy here, and it felt good to be back. Memories of Honolulu and the implications of what they had seen there loomed ominously over him, but he pushed them away. Once he fully processed everything, maybe he'd feel differently. But for now, for this short moment in time, things were okay.

When he got to the beach he turned towards the patch of jungle to his right, pausing only to admire a pretty girl in Goth getup—pale skin, black hair, black lipstick, long skirt and leather tank top, also black.

"Hello," he muttered, though she was too far away to hear him. "Where have you been hiding?" He wondered how Yael would look in Goth clothing, and decided he would have to find out one day soon.

Passing through the patch of jungle, he was so shocked at what he saw that he drew his pistol before he knew what he was doing.

Just ahead, about where he had grabbed the dog after crawling half way through the barrier, someone had mounted a wooden pole in the sand. Tied to the pole was a man, obviously dead for some time. Dried blood and vomit covered him from chin to groin and spread out in a small circle around him.

Whatever feelings of relief at his homecoming he had harbored were gone, and Alex was hit with a sudden and sickening realization: the man had been executed. *Using the barrier.*

Chapter 17

He found Max in his oversized cabin, sitting at his desk—which was setup so that he would face the entrance like in some kind of damned office. Bob and Reynard weren't around, but some other guy he didn't know tried to stop him at the door. Alex ignored him and marched in.

He glared at Max, but didn't say anything. He told himself, again, that he didn't know the details of what had happened, and acting on assumptions was what stupid people did.

"This is about the man on the beach," Max said, not the least bit flustered.

"Sorry, governor," the man by the door said. "I tried to…"

"That's okay, Kristoff, Alex can come in whenever he wants to. Close the door please."

"Sure thing," Kristoff said, sounding confused. Alex heard the door click behind him.

"Something terrible happened while you were gone," Max said with a dramatic sigh as he leaned back in his chair. "Do you know Michelle?"

Alex shook his head. "I don't know most of the people in the colony."

"Lovely young woman," Max said, with clear regret. "The man you saw tied to the pole, he raped her. Beat her badly also. I've already let Barbara know, and she will examine her when she is done with your man."

Alex was taken aback. "Raped?" he asked stupidly. His anger was replaced by confusion.

"Yes, I'm afraid so. He forced his way into her cabin, beat her, raped and sodomized her." Max pursed his lips in distaste. "He didn't even deny it, acted like he had done nothing wrong."

"So you…" Alex was horrified by the images Max's story conjured, but killing a man? With the barrier? What right did he have?

"We tried him, of course," Max continued. "As I said, he didn't deny the charges and made a mockery of the proceedings."

Max's expression changed, and though Alex couldn't read it, he knew he didn't like it. "But he changed his tune very quickly when I pronounced sentence." Max seemed self satisfied, smug even.

"You executed him with the barrier," Alex said, aware that he was stating the obvious. He needed to say it out loud, it was important to do so for some reason he couldn't understand.

"Yes, I did. Would you not have done the same?"

"I don't know," Alex admitted. "I guess I don't understand what gives us the authority to do things like that. I told my guys I'd shoot them if they disobeyed orders, but..." He wasn't sure why he was telling Max this. He wasn't sure of a lot things, it seemed.

"I applaud the fact that you would ask such a question, but that answer will be apparent to you soon enough. It's what I wanted to talk to you about."

"Oh?" He didn't want to gloss over the execution, but he didn't know what else to say. If the rapist hadn't denied guilt, and if everything else Max said was true, hadn't Max done the right thing? Wouldn't Alex himself have just shot the bastard in the head? That was the thing though. *Was* Max telling the truth? He would have to ask around and find out.

"I received a transmission yesterday afternoon. It contained a list of instructions and a video. I watched the video, but I haven't shown it to anyone else. I wanted to wait until you returned."

"A video? What was on it?"

"A presidential address," Max said.

"A *what*?" Alex's mouth fell open. "A presidential address? What president? Of the United States?"

"It's the former vice president," Max explained. "And yes, of the United States." He raised his hands, fending off the barrage of questions Alex was about to unleash. "You'll just have to watch it. Do you want to do it now, or with everyone else? I plan to play it for everyone after you give your report."

Alex thought it over. "I guess I'll watch it with everyone. You already know what I'm going to tell you, don't you?"

"Not the details, but yes," Max admitted. "It was all part of the address."

"You mean," Alex asked. "It tells us what...what we're doing here? What happened to the rest of the world?" Surely it wasn't going to be so easy? All the answers conveniently packaged in a single video?

Max nodded. "Yes it does, and it changes everything." Alex wondered what he meant by that, and then remembered that the guy at the door, Kristoff, had addressed Max as "governor." Back at the beach when Alex had thwarted the vote, Max had referred to himself as a temporary leader.

Alex took a step back and grabbed a dresser near the door. "Fuck."

"Shall we go outside now?" Max asked, motioning towards his monitor. "Looks like almost everyone is here." So he did have at least some cameras in the facility after all.

"Yeah," Alex said weakly.

The sun was in Alex's face as he stepped through the door, and he held up his hand to shield his eyes. People were still arriving, but the crowd gathered in the small clearing in front of Max's house was the biggest he'd seen since waking up in this place. It felt good to see so many people after the desolation of Honolulu, but also strange, as though it wasn't normal for so many living human beings to be in one place. Perhaps it wasn't normal anymore.

They waited a few minutes for the stragglers to come in. Yael was one of the last to arrive, and she brought the little dog with her. Barbara wasn't there, and of course neither was Ryan.

"If everyone is ready," Max said. "There are a lot of important things we have to tell you, and something to show you. Alex will begin. Alex?"

"Just outside the facility," Alex began without ceremony. "Are a bunch of ruined buildings…collapsed houses, piles of rubble, that sort of thing. No sign of people, though there are roads and a park and power lines, or at least poles."

He continued, telling them about how they found the boat and took it to Oahu, and what they found there. He looked into their faces as he talked and saw a mix of disbelief, shock and a steadily growing terror. Until a moment ago, most of these people had probably thought that there were lives for them to go back to. Alex didn't know how far the destruction spread, but he held on to no illusions that there was any part of home to which any of them could return.

"What the hell do you mean, gone?" the long haired loud-mouth demanded. "A city can't just disappear!"

"I don't know," Alex said. "It was just gone. There was some debris, a lot of garbage and holes in the ground where the foundations used to be. I haven't the slightest fucking idea what could have done that, only that it happened."

"How do we know you're telling the truth?" the loudmouth continued. "What if you're lying to get us to stay here?"

Alex almost laughed, but all that came out was a derisive snort. "You think I'm lying? Go! Go out there and see for yourself! No one's going to stop you. Now do you want to hear the rest or are you going to run your god damned mouth all day?"

The man glared at him fiercely, but didn't say anything.

"There were survivors," Alex said. "The retarded man we brought back was one of them. The other…" He felt the pain of her death as though it had just happened. Her face was clear in his mind's eye, and it was not contorted in a snarl. There were no bloody teeth seeking flesh. She looked sad, pleading. Perhaps asking him to spare her, to give her a chance.

He continued his story, up to the part about the attack in the jungle.

"So there are survivors," someone said. "Normal ones I mean."

"There *were*," the loudmouth muttered. "Before Captain America over here shot them."

"Why don't you just shut up?" someone from the crowd said to the loudmouth, and there were several assents.

"That's all I have to say," Alex said, biting back harsh words. He looked at Max and motioned for him to take over.

"Thank you, Alex," Max said in a booming voice. "You and your team did a very brave and necessary thing. It is your expedition that will allow us to properly evaluate what I am about to share. I received a transmission a little while ago. An address from the current president of the United States. An address to us."

The gathered crowd erupted in a mix of gasps and outcries demanding an explanation. Max raised his hands, calling for calm. "Please, please, settle down. There will be plenty of time for questions after we watch it."

Max turned to the wall of his cabin and pushed something near the door. A panel slid open, revealing a smooth gray surface about fifty inches wide and thirty inches tall. Judging by its aspect ratio, it was some sort of video monitor. Max pushed another button, and an image appeared. It was the seal of the president of the United States.

Immediately the crowd fell silent, waiting. Alex moved to the back and found Yael. The dog reared up onto his legs, and he gave it an absent minded pat on the head.

"What is this?" Yael whispered. "Is it really…"

"I think so," Alex said. "I haven't seen it yet. I didn't want to watch it without you."

The display changed to show a man Alex immediately recognized, the former vice president. He was sitting at a desk in front of a draped window. Behind him was an American flag and framed photos, presumably of his family. It looked so normal that it bordered on absurdity.

"My fellow Americans," the new president began. "It is with the greatest sadness and weight of responsibility that I address you in this time of unprecedented crisis. You have many questions, and I will humbly try to give you answers, but I must first warn you that what you are about to hear will not be easy, not for me to say, and not for you to accept."

Alex felt Yael's hand on his and turned it so that she could grip it.

"Approximately two weeks ago, without warning or provocation, in an act of historically unprecedented cowardice and evil, the People's Republic of China unleashed a weapon upon the world, a weapon so devastating, so destructive, that it could not have been imagined by sane men."

Yael's hand tightened on his.

"The destruction was almost total, the loss of lives measured in the billions. It was an act of savagery the likes of which the world has never seen…"

Alex tuned out the words, though he could no more keep the message from reaching him than he could keep the sun from warming the back of his neck.

"Oh my god," Yael said, her voice shaky, lips pressed flat,

eyes tearing. "It wasn't just Honolulu. Oh my god."

He reached out to her, and she grabbed his shirt, her fingers clenching so tightly that he felt the fabric constrict his neck. *It wasn't just Honolulu.* The town he grew up in now lay in ruins, holes where his home once stood, the streets where he had played as a child now covered in garbage and bloody clothing. The mall where he had kissed a girl for the first time, gone. The old mountainside resort where he had told his then girlfriend Megan he was leaving for military service, now nothing but rubble. Megan herself was an empty dress flapping in the wind. Or perhaps a raving lunatic, shitting in her pants while munching on the faces of what few people were left with wits intact, waiting for someone to come and cave in her skull.

"...retaliate by conventional means using our strategic defenses, including but not limited to our nuclear arsenal..."

"Oh my god," Yael repeated, her voice a high pitched whine. All around them, people were holding each other, crying. Some were shouting, cursing. It was too much for Alex, he felt numb, as though he were watching from afar, a detached observer engrossed in a television drama. He saw the gathered colonists, but also the ruins of the hospital where Haag was treated, the parking lot where Campbell used to park his beat up old Lexus. He saw the sands of the Mojave sweep across the remains of Fort Irwin.

"...limited capacity, forcing us to make difficult choices, the most difficult decisions of our lives. The result of those choices are all of you, in this facility and the many others like it scattered throughout the former United States..."

Yael's body shook violently with each sob, and Alex held her tightly, just as she had held him by the walls of the cathedral. The disturbing images faded from his mind, replaced by a steadily strengthening conviction that something wasn't right. The things he had imagined were true to some degree, he had no doubt of that, but there was something about what he was hearing that he just couldn't accept.

"...will soon be functional, and we will be able to provide you with additional supplies. However, our capacity for agriculture and manufacturing has been severely compromised, and over the next few years you will have to learn to grow your own food, hunt and fish as necessary. Life will not be easy, but we will survive where our enemies have not. We will prosper, and we will rebuild. The same pioneer spirit that guided the founders of this great nation is alive in all of you, and I have every confidence that we will build a new tomorrow together. I salute your courage, and your perseverance in the face of this great tragedy..."

"I can't…" Yael said, pulling away from him. "I can't do this." She started back towards her cabin.

"Yael wait…what are you going to do?"

"I need to be alone," she said. "Please, Alex, let me be alone. I need to sit shiva…to mourn." She reached up to the right side collar of her t-shirt, gripped it with both hands and pulled as hard as she could, tearing the fabric.

Alex stopped following her and watched her walk away. He felt tears on his face, but they were not for the world, or his family—he had shed those back in Honolulu. These tears were for her. For all of them.

"It really hit her hard," Tom said behind him.

"Yeah."

"Me too, I guess. I thought I did all my crying back at Honolulu, but this…"

Alex nodded. "It's official now, or so it seems."

"What do you mean, 'or so it seems'?" Tom asked, a small glimmer of hope in his eyes.

Alex turned to look at him.

"I think it's fucking bullshit."

Chapter 18

Alex knocked on the door, and when he didn't hear anything, he knocked again, louder.

"Who is it?" a woman's voice asked. She sounded weak, hesitant.

"It's Alex," he said. "Um, Captain Meyer. The…uh…army guy."

After a few seconds, the door LED turned green. Alex waited a bit, then pulled on the handle and stepped inside. Michelle was sitting on the bed, looking at the floor. Her face was a mess of dark purple bruises and bandages. There were more bruises on her arms and legs, perhaps more still hidden under her crimson bath robe.

"Hi," he said, hesitantly.

"What do you want?" she asked, without looking up. He was suddenly struck with a sense of familiarity.

"You're one of the girls from the beach. The ones watching when I put my team together?"

She nodded. "Yeah." Her voice was strained, weak. She refused to make eye contact.

"It's true, then?" he asked. "What Max said? About…"

She nodded. "Please don't ask me any questions."

"I won't. And…I'm very, very sorry."

"For what?"

"That I wasn't here. To stop it." He turned to go and was about to close the door behind him when she spoke.

"Thank you."

"For what?"

"For giving a shit." There was something in her voice that chilled him. He turned around and went back inside.

"Listen to me," he said. "We all give a shit. What happened to you…it will never happen again, not here, not while I'm alive. Don't you do anything stupid, do you hear me?" He realized as he spoke to her that he felt a sense of responsibility that hadn't been there before. She was one of his people, one of those with whose safety he had been entrusted. It didn't matter that those doing the entrusting had lied to them, kidnapped them. What was important was that these people needed him, whether some of them knew it or not, and he needed to start taking that responsibility seriously.

"What, you think I'll kill myself?" He words suggested she wouldn't, but her tone was not in agreement.

"I hope that hasn't crossed your mind," he said.

"What is there to live for? I watched the address on the laptop. My family, everyone that ever cared about me…they're all dead. The world is dead." She spoke with no emotion, which made it worse.

Alex knelt in front of her, low enough to meet her gaze, and took her hands in his. She flinched, but didn't pull away.

"Listen to me," he said. "There are people here that care about you. *I* care about you. The piece of shit that did this, you know what happened to him?"

"They told me."

"He suffered, believe me. I was in that barrier twice. To die like that…" He shuddered. "It's probably worse than being burned alive."

"That doesn't make me feel better." She hesitated, blinking away tears. "I didn't want him dead, especially not like that. To suffer, to pay for what he'd done yes, but not dead. I don't need to deal with that shit too. That bastard Max!"

Alex raised an eyebrow at her, but decided not to press her. An odd attitude, but then what did he know? He had no idea what she was going through.

"Michelle, just promise me you'll hang in there for a little while, okay? Just a little while. There are good people here, people that will help you in any way they can. If you need anything, anything at all, find me and I'll make sure you get it."

"Okay."

"Promise me."

"I promise."

"Good," he said. "I'll check in on you later."

Satisfied, he left her and headed straight for the arms room. He passed many people along the way, most of them gathered in small groups, looking glum. It had been quiet in the colony ever since

Max aired the address. People were busy coming to terms with their new reality, and judging by what he saw, they weren't having an easy time of it.

Once he was past the airlock, he checked the arms room computer and found an update to his general orders. There was nothing new, just a more detailed and formal version of the same old thing. There was a menu that wasn't there before, and he found that he could control the barrier and fusion reactor from his station. He messed around with the reactor menu, just to see what kind of options he had, but didn't understand enough to work it. Just as he was about to turn away, he noticed something else—a security menu. It gave him the option to override door locks, and scanning through the list he noticed that he had access to every cabin, even Max's. Each cabin had an assigned number and an associated name, except for number thirty seven, which was listed as vacant.

"He's quick," Alex mumbled, assuming Max had updated the database to remove the rapist's name. There were also controls for a bunch of exterior cameras, and one interior camera that covered the warehouse hallway. There were no other interior cameras, but of course he had no idea if they didn't exist or if he just didn't have access to them.

Along with camera controls, the security menu had a public address option. Looking over the terminal, he found what could be a microphone.

"Interesting," he mumbled, though he had no use for a PA system, at least not at the moment.

After getting what he needed, he left the warehouse and made his way to Yael's cabin.

"Who is it?" she asked after he knocked. He heard the dog barking excitedly and scratching on the door.

"Alex."

There was a pause. "Alex, I told you I wanted to be alone."

"Yeah, yeah, I know. I just brought you some stuff. Let me give it to you and I'll go away." It rankled him that she didn't want to see him, especially now that they had just started to form a connection.

The door opened and she stood blocking the entry, just as she had the first time he visited. She was wearing the shirt she had torn earlier, along with what looked like a homemade black ribbon, also torn. The dog tried to run out, but she blocked its egress with her legs.

He frowned. "I need to come in for this."

"Alex, please…"

"Look," he snapped. "I just want to give you something and then I'm gone, okay? I can't give it to you out here." She looked down at the bundle he was holding, wrapped in a camouflage shirt, and stepped aside, letting him enter. He closed the door behind him and reached down to pet the excited canine, who was jumping up onto his legs.

"Have you heard about what happened to Michelle?" he asked. Her cabin looked very different than the last time. All of her decorations were gone, including the hanging dresses. It was also a mess, with clothing piled in heaps all over the place and unwashed dishes on almost every surface.

"No. Who is Michelle?" She looked almost as disheveled as her cabin. There were dark circles under her eyes and her face was unusually pale.

"One of the girls that was watching us on the beach when I was doing my test."

"You mean one of the ones you were ogling? What happened to her? Is she okay?"

"She was raped, beaten."

Her eyes widened. "What? Raped? Here? You have to do something!"

"It's done," Alex said. "Max had him executed in the barrier. And Michelle is okay, considering. I just went to see her."

"Oh," she said, calming down. She looked away and wrung her hands together. "I'm glad she's okay." He knew what she really wanted to say, that there was something else for her to worry about now. "In the barrier you said? That's…brutal."

"That's why I'm here," he said. "I mean the rape, not the execution. I brought you these." He moved past her and set the bundle down on her unmade bed, then unwrapped the shirt. He removed a pistol, four spare magazines and a fixed blade combat knife.

She stared at the items, but didn't say anything.

"This," he said. "Is a 9mm. You probably used this type of

weapon in your kibbutz. It doesn't have a lot of recoil and holds a lot of rounds."

"I did," she said. "Use it I mean."

"Good. Keep this in your cabin. Hide it. I gave you some spare magazines just in case." He set the pistol down on the bed, then picked up the knife. "Keep this with you also. You can swim with it, get it wet, whatever." She took it from him and set it down on her desk. "Don't be afraid to use it. Just stab the bastard wherever you can and keep stabbing him until he stops moving, then stab him some more."

"You're worried?" she asked. "That it might happen to me?"

"A little," he admitted. "I don't think there's much of a chance, I mean how many assholes can there be in a handpicked group of fifty? And after what happened to that guy…" She didn't catch the sarcasm in his voice when he mentioned the handpicked group, but that was just as well. He had no interest in depressing her further, there would be time enough to discuss his ideas with Tom and Barbara later in the evening.

"Why do you care so much about me?" she demanded. "I don't want to assume anything, but the way you've been acting…"

"There's nothing to assume," he said. "I do care about you, more than anyone else in the world, which may not be saying very much right now, but it's all I've got."

"Why?"

"Don't be dense," he said. "We don't have to have this conversation now, but you know damn well how I feel about you." He had intended to play it cool and let things take their natural course, but she was pissing him off with her insistence on being alone, even though he understood that she needed to do something to deal with the loss of her family. He needed to do something about his own grief, but putting it off would have to do for now.

She looked away. "You're right. We shouldn't have this conversation now. I have to sit shiva, and it's not appropriate."

"Fine. I'll go. Just be careful, leave your door locked and don't let just anyone in, especially at night." He turned to leave, then felt a hand on his arm.

"Alex," she said softly. "I want to have the conversation. If you can wait until my shiva is over. It's four days."

He didn't turn around, but he was afraid his racing heart would betray his excitement.

"I'll wait as long as it takes, Yael. You just do what you need to do."

"Thank you."

He left her cabin and closed the door behind him.

* * *

"Here," Tom said, handing him a plastic cup filled with water. "Don't spill any, it's priceless."

Tom was sitting under a palm tree on the outskirts of the beach. There was a plastic bowl next to him, also filled with water, and a few more cups. The sun was dipping below the western mountains and its light covered the ocean's surface with rivulets of gold.

"Water is free, Tom," Alex said, taking the cup as he sat down against another tree. "I'm pretty sure the colony water system taps an underground spring or has a desalinator or something."

Tom grinned. "Who said anything about water?"

Puzzled, Alex brought the cup to his nose and took a whiff. It smelled like rubbing alcohol.

"Holy shit!" he said. "Where did you get this? Is it safe? I mean is it denatured?"

"No, it's not denatured," Tom said. "There's about a thousand gallons of the stuff in the warehouse, it'll last us for decades. King Max hasn't told anyone about it, but that's never stopped me before. You should have seen the look in that douche bag Bob's face when I walked out of there with a bowl of this stuff and said, 'This is my one item for the next two days, your holiness.'"

"Hi guys," Barbara said, walking up from the beach.

"Hey," Alex said, sliding over to make room.

"Hi Barb," Tom said. "What did you do with Wawa? I half expected you to bring him along."

"He's in the vacant cabin," Barbara said as she sat down next to Tom. "I taught him to use the potty. Didn't take long. He's not as far gone as I thought, he must have just been confused and scared."

"Good deal," Tom said. "I'd hate to see you on twenty four hour diaper duty to a fifty year old baby."

"That's so nasty," Alex said. "I need a drink just to stop thinking about it." He exhaled, braced himself and took a sip. He almost coughed it out. "Fuck!" he swore. "This stuff is strong!"

"Alcohol?" Barbara asked, suddenly brightening. "Is there enough for me?"

"Sure is," Tom said, handing her a cup. "Just be sure to get more with your ration allotment, 'cause this stuff ain't gonna last the night."

"I'll say," Alex said and downed the whole cup. "This is so strong it'll probably evaporate before we can finish it!"

"Take it easy, Chief," Tom said. "I'm pretty sure it's at least ninety percent alcohol."

"Pretty sure?" Barbara said with a grin. "You're a pretty shitty fake biochemist."

"Oh? I had a good thing going before I was kidnapped."

"Okay," Alex said. "Before this stuff hits my head, and before we talk about the bullshit presidential thing, spill it. Tell me why you were posing as a scientist. Who the fuck poses as a scientist?"

Tom laughed, leaned back against the tree and put his hands behind his head. "I'm a Ripper."

Alex frowned. "A what?

Barbara leaned forward. "Wait…hold on. I've heard that before, on TV. I think it was the news."

"Yeah, the news is about the only place you'd hear that stupid word. The media coined it."

"So what is it?" Alex asked.

"It's easy to explain, but hard to understand," Tom said. "To make it simple, I'm a hacker. Ripping is a way to steal money without giving it to yourself, which is how they get you. Fuck, they've got me using that word now. It's kinda catchy, though, ain't it? Ripper? Ripping?"

"Is that more of this shit in the bowl?" Alex asked, holding up his empty cup. He was starting to feel light headed. This was potent stuff.

"Yeah, help yourself."

"Thanks. So…why would you want to steal money without giving it to yourself?"

"You can't steal money," Tom said. "That's a big hacker myth."

"You just said…"

"Okay, let me be clear, you *can* steal money, meaning you can take it out of somewhere and put it somewhere else, but you can't give it to yourself, or you're done. Why do you think money laundering is such a huge business?"

"Can't you just take it out as cash and go to Mexico?" He downed the second cup, but decided not to drink anymore, at least until after they had their conversation. Barbara was still on her first and taking it slow—she was a smarter drinker.

"I suppose" Tom said. "But then you'd have to live in Mexico, and not for long, because they'd still find you."

"Okay, so launder it then."

"Yeah," Tom agreed. "I suppose we could launder it, but hackers aren't typically real criminals. I mean we steal money, yeah, but we steal from banks and other assholes that stole it from people in the first place. We don't exactly have legions of scummy gangster friends we can turn to for money laundering."

"Okay, I'll buy that," Alex said. "So what is Ripping then, and what does it have to do with you being a biochemist?"

"First," Tom said. "I don't steal money."

"But you said…"

"I said that's what Ripping is…usually. That's how it started, but not all of us do it for money. The idea is you create an identity and give that identity the money."

"Like identity theft?"

"No, we don't steal people's identities…we make new ones. Social security numbers, driver's licenses, credit cards, all that good stuff. It's hard work. You make this guy John Fucklubber, say he's a doctor, and you give him the ten million bucks you stole from some scum bag hedge fund manager. Then you wait, three months, six months, a year. If the FBI doesn't come looking for Fucklubber, you become Fucklubber and spend the money, living Fucklubber's life. If they come for Fucklubber, and you'll know because you set it up so you know, then the money is gone and you start all over, but nobody knows who the hell *you* are so you're safe at home. You could have several Fucklubbers going at the same time, in case some get popped."

Alex nodded appreciatively. "Pretty clever. But you said you don't steal money, so what do you do it for?"

Tom grinned. "Some of us just like the challenge. It's hard to make a life and then try to live it. House, job, everything. Can't hack a wife, though, bummer." He grinned, and Barbara punched him lightly in the arm and giggled. Tom continued, "I don't know the first thing about biochemistry, but I lived as a chemistry professor for more than a year."

"How the hell did you manage that? And didn't you learn anything while trying?"

Tom laughed. "I tried not to, more fun that way. As for how, I downloaded lectures and then repeated the whole thing almost word for word. I have a good memory, almost eidetic. I taught two or three classes a week so it wasn't a bad gig."

Alex shook his head. "But what if someone asked a question?"

"I'm the professor, I'll answer questions when I feel like it. Besides, you'd be surprised at how often the same questions get asked, which means most are in the videos. Look, I taught basic chemistry and biology to undergrads. It was a piece of cake. I had it all set up where I did this important research that took up most of my time. Fucked if I understand what it was, but it was really important! They thought they were paying a lot for it, but the money was fake, I don't steal. Well, except for my salary, but I like to think I did a pretty good job, considering, so I think I earned it."

"What about hobnobbing, social gatherings, your fellow professors?"

"Avoid them like the plague. But it's all part of the fun. You *will* get caught. Sometimes right away when they ask themselves why they never heard of Dr. Fucklubber, the guy their computer tells them they hired, or another way to fuck up is to put in something that doesn't make sense, like stem cell research for a space physicist. I got nailed that way once. This time I did my homework."

"I caught you," Alex said, grinning proudly.

"Yeah," Tom admitted. "You did. But to be fair I was a little distracted, what with the whole kidnapping thing."

"So the people that put us here," Barbara said. "The government. They thought you were a biochemist? And that's why they picked you?"

Tom nodded, grinning widely.

"Did you get any instructions? Like Alex's general orders? To tell you what you're supposed to do?"

"Yeah, but it's real weird stuff," he said. "I have no idea why they want me to do it."

"What is it?" Alex asked. "Maybe it will give us a clue as to what we're doing here."

Tom shrugged. "Can't hurt to tell you, but I don't understand most of it. Essentially I'm supposed to study microscopic multicellular organisms and look for certain characteristics. I don't know the details, it's very technical stuff, over my head. But they made it sound pretty important." He ran a hand through his hair and grinned sheepishly. "I kinda feel bad that I can't do it, but there's no helping that. I wish I knew how, but…"

"Fuckin' A," Alex said. "Serves those bastards right."

"Yeah, I guess it does," Barbara agreed. "But if they thought it was important, maybe it's important to us."

"Not Tom's fault, theirs."

"You realize," Tom said. "That we're talking about a world that doesn't exist anymore."

"Yeah," Alex said, feeling a bit of the alcohol induced euphoria slipping away. "About that…"

Chapter 19

"Okay," Barbara said. "So you think it's bullshit. Why?"

Alex took a small sip from his cup and leaned back, letting the tree support his weight.

"For starters," he said. "No way this whole getup..." He spread his arms, indicating the colony. "Was some last ditch, minute to midnight emergency response."

"Okay," Tom said. "Let's start with that. Why? I mean I know it doesn't seem likely they could pull this off last minute, but let's hear some concrete reasons."

"Okay, here goes," Alex said. "I'll do one at a time, and the first one's easy. Let's forget about the fully stocked warehouse, the terminals with general orders and the nutrient paste I've never heard of. All that could have been part of some emergency doomsday stockpile, as could these little cabins, the DNA locks, everything. Maybe they were planning for some asteroid impact, or some other catastrophe. So all that is plausible, though I'll say it's too much to do for some wacky contingency. I mean this crap must cost serious bank."

"Yeah," Tom agreed. "There's some pretty impressive tech at work here."

"Right. So forget about all that. I'll even give them that it could have been sitting here, just waiting for us to come along, and that they had time to get our DNA and code the locks. All possible. There's still no way they pulled this off in less than four or five months at least."

"The clothes," Barbara said. "You're talking about the clothes."

"Bingo," Alex said, grinning proudly like he'd just discovered the cure to cancer. "That's number one. My clothes were pretty generic, but they all fit. It was something Yael said that got me thinking. She said, 'They are like the clothes I'd wear.' Except they weren't hers. Everyone here dresses pretty distinctively. Max with those ridiculous dress shirts, you, Barb, with your capris.

Tom, that long sleeve t-shirt with the short sleeve one over it…this is like the stuff you used to wear, right?"

"Right," Tom said. "I see where you're going with this. How did they know what kind of clothes we wore unless they watched us for a while."

"Or just gone through our drawers?" Barbara suggested.

"Then these clothes would have been ours," Alex said. "Not just like ours."

"Ah," she said. "You're right. They must have prepared all of these for us ahead of time."

"Not something you do when you're trying to save civilization in a hurry," Alex said.

"That's good," Barbara said. "Do you have more?"

"Only one," Alex said. "But it's a doozy. The night on the beach in Oahu, I couldn't quite fall asleep and I heard people talking. Ryan and Patrick were arguing over Sandi, and they brought up IQ tests they both took recently. Ryan said his IQ was one forty five and Patrick said his was one forty four and that a single point didn't matter because it was within the error margin."

"Wait a sec!" Barbara said. "The hospital had us take an evaluation test about a month ago. They only posted the results a week before we came here. I remember thinking it was odd, since it turned out to be an elaborate IQ test. What the hell did they need to know our IQs for?"

"Holy shit," Tom said. "The university gave the faculty IQ tests a while back…they said it was for the psychology department, to help them with their research! Everyone at the university had to take them."

"Yeah," Alex said. "You see it now, don't you? The army gave us an in-service ASVAB. That stands for 'armed services vocational aptitude battery.' You take one when you join…but they said they were giving one to people already in because they needed to fill some key roles and were looking for candidates. The biggest part of that test was…three guesses…"

"An IQ test," Tom muttered.

"So," Alex continued. "We all took an IQ test. I'll wager everyone in the colony took one. What did you get, Barb?"

She frowned. "One forty three. I can't believe those two are smarter than me."

"They're not," Tom said quickly. "IQ tests are bullshit. What did you get, Alex?"

"I have no idea," he said, still bothered that he hadn't made it to the board in time, especially now that he would never know. "They posted the results the day before I got here, or at least the last day I remember, and they called formation before I could get to my name. I usually do very well on IQ tests, though. What about you, Tom?"

He shrugged. "It was high, like the rest of them."

"Oh ho!" Barbara teased. "He doesn't want to tell us. Spill it, Professor Bullshit, right now!"

"I like that," Alex said, laughing. "Professor Bullshit. That's your new name, Tom."

"Yeah it's funny. I'll take it."

"Spill it," Barbara insisted.

"Fine, I got a one sixty three." He grinned sheepishly, trying to look modest.

"Wow," Barbara said. "Impressive. We've got ourselves a genius."

"Well technically," Alex said. "He's a super genius. One forty is genius."

"It's all bullshit," Tom said. "I should know, I'm the professor. It's mostly spatial reasoning, some people are better at that than others, doesn't mean they are smart."

"Okay, so there are the clothes and the tests…what does that tell us?" Barbara asked.

"It tells us," Alex said. "That we were carefully chosen, at least a month before, probably more. From among the best and brightest, it would seem, though I wish I knew what my score was. Then we were watched, studied and given things that remind us of our lives back in the world."

"Why?" Barbara asked. "Why go through the trouble."

"Psychological," Tom suggested. "They probably wanted to ease our transitions as much as possible."

"Why not take our real clothes?"

"I dunno," Tom admitted. "Seems like it would be easier."

"I think," Alex said. "That the people who took us had no idea what was about to happen to the rest of the world, to them. It would take at least two, maybe three people to get each of us and bring us in. If they were saving a select few, odds are they didn't have enough room for three support personnel for each candidate. So they probably told those people some story, like we were terrorists or something, and they came and got us. Maybe it was homeland security goons. So then…"

"If they told them to take our clothes," Tom cut in. "It would look really suspicious. Why arrest a terrorist and take his clothes too?"

"And what if our clothes were in the wash?" Barbara added. "That would complicate matters. They probably didn't want to wait around for the laundry."

"Good point," Alex said. "I hadn't thought of that one. But it all boils down to the same thing. This was no last minute contingency. They planned this."

"Maybe they had advance warning of the Chinese weapon," Barbara suggested.

"Nah," Tom said. "If they did they would nuke the shit out of them, not build Star Trekian mobile homes in Hawaii."

Alex laughed. "Star Trekian mobile homes! I love it! But yeah, you're right. Also, I don't buy that this is a Chinese weapon. The Chinese are not that advanced. Whatever did what we saw in Honolulu, that was some high tech stuff. Like sci-fi shit. Furthermore, whatever the cause, they knew about it for a long, long time. Enough to plan and execute this absurd little plan of theirs."

"Speaking of," Tom said. "Barb, did you get a chance to look at the samples we brought back?"

"No, after Ryan's surgery I had to look at Michelle, and then I just took a nap. I was beat. I had to set the alarm clock to meet up with you guys, or I'd still be asleep."

"We have an alarm clock?" Alex asked.

"Yeah, it's an app on the laptop," Tom said.

"I'm such a moron. It probably tells us the time, too. I never even thought to look."

"Um, it would have to tell time to be an alarm clock, Chief," Tom said, grinning.

"Sure, rub it in, super genius."

"So what do we do about this?" Barbara asked.

"We learn all we can," Alex said. "Barb, you need to take a look at those samples first thing tomorrow, if you have time. I think that will be our starting point. Tom, maybe you can hack your way into the computers or something, see what you can see."

"I need to get to a terminal," Tom said. "The laptops won't cut it."

"I thought they were connected to something," Alex said. "The movies…"

"Nope, it's all local. I need something like Max's terminal. Or the one in your arms room. Can I take a look at it?"

"It's fine with me," Alex said. "But I don't think it will let you in. The door works like an airlock. I open the first one, and if there's anyone in the corridor with me, then the second one won't open."

"Hmm," Tom said, rubbing his chin. "Maybe we can try pressing close together to fool the sensor, like arm to arm, leg to leg."

Alex shrugged. "Worth a try. Wanna go now?"

"Nah. I'd rather just sit here and get drunk, then fall asleep under the stars."

"Good plan," Barbara said. "Want company?"

"Well now!" Tom said, leaning forward excitedly. "Are you asking to sleep with me?"

She laughed, and punched him in the arm again. "I don't think it works that way…I'm the girl. You're supposed to ask me."

"Get a room," Alex said. "But not until I get piss drunk. Give me more of that stuff."

By the time they got through half the bowl, Alex could barely see straight. All talk of plots and lies was put aside, and he allowed himself to relax and enjoy casual conversation, the sounds and smells of the ocean and most of all, the freedom. Freedom from having to work, from responsibility, from life—even if only for a little while. The drink made it easy to ignore, but it was all there, waiting for him at the edge of awareness. The death, the devastation, his family. A part of him knew that one day soon he would have to face what happened and acknowledge what it meant for him. He tried to convince himself that he could not be certain that it was not limited to Hawaii, but he knew better, even as drunk as he was. If there was one thing from the presidential address that he did believe, it was that whatever had destroyed Honolulu and its people had indeed affected the entire world.

"Dinoflagellates!" he said suddenly. "I read a book where dinoflagellates—primitive marine bacteria—were forming huge swarms and dissolving people!" It was hard to talk, but if he concentrated he could get it out without slurring or stumbling.

"That's dumb," Barbara said. She was swaying back and forth, humming some obnoxious love song that Alex didn't recognize. "Dino…dinoflaga….dinoflawhatsits are just harmless microscopes."

"You mean microorgans?" Tom slurred.

"Yeah," she said. "Micro organs…you have a micro organ!" She burst out laughing, quickly put a hand over her mouth, turned her head and threw up.

"Fuck!" Tom said. "Now we can't shleep here. We have to find a new plashe."

"On that note," Alex said, climbing to his feet. It was difficult to stand and he almost fell. "Goodnight you two. I'm gonna go home."

"Stay here," Tom said. "We're gonna shleep under the shtars!"

"Nah, gotta go."

"Night," Barbara said, and laughed again. "Tom has a micro organ!"

Alex stumbled to his cottage, closed the door behind him and collapsed on the bed. He was asleep in seconds.

Chapter 20

Alex paused just outside his cabin and watched the strange procession. There were a dozen people, most of them familiar. They carried what appeared to be an assortment of farming implements: rakes, oddly shaped shovels and other tools he didn't recognize. Bob walked behind them, wearing one of the pistols Alex had given Max.

"What's going on?" Alex asked him. The big man stopped and frowned at Alex, his irritation clear.

"Were going to start clearing some land," he explained. "Get it ready for planting."

"Outside the barrier?"

Bob nodded.

"Max's idea?" he asked. It seemed a bit too soon to start something like this. Alex would have given them some more time to deal with the announcement and its implications. Then again, getting out there and doing something could do them some good. He hated the idea of making such decisions for others, which was a large part of why he was content to let Max run things.

"Yeah."

"How'd he get them to do it?" Alex asked. "I mean are they volunteers?"

"You'll have to ask him about that," Bob said tersely, then walked away after the others.

"I plan to," Alex muttered, though Bob was out of earshot. He headed towards the "governor's mansion," keeping an eye out for members of his team. He had met up with Tom just shy of noon when he'd crawled out of bed with a miserable headache, and the two had tried to trick the airlock sensor to get Tom into the arms room. It didn't work, and Alex hadn't seen Tom since, or any of the others. There seemed to be few people around, and everyone he saw was in a hurry to get somewhere.

He found Max behind his desk, his door open. Reynard was sitting across from him, his back to Alex. There was something about that trio—Reynard, Bob and Kristoff—that Alex just didn't like. He couldn't quite put his finger on it, but the very idea of them disturbed him. He hated the way they followed Max around and did everything he told them without question. The world was divided into sheep and wolves, but some wolves were content to attach themselves to those of higher status, following them blindly. He had known soldiers like that, men he served with, and they were dangerous people. He would never turn his back on any of those three, and the more he thought about it, the less he liked the idea of them walking around armed.

"Alex," Max said, spotting him. "Good morning. What can I do for you?"

"I'd like to speak with you," Alex said with a glance at Reynard. "Alone."

"Certainly," Max said with a good natured smile. "We were just finishing up here." He turned to Reynard. "I'll see you here at four, then."

"Sure thing boss," Reynard said, sparing a moment to frown at Alex on his way out.

"Captain," Max said. "Have a seat. What's on your mind?"

"The guns," Alex said, lowering himself into the chair Reynard just left. "I'd like to get them back, now that we've returned." The chair was warm from Reynard's ass, and Alex tensed, finding even such indirect contact distasteful.

Max frowned. "Whatever for?"

"You wanted them for protection while we were gone," he explained. "But now we're back. In light of what happened, I'm going to make a security force out of my people. Patrick, Sandi, Tom. And Ryan, of course, once he's better."

"I think that's a great idea," Max said, leaning back in his chair. "But I've made Reynard, Bob and Kristoff my assistants, and I'd like for them to be armed as well. As governor, I have the authority to make that decision."

Alex frowned, trying to think of a retort. Max was infuriatingly accommodating, which was part of what made him dangerous. Alex had no doubt whatsoever that Max was manipulating him, or trying to, but there wasn't much he could do about it. He was the governor, however much Alex didn't like it.

"I don't believe that to be the case," Alex said in a measured tone. "My orders are clear, I am to support you, but maintain control of the arms room, and I interpret that to include everything in it. I see no reason for your assistants to be armed, and I want my guns back."

Max narrowed his eyes at him. He held his hands over his lap, fingertips touching, and watched him in silence for a moment. His expression changed subtly, became more confident, as though he had expected this and had prepared himself.

"No," Max said finally. "I don't agree. You are to maintain control of the arms room, yes, but I am in charge of the facility, and that includes, to borrow your own words, everything in it. This is not open to discussion, I also have my orders. You may arm the people from your team, and your idea for a police force is a very good one. I cannot spare any of my men for such work, they are far too busy organizing and supervising our efforts to become self sufficient."

Alex didn't like the word "police." Police served the politicians, and he wasn't about to do Max's bidding or enforce his decrees, he was only interested in protecting the people of the colony. He started to speak, but Max raised his hand to hush him. "Do not forget that we are not, as we first thought, alone. I have been in contact with the government, or more accurately what is left of it, and I have been assured that we will receive their full support and attention once things settle down. If you have a problem with the responsibilities and duties that you have been given, I have no doubt I can find someone to replace you. The DNA locks, while out of my control, are not out of theirs, and they can be reprogrammed remotely." It didn't sound like a threat. The way Max spoke he could have been asking Alex if he was tired and wanted to sit down.

Alex stared at him, stunned. It had never occurred to him that he could be replaced, but the more he thought about it, the more obvious it seemed. The "government," a charitable term for whoever was left in charge, clearly had a link to the facility, since they had updated his orders, given them control of the barrier and broadcast that ridiculous presidential address. There was something about the idea that didn't quite add up, but he couldn't put his finger on it.

"Let's not end this on an antagonistic note however," Max continued. "You've done a good job so far, and you can hardly be blamed for misinterpreting your role here. After all, it's not like your position came with a 'how to' manual. Go ahead and create your police force, and report back to me first thing tomorrow morning with a status report. You can use all the people you took with you on the expedition, except of course for Barbara. Her talents are too precious to waste on such matters. And you can only have Tom until we figure out what his purpose here is supposed to be."

Alex got to his feet. "Fine, I'll do that." He turned to leave.

"One more thing," Max said. "Before you go."

"Yes?"

"Don't ever lay a hand on one of my men again. I heard what happened with Bob at the warehouse, and I've decided to overlook it in this one instance. I'd also suggest you stay away from the alcohol, especially when armed. You weren't doing anyone any good last night. Someone else could have been attacked, and you would have been too drunk to notice. You may go now."

Alex had to stop himself from answering or nodding. He walked out, and didn't stop walking until he was sure he was out of earshot.

"Fucking dick," he swore, turning around to glare at the direction he had come from. There was no one around, which was good, because he was in no mood for spectators. He was furious, mostly because he knew that Max had cowed him. Throwing that curve ball, the idea that he could be replaced, had so unsettled him that the rest was child's play. Max was a master manipulator, alright. He had played Alex like a violin.

He started walking, his hands clenched in fists. When he saw Yael's cabin, he stopped. He had been on his way there without realizing it. As much as he could have used her company, he decided to honor her wish to be left alone. He had to deal with this on his own, and the more he calmed down, the clearer his course became.

"I'll give him a fucking status report." It was his turn to do the manipulating, and the first part of that would be not giving Max what he wanted. When the so called governor confronted him, Alex would play it off as though he had forgotten. Max was very well suited for his role, but then so was Alex. Toying with his superiors had been one of his more enjoyable pastimes in the army, and he had gotten quite good at it—Medlock hated him for a reason. Max didn't know who he was fucking with.

Alex had some pretty strong advantages to work with. There was no reason at all to believe Max knew the contents of the arms room, and that gave Alex a lot of leverage and wiggle room. There was also the fact that Max was not very well liked in the colony—the response he had received when he'd called for a vote made that clear. Alex wished he had never interfered, but then things probably wouldn't have turned out much differently, not after the presidential address.

If Max wasn't going to give back his guns, Alex would have to settle for making sure that his people were much better armed than Max's goons.

He looked for Patrick and Sandi, but couldn't find them anywhere. Just as he was about to head to the arms room to use the security cameras, he spotted Kristoff by the beach, arguing with three young women who had apparently been sun bathing. The newest of Max's lackeys was tall and thick, though not nearly as big as Bob. He had short cropped blond hair and a goatee, and despite his long and pointy nose he probably would have looked a lot less goofy without his gold wire rimmed glasses.

"Go get changed and report to the barrier gate," Kristoff said. "This isn't a god damned vacation!"

"Go fuck yourself!" one of the girls said. "I don't know who the hell you think you are, but you can't order us around."

"Problem?" Alex asked as he walked up.

"Yeah," the girl said, and Alex immediately recognized her as the other of the two who had watched his test, Michelle's companion. "This asshole wants us to go dig up some field. Tell him to leave us alone."

"Or better yet," another one of the girls said. "Shoot him."

"Stay out of this," Kristoff told him. "Unless you're here to help me."

"Help you?" Alex said. "Why would I do that? These ladies

want to be left alone." Alex relished opposing the goon, but he knew he had to get himself under control. Nothing would be served by openly defying Max, at least not yet.

"Max has made it clear," Kristoff said, obviously annoyed. "That everyone has to pitch in. This isn't a game, we're all alone here. Everyone has to work to grow food, or when we run out of nutrient powder we'll starve to death."

"These people just found out the world is gone," Alex said. "Give them a fucking break."

"Yeah," the first girl said. "Asshole."

"I told you to stay out of this," Kristoff said. "If these bitches don't get off their lazy asses—"

"What the fuck did you call me?" one of the girls shouted as she jumped to her feet. She started walking towards Kristoff, fists clenched.

"Hold on now," Alex said, putting himself between them. "Let's not start fighting."

"This little faggot called me a bitch!" she said. "Tell him to say it to my face!" She wasn't particularly large, but that attitude hadn't come from nowhere. Kristoff was confused by her sudden hostility, but Alex noticed the slight shift in posture that indicated he was ready for a fight. He was almost sorry the lackey didn't go for his pistol, which would have given Alex an excuse to take it away from him.

"He's sorry," Alex said, holding his hands up to keep them apart. "And he's going to apologize, aren't you Kristoff?" The pointy nosed man started to protest, but shook his head and cursed under his breath.

"Fine," Kristoff said. "I'm sorry I called you a bitch. But if you don't work, you don't eat. When the powder in your dispenser runs out, don't go to the warehouse for more. You won't get any."

The girl seemed to deflate, and looked questioningly at Alex. "Can he do that?"

"Yeah," he said. "I think he can. As much of an asshole as Max is, he has a point. We have to work together."

"Don't talk that way about the governor!" Kristoff protested. "He's doing the best he can to make sure we survive!"

"Yeah, sure," Alex said. "He's a real humanitarian."

"I'm not a construction worker," one of the girls said. "Making me dig holes is fucking cruel."

"If you don't want to dig," Kristoff said. "You can help the others make boats."

"Boats?" Alex asked.

"There were plans and tools in the warehouse for outrigger canoes," Kristoff explained. "There's a party outside the barrier that way." He motioned towards the patch of trees on the western edge of the beach. "They're cutting down trees to build the boats."

"Are Sandi and Patrick there by any chance?" Alex asked.

"Who?"

"Two of my group, the ones that went out exploring."

"Oh, yeah, I think so. At least the girl is. The guy—Patrick—he's with the first farm detail."

"Good, go get them for me."

"Excuse me?" Kristoff asked, raising his eyebrows. "Get them for you?"

"They're not workers," Alex said sternly. "They're soldiers." He looked down at Kristoff's waist and saw the radio clipped to his belt. "Get whoever is in charge out there on the horn and tell him to send those two back here right now."

"On whose authority?" Kristoff demanded.

"Mine. Do you have a problem with that?"

"I'll have to ask Max."

Alex was about to snap at him, but stopped himself. There was no point in letting his ego make matters more complicated than they needed to be. He had Max's approval, however much needing that approval rankled him. He wasn't ready for the rank they had given him, or the responsibility that came with it—he knew that. He was too young, too irresponsible, too impulsive. He was, however, the only thing standing between these people and a man he was starting to believe might just be a tyrannical lunatic, and he had to man up to the job.

"You do that," he said.

He watched Kristoff bully the three girls into going to their cabins to get dressed for work, then waited while he radioed Max to confirm Alex's request—and he had to consider it a request since he apparently lacked any real authority in Max's eyes. Finally Kristoff asked that Sandi and Patrick be sent back to the beach. Alex asked about Tom, but Kristoff didn't know where he was, and a quick radio conversation confirmed no one else knew either.

"Thanks for getting us out of there," Patrick said as soon as Alex met him and Sandi by the barrier. "I appreciate it." There was a guard stationed on the colony side of the barrier with a radio, acting as a gate keeper.

"Me too," Sandi said. "I felt like a damned slave."

"Don't mention it," Alex said. "We have work to do. A lot of work."

They searched for Tom for almost half an hour and finally found him hiding out in Barbara's infirmary room in the warehouse. Ryan was there too, resting in bed, his shoulder covered in clean white bandages. Wawa was sitting on a stool, grinning and staring at the newcomers.

"Alex," Barbara said as soon as she saw him. "I've got a lot to tell you!"

"In a sec," Alex said. "First I have to speak with all of you."

"You're going to want to hear this, Chief," Tom said. "She's found something big, real big."

"What is it?"

"We may not know who destroyed the world," Barbara said. "Or why, but I think I may have found an important clue as to how."

Chapter 21

"What am I looking at?" Alex asked, straining to keep the image in focus. He had never been good at looking through microscopes, though this was the finest such instrument he had ever used. The level of detail on the tiny piece of cloth was amazing. He tried not to think about what that piece of cloth actually was.

"I wish I knew," Barbara said. "They were all over the samples I recovered. Rocks, concrete fragments, even the dust. I found them on the dog collar too, but at the time I thought it was just some kind of infestation."

"They look like water bears," Alex commented as he messed with the focusing knob. The tiny creatures, apparently dead, looked like flabby eight legged monsters with wrinkled skin and thick heads. Their fat stubby legs were tipped by either whiskers, claws or spikes—Alex couldn't tell. They were mostly translucent under the strong light, and he could actually see a brain in their heads, right next to a pair of eyes. There were also things in their bodies he couldn't quite identify, odd looking organs with unnatural shapes. They were strange little creatures.

"Yes," Barbara agreed. "Tardigrades. Fascinating animals, though none of what little I know about them would even begin to tell me why the hell they are all over every piece of debris."

"What are tardigrades?" Ryan asked.

"Little animals," Barbara explained. "These are tiny, a fraction of a millimeter, though some species grow to one, one and a half millimeters. They can survive very harsh conditions, even the vacuum of space, or stay desiccated—dehydrated—for years."

"Where do they live?" Sandi asked. "And why are they called water bears?"

"Because they walk on their legs like a little bear," Alex said. "I saw something about them on the Discovery Channel. Here, have a look." He stood back, allowing her to use the microscope. Patrick moved behind her, eager for his turn.

"Gross," Sandi said. "Where do they live?"

"All over the place," Barbara said. "But nothing like this. You can find a few almost anywhere, but I've never seen so many everywhere. I did a biology paper on them in college, before med school. And these look different from any I remember, though admittedly there are many species of tardigrades, most of which I haven't seen."

"You think these are something else?" Alex asked. "A new species?"

"I don't know," she admitted. "But they obviously have something to do with what happened in Honolulu."

"Do they live in the ocean? Maybe a tsunami left them behind."

"I don't know," Barbara said. "It was an undergrad paper... need I say more? I really don't know that much about them. But I don't think a tsunami destroyed the city. It was too…well… surgical, whatever it was."

"Yeah," Tom agreed. "But Alex has a point. Maybe not a tsunami, but something left these things behind, and left them dead. They're supposed to be tough, right?"

"Yes," she said. "Very tough. Extremes of temperature, radiation, climate."

"What are you going to do now?" Alex asked.

She shrugged. "I'm going to run some tests, try to get a closer look at them. I wish I had an electron microscope, but this bad boy is all I've got to work with. It's pretty powerful, but I need to figure out a way to get in close without depth of field problems. These things are too three dimensional for their own good."

"What is it you wanted to tell us?" Tom asked. "When you came in here?"

"Oh," Alex said, frowning as he remembered the Max situation. He took a peek out into the corridor, and finding it empty, he closed the door to the infirmary.

"I wanted to talk to you guys about Max."

"He's lost his fucking mind," Tom said.

Alex smiled. "Agreed. How about the rest of you?"

"If you want to know if I'm with you or him," Sandi said. "I'm with you. All the way."

"Me too," Patrick said.

"And me," Ryan said from the bed. "When I can get out of here, at least. For now it will have to be in spirit."

"Wawa," Wawa said, perhaps picking up on the energy of the moment.

"I'll go along with whatever you're planning," Barbara said. "I like our little group, I trust you guys. I don't trust Max. I don't like what he's doing with the farms and boats. People should work because they understand the situation and want to, not because he threatens to starve them if they don't."

"Heard about that, huh?" Alex asked.

"I filled her in," Tom said. "And it should be obvious I'm with you."

"Thank you guys," Alex said. He was so grateful that he had a hard time keeping his voice level. If Yael had been here it would have been perfect, but he didn't need to hear her say it to know she was on his side. He felt his bravado rising and felt the desire to make bold declarations. He steadied himself, took a deep breath, and possibly for the first time in his life, acted with foresight and thought.

"But let's not get ahead of ourselves," he said. "He is the governor, and as much as we may not like it, we have to realize that the same people that put us here also gave us food and shelter and the means to defend ourselves, and those are the people that put him in charge. They are in control of what happens here, not us. At least for now. What we need to do is introduce balance to the equation."

"Balance would be nice," Barbara said.

"He threatened to have me replaced," Alex continued. "If I don't go along with him. So that's a problem we'll have to work around."

"Can he do that?" Barbara asked.

"I'm not sure, honestly. It makes sense that if he's the governor and he can communicate with the bastards in charge, then he can have me replaced if he wants to."

"I'm not so sure," Tom said.

"Why not?"

"Because whoever set this up locked King Fuckwad out of the arms room for a reason."

"Good point," Barbara said.

"Think about it," Tom continued. "First, who the hell can use a tenth of the shit you told me is in there other than you?"

"Yeah, I guess…" Alex said.

"Second, they didn't just give you access, they made damn well sure you're the only one who can get in there. Not the only one who can open it, the only one who can get in. You couldn't let someone else in there with you if you tried, as we found out this morning."

"But what does that mean?" Alex asked. "It could just be a security thing."

"I think it's a checks and balances thing," Tom explained. "You told us that your general orders told you to support him unless he endangers the welfare of the colony."

"Yeah, so?"

"Well, checks and balances don't work if he can just replace you and appoint one of his stooges who will go along with whatever he says. The whole system falls apart. Whoever set this up believed in that system, or they wouldn't have gone through all that trouble to build the 'air lock.'"

"Good point," Alex admitted. "I hadn't considered that."

"Super genius, remember?" Tom said with a broad grin. "So now that that's out of the way. How do we keep King Fuck in check?"

Alex smiled. "First, I have his majesty's approval to turn you people into a security force." He turned to Barbara. "Except you, you're the doctor."

She smiled. "At least that means I don't have to work in the fields."

"Right." He turned to the rest of them. "Don't just say yes. It's not going to be easy. We're going to wake up early every day and do PT. Running, pushups, sit ups, that sort of thing. I used to hate that shit, but I can run circles around any of you and do it all day long, so I guess it has its place. I'm also going to train you, shooting, close quarter combat, hand to hand, all that good stuff."

"I say yes!" Sandi said with enthusiasm.

"Me too!" Patrick and Ryan said almost at the same time.

"Count me in, Chief," Tom said. "I'm gonna rip the shit out of being a soldier." Some of the others raised eyebrows at him but he ignored them, apparently content to keep it as an inside joke.

"Good!" Alex said, nodding proudly. "So the first thing I'm going to do is to arm the fuck out of all of you. M4s, body armor and side arms. And you'll take them home. Keep them locked up though. Barb, I'm going to give you a pistol, keep it here, out of sight. Everyone okay with that?"

"Super," Tom said, and the others agreed in unison.

"Our primary job," Alex continued. "Is going to be to keep Max's goons in line. They're bullying people into working, but I can live with that for now. I won't stand for people being abused though. If you see that going on, stop it. There are four of us right now, soon to be six. We work in pairs, never alone. If something happens, radio the others before acting."

"Six?" Barbara asked. "Do you plan to draft me after all?"

"Well I like to think you're on the team, even though you're not going to be active, but I was talking about Yael."

"Thanks, I'd like to think so too. And yeah, I should have realized. Poor girl, she was real close with her family."

"Yeah, she was," he said. "It's odd, though, most of us don't seem to be too broken up. I mean I'm holding out hope my folks will be okay, and I'll be in a world of hurt if they're not, but I haven't seen them in more than a year. It's not the same as her, she was with her family right before they took her."

"My folks are dead," Barbara said. "I have a sister in Tulsa, but I haven't seen her in years."

"I'm all alone," Tom said with a half smile. "No one to cry over."

"I was in college," Sandi said. "I hope my parents are okay, but like you I haven't seen them in a while. I have a brother too. He's a dork, but I love him."

"I'm an orphan," Patrick said. "My foster parents were nice, but kinda distant. I miss them and all, but I'm alright."

"My dad," Ryan said. "I really hope he's alive. My mom died when I was three, and my sister was killed in Iraq."

"No wives," Alex said. "No husbands, no children. Interesting."

"What do you mean?" Patrick asked.

"We have some theories," Alex explained. "About that bullshit presidential address, but now's not the time. Let's get you guys squared away first, then let's get out there and do some damage. Let Max's goons know we're watching them."

"Yes sir!" Sandi said enthusiastically.

"One thing," Alex warned. "Don't do anything to them unless they cross the line. You don't have to listen to anything they say, you report to me and only me. However, if Max gives you an order, say 'yes sir' and make believe you're going to do it, then call me right away. We don't want to openly defy him. If he backs off and mellows out, we'll work with him."

"If not?" Tom asked with a wolfish grin.

"I'm sure he will," Alex said. "He's not crazy, and he'll see that working with us is better for everyone in the long run. The guy was a law professor for fuck's sake."

"Well," Tom said, grinning. "As boring as that is, I guess you're right."

* * *

Alex spent the rest of the day outside the barrier with Tom, watching the farming party at work. There was an area of cleared forest, mostly flat, not far from the colony. Perhaps it was once a parking area for the beach. Bob was supervising as people worked it with plows and shovels while others used axes to cut down more trees to expand the useable land. Alex didn't understand what they were doing—he didn't know the first thing about farming—but some of the workers apparently did. They were giving instructions and walking around making sure people were doing what they were supposed to do, helping where help was needed. Bob seemed to be completely useless. All he did was hover menacingly and make sure no one slacked off.

When Tom and Alex first arrived, brandishing slung rifles and wearing body armor and Kevlar helmets, Bob glared darkly at them and spent several minutes on the radio talking to Max. That was exactly the effect Alex was hoping for. Scare them, but don't do anything that would give the governor grounds to complain.

Towards late afternoon, two women and one man sat down and

announced they were on break.

"Get back to work," Bob barked.

"This isn't a prison camp," Alex said immediately. "They break when they want to. We have enough rations to last for years and the weather here is almost the same year round. There's no hurry."

Bob scowled and looked like he wanted to say something, but turned away and got back on the radio.

"Thanks," one of the women said, a pretty young black girl in shorts and a dark red t-shirt.

"That's what we're here for," Alex said, smiling. He had noticed that all the women of the colony were well above average in looks. He wondered if that had been one of the selection criteria. The thought of some old bastards in Washington looking over photos of bright young women and passing judgment based on appearance made him angry.

"I thought maybe you guys were here to back him up," she said, glancing at Bob distastefully.

"That asshole? No, we're here for you."

Once Alex's intentions were clear, people began to slack off, and eventually a big group got together and announced they were done for the day. It was about four or five in the afternoon.

"You guys did great," Alex said quickly, before Bob had a chance to respond. "You've accomplished a lot. I think this calls for some of that alcohol."

"Now you're talking!" someone said, and Alex saw that it was the long haired loudmouth. "After a whole day of this crap it would be nice to unwind."

"You deserve it," Alex said, and smiled. "In fact there should be extra alcohol rations for everyone who works. That'll give people some extra motivation." Bob frowned, but didn't say anything, at least not to Alex. He was on the radio seconds later.

That evening there was another bonfire, and most of the colony was there, drinking alcohol and talking. Alex had sent two of his people to the warehouse to make sure no one stopped them from taking the stuff. The tension of the morning was gone, or at least lessened. Dark looks were cast at Max's goons, and at Max himself when he finally joined them.

"Alex's idea of extra alcohol rations is a good one," he announced. "And I'm going to implement it right away. People deserve to unwind after a long day's work."

"Good," someone said.

"But I stress a 'long day's work.' The work is for everyone's benefit, and extra rations will be contingent upon honest labor and sincere effort." Alex saw this for the impotent power play that it was—there was no effective way for Max to enforce such a limit—but it had its desired effect. Max had effectively taken the credit for the alcohol and added yet another incentive for people to do what he wanted. This did not disturb Alex in the slightest. He had accomplished what he'd set out to do. Max's goons could not stand up to him and his people, and Max didn't make any effort to curtail Alex's actions. That told him that either Max could not replace him, or that doing so was difficult. Just how difficult was something Alex was certain he would find out soon enough.

Chapter 22

The next few days brought the tedium of a fixed routine, broken only by occasional chances to stick it to the governor in ever more subtle ways. One of these was to allow people to leave the colony to explore the island. Max had summoned him to complain, but when Alex asked him if he wanted him to keep people from leaving by force, the governor balked, then smiled and said, in his infuriatingly affable tone, "Of course, Alex, you're probably right. Keep me posted."

Everyone who left came back the same day, their faces grim, repeating the same story over and over again—everything destroyed, no signs of human life. After the first three groups returned, people stopped exploring and turned their attention to other tasks, like fishing on the beach or working in one of the camps. Once Max's goons were relegated to fringe roles, what started as forced labor became a relaxed but focused effort to improve the quality of the food supply. Everyone—Alex included—was growing sick of the nutrient powder, and the governor's tight rationing of the dehydrated foods offered scant relief. After the first boat was launched into the sea and came back with nets full of fish, efforts in the work camps nearly doubled.

Not everyone shared in the enthusiasm, but that was to be expected. On the afternoon of the second day, Reynard caught a few people sneaking off to rest on the beach not far from the boat building camp. It was the same three girls that Kristoff had bullied into working.

"I want them flogged!" Reynard had screamed. "This is bullshit! Everyone works!"

Alex put an end to that notion right away, and Reynard had been forced to settle for depriving them of alcohol rations for the next three days, which had upset them almost as much as the idea of flogging.

After that, the governor's stooges finally understood that their leader's authority had definite limits, and that Alex was standing firmly on that boundary making sure he didn't cross it. This made Alex's job a lot easier, and more monotonous.

Max made his rounds at least once a day, coming by both work areas, smiling, saying words of praise. Alex marveled at the man's calculated style. He was never the one to crack the whip—he left that to his minions. Max was always cheerful, supportive, even kind. People started to warm up to him after a while, their hatred reserved for the goons that did his bidding. Despite that, two more people joined Max's retinue. A short chubby kid with a fuzzy beard that couldn't have been more than eighteen or nineteen, and a slightly taller man in his early twenties. The latter was thin and stoop shouldered, with small eyes that were hardly more than slits sitting above a long nose with a bulbous tip. He reminded Alex of a young and obnoxious looking Richard Gere.

The chubby one, Jonathan, was the most annoying of the lot. Where the others were nothing more than eager underlings, he was a true sycophant. Alex found it difficult to insult Max, even subtly, without hearing an earful of how great the man was. Unlike Kristoff, who had defended the governor's actions, Jonathan always spoke about Max himself as though he were a mythological hero lowering himself to walk among ordinary folk.

The skinny guy, appropriately named Richard, was hard to read. He was polite enough, but there was something behind his all too easy smile that made Alex suspicious. He liked him the least of all of Max's posse, though the man hadn't so much as complained about Alex or the things he was doing.

On the morning of the fourth day after the presidential address, Alex was by the boats, pacing anxiously along the beach. Sandi was with him, though she was busy watching Kristoff, who was supervising the workers. Using cordless power tools, they had built workbenches and saw horses and were cutting trees into lumber of varying sizes. The foreman, a curly haired man with a lanky worker's build, had the plans on a tablet PC and worked furiously with a measuring laser and marker to make sure the lumber was exactly the right size. He should have been in charge, not Kristoff, who like his counterpart at the farm was completely useless.

"Everything okay, Captain?" Sandi asked, turning to look at him. Her lips curled into a concerned smile, and Alex noticed how pretty she looked under her Kevlar helmet. Like the rest of his people, she had complained about having to wear it, but after a couple of days she'd grown accustomed to the extra weight.

"What?" he asked, momentarily forgetting her question. "Oh. Yeah, I'm fine."

"You're pacing," she said. "And looking back towards the colony. Anything I can help with?"

"No," he said, then frowned. "It's Yael. Her shiva is over today, and she could be out any minute."

"What's a shiva?" she asked, pursing her lips cutely. Alex realized that his hormones were starting to complain about his prolonged celibacy, and though serving in the military had provided him with a measure of tolerance, being surrounded by so many pretty girls was wearing away at him.

"It's a Jewish thing," he explained. "A mourning period."

"Oh. I could use one of those." She looked away, her face changing color slightly.

"If you want time off…"

"No, I'm fine. I haven't given up hope."

"Me either." Though that was a lie. He knew his parents were dead, and every now and then the grief overwhelmed his defenses and forced a reckoning. He cried most nights in his cabin, though the grief would often fade as quickly as it had come, leaving him able to sleep. Being in the colony was so surreal that it made it difficult to maintain a connection to the past, even one as important as his love for his family.

"If you want to go check, I can handle things here," she said.

He shook his head. "Nah, I'm good. I can always talk to her when the work day ends." He was about to thank her for the offer when his radio went off.

"Purple Power to Awesome One." It was Ryan. He'd chosen that call sign after Alex awarded him a Purple Heart. There was an assortment of medals in the arms room desk and giving them to his people seemed as a good a use for them as any.

"Go ahead Purple Power," he said into the radio.

"Alex…I mean Awesome One…you have to get over here!" he said. After his surgery, Ryan had recovered surprisingly quickly, though his left arm was still in a sling.

"Give me a sitrep."

"Max is having David flogged…they're tying him to a post!"

Alex turned to Sandi. "Who the fuck is David?"

"He's the long haired guy that doesn't like you. The one who gave you lip when you were making our team."

"Oh, that guy." He spoke into the radio, "Purple Power, what is your position?"

"Just outside Burger King," Ryan shouted. "Come quick!" Burger King was their nickname for Max's cabin.

"On my way," he said, then turned to Sandi. "Come with me."

They ran to the barrier, where Jonathan the chubby sycophant stood guard.

"Lower it," Alex ordered.

Jonathan hesitated, but finally brought the radio to his mouth. "This is Jonathan, lower the barrier."

"It's down," someone replied.

Wasting no time, Alex ran to Max's cabin with Sandi in tow. There was a small crowd gathered, made up mostly of people taking advantage of the rotating days off Max had implemented at Alex's insistence. It was yet another of his ideas the governor had taken credit for. Alex pushed past the crowd and saw Bob and Reynard digging a hole while Richard stood watch over the long haired loudmouth, David, who had his hands bound in front of him with a white zip tie. Richard was holding his pistol, pointed at the ground.

There was a thick wooden post lying next to the hole. It was a about ten feet long and had a big nail sticking out near the top. Max was standing by the door of his cabin, watching, while Ryan stood nearby, his good hand hovering near the butt of his holstered sidearm. The gathered crowd was silent, but many people exchanged troubled glances. Alex noticed Yael among the gathered throng, and for a moment stood frozen, eyes interlocked with hers. The situation forgotten, he started to move towards her.

"About time, Captain America," the loudmouth said. "Get me the hell out of here!"

"Alex," Max said. "There is no need for you to be here. You've left one of our work camps unguarded." The governor's voice snapped him back to the moment, and he turned to glare at

Max.

"What the hell is going on here?" he demanded. "What are you going to do with that post?"

Max narrowed his eyes. "We are going to carry out a punishment. That man there…" He pointed to David. "Is going to be flogged."

"That's bullshit!" David screamed.

"Flogged? What the fuck do you mean flogged?" What was it with these people and flogging?

Max was unfazed by Alex's interrogation. "I mean tied to that post, as soon as Reynard and Bob finish installing it, and beaten with a fiberglass fishing rod. I would have preferred a whip, but we don't have one handy."

Alex blinked, not sure how to respond. Dealing with Max was most unlike dealing with one of his flunkies. He had to be careful, lest he give Max an opportunity to discredit or embarrass him. Or worse.

"What's he done?" Alex asked.

Max smiled. "Now we're getting to the heart of it, aren't we? Let's try being reasonable out of the box next time, shall we? Instead of coming out half cocked? What he did, Alex, was to steal from the warehouse." The way Max glared at him almost made him cringe. There was more than a hint of accusation in that tone, directed squarely at Alex for the incident with Bob.

"Steal?"

"That's right. He entered the warehouse a little while ago, claiming to want his ration of dehydrated meat, and came out, carrying a single package. Or so it appeared. The warehouse guard quickly searched him and found five more packages hidden on his person. That is fifteen days worth of extra rations. An example must be made."

Alex frowned. "Flogging, that's…well…harsh. Uncivilized. Can't you think of something a bit less cruel and unusual?"

"We could always confine him, Alex, if that would make you happy. But for how long? What is an appropriate sentence for a man who would steal from his community and endanger its people?" Max was on a roll, chest thrust out and eyes blazing with self righteous fire. "How long shall we lose a valuable worker? And as

I have no way to lock a door to prevent it being opened from the inside, how long shall we lose a guard to stand watch? Can you spare one of your people for a week? A month?"

Alex was about to protest, but he realized that Max had outmaneuvered him. There was no way to be sure if Max was telling the truth about being able to lock doors, but Alex had no choice but to believe him, at least until he could verify it using his own terminal. He knew he could call off the flogging, but then Max would score a crucial victory in their power game—he would establish the dangerous precedent of being able to allocate Alex's soldiers to his own tasks. He could easily neutralize one of his people by confining David for a month and forcing Alex to set a round the clock guard. More like three people, considering watch rotations, though Max didn't seem to be aware of that.

"I guess you're right," Alex said grudgingly.

"What?" the loudmouth demanded. "You're going to let him flog me?"

"You shouldn't have stolen the food," Alex replied without much enthusiasm. He turned to Yael and saw her watching him, but he wasn't certain if it was concern or criticism he saw in her eyes. He felt shame nonetheless. Every time he confronted Max directly, the man defeated him soundly.

Reynard held the post in place while Bob, standing on a short wooden ladder, struck it with a sledge hammer until it sunk several feet into the ground. They pushed a struggling David to the post, then hooked the zip tie binding his hands to the nail near its top, now about seven or eight feet off the ground. With his hands secured up high, David was held firmly in place, facing the post, his back to the crowd.

"I'll kill you!" David screamed, tugging at the post, which leaned under the strain. Reynard drew his pistol, raised it in the air and fired a shot. Alex cringed from the blast as the crowd pulled back, clasping their ears. David stopped struggling.

"There will be no more of that," Reynard commanded, then put his pistol away and picked up a fishing pole, which had been stripped of all of its fittings. It was a thick fiber glass stick, longer than the post was tall. Reynard took his place behind David while Bob pulled the man's t-shirt over his head and left it hanging off of his arms before stepping out of the way. Reynard looked at Max.

"Begin," the governor said.

Reynard pulled the pole back, then whipped it forward, blindingly fast. It whistled as it pierced the air and struck David's back with a sickening slap. The loudmouth's head snapped back and he howled in pain, a primal scream of terrible agony that made Alex recoil. He was reminded of Haag's cries after the artillery simulator had shredded his left hand, but somehow this was worse.

Reynard hit him again, and again, and each time he screamed, each time louder than before. David's face was contorted, wet with tears and sweat, his back red with blood that welled freely from split skin.

"Enough!" Alex shouted, but Reynard continued. Again he hit him, and again.

"Enough!" Alex screamed louder. Reynard hesitated and looked at Max, who motioned him to continue. Reynard pulled back even farther and hit him once more. David's scream was an inhuman shriek, terror and pain combined. Those watching recoiled from the sound, and Alex saw a tear roll down Yael's face.

"I said *enough*!" he roared, and took up his carbine. Flicking the selector to auto, he pointed the weapon in the air and held down the trigger. Sonic booms thundered across the open sky as the weapon kicked in his hands, a fountain of ejected brass arcing through the air. One shiny case for each thunderbolt, impossibly loud, an atomic fireball to the stick of dynamite that had been Reynard's pistol blast. Fifteen shots, maybe twenty, and Alex released the trigger and lowered the weapon, though he still held it menacingly. He glared at Max, who was cringing, hands over his ears, along with most of the others. Only Sandi, Ryan and Yael stood their ground.

Reynard stepped away from David, the pole laying discarded at his feet.

"I said that's enough," Alex repeated, softly, and this time everyone paid attention.

The look of hatred on Max's face would have been frightening if not for the adrenaline coursing through Alex's body. At that moment, he wanted nothing more than for Max to order his goons to attack him so that he could put them down once and for all, then turn his weapon on the governor and put an end to a life of tension and conflict.

"You've made your point Alex," Max said, his tone impossible to read. "Reynard, take David to the infirmary and have Barbara patch him up. I trust that the example has been made, despite the rather loud interruption by our military liaison." He turned to Alex. "I want to see you in my office first thing tomorrow morning. I have something of importance to discuss." His voice was venomous, but Alex found himself nodding. The ebb of adrenaline left him shaky and uncertain.

Max turned and walked into his cabin, slamming the door shut behind him. His goons, still glaring at Alex, took David off the pole and led him away. He was complacent, beaten, cringing at every touch and movement. Alex should have stopped it sooner.

Chapter 23

As the crowd began to disperse, mumbling and looking over their shoulders, Yael walked up to Alex, her arms folded across her chest. She seemed hesitant and unsure.

"Hi," he said, trying to smile, but wasn't sure if he succeeded.

"Hi," she echoed, and looked down at his hands. He followed her gaze and realized he was still holding his rifle. He set the weapon to safe and released it, letting it hang free on its single point sling.

He started to speak, but couldn't come up with anything and closed his mouth. Being close to her thrilled him, but it had been so long since he'd seen her, he didn't know what to think. She had been absent from his life for as long as she had been in it. How he felt had not changed, but what of her?

"Do you have some time?" she asked. "To talk?"

Alex turned to Sandi and Ryan. "Can you two go back to the boats? Ryan, I know it's your day off, but…"

"No problem, sir," he said quickly. Alex handed Ryan his rifle, and he and Sandi set off at a brisk pace towards the barrier. Yael turned and started walking towards the beach. Alex followed.

"Are you okay?" she asked. "That must have been hard on you. I mean you must have felt responsible."

"I guess," he said, and wondered how she understood so clearly. "I wasn't the one being beaten though."

"We can wait," she said. "Talk later, when you're feeling better."

He shook his head. "Nah. I'm fine. How was your shiva?" He felt stupid for asking, but didn't know how else to phrase it.

"Hard," she said softly. "Very, very hard."

"I'm sorry. If you want to wait…"

"So I understand I'm supposed to work," she said, ignoring the offer. "Do you recommend the boats or the farm? Or maybe fishing on the beach? I have to do that anyway, I'm sick to death of the powder."

"Are you kidding?" he asked, surprised. "You've been drafted, young lady. You're on my team. We could use the help, too. Working in pairs leaves only one person in the village and not enough down time. And I still need a lieutenant."

She nodded. "I didn't want to assume."

He stopped and put a hand in front of her to halt her. They were at the outskirts of the beach next to a stand of palm trees. The broad leaves provided some shade from the sun, which was almost directly overhead. Alex took a look around and didn't see anyone. That was just how he wanted it.

"That's ridiculous," he said. "Of all the others, you would always be my first choice, even if I didn't…" He didn't let himself finish.

She put her hands on her hips. "Even if you didn't what?"

"Are we having that conversation now? The one we discussed last time we saw each other?"

"I suppose we are."

He nodded. "Good. Then you go first. You know how I feel, I've made it obvious, but you've been dodging the bullet ever since I started shooting."

"Is everything about guns and violence with you?" she asked, narrowing her eyes. He recognized her mood, she was digging in for a fight, and it wouldn't do, not now.

"Is everything about avoidance with *you*?" he countered. "You asked me to talk, but now you're the one looking for a way to back out of it. Well I won't give it to you. I haven't stopped thinking about you since I met you. I'm in love with you, and you're going to have to deal with it." He glared at her as he said it. She took a step back and her mouth fell open.

"You're…" she said, hesitating, clearly shocked. "You're in love with me?"

"Does that surprise you?" he demanded, still angry.

"Yes!" she said, reclaiming lost ground with a step forward. "You don't even know me! You don't know anything about me! You don't know what my favorite color is, what I like to eat, whether I'm a democrat or a republican, nothing!"

"All that stuff is bullshit. It means nothing. I know what I need to know."

"I'm a democrat," she said, turning away.

"What?"

"A democrat. Social safety nets, universal heath care, that sort of thing. But I don't believe in gun control, if that makes you feel better. I think it's stupid."

He tried to stop himself, but couldn't, and burst out laughing.

"What's so funny?" she demanded.

"Nothing," he said, calming himself. "Everything. I tell you I love you and you tell me you're a democrat. Can we get on with it now?"

"Get on it with what?"

"This conversation we're supposed to have."

"I don't know what else to say."

He stared at her and sighed. "Fine, if you want me to do all the work. How do you feel about me? Does it matter to you that I'm not Jewish?"

She looked up at him, her expression unreadable. "Yes, it matters."

Her words hit him hard, and he felt his legs turn rubbery. "I was afraid it would. Is there anything I can do? Convert, maybe?"

She studied him uncertainly. "You would do that for me?"

"I would. I mean I can't change what I believe, or rather what I don't believe, but I'd do whatever else I could to make it work."

"No," she said, shaking her head. "No, just going through the motions wouldn't be right. Besides, I would never ask you to do that."

"If it means we can be together…"

"It's stupid," she said, and he saw her eyes moisten. "I'm probably the only Jew left alive."

"I'm sure that's not true," he said. "There are other colonies."

"So what I'm supposed to leave this one and go find them? Just to find a Jew? When the person I love is right…" She stopped and put a hand over her mouth, eyes wide.

He stepped towards her and grabbed her by her shoulders. His fingers felt the ridge of a bra strap through the thin cotton fabric of her shirt.

"What did you just say?" he demanded, smiling triumphantly.

"You heard me."

"You just nearly had a shit fit after I told you I loved you, and all this time…"

"I just didn't think you had it in you," she said, but it was obvious she wasn't serious.

"Say it," he said. "I want to hear you say it."

She looked up at him and sighed, resigned. "Fine. I love you. Are you happy now?"

"Yes." And it was true. He was extremely happy, much more than he had a right to be in his situation. Max, the government, the world, none of it mattered.

"What if we have children? Can I raise them with my beliefs?"

"Whoa there!" he said. "Aren't we getting ahead of ourselves?"

"There's no sense in starting something you can't finish. I don't do flings, so if you're not serious tell me right now."

"Good point," he said. "And I've never been more serious about anything or anyone. If we don't kill each other long enough to have children, you can teach them your traditions, and I will teach them my way, and they can make up their own mind when they get older."

"Fair enough," she said. Her hands pushed forward and wrapped around his waist. "Can we observe the Sabbath? Holidays?"

"You can," he said. "I'll participate, but I'm not fasting or not working on Saturday and stuff like that. Is that okay?"

She nodded.

"Do I get to kiss you now?" he asked, leaning forward. "Or do we have to get married first?" He caught the scent of strawberries in her hair and his pulse quickened as he squeezed the firm flesh of her shoulders.

She smiled. "You can kiss me, dummy."

He pulled her close and wrapped his arms around her as she rose up on her toes. Their lips met, and he felt such an intense release of pent up desire that he lifted her off her feet, holding her so tightly he was afraid he would hurt her. About to lose himself to a lust that threatened to overwhelm him, he pulled away and set her down, though he couldn't bring himself to let her go.

"I didn't know you were allowed to do that," he said.

She raised one eyebrow. "Do what?"

"You know, the tongue thing."

She smiled. "I'm not a religious nutcase, Alex. Jews are allowed to have *some* fun."

"That's good to know," he said. "But we'd better not do that again."

"Why not?"

"I don't know if I can control myself," he admitted.

"Who said I want you to control yourself?"

He blinked. "But I thought… I mean religion and sex…"

"Did you lie when you said you loved me?" she asked.

"No way."

"Neither did I. This isn't a casual affair."

"So we can…"

"I think we should stop talking now," she said, and kissed him again.

He scooped her up under her knees and carried her to his cabin, fortuitously close by. Locking the door behind him, he fought her all the way to the bed as they struggled to discard their clothing. She tugged furiously at his chest rig, working zippers and fasteners as he snaked his way out of his sling and piled his weapons and gear on the floor. He almost tore her shirt as he pulled it over her head while she kicked off her skirt and panties.

Her passion was as combative as her personality, and he found that this excited him in a way he had never before experienced. Everything with Yael was a struggle, and as he muscled her down onto the bed the thrill of physical dominance coupled with desire in a primal cocktail of sexual fervor. Worried that he was going too far, he forced himself to withdraw, but she glared at him impatiently and pulled him back to her. Thus reassured, he renewed his onslaught with full intensity.

Her fingers dug into his back, her teeth sank into his chest and shoulders almost hard enough to make him cry out. She was guiding him, telling him what she wanted, letting him know her limits. Holding back his release was torture, but he needed to defeat her, to force her to orgasm before he succumbed to the overwhelming pleasure of the struggle. This was a type of lovemaking he had never imagined, so much more than the simple and almost casual coupling of his past relationships.

She did not hide her pleasure from him, and when he was satisfied that he had accomplished his objective, he dropped his resistance and the explosion that followed was almost too much. Darkness flashed before his eyes as he teetered on the edge of consciousness, and when he found himself in her arms, panting, listening to her heart beat with his ear pressed to her glistening left breast, he realized that he had crossed it.

"Are you okay?" she whispered over labored breaths. "You passed out for a second."

"That was incredible," he said, lifting his head to look at her. Her skin glowed with the sheen of perspiration that enhanced the contours of her sylphlike body. "I can't believe how tired I am."

"Are you sure?" she asked, her expression a mix of uncertainty and vulnerability. "I've never…I mean I haven't…"

"You were a virgin?" he asked.

"Yes. Does that bother you?"

He shook his head and smiled. "The only thing I care about is that we're finally together."

"I'm glad," she said, and rewarded him with a truly warm smile devoid of conflict.

"And you're just as much of a hellion in the sack as you are out of it."

She punched him the arm, but lightly. "I'm not a hellion."

"I wouldn't have you any other way," he said, and kissed her. "So what now?"

"What do you mean?" she asked, confused. "What now what?"

"I don't know what I mean," he admitted. "I guess what I'm saying is I don't just want to go back to the way things were. I want to go and bleed Max and his moronic goons so that they leave people the fuck alone and I can stay here in bed with you and not have to babysit the workers all day long. Is that wrong?"

She laughed. "If 'bleed' means kill in your colorful and somewhat infantile military parlance, then, yes, Alex, that would be wrong. But it feels good to hear you say it."

"Tell me to kill Max," he pleaded playfully. "Just say it and I'll go right now."

"Stop it," she said, nudging him on the side of the head.

"Fine, fine. What do you want to do now?"

She shrugged. "I've never done this before, so I don't know the rules."

"Rules?"

"Yeah, like when can we do it again."

He stared at her. "You want to do it again?"

She bit her lower lip. "Do you?"

He felt himself stirring, despite his exhaustion. "God yes, but if I die, it's your fault."

Chapter 24

"Good morning, Alex," Max said, grinning ominously. Alex brushed past a young woman on her way out of Max's cabin. He recognized her as the Goth girl he had seen after he returned from his expedition. She looked embarrassed and withdrawn, and the lingering scent of perspiration betrayed what had been going on. He turned to watch her go, his face darkening with resentment. He didn't know what Max had done to get her in bed, but knowing what he knew about the man he doubted he would approve.

"You don't look so good," Max continued smugly. "Were you out drinking again?"

"Something like that," Alex said, rubbing his eyes as he lowered himself into the chair opposite Max's desk.

"I didn't ask you to have a seat," Max said.

"No," he said. "You didn't." He yawned, trying to clear the lingering grogginess. He had set his laptop alarm to ten o'clock, which he figured was early enough to be considered morning yet late enough to annoy the governor. With Yael on duty, he had enough people to leave one in the village and two at each camp, which gave him some free time to waste with Max.

The governor's smile deepened, as did the level of threat Alex perceived from him.

"I was not pleased with your outburst yesterday," Max said. "Back in the real world, we would have called that felony menacing, unlawful discharge of a weapon and reckless endangerment. Those charges carry a stiff penalty."

"Really?" Alex asked facetiously. "What did you call it when Reynard did it?"

Max nodded appreciatively. "I see you're on your toes this morning. That was a most excellent retort. However, it doesn't change the fact that you openly defied my authority, and I just can't have that. Something must be done."

Alex's eyes narrowed. He was tired of playing cat and mouse with this petty tyrant. A part of him screamed for caution, but he was too distracted to care. All he wanted to do was to get back to his girlfriend.

"Come get some," he said, his tone an artful mix of casual and menacing.

Max was taken aback momentarily, but his smile quickly returned.

"Okay then," Max said. "Let's not screw around anymore, Alex. Let's just cut right down to the chase."

"Let's," Alex agreed. "Why did you call me here?"

"To be perfectly honest," Max said. "I don't like you. I've never liked you. I think you're stupid, reckless and irresponsible. I think that you are grossly unqualified for your position, and frankly I don't see why I should be burdened with you. You are also dangerous and undisciplined."

"And ugly," Alex added, emboldened by the overt hostility. Max's mind games unnerved him, but such open confrontation was much more to his liking. "You forgot 'ugly.' I probably smell bad too, and my mother dresses me funny."

Max leaned back in his chair, once more holding his hands before him with the fingertips touching. Alex wanted nothing more than to grab those fingers and break them.

"I really like this sudden honesty and openness between us," Alex continued. "I think it's a refreshing change."

"Oh?"

"Yes, and while we're doing this, I don't like you either. For starters, you're an asshole. All you care about is being in charge and having people ask 'how high' when you say jump. You've surrounded yourself with ass-kissers and sycophants, which I suppose is a public service, because it lets us filter out the garbage among us. If you had your way you'd turn this place into a prison labor camp with you as its warden."

"Are you quite finished?" Max hissed, his tone venomous.

"No," Alex continued undaunted. "I'll let you know when I'm finished. I think *you* are grossly unqualified for your position. Whoever thought a glorified lawyer would make a good governor obviously watched too much network television. You don't know the first thing about being a leader. Sure, you're a great manipulator, you lie and scheme and twist people into knots until they do what you want out of fear and confusion, but you have no idea how to really motivate people, how to inspire them. This place would be a whole lot better off if Yael's dog were in charge. At least it would have the good sense not to shit where it sleeps. And if you're the kind of egotistic dipshit that passed for a judge back in the world, then a part of me is glad that shithole is gone and your ilk along with it."

Max's lips pulled back, baring his teeth.

"Now I'm finished," Alex said. "Tell me why you called me here or I'm leaving. I have work to do, like keeping your dogs from biting the humans."

Max glared at him a moment, the veins in his temples pulsing, then relaxed and regained his composure.

"I'm not here to trade insults with you, Alex," he said. "Yesterday afternoon I sent a request through channels to have you removed from your position."

Alex tried hard not to flinch as he felt his world crumbling around him. He had all but decided that Max was bluffing, that he couldn't have him removed. Yet if that were so, why had he called him here? Why had he dropped the pretenses? There was no stopping it now, not after what he said, and yet he couldn't bring himself to regret his words.

"And?" Alex asked, doing his best to keep his voice steady. His heart raced as he came up with a contingency plan in the event he was locked out of the arms room. He had three rifles in his cabin, not including the one he used when on duty, and several thousand rounds of ammunition. His people were still armed and equipped. If all of Max's stooges were as heavily armed as they were—

"And I was told, in no uncertain terms," Max answered, interrupting his thoughts. "That I could not replace you so long as you obeyed your general orders."

Alex exhaled sharply, not bothering to hide his relief, then grinned triumphantly. "So we're done here?"

"Not quite," Max said and leaned forward, like a cat about to pounce. "I was also told that if you disobeyed a single order from me, they would indeed replace you. Of course such an order would have to be for the welfare of the colony, and not something arbitrary and pointless like 'shoot yourself' or 'jump off a cliff.' Pity, that would have been a lot simpler."

Alex nodded. "So then. Go ahead and order me to do something that would benefit the colony. I may do it myself, or I may delegate. Or, better still, I may co-opt one of your people to do it. My general orders aren't very specific on that issue, but I'm betting I have some wiggle room." Now that he knew his position was secure, he was eager to push its boundaries. Though he wondered why Max had told him that his request had been refused. It didn't make sense to give him that information freely. Unless he were planning something.

Max's toothy grin was unnerving. "Absolutely, Alex, you may delegate or co-opt as you wish. As long as you carry out my order."

"Well then, what is it?"

"The mentally challenged survivor," Max said, his voice almost a hiss. "What did you call him?"

"Wawa," Alex said nervously, not liking where this was going. "What about him?"

"He represents a drain on our resources, by which I mean our food and our surgeon's time, both of which can be better spent elsewhere. Over a few days, such drains are insignificant, but over time, they add up, until this 'Wawa' amounts to a significant threat to the survival of this colony."

"Bullshit."

"Perhaps, but I have conferred with our 'friends' and they see it my way."

"So what do you want me to do? Stop feeding him from the rations? I'll get fruits…"

"No, Alex, I want you to kill him. I want you to take him into the jungle and blow his fucking brains out. That is an order."

Alex jumped to his feet. "Fuck you, I won't do it."

Max nodded, his teeth bared once more. "Oh, Alex, I'm counting on it. You have until the end of the day to carry out my order…or not. Now get the hell out of my house."

Alex stared at him, unbelieving. Once again, Max had completely and utterly outmaneuvered him.

"I said get out," Max said. "Or you won't need to kill Wawa, because I'm pretty sure failing to respect the sanctity of my home and office will also do to have your sorry ass replaced."

Alex trembled with impotent rage, his hands itching to draw his sidearm and empty the pistol into the governor, but he forced himself to turn about and walk outside. There was work to do.

He went to the arms room and located Wawa on his security cameras. The man was walking in the jungle near his cabin, the one that used to belong to the rapist. He was holding a stick and poking the ground. He smiled with each touch, as though delighting in the fact that he still had the ability to affect the world around him. They had found him in an art school of some kind, Alex remembered.

Radioing Patrick to meet him, Alex grabbed some things he needed and took Wawa down to the beach. The man was happy to go along with someone he knew.

"What is it?" Patrick asked, looking at Wawa uncertainly.

"The boat," Alex said. "Help me get it in the water.

Patrick looked at Alex, then at Wawa, and swallowed nervously.

"Sir, what—"

"Don't ask questions, Patrick, not right now. Sometimes we have to do things we don't want to do, for everyone's benefit." Even as he said it, Alex knew those very words, in one language or another, had been spoken at the scene of every atrocity in the history of mankind. The sprawling wilderness of human civilization had been burned away, leaving just a few tiny seeds behind. Here, in one such seed, the offspring had already begun to emulate the parent.

"Okay, Alex, I trust you." Together they got the boat in the water, and after helping Wawa board, Alex got the motor started and idled past the rocks and reefs, cringing at every scrape. As he cleared the obstructions and pushed on the throttle, he turned to look back at Patrick, who was still on the beach, watching him pull away.

"I'm sorry," Alex muttered, though he wasn't sure to whom he was speaking.

* * *

There was a small crowd waiting for him when he returned. He guided the boat gently onto the beach and looked at them apprehensively. Barbara stood in the lead, hands on her hips, glaring at him with such anger that he was almost afraid to get out and face her.

"What have you done?" she demanded, wasting no time. Behind her, Yael stared at him, her face red and puffy, probably from crying. Tom and Sandi stood next to her, looking glum, but there was no one else from his team. Max looked on from beyond the beach, obviously pleased. He was flanked by Bob and Kristoff, who looked smug. They were enjoying their payback.

"Where is Wawa?" Barbara continued as Alex climbed over the side and jumped down onto the sand. "You better not have done anything to him, you bastard!" She walked up to the boat, and looked over the gunwales. "Where the fuck is he, Alex?"

"He's gone," Alex said softly. "I'm sorry, I had no choice. Max—"

Barbara slapped him across the face, hard, and while he could easily have voided the strike, he chose to let it hit. It hurt, a lot, and he wanted to cry out, but held himself back. She turned around and walked away, holding her face as she cried.

"Chief," Tom said, shaking his head. "That's not cool, man."

Alex ignored him and started for his cabin, sparing a regretful look at Yael. To his surprise, she fell into step behind him.

"That'll do, Alex," Max said as they passed him. "Not quite a bullet in the head, but I like it." Alex ignored him too and kept walking. If he looked back at the governor, if he tried to speak to him, he would kill him.

After they left the others behind, Yael said, "How could you, Alex? How could you do it?"

He opened the door to his cabin, and she followed him inside.

"I suppose this means it's over between us?" he said, turning to look at her as he closed the door. "I wouldn't blame you."

"If she hadn't slapped you," Yael said. "I would."

"You can, I deserve it."

She slapped him, though not nearly as hard as Barbara had. It still hurt.

"Is that what you want?" she said, her voice even. "An easy way out?"

"No," he said. "How could you even think that?"

He stepped back as she came at him again, but it was not to strike him. She put her hands on his shoulders.

"Then we'll get through this," she said. "I really wish you hadn't killed him, but we'll figure it out somehow."

"You would stand by me?" he asked. "Even after something like this?" All else momentarily forgotten, he stared into her eyes and was overwhelmed. When she had stood by him outside the ruined cathedral, he had crossed the boundary between infatuation and love, but now he felt yet another boundary fall behind him, and he was in a new territory, an undiscovered country. He had no words for how he felt for her.

"I don't know about you," she said. "But when I told you I loved you I meant that I'm with you, always, no matter what. Even when you do something as terrible as this, though it breaks my heart, because I thought you were better than this. I can't believe it, that you would do it, but I trust you, and I'm sure you had your reasons."

"I am," he said.

"You are what?"

"Better than this. And I can't tell you how much what you just said means to me."

"What do you mean you're better than this?" she demanded, pushing away from him.

"I mean Wawa isn't dead."

Her hand was quick, almost too quick, but he caught her slap just before it hit him.

"You bastard!" she cried, though he could see the relief in her eyes. "What did you do with him?"

"He's on that trawler, that big boat we found with the useless diesel. I gave him water, a bunch of nutrient powder and some dehydrated food. He'll be fine for a while, and we can figure out what to do with him later."

She shook her head. "How could you keep me going like this? You could have told me what you were planning! You should have told Barbara! She was hysterical! She really cares about Wawa!"

"No. I needed an honest reaction. Max has to believe I killed him, or it will give him grounds to have me replaced. And we can't afford that. What that man would do…"

"You could have told me once we were alone."

"Yeah," he admitted. "I could have. But I wanted to know what you would have done if I'd really killed him. I'm sorry, it was cruel, but I couldn't help it."

"Asshole!" she said. "Don't you ever do that to me again!"

"I won't. But I'm really glad I did. Really glad!"

"We have to tell Barbara," she said. "And the others."

"Yes we do, but they may not listen to me right now. Get them on the radio, tell them to go to the warehouse. I'll meet you there."

Chapter 25

"I can't believe you did that to me!" Barbara cried, but this time they were tears of relief. "The thought of you pushing poor trusting Wawa overboard and leaving him there to drown…I couldn't handle it." She leaned against the recovery bed that Ryan had occupied, glancing nervously at the "hospital" room door.

"Well I wouldn't have just left him there," Alex said, trying to make her feel better. "I would have shot him first."

Yael shook her head, then said to Barbara, "He has a way with words, doesn't he?"

"You could say that, yeah." Barbara smiled, then turned to Alex. "I want to see him! After I thought you killed him…"

"Sure," Alex said. "But not today. Let's wait a little while, until Max forgets about this. He may suspect I stashed him somewhere, so he'll probably have his dogs on the lookout. And you won't have to swim to him either. I found a small folding rowboat on the trawler and dumped it on the beach. I only found one oar, but it's better than nothing."

"But he'll be scared, alone!"

"But alive. Remember Max's people have guns too, and if they figure out where he is…"

She nodded. "Okay, we'll wait."

"Chief," Tom said, shaking his head and smiling. "I gotta hand it to you. You had me going. That was a great idea, putting him on the trawler."

"I'm so glad you didn't actually kill him," Sandi said. "I don't know if I would have been able to trust you again if you had."

"That's fair," Alex agreed. "It would have been a bastardly thing to do."

"I'm glad too," Patrick said. "Back at the beach, I thought for sure you were going to kill him, but I just couldn't believe it."

"Yeah," Ryan agreed. He was standing by the operating bed, messing with the sheets with his good arm.

"Thank you for your trust," Alex said.

"I almost forgot!" Barbara cut in excitedly. "I found something big. Very big. But with all this Wawa business I completely forgot."

"What is it?" Alex asked.

"Remember I told you I had to figure out a way to get these things on a slide without crushing them so I could get a better look?" When she saw his confusion, she added, "The tardigrades? Water bears?"

"Oh. Yeah. What about it?"

"Well I got one positioned just right without a slide cover and got a much closer look. There's no way these things are tardigrades, no way at all."

"So they're some other species?" Tom asked. "How is that big? I mean I'm sure it's scientifically fascinating and all that, but…"

"Just hang in there," Barbara assured him. "It gets very interesting. First, these things aren't natural." She stared at them, as though building suspense.

"What do you mean?" Alex said.

Barbara motioned to the microscope. "I have one under there now. I'm going to put it on the monitor." Alex looked around and noticed a flat panel monitor integrated into the wall. It came to life as Barbara fiddled with the microscope. There was a water bear taking up most of the screen. It appeared to be intact, unlike the ones she had shown them previously, but inert. Either dead or dormant.

On its side was a pattern of discoloration. It looked pixelated, like a video game from the 80s, but Alex could tell it was the letter F, surrounded by a circle. It took him a moment longer to realize what it was.

"Holy shit!" he said.

"What is that?" Tom said, squinting at the screen, as though the blurry image was a product of his vision.

"Fonseca!" Yael said. "That's their logo."

"Are you sure?" Barbara said. "I knew it was a logo of some sort, but I didn't recognize it."

"Yes," Alex said. "The nutrient powder canisters, they have this same logo. And the laundry detergent, or whatever the fuck it is. Do all of the waterbears have it?"

Barbara nodded. "I checked a couple of dozen. Random samples. They all have it."

"But…" Yael said, hesitating, unsure of how to phrase her question. "How is that possible? How can they mark these tiny things? How can they mark all of them?"

"It's genetic," Tom said. "Epigenetic to be exact."

"But how?" Yael said. The question was really important to her. Alex wondered if she was curious or if it had something to do with her religion. He instantly felt guilty. She was smart, smarter than he was, and he needed to stop second guessing her.

"Well," Tom said. "The easiest way is to change the color of its skin. You do that by getting the cells of a specific area to express certain proteins that contain the color you want. Then you adjust the epigenetic markers such that each gene is expressed at the right time and place to make the logo. This is cutting edge tech, but it's real."

"You are the best fake scientist of all time," Alex said, smiling.

"Thank you, Chief. But don't think I understand any of the words that just came out of my mouth."

"So then," Alex said. "We know three things. One, these things were genetically engineered. Two, Fonseca is responsible. And, three, there is also a chance that Fonseca is behind this installation, since their logo keeps popping up. But what does that tell us? What are they for?"

"We know one more thing," Barbara said. "And this one is big."

"Spill it!" Alex said. "No more dramatic pauses!"

Barbara smiled. "Okay, okay. When I decided to try to get an even better look and put a slide cover on it, I crushed one of them." She paused again.

Alex pointed a finger at her, and she raised her hands in a gesture of surrender.

"Fine! You are taking all the fun out of this. So…I crushed it, and something oozed out of it that dissolved the slide. Ate away at it. Then it ate through part of my microscope. A very, very small part, I had to use a magnifying glass to see it, but it dissolved solid aluminum. Can you believe that? A micro organism secreting something that dissolves glass and aluminum!"

"Calcium oxide," Tom muttered.

"What?" Alex said.

"Calcium oxide," he explained. "It's made from limestone, and is an ingredient in glass. In commercial form it also contains small traces of aluminum oxide. Portland cement, the most common form of concrete, also contains calcium oxide, as well as aluminum."

"The dog's collar," Barbara said. "Same pattern as the damaged microscope, and the concrete."

"Oh my god!" Yael said, catching on first. "That means…"

"These things," Alex finished. "They weren't left behind by whatever destroyed the city. They *are* what destroyed the city!"

"The collapsed houses…" Yael said, looking distant.

"Wood and stone!" Alex said, realizing what in hindsight should have been obvious. "All that was left were the wooden foundation and the roof shingles! Both naturally occurring substances! And the buildings, the ones still standing in Honolulu…they were made of stone. Tom, you brilliant bastard, I thought you said you tried not to learn anything as a biochemistry professor."

Tom grinned sheepishly. "I tried my best, but this is from one of the last lectures I did, it talked about how common certain substances were in modern industry. Substances like oxides of calcium, silicon, aluminum and iron. These things, if they can somehow destroy those substances…"

"Nanomachine disassemblers," Alex said, remembering something he'd read.

"What?" Yael asked.

"It's from a sci-fi book," he explained. "It was about a war in the asteroid belt in the near future, between mega corporations. Some of them designed nanomachines that were supposed to make mining cost effective by stripping down asteroids, but they went haywire and destroyed the ship carrying them and everyone on it. They were self replicating and all that jazz."

"I know what nanomachines are," Yael said. "I just…I mean…it's crazy! You said it yourself. Science fiction."

"These are way too big to be nano-machines," Barbara said.

"Nanomachines would be measured in nanometers, while these things average about a tenth of a millimeter."

"That's one hundred thousand nanometers," Yael said.

"Besides," Barbara said. "Nanomachines don't exist. And these are not machines, they are organic. If Fonseca made these things, then they used genetic engineering, not nanorobotics. The Chinese weapon theory…maybe it was a weapon, just not Chinese."

"Chinese weapon *theory*?" Yael said. "You guys want to fill me in?"

"Right," Alex said. "Sorry." He told her about their conversation, and as she listened and nodded, her expression darkened.

"You okay?" Alex asked.

"I don't like being lied to."

"So," Barbara said. "We now know three things."

"They are genetically engineered," Alex said, piecing it together. "They were made by an American biogen firm, and they can destroy industrial compounds by secreting some kind of acid…but, can acid do that? Dissolve such very specific things?"

"No," Tom said, shaking his head. "Not that I know of."

"I don't think so either," Barbara said.

"So what are we left with?" Alex said.

"Nanites," Yael said. "Or some kind of bacteria that may as well be nanites."

"But you said—"

"When you have eliminated the impossible, whatever remains, however improbable, must be the truth."

"Quoting Sherlock Holmes?" Tom said.

"Why not?" she said. "We're trying to solve a mystery."

"Speaking of," Alex said. "Fonseca. They made this weapon, and they also make our nutrient powder and our laundry enzyme—hey!" He suddenly realized that there was a possible connection. "The thing that does the laundry for us, the powder, is it….is it like these things?"

Barbara shook her head. "That was the first thing I looked at. It's just an advanced enzyme mix. No nanotech."

"Okay," Alex said. "Good. But going back to my point, Fonseca is involved, not only in what destroyed the world, but with us.

It’s too much to be a coincidence.”

“Agreed,” Yael said, her brows wrinkling as she stared off into space. “I don’t like where this is going,” she said. “An American biotech company makes a weapon and destroys the world? Why? That doesn’t make any sense.”

“I know,” Alex agreed. “That can’t be what happened. It just…it can’t.”

“We need answers, Chief,” Tom said. “We can’t go on guessing like this or who knows what kind of crazy shit we’ll come up with? We have to get to Max’s terminal. I’m sure I can get some answers there.”

Alex nodded. “Yes, we do. Give me some time, I’ll come up with a plan to get you in there. I can override his door lock, but we need to make sure no one sees us.”

“Sounds good,” Tom said. “We can’t just let this go.”

“No,” Alex agreed. “We can’t.”

Chapter 26

The next four days were agonizingly slow. The tedium of routine guard duty ate away at Alex as he constantly looked up at the sun and wished it would move faster across the sky. He never paired himself up with Yael as it would have been too distracting, and he couldn't wait to see her when their work day ended. Tom had convinced her that the alcohol in the vats was potato based, which was apparently okay for her to drink on special occasions, and the group had taken to gathering on the beach by a small fire every night after the work crews went home. Tom drank until he could barely walk and Barbara and the others consumed almost as much, but Yael never overindulged and rarely drank more than a single cup, sometimes less. Alcohol was apparently acceptable in Judaism, but over indulgence was not, which made sense to Alex, even if he did not agree with the source of the limitation. The little she drank was enough to loosen her up quite a bit, and their nights together became even more intense.

Sometimes, after making love, they would talk about what happened, about their families, and she would cry as he held her. Most of the time it was her crying, but not always.

Alex had someone watching Max throughout the day, as inconspicuously as possible, looking for opportunities to get into Burger King unobserved, but nothing presented itself. The governor was pretty good about locking the door behind him.

On the morning of the fifth day after the Wawa incident, after the team did a brisk run around the interior barrier perimeter and some quick shooting practice, Alex looked at his laptop calendar and noticed that it was Saturday. He decided to annoy Max by declaring it a weekend. He showed up by the barrier gate before the work parties gathered and dismissed Rich, who was acting as gatekeeper that morning. As the workers began to assemble, he made his proclamation known, and despite protests from Bob and Reynard, the colonists dispersed and went about their business, delighted by the prospect of two days of rest.

"Max wants to see you," Bob said angrily after getting off the radio.

"Ask him how it feels to want," Alex said as he and Yael walked away. "But tell him I'll see him first thing Monday morning." The smile on his face was hard to contain. Knowing the limits of the governor's power made it easier than ever to toy with him. Perhaps Max had not been the one to do the outmaneuvering this time around.

"This is our first weekend together," Yael said. "What do you want to do? Anything but work, that is. I've been far too lax in my observances."

"Besides the usual?" he asked, grinning. She smacked him lightly on the arm.

"Yeah, besides that."

"Let's get the dog and go swimming!" he suggested.

"That sounds great!"

They spent the day enjoying the beach and the water, then got together with the others for their nightly bonfire ritual. As usual, there was more than one fire with distinct groups gathering at each. They were forming cliques, Alex realized, which was dangerous and divisive for the community. If Max had been a real leader, he would have taken steps to unite the colonists. Maybe hold celebrations, dances or other festivities. Of course Max probably preferred them divided, it made them easier to govern by intimidation.

Enjoying the prospect of sleeping in, Alex and Yael stayed out later than usual, then retired to his cabin, where they made love before drifting off to the first night of peaceful sleep he'd had in a long time.

In the morning he was woken by a frantic voice shouting through his radio.

"Awesome One, this is Beach Bunny!" Sandi shouted. "Alex! Come in! Oh god please come in!"

He was out of bed in an instant.

"Beach Bunny, Awesome One, go ahead."

"They have Tom! They're taking him away!"

"Say again?" Alex demanded, not quite able to grasp what she was saying. He had never been a morning person.

"Tom!" she repeated. "They caught him sneaking into Burger

King! They took his guns and they're going to punish him!"

"Beach Bunny, what is his location?"

"They're leaving Burger King and headed to the beach!"

"Fuck!" Alex swore, then into the radio, "On my way!" He switched the channel on his radio and said, "Awesome One to all call signs, get up, get dressed! The holiday is over!"

"What is it?" Yael asked, just waking up. "What's wrong?"

"They've got Tom!" he said as he slid into his pants and reached for his shirt. "Gear up! We're going to get him."

They were dressed in less than a minute, and a minute after that they had their gear and weapons and were out the door, running towards the beach. They saw Tom, hands zip tied behind his back. Kristoff and Bob were shoving him along, pistols drawn, and Max and Reynard walked behind them. A small crowd of onlookers trailed them, though they held back quite a bit, as though afraid to get too close.

"What the fuck is going on?" Alex demanded as he ran up to Max. "Release my man at once!"

Max's face darkened, and Alex realized that this was not the usual cat and mouse game. The governor was angry.

"Stand down, Captain," he commanded. "Your 'soldier' was caught in my office, attempting to gain access to my terminal."

"Sorry Chief," Tom said with an apologetic shrug. "I saw a chance, and I took it."

"I'll deal with him," Alex said. "You can rest assured he will be punished."

"I'm afraid that just won't do," Max said. "As governor, carrying out justice is my responsibility, not yours."

"You're not going to flog him," Alex said sternly.

"No," Max agreed. "I'm not. His crime was much more serious than David's." He looked over at the long haired loudmouth, who was among the onlookers, and the man took a step back, clearly cowed. Alex hadn't heard much from David since the flogging. The man had mostly kept to himself.

"What are you going to do with him?" Alex demanded.

"The barrier," Max said. "I am going to put him in the barrier, a quarter of the way in, for thirty minutes. If he survives, we shall consider the matter settled."

"What?" Tom shouted. "No fucking way! You're not putting me in there! Chief, do something!"

Alex's mind raced as he struggled to remember what it felt like being a quarter of the way into the nausea field. That was a little more than half the distance he had managed to penetrate, and he remembered it being very severe, but just how severe he couldn't be sure. However bad it was, he was only in there for a few seconds, a minute tops. Max was talking about half an hour!

"Max," he said, the desperation clear in his voice. "I'm begging you. I know this is about you and me, and if you let him go, things will be different, I promise. We can work together, I'll stop doing things to piss you off."

"It's nice that you acknowledge that the totality of your existence here is as a thorn in my side, Alex," Max said icily, then turned to Bob. "Get on the radio, get the others here, and tell them to announce what's happening on the way. I want people to see this."

"Max, please," Alex begged.

"No, Alex, I will not let him go. He has committed a serious crime, and for the welfare of the colony, he must be punished." *For the welfare of the colony*. He still knew how to push all the right buttons.

The governor turned and continued towards the beach, angling to the right, in the direction of the patch of jungle behind which the rapist had been executed. "We're going to need to move the stake a little closer," he said to Bob, who was talking on the radio. "Make it happen."

Alex didn't follow him. He stood in place, watching them lead his friend away. Tom looked back over his shoulder, his eyes wild with fear, and stumbled as he walked. Kristoff shoved him violently forward and he almost fell.

"Alex," Yael said. "I'm with you, whatever you do." He nodded, and picked up the radio.

"Awesome One to all call signs, roll call, repeat, roll call."

"Dark Knight here," Patrick said immediately. A few seconds later, Purple Power and Beach Bunny checked in.

"Doctor Who here," Barbara's voice crackled, surprising him. He hadn't expected her to answer, but why not? She was a member of his team, and it was time to call her to duty.

"All call signs," Alex said. "Proceed to the warehouse ASAP. From this point on, you are cleared to engage the enemy. I say again…you are cleared to engage the enemy."

"Alex…" Yael said, but then stopped herself and nodded. She hefted her M4 and flicked the selector switch from safe to semi. She was adorable under her Kevlar helmet, and for a moment Alex was tempted to order her to go and hide somewhere where she would be safe.

"Awesome one, this is Dark Knight," Patrick said through the radio. "Who exactly is the enemy?"

"Anyone who gets in your way," Alex said.

Chapter 27

They came out of the jungle like a pack of predatory baboons, hunched over, moving quietly, quickly. The weight of body armor and weapons hardly slowed them, attesting to the effectiveness of the brief but intense training that Alex had subjected them to. Upon seeing them emerge from the trees, Alex signaled his group to advance from the other direction. Neither Max nor his people saw them until it was too late.

"On the ground!" Alex shouted as he charged them. "Get down on the fucking ground!" Max whirled, eyes wide. Kristoff looked up from where he had been securing Tom to the pole, frozen like a deer in headlights while Bob fumbled for his gun.

Pointing his carbine at the ground at Bob's feet, Alex fired a short burst. Bob flinched from the piercing cracks and flying sand and dropped his weapon.

"On the ground!" Yael shouted as her party closed from the other side.

"Get down!" Patrick yelled behind her.

Reynard, who was standing next to Max, reached for his radio. Alex, now in range, jerked his carbine forward and struck Reynard in the temple with his weapon's flash suppressor. The stooge crumpled like a severed puppet and lay on the ground, clutching his bleeding head and looking up in confusion.

"I said get down!" Alex shouted at Max, who was frozen, not moving. He kicked the governor in the back of the knee, and the man collapsed almost on top of Reynard. Every one of them was now face down in the sand.

"Secure the prisoners," Alex ordered. "We have two more unaccounted for."

"Just what do you think you're doing?" Max demanded, clearly shaken as Patrick ziptied his hands behind his back.

"Taking over," Alex said. "Something I should have done a long time ago."

"You'll never get away with this!" the governor shouted.

"When they find out about this—"

"Shut the fuck up," Alex barked. "Before I blow your fucking head off!" Max glared with pure hatred, but didn't say anything else.

"Thanks a bunch, Chief," Tom said, clearly relieved, as Sandi and Patrick went to each of the prisoners and zip tied their hands and feet, then collected their weapons.

"No problem," Alex said, and smiled. "Remind me to kick your ass after we celebrate."

"Will do."

"Barbara, Ryan," Alex said. "You guys cut Tom loose and guard these assholes. The rest of you, we have two stray dogs to bring in."

They found Jonathan guarding Burger King, frantically yelling into the radio. As soon as the kid saw them coming, he turned and started to run. Another burst of rifle fire scared him enough to freeze him in his tracks, and Alex knocked him to the ground the same way he had the governor. Once he was secured and his weapon confiscated, Alex picked up the sycophant's radio.

"Hello, Richard," he said. "Where are you?"

"Who the fuck is this?" Rich's whiny voice blared through the radio's tiny speaker. "What's going on?"

"Awesome One, this is Rip Ranger," Tom said through Alex's radio. "Richard was just here. He saw us and bolted towards Burger King."

"Understood," Alex said, discarding Jonathan's radio.

They saw Rich a few seconds later. As soon as he spotted them he froze.

"On the ground!" Alex shouted. Yael, Patrick and Sandi advanced towards him, rifles pointed at his head.

He looked from one to the other, then dropped to his knees. Yael walked up behind him, took his pistol and shoved him down onto his face. Within seconds they had the last of Max's goons tied and helpless.

Alex lowered his weapon, smiled, and let out a long sigh.

"Wow," he said. "We really should have done this a long time ago. Let's get these guys locked up and get all the guns, especially the stuff they took from Tom."

They gathered up the prisoners and Alex used the arms room terminal to lock them in their respective cabins, except for Max, whom he put in the empty one. The former governor had indeed been lying when he told Alex he had no way to lock someone in. It was one of the top level options in the security menu.

"Stew in here for a few days," Alex said to Max. "I'm going to let you out eventually, but when I do, you're just a regular colonist. You're done as governor. I'll get your shit and bring it to you here…this is your new home. If I see you near your old 'office' or if you cause any trouble, I'm going to kill you. Do you understand?"

Max nodded, still glaring.

As he and Yael made their way to Burger King, a lot of people were coming out of their cabins, confused by the gunfire.

"Change in administration," Alex announced. "Nothing to worry about."

"Captain Meyer?" someone asked, and recognizing the voice, he turned around. It was David, the long haired loudmouth.

"Yes?"

"Is it true?" he asked timidly. "That you killed Max?"

"No," Alex said with a twinge of regret. "He's alive, but he's not the governor anymore."

David nodded. "Thank you."

"You're welcome. Feel free to kick his ass a little bit when I let him out, but don't hurt him too much."

The loudmouth smiled, and Alex felt good. If *this* guy could come around to his side, he must be doing something right.

As word spread, people started to express shock and disbelief, though there were few actual protests. Some people demanded to know what right he had to take over by force, but those were a clear minority and he ignored them. The rapport he had built over the last week or so was paying off. Despite Max's spin, most of them knew who their friends were.

By the time he got to Burger King, Ryan and Patrick were already standing guard outside, while Tom sat at the governor's desk, clicking away at the keyboard while Yael, Barbara and Sandi hovered over his shoulder.

"Chief," Tom said without looking up as soon as Alex walked

through the door. "These security measures are a joke. It's almost like they didn't expect any hackers to survive." He grinned.

"I wonder why. How long do you think it will take you?"

"Not long, maybe a couple of hours. The security may totally suck, but this connection is slow and cumbersome. You guys can go, I'll radio when I've learned something."

"Okay," Alex said. "I'll leave a guard outside, just in case."

"In case what?" Barbara asked. "Didn't you lock them up?"

"Yeah, the ones we know about. How many more fans does that snake oil salesman have? Or maybe some misguided morons could try to 'do what's right' and free him, or attack us."

"Just in case," Barbara agreed. "This is why you're the captain."

"You're the Burger King now, Chief," Tom said, without taking his eyes off the monitor.

"Right," Alex said with obvious distaste. "We'll have to talk about that later."

"I can tell you something right now," Tom said.

"What's that?"

"Max's talk about having you replaced…it was bullshit."

"Really?" Alex turned back to the terminal and looked at the screen.

"Really," Tom said. "See the communications log? It's all one way. Outgoing communication isn't even enabled."

"Motherfucker!" Alex swore, shaking his head. "He had me going the whole time! What a manipulative, nasty bastard he is!"

"And apparently," Yael said. "He was just clever enough to orchestrate his own undoing."

Alex turned to her and smiled. "You turn me on when you use big words."

She rolled her eyes. "You're not as dumb as you look so stop fooling around."

"Well I feel pretty dumb after the way he played me."

"You shouldn't."

"Wait a minute!" Alex said. "That's why he ordered me to kill Wawa. Now it makes sense. He told me that he tried to have me replaced, and that they wouldn't let him unless I disobeyed one of his orders. I wondered at the time why he would tell me something like that. Then he gave me an order that he knew would fuck my head up. He was going to have a man killed just to keep me believing that I was under his control. That piece of shit! I kinda wanna go shoot him now."

"It's what he does," Tom said. "He's a freakin' lawyer. I should know, I used to play one. Now leave me to my business, you bunch of circling vultures. I need room to stretch my wings."

"Right," Alex said as he followed the others outside. "So you can crawl out of your cocoon and become a beautiful butterfly."

"You got it, Chief."

Once they were outside, Alex turned to the others. "I need two volunteers to stay on duty, guard Burger King while Tom does his business."

Patrick and Sandy immediately stepped forward.

"Good. As for the rest of you, go relax, unwind. You did good work today, and with Max out of the picture our lives are going to get a lot easier. No more standing around in full kit…from now on we can get that stuff when we need it."

Alex watched them disperse. They were weary but obviously very proud.

"I'm going to go shower," Yael said. "Meet you at your place?"

"You could shower at my place," he said suggestively.

"Yeah, but I actually want to get clean."

He chuckled as she walked away, and started for his own cabin. He felt lighter, and despite the weight of his kit there was a slight bounce to his step, an expression of the childlike joy he felt. The sun was climbing over the mountains, warming the steady breeze that carried the tang of salt water. People were everywhere, talking, pointing. He had never seen such energy in this place. While not all of it was positive, he decided it was a good thing. People didn't have to like freedom, they just had to have it.

"Live free or die," he muttered, and it suddenly occurred to him that for the first time in his life, he was actually, totally free. Alex was a product of the public school system, and since childhood he'd been taught that America was a free country. The older he grew, however, the more he realized that American freedom was an idea more than it was an actuality. He had the right to bear arms, but only if the government let him. He had the right to protest, but only with a permit and in designated areas—even his freedom of speech was subject to the will of the courts. Small things like going camping, fishing or walking down the street with a beer were subject to constant government meddling. He wasn't a right wing nutcase, he could entertain the notion that some restrictions were a necessary evil brought about by an increasingly complex society and a growing population, but that didn't mean he liked it, or that he didn't resent the lie.

"Regulate this," he said, hefting his rifle.

He thought of all those that had died, the exact number of which he could only guess at, and felt somewhat ashamed for his joy. Whoever had unleashed this destruction upon the world had committed a crime beyond his ability to measure, and yet out of the ashes of that evil something good had emerged, at least for him. When he looked around, he didn't just see the idyllic location or the beautiful greens and blues that painted his world in shades of natural splendor, he saw the faces of the best friends he'd ever had, and the face of the woman he loved. Would he give it all up to restore that which had been lost? He didn't want to press himself for the answer, sure that he wouldn't like it, regardless of what it was.

He turned a familiar corner and came within sight of his cabin. Max was standing there, right in front of his door.

Chapter 28

Alex stared at him, frozen, uncertain. What the hell was he doing there? He wanted to rub his eyes to emote his confusion, but instead he brought up his rifle and aligned his targeting dot with Max's head.

"Hold on Alex," Max said calmly. He turned and motioned. Bob came out from behind the cabin, his meaty arm around Yael's throat, pinning her to him. In his other hand he held a pistol. The same pistol Alex had given her to protect herself.

"Put your weapons down," Max said. "Or he'll kill her."

Yael clutched at Bob's arm, her eyes glaring with hatred, though he could clearly see the fear within. His whole life, spent searching for her, to end like this…

"Shoot him!" she hissed, and in response Bob tightened his arm until her eyes bulged and she gasped for breath.

"Give him three seconds," Max said. "Then kill her." The corners of Max's lips curled up ever so slightly as he looked at Alex. "If you surrender now, you have my word that she will not be harmed."

Alex aimed at Bob's head but he shifted his position, still partially hidden behind the wall of the cabin, and he couldn't get a clear shot.

"One," Max said.

Bob was big, almost fat, and Alex could easily hit his leg or torso, but that would give him a chance to pull the trigger, a chance he wasn't willing to take.

"Two," Max said.

"I'll waste this fucking kike whore," Bob snarled. "Don't think I haven't wanted to since I met her." The shock of those words undid him. Whatever strength he had, it flowed out of him like water out of a fractured barrel, replaced by fear, and hatred. He dropped his rifle, then unclipped it from the sling, letting it fall to the ground with a thud.

"Get his weapons," Max ordered, and Kristoff came out from

behind the cabin and grabbed Alex's rifle, pointing it at his head.

"How did you get out?" Alex asked. It only mattered to his guilt, for he had failed to anticipate it, and now everything was falling apart.

"I told you that you were stupid, Alex," Max said smugly. "My DNA opens any lock in the colony, even one you override. Except for the arms room, and your cabin, of course, though we'll see what we can do about that. I'm the governor, Alex, you're just a soldier. If you'd figured that out for yourself, we could have avoided all of this."

"Your pistol," Kristoff said, reaching out with his left hand. Alex reached for it, slowly, and handed it to him. He had never known such hatred, such seething, pulsating wrath. It was alive, a serpent coiled around his spine, squeezing, crushing him. He could say nothing, do nothing, so intense was his desire to kill, to rip these men apart with his bare hands and tear into their beating hearts with his teeth. Turning away from the objects of his rage, he looked at Yael, and she at him. She looked remorseful, conveying her regret through moist eyes obscured by unruly locks of auburn hair. He wasn't sure what burned more, his failure or her adoption of the blame.

"Open your door," Max commanded. "Then go inside and unlock your gun cabinet, the one under your bed." As he spoke, the others—Rich, Jonathan and Reynard—came out from behind his cabin to stand around their leader. They leered at Alex, their faces ripe with contempt.

He considered his options and realized he had none. The price of freedom was eternal vigilance, and he had let his guard down. Forcing his legs to respond, he shambled towards his door and put his thumb on the green pad. The familiar chime sounded, and he pulled it open. Someone shoved him inside, and he knelt before his bed and pressed his thumb to the DNA pad. He knew that by surrendering he doomed the others. He had sacrificed the many for the one, but there had never been any other choice. His friends were more important to him than his own life, but nothing mattered more than her.

They pulled him away, knocking him to the ground. He did not resist, only watched, helpless, as they pulled open the drawer and yanked out the three carbines. Reynard turned him over, wrenched his arms behind his back and secured them with zip ties. He bound his legs then dragged him against the wall, turning him over again as he shoved him into a sitting position, his back to the plexiglass divider.

Kristoff pushed Yael inside and forced her down by the foot of the bed.

"We should waste them both right now," Bob said. "We shouldn't make the same mistake they made with us."

Max looked at him reproachfully. "Robert, did you not hear me give Alex my word?"

"Yeah, but—"

"The girl will be unharmed, as I have promised. As for young Captain Meyer, rest assured his life is forfeit. Killing him here, however, will only make our task more difficult."

"Whatever you think is best," Bob said, looking down at Yael with regret. How had normal men become so vile? Or were they always this way, under the surface, just waiting for the right moment to expose the malignancy within?

Once the weapons had been distributed, Max motioned to Reynard and Rich, who ran out the door and out of sight. He then walked over to Alex, reached down and took his radio.

"This is Max," he said into the device. "We have your captain, and your lieutenant. Go to his cabin immediately and drop your weapons by the door. You have five minutes, or we're going to kill them, starting with the girl." Max turned to Alex. "A necessary bluff. I have no doubt that they will comply." And Alex had no doubt that Max would break his word and kill Yael if they didn't. Men like Max only played at honor and could justify anything to themselves, no matter how horrific.

Confused chatter blared through the radio as the others tried to make sense of Max's broadcast. "Four minutes," Max said, looking at Alex's laptop to monitor the time. "You have my word none of you will be harmed as long as you surrender. I have men armed with rifles hidden throughout the colony, and after our hostages are executed, they will hunt you down like animals. You are good at playing soldier with your leader around, but without him you are a hopeless band of misfits, and you'd better wake up to that fact before someone gets hurt."

"Alex," Yael said. "I'm so sorry…they were waiting inside my cabin when I got there, I tried to fight them, but…" He suddenly noticed her split lip, and the dried crusty blood on her chin.

"It's not your fault," he said. "It's—"

"Shut up," Max barked. "Or I'll have Robert break her jaw."

So much for promises.

"How do we know they're still alive?" a voice crackled through the radio. It was Tom.

"You're at my terminal," Max said. "Do you have access to the interior cameras?"

"No."

"My password is terranova202," Max said, and waited.

"I'm in," Tom said.

"Access the camera for unit 2." So there were interior cameras, even in his cabin!

Bob walked up to him and knelt down so that his face was next to Alex's. With a look back to make sure Max was distracted, he whispered, "I watched you, fucking her. We all did. Can you guess what we did?" He made a rude gesture implying masturbation. "She's a dirty little whore for a stuck up Jew bitch, isn't she?"

Alex didn't react, he didn't want to give him the satisfaction. If it were not for the fact that Bob would take it out on Yael, he would have torn off his face with his teeth. Not too long ago the thought of such savagery would have shocked him, but now he hungered for it.

"I see you," Tom said. "How do we know you'll keep your promise? That you won't kill us, and them, as soon as we surrender?"

"I gave you my word," Max said. "I'm many things, but I am not a liar. Besides, there aren't many of us, and we can't afford to murder needlessly. I'll also grant you amnesty, Tom. You will not be punished for trying to break into my terminal."

"That's not good enough," Tom said.

"Then watch them die. Robert, cut Yael's throat."

"With pleasure!" Bob said, and started towards her.

Alex lurched forward, straining against his bonds. "No!"

"Wait!" Tom shouted through the radio. "Don't! We'll surrender! We'll trust you!"

"Stand down, Robert," Max said. The big man stopped with obvious displeasure.

Long, agonizing minutes passed until Alex heard sounds from outside. The others had arrived, and they were laying down their weapons. It was over.

* * *

They had chosen a different location to place the pole, closer to the warehouse on the jungle side of the colony's perimeter. Alex was unfamiliar with the area, but he could guess how far into the barrier the pole was—right in the middle.

Bob led him with a callous hand on his arm as the crowd looked on. It was as big a gathering as the one that watched the presidential address. The many faces stared solemnly at him as he walked past. He was surprised to see that some were crying. Why any of them would shed tears for him, he had no idea. None of his people were there. Max had confined them to their rooms, exactly as Alex had confined him just a few hours before. Max had kept his word, at least so far, and none of them had been harmed.

"I tried," Max said to the crowd as Bob cut the zip tie holding Alex's hands together. "To lead you towards a greater good, to make sure that we would survive, that the devastation that befell the rest of the world would never find us here."

Alex thought about grabbing Bob's weapon, but Kristoff and Reynard were a few feet away, pointing rifles at him. *His* rifles.

"I tried to ration our supplies so that they would serve us as long as possible, to keep a selfish few from taking for themselves what rightfully belongs to all of us. I tried to make sure everyone worked, everyone contributed, so that we would thrive as a colony."

Bob pulled another zip tie from his pocket and secured Alex's hands behind the pole, then kicked him in the side of the knee so that he collapsed. There was pain, but it was distant, beyond his concern. All he could think about was leaving Yael and his friends in the hands of these animals.

"Yet this man, Alex Meyer, thought himself above such concerns, and conspired to interfere with my efforts. When that proved insufficient to satisfy his anarchistic nature, he abused the trust placed in him by those who put us here, who saved us from the Chinese attack, and attempted to oust me, this colony's legitimate governor, by force."

Bob and the others backed away, leaving him alone in the barrier's kill zone.

"Take a good look. This is what happens to traitors. And with Alex out of the way..." He motioned to his men, all of whom were now armed with M4 carbines. Jonathan and Rich were hunched over under the weight of their ill fitting body armor. Bob wore Alex's chest rig and had to leave it unfastened. Correct sizing of load bearing gear was critical for its function, and Alex took some small pleasure in knowing that these pigs were stuck with the wrong gear. If Max had lied about being able to communicate with the government, then perhaps he would never be able to get into the arms room.

"I will finally be able to run this colony in the manner it needs to be run. This is a survival situation, not a tropical resort, and it's about time you people learned that the hard way." He glared at the crowd, as though daring someone to speak out so that he could make an example out of them. No one did. Satisfied, he turned to Alex.

"*Mr*. Meyer," Max announced. "You have been found guilty of treason against the government of the United States. Do you have anything to say for yourself?"

"Someone," Alex growled. "Anyone, please slit this pig's throat before he turns you all into slaves."

Max smiled at him. "Fitting last words for a rabid dog that is about to be put down." He raised the radio. "Prepare to activate the barrier."

"Ready," Rich's muffled voice echoed across the emptiness between Max and Alex, emptiness that wasn't going to remain so for much longer. Alex braced himself.

"Activate."

Chapter 29

Pain.

Blinding, unbearable pain. It hit him like a derailing bullet train, so sudden and brutal that there was no way to prepare. His gut clenched as its contents sprayed from his mouth, his stomach heaving, desperate to expel every last drop.

His vision blurred, his ears rang. There was no light, no darkness, except the flashes that accompanied each spasm, each wave of agony. Devoid of its contents, his stomach clenched down harder, as though trying to push out his intestines. He was only vaguely aware of his surroundings, of the gasps of horror from the crowd. Time passed, the crowd grew smaller, the pain got worse.

He fought it, harder than he had ever fought anything. Part of him screamed to let go, as though that could make a difference. He would die when he died. Life, it was all he had, all he was. He couldn't let it go. His pain was a constant companion now, and the only relief would be death, and yet he fought.

They were all gone now, except one. Short, chubby, holding a weapon he didn't know how to use. Jonathan. How great did he think Max was now? Or perhaps this act of brutality had elevated the governor in the kid's eyes. How was Alex to know? All he knew was agony.

Time lost all meaning. A minute, an hour, did it matter? There was no relief, no subsiding, just constant and unyielding anguish. He should be dead, but he wasn't. It couldn't be long now, but the end would never come. There was only this moment, and the moment was as unceasing as the pain that defined it.

Yet, despite his conviction that he would endure eternal damnation, there was change. The spasms became worse, more frequent. The pain steadily increased, but it was growing distant. His body had suffered too much and was shutting down. He forced his eyes open, forced himself to see the world one last time before he died. His vision cleared, little by little, until he could just make out Jonathan's face. And something else. Someone else.

Yael.

Of course it couldn't be her, she was locked in her cabin, but it didn't matter. Maybe she was an angel, sent down from a heaven he didn't believe in to deliver him from his suffering. Or more likely a vision, conjured by a mind desperate for solace. It worked, at least a little. The sight of her calmed him, soothed him, and though the intensity of the pain did not change, it grew even more distant.

He managed to twist his bloody lips into a smile as he watched her. She was moving strangely, like a stalking cat, walking up behind Jonathan. She pounced, and he remembered the little dog and how it played with Yael's shoes. It would take one and bring it to its bed, a pile of dirty laundry she had set aside for it. It would growl, shaking its head, then toss the shoe aside, only to skulk towards it and pounce once more. He wasn't sure if he was watching Yael smashing Jonathan's head with a rock, or if he was watching the dog bite down on a shoe—

Suddenly his mind cleared, and he screamed, for the pain became too real, too close. He saw Jonathan collapse, saw Yael reach down and take his knife and pistol. How was this possible? How had she gotten out of her cabin?

She started toward him, and he tried to reach out to her, though his bonds held firm. When she flinched and momentarily stepped back, he realized what she was doing. She was going into the barrier.

He wanted to scream, to tell her to stop, but he didn't have the strength. A sound came out, but it was a bestial shriek, unintelligible.

She vomited, more than once, but she kept coming. Halfway through, she collapsed to her knees, unable to continue. He saw her tears, saw her face contorting, and the pain he felt was no longer his own. It was hers, and it burned twice as much as before.

After hesitating for a moment, she pushed on, slowly, steadily. She still held the knife, and she used it like a mountain climber would use a spike, stabbing into the dirt, pulling herself along. Each movement forward was shorter than the last one. Her hair hung before her face like a soiled curtain, flecked with bits of vomit and soaked with sweat. He could see her body tremble, her arms shake, and yet she pressed on.

Almost, she made it, but just before she reached him she collapsed and lay still.

"Yael," he tried to say, but only a gurgle came out. "Go back." More gurgles. "Please."

She rose, and with one last burst of strength she collapsed on his lap and reached behind him with her knife hand. Desperately she searched for the zip tie and found it, jamming the knife blade between it and the pole. He felt her body tighten as she rolled aside, still holding onto the knife, and the zip tie burst.

He was free.

Free, but too weak to move. How long he had been in the barrier, he couldn't tell. Too long, that was for sure. He could hardly turn his head to look at her. She had given her life for him, but it was only a gesture.

They would both die in the barrier.

"Get up Alex," his father said, kneeling by his side. "Wake up son. Time for school." A memory, and though it had not always been a fond one, it was so now.

"Move your ass soldier!" Sergeant Medlock shouted, towering over him imperiously. More recent, and less pleasant, but Alex smiled nonetheless. Medlock had tried to do right by his men in the only way he knew how, and Alex was grateful.

"Come on, man," Lieutenant Campbell said. "Medlock will see you slacking off." The voice of a friend, helping him along as he always had, and yet he had no strength with which to respond. Why did Yael have to do this? He had given up everything so that she could live, and now…

"Why?" he tried to say, and this time, it did come out.

"I…" Yael whispered softly, without moving her head. "Love…you." He felt her body tense, once more overcome with spasms. She did not have his tolerance, and she would not survive much longer. He had killed her.

"Sometimes," his mother said. "When no one else believes in you, you have to believe in yourself." It was the night of his high school prom, when his girlfriend had dumped him for a popular jock. "You're special, Alex, and I don't care if no one else sees it, because I see it. You will do something great one day. I know you will."

"You're going to die here," Bob said, leering. "You and your whore."

"Get up!" a voice shouted, though he was too far gone to make out who it was. Maybe he was talking to himself.

"I can't!" he cried. "I don't have the strength!"

"Yes you do! Fight it!" Was it a woman's voice? Was it her voice?

Alex grabbed the pole. He had no strength, and yet his arm moved.

"You can beat it! I know you can!"

He spun around, onto his knees, and stood. His body was frail and weak, and yet his legs carried his weight.

Reaching down, he grabbed Yael and heaved, slinging her over his shoulder. His legs were rubber, his arms were limp ropes, and yet they held, and they moved, driven by discipline, by hatred, by desperation and by love.

He willed one foot in front of the other, and it moved. Yael was too heavy, and he started to fall, but he pushed her body forward and kicked his foot out to catch himself. And it moved. It held, but he was still falling, so he did it again, and again. Each step brought some relief, and some more strength, and he realized that he was running.

Just like that, he was out. He set Yael down and dropped to his knees, panting. His stomach still burned, but it was the ache of cramping muscles, free of the effects of the barrier. She stirred, coughing. They both reeked of vomit. Their clothes were covered in it. Alex's shirt was flecked with blood, but there was less than he thought there would be.

He looked over at where Jonathan lay. She had hit him hard. His lifeless eyes were cloudy, staring up into the burning orb of the sun. The back of his head was a mess of blood and matted hair. Alex looked for his rifle, but didn't see it. He must have put it away at some point. The pistol Yael had taken was still by the pole, in the middle of the barrier.

"Alex," Yael gasped, climbing to her feet. "You have to go."

"I know," he said, helping her up. "Yael, what you did…" Yet another boundary crossed.

"No time," she said, shaking her head. "Go!"

"What about you?"

"I'll go back to my cabin, it's not far. Go now!"

"No, I can't just leave you!"

"Alex!" she barked. "Go or we'll both be killed! I can't follow you into the arms room, and it's the first place they're going to go." As if to validate her point, someone shouted in the distance. They had been spotted, and word would spread.

He turned and ran to the warehouse, sparing a long look back. She was moving slowly, limping, in the opposite direction. Within seconds she disappeared behind a corner and he was alone.

There was no one at the warehouse, at least not outside. Alex approached cautiously, then pulled one of the doors and risked a glance inside. Empty.

He was at the arms room door in seconds, pressing his finger to the pad. Had Max had time to lock him out? Was that even something he could do?

A chime sounded, the negative one. Alex's face paled, his heart thundered. Was this how it would end? They had both endured so much, only to be locked out of the only place that could offer salvation.

No. It couldn't be. He tried again. Negative chime.

Desperate, he looked at his finger. It was covered in vomit and grime. He looked for a clean spot on his clothing and found none, so he put the finger in his mouth and licked it clean. He didn't even notice the taste.

He tried again. Positive chime. The lock clicked open.

Alex bolted into the airlock corridor, clenching his fists impatiently.

"Come on, come on!" he cursed, glaring at the door behind him. It finally slid closed. Wasting no time, he pressed his thumb against the inner door.

A negative chime sounded.

"No!" he cried. "No, no, no!"

There had been no prick. He had missed the hole. He tried again, and the door opened.

Sighing with relief, he grabbed a rifle off the rack and dumped it on the table, then went through the aisles gathering equipment.

He was frantic, desperate. He had to get back out there before one of them hurt her.

There was no time to get fancy, so he put together a basic kit: modular tactical vest with plates, rifle, ten magazines, sidearm, some flashbangs and a few frag grenades. Just as he was about to leave, he decided to check the cameras. He pushed the chair away, leaned over the terminal and activated the security menu.

There was no one in the hallway, but two armed men were approaching the warehouse. He couldn't be sure, but they looked like Kristoff and Reynard. Returning to the menu, he selected the camera that overlooked Yael's cabin. The image flicked on, and he froze.

Her door was open, and a limp arm hung over the threshold. Her arm. Bob was walking away. The image was in color, and there was no mistaking the spreading area of red by the doorway.

Yael's blood. She wasn't moving.

I'll waste this fucking kike whore. Don't think I haven't wanted to since I met her.

He turned away, not willing to accept it. "No."

Unable to resist, he looked again, and nothing had changed, except her murderer was gone.

"Please god!" he cried, aware of the irony of his prayer. "Please no!" An image on a screen, and his life had lost all meaning. The world, devoid of all those teeming billions had seemed so full with her in it, but now it was empty. Completely, utterly empty. It wasn't a world he wanted to live in.

He had killed her. Not Bob, not Max, him. Alex. He had sent her to her death. She had insisted, but *he* was the soldier, he was the one who was supposed to know what to do. He started to cry. His body convulsed as strongly as it had in the barrier, but he stopped it, stopped the tears. There would be time for grief later. Now was the time for death.

He walked through the aisles again, this time paying attention. He picked what he needed, including a heavier but more effective armored vest. It was called Dragon Skin Mk II and it was made of small overlapping armored plates that offered greater coverage and increased mobility.

Long minutes passed as he prepared to leave the arms room.

He was carrying over a hundred pounds of gear, but it wasn't anything he hadn't done before. A steadily burning rage gave him all the strength he needed, enough to hardly feel the weight. He checked the cameras one more time. There was still no one in the hallway, but Reynard and Kristoff had taken positions outside, behind trees, pointing their rifles at the warehouse exit. They were waiting for him.

Returning to the computer, he brought up the security menu, unlocked the doors to his friends' cabins, then activated the PA system and spoke into the microphone.

"This is Alex." His voice was cold, alien. "Everyone, get in your homes and stay there, for your own safety. Max, the others…I'm coming for you. Pray, run, hide, it doesn't matter. Nothing can save you now." He released the talk button and headed for the airlock.

On his way out he saw his reflection in the mirror by the door. What was leaving that arms room was more tank than man, and the look of hatred in its eyes—his eyes—would have scared him, if he were still capable of fear.

Once he was in the hallway, he let his rifle hang free and took two fragmentation grenades from his vest. Holding one in each hand, he pulled the pins with his teeth, one at a time, taking great pains not to lose his grip. As long as he held the grenades, the spring loaded safety levers would remain attached, and they would not explode.

He paused by the side of the door, then kicked it open. Gunfire erupted almost immediately. Bullets slapped against the metal walls inside the warehouse and left dimples. The mystery metal was definitely not aluminum, more likely titanium. This was important information, especially now—titanium walls would stop bullets, aluminum walls might not. As the dimpled doors swung back, the gunfire stopped. As he had expected, the untrained fools had emptied their magazines and were now reloading. He stepped into the doorway and threw both grenades out as far as he could.

"Oh shit!" someone screamed as Alex pressed against the inside wall and covered his ears.

The ground shook with two nearly simultaneous detonations, like the grand finale of a fireworks extravaganza. He felt the shrapnel pepper the reverberating walls and, grabbing his rifle, burst through the doors.

He caught movement, and fixed on it. One of them was running into the jungle. He gave chase, and despite the weight of his gear, he quickly caught up to him. It was Kristoff. The stooge turned back to look at his pursuer and then tripped over an exposed root, dropping his rifle, which had no magazine in it. He wasn't wearing his body armor.

"Please don't…" Kristoff started to say as he lifted one hand over his face. The other hand moved towards his pistol. Alex didn't let him finish. He fired a long burst that struck Kristoff in the chest then walked up to his face, where the bullets tore open his jaw and left his head a ruined mess. Turning, Alex ran towards the warehouse, looking for Reynard. He saw some blood by one of the trees and immediately took cover behind the thickest trunk he could find. The crack of automatic rifle fire came from a nearby cabin. Leaves and bark showered down on his helmet as he raised his carbine and positioned his hand over the trigger of the underbarrel grenade launcher. He caught movement by the side of the cabin, aimed at the ground just beyond and fired. The weapon thumped as the 40mm projectile flew to its mark and exploded into a cloud of dust.

His protesting knees pushed Alex upright and he ran to the other side of the cabin, where he circled the corner until he saw Reynard, pressed against the wall, looking the other way through the dust. He heard Alex approach and whirled around, but it was too late. A long burst and he was down, his body limp save for his right foot that kicked feebly into the wall of the cabin as his blood rushed into the soil. Reynard had not discarded his armor, but repeated impacts had shattered the ballistic plates. Alex dropped his nearly empty magazine and replaced it. The smell of feces wafted from the corpse, from either a release of the bowels or a ruptured intestine.

He put a bullet in Reynard's head, just to be sure, then loaded another grenade into the M203 and headed towards Max's cabin—Burger King. Yael had thought up the name. He stopped for a moment, overcome with pain, but he forced himself to go on.

His PA message had apparently gotten through—he didn't see

anyone outside. Spotting the governor's cabin between two others, he was about to circle around to get a better look when he heard shots behind him and felt something slam into his lower back with almost enough force to knock him to his knees. It struck him just between the back and side plates of a standard IOTV body armor vest. He started to panic, afraid that he would die before he could exact his vengeance, but then he remembered that he was wearing Dragon Skin. The pain was intense, but the armor held. He whirled around, still moving, and fired, though he hadn't yet spotted anyone. Movement betrayed someone hiding just behind one of the cabins. Someone big. Bob.

Alex stopped running, turned around and started walking towards the man who had killed Yael. Bob peeked around the wall and tried to bring his weapon to bear, but Alex shot at him. The bullets bit into the wall of the cabin and Bob ducked out of sight.

Circling the other way, Alex cleared the corner just in time to see someone being shoved out of the cabin as Bob disappeared inside and closed the door behind him. The girl Bob had pushed out, the Goth that Max had forced into his bed, looked at Alex and her eyes widened. She cried out, scrambled to her feet and ran.

Alex walked around to the front of the cabin, then released his rifle and unslung the AT-4 rocket launcher that was strapped to his back. He backed away, and after looking over his shoulder to make sure that nothing and no one was behind him, he unfolded the sights and aimed the weapon at the wall near the door. Disengaging both safeties, he cocked the mechanical firing pin and pressed the trigger.

The weapon belched a cone of smoke and fire as the rocket's wake buffeted his face. His knees trembled from the blast as a flash of light flared from the side of the cabin, accompanied by a sharp crack so loud that a jolt of pain coursed through his ringing ears. Smoke and debris exploded in all directions as Alex dropped the empty launcher and took up his rifle, advancing towards the ruined building. He could barely make out a blackened hole in the wall through the smoke. The force of the explosion had blown out the door and all the windows. Bob was crawling out, one arm dragging limply by his side. His face was black, burned, ears bleeding.

Alex knelt over him and unclipped his weapon from the sling.

"I didn't kill…" Bob started to say, but didn't get to finish. Alex smashed his head with the butt of his rifle, raised it, hit him again, and again. He felt the skull give way as the head deformed under his blows. Dark blood flowed freely from Bob's ears and mouth.

A part of Alex was disgusted by what he had done, yet another part relished in his vengeance and thirsted for more.

"Two to go," he said, then heard gun fire. Turning around, he circled the smoke filled building for cover and saw Richard in Burger King's open doorway, shooting in the direction of the smoke. Alex took careful aim and fired once. Richard collapsed, screaming and clutching at his stomach. Lining up the red dot with his head, Alex remembered that Rich had been the one to activate the barrier. He waited a moment and let him feel the pain of his wound, then put him out of his misery with a bullet through the brain.

Max walked out of his cabin, unarmed, and stepped over Richard's lifeless body.

Alex approached him. He caught movement in the periphery of his vision and saw that there were several people watching from their cabin doors.

"I surrender," Max said confidently, raising his hands. "There is no need for anyone else to die here."

"You were dead the moment your dogs touched her," Alex said, then raised his rifle and emptied his nearly full magazine into Max's chest in one sustained burst. It nearly cut him in half. What was left of the governor lay twitching in the bloodstained grass.

Turning away from the carnage, he forced himself towards Yael's cabin. He saw the open door, the blood, but not the arm. Tom and Sandi were standing outside. As soon as they saw him, they ran to him, asking questions, saying things, but Alex didn't hear them.

As he got close to the house, he saw Barbara, leaning over Yael, and he stopped, staring in disbelief. Yael was moving, talking, as Barbara was wrapping her head in clean white bandages. She saw him and immediately got to her feet and ran towards him. Barbara was forced to let go of the bandage, which trailed behind

Yael like the tail of a kite.

"Oh, Alex!" she cried as she jumped into his arms. "You're alive!"

He held her tightly and wept. She was alive. Nothing else mattered.

Chapter 30

"We should get going," she said, still holding him. "The others are waiting."

"I thought I lost you," he said, unable to release her. The frosted windows lit the room with morning's light, banishing the comforting darkness. Too exhausted to talk or make love, they had slept through what remained of the day and all of the night. The radio broke their slumber moments ago, when Tom announced that he had successfully hacked into the server that controlled Max's terminal.

"I thought I lost you too," she said as her body tensed, then shuddered slightly before relaxing. "In fact I was sure of it. Until I saw you in there. How did you survive for so long?" She stroked his head, her eyes fixed on his hair, as though she were counting the strands.

He shrugged. "It didn't seem like a long time, maybe a couple of minutes."

"You were in there for just over twenty minutes!"

"Really?"

"Yeah," she said, shaking her head. "You amaze me sometimes."

"You came for me," he said. "You crawled through the barrier. You could have died. What do you say to someone who does that for you?"

"There's nothing to say. What you did…"

He cringed. "Yael, I'm very sorry, I lost control." Their dead and deformed faces haunted him, especially Bob's. The brutality of what he had done was too much, and he wasn't sure how much longer he could stand the images without bursting into tears.

"Don't be sorry," she said. "Don't ever be sorry, not for that."

"You don't…" he started to say, unable to get it out. "I mean you don't think I'm…"

"I think you're a hero. You saved us all. Some of the others might not see it that way at first, but eventually they'll come around."

"Heroes don't cave in people's heads. I could have let some of them live. Kristoff begged for his life." Even as he had reached for his weapon, but that didn't matter now, not when it was guilt's turn at the wheel.

"And the ones you spared could have shot you in the back," she said. "You let them *all* live, remember? And how did they repay you? Did even one of them say 'don't do that Max, that's not right'?"

"I guess not," he said, grateful to whatever god or force of the universe that had kept her from harm. He didn't think he could deal with what he had done without her support. Her head was still bandaged, but the wound was small, and there was no concussion. Bob had hit her with the butt of his rifle as soon as she walked into her cabin. He could have easily killed her, but he had chosen not to for reasons Alex would never know, or understand. He doubted it was anything benevolent, considering what he knew of the man.

"What about you?" he asked. "Are you okay? About Jonathan?"

Her eyes welled with tears. "I didn't mean to hit him that hard." He instantly regretted his words. What a bastard he was, to try to find comfort in shared guilt!

"It doesn't matter," he said quickly. "I would have killed him if he'd survived. You are without blame."

She shook her head, but managed to smile. "Thank you for trying."

"I'm just so sorry it had to come to that." She nodded, and they lay still for moment. The dog sighed contentedly from the base of the bed. Alex was glad that it had stayed out of sight during the troubles. He wasn't sure what Max's goons would have done to it.

"Shall we?" she said finally.

They got dressed and left his cabin, armed only with pistols. With Max and his men gone, there was no need to walk around like they were in a war zone. Tom had taken charge of securing all of the weapons from the battle, and there had been plenty. The only threat now would most likely come from outside the barrier. Or through whatever lines of communication the "government" used to access the colony.

As they walked to the former governor's house he noticed the stares, different from anything he had seen before. Some looked at him with fear, others awe. Most were a combination of the two. No one wanted to meet his gaze, and most took a step back, or went in a different direction when they saw him coming.

"Alex," someone said. "Um, Captain Meyer, sir?"

He stopped and turned, and saw a familiar face. The man was lanky, with wavy brown hair.

"You're the guy from the boat building detail, right?" Alex asked.

"Yes sir," the man said nervously. "Name's Joe."

"Just call me Alex. What can I do for you?"

The man shifted his weight apprehensively. "Well, I was wondering if it would be okay to get started working on the boats again, maybe with the same people. I know most of them would want to do it, and with the amount of fish the one boat is bringing in…"

"Sure," Alex said. Why was he even asking? "Of course you can. I was going to put you in charge of that anyway. You were the only one who really knew what the fuck he was doing over there. Do whatever you think is best. I'd like at least three more boats built, considering how many people we have."

Joe smiled. "Great! I'll get started right away. Thank you!" He headed off towards the beach, obviously excited.

"You're going to have to get used to that," Yael said.

"What?"

"People turning to you for leadership."

"Yeah," he muttered. "Serves me right, I guess."

When they were in sight of their destination, Alex turned to look at the house Bob had tried to hide in. It was gutted. Windows shattered, interior destroyed. The Goth girl walked out, carrying a broken food dispenser. She was trying her best to clean the place, and judging by her haggard features, she hadn't slept.

"Miss," Alex said. She startled, then turned to see who had spoken and gasped, freezing in place.

"It's okay," Alex continued. "We'll get you a new house. What's your name?"

"Gigi," she said apprehensively.

"Well, Gigi, as soon as I get to Burger…I mean the governor's house, I'll have Tom reprogram the locks on one of the vacant cabins. I'm sorry about yours. You can let him know which one you want…there are plenty to choose from." Because he had killed a lot of people, but he had the good sense not to say that out loud.

She seemed surprised. "Thanks."

He nodded, then resumed his trek to Burger King.

Tom was seated at the Terminal, and the others stood around him. Including Wawa.

"I went and got him," Barbara explained. "As soon as we finished cleaning up the mess."

"Sorry about that," Alex said. "I didn't mean to cause so much damage."

"No way," Barbara said, shaking her head emphatically. "They deserved it."

"It was fucking awesome!" Ryan said, then noticed how the others looked at him and reddened. "Sorry sir, I don't mean to make light of it."

"No problem. I'm just glad none of us were hurt."

"Chief," Tom said. "Sorry to interrupt your guilt trip, but you're going to want to hear this."

"First things first," Alex said. "How did Yael get out of her cabin?" He had asked her the day before, but all she knew was that her door hadn't been locked when she tried it. "I can't believe Max would have been so careless, especially after how I fucked up trying to lock him in." Saying his name was strange. He had gotten so used to complaining about him when he was alive that it was hard to adjust to him not being around. It was even harder to adjust to the fact that he had murdered him.

Tom leaned back in the chair and grinned. "Remember when I told him I couldn't get into the cameras?"

"Yeah…"

"Well I lied. I was already in. But I didn't have full access yet, not to the other stuff."

"So he gave you his password! You clever bastard!"

"That's right," Tom agreed. "I am a clever bastard. But I only had time to do two things. One was to reprogram our cabin locks to no longer respond to an override, though of course I had to make it look like they did."

"What was the other thing?" Alex asked.

Tom's smile deepened. "You're gonna love this one, Chief. I lowered the intensity of the barrier."

"That's how you survived!" Yael said excitedly.

"I tried to lower it to the same levels we use when we go through it," Tom continued. "But there was no way to do that and hide it, so I just kept trying numbers until I got the lowest one it would take without triggering an alert, which was seventy one percent."

"That's still pretty high," Yael muttered.

"Yeah," Alex agreed. "But it's a lot better than a hundred. Tom, I don't know what to say."

"If you want to thank me," Tom said. "Then shut up and hear me out. I found a lot of stuff on the servers. I think we have enough to piece it all together. What really happened, I mean."

Chapter 31

"Okay," Tom said, wringing his hands. "So the way this terminal is set up, you're not supposed to be able to access the backend, the server, but there are always open ports, and I was able to write a simple program to piggy back on data packets and upload a copy of itself. Once it was there, I had a two way connection and was able to poke around. This is very simple stuff, hacking 101 if you will. They had no firewall, rudimentary passwords…these people really didn't expect anyone like me around."

"I guess they think they have no one to hide it from," Alex said.

"And they're right," Tom said. "Who am I gonna call? The press? The UN?"

"Be that as it may," Alex said. "There's still us, and maybe, thanks to you, we can learn the truth. I'm glad you chose to be a fake biochemist, Tom. If you hadn't, none of us would have had a chance at getting the data. Ports, packets. I have no idea what the hell you're talking about."

"I'll second that," Barbara added. "To borrow the cliché, it's all Greek to me."

"It's weird to be appreciated," Tom said, smiling. "But I like it. So anyway, once I was in there, the first thing I did was to figure out where 'there' was. California. Marin County, to be precise, in what used to be Federal park land. I gotta tell ya, Chief, they sure know how to pick 'em. That's some beautiful country up there."

"So that place," Alex said. "That's where the people who built this facility are? The ones we've been calling 'the government'?"

"Yep," Tom said. "That's them."

"Okay, what else did you find out? Who did this? Why?"

"Not so fast, Chief. I don't know any of those things. But that doesn't mean we can't piece it together. I mean…I've got my theories based on what I know, but my head's been reeling, so I'm not the clearest thinker right now."

"Alright then, lay it on us." Alex wasn't sure he'd be a particularly clear thinker either. His thoughts were churning too fast, out of control. They were discussing the destruction of all of human civilization. He didn't think any of them had yet wrapped their heads around it. He wondered how long it would take for them to truly accept it, and whether that acceptance would be measured in months or years.

"Okay," Tom continued. "I found a bunch of shit. First, the water bears that Fonseca made. I found data on them. Patent filings. They're called Fonseca 'WasteAway' ED REV 3 Transports, U.S. Patent number...um....I forgot. Doesn't matter. The patent files are full of details, but there's little there that we haven't already figured out except technical stuff. So basically, yay us, we were right…mostly."

"So they're not a weapon like we thought," Yael said, her brow furrowing. "They're a waste disposal system?"

"Yep," Tom said. "At least they were, originally. Genetically modified tardigrades that organically synthesize fast acting nanotech disassemblers that target substances found in our building materials, like calcium oxide, aluminum oxide, and so on. They make the shit like we make mucus and store it in an inert state. Until triggered, they breed like normal water bears, only faster. That makes them self replicating. And until they kill themselves releasing their payload, they're nearly indestructible. Hot, cold, doesn't matter. Like real water bears they can even survive in a vacuum.

"They also communicate, in a rudimentary way. Each one is like a tiny relay…passing information to the one next to it through bioelectromagnetism—that's a mouthful, ain't it?"

"But I thought we established that nanorobotics is science fiction," Barbara protested. "It doesn't exist!"

"Neither do fusion generators the size of minivans," Tom pointed out. "And yet we have one here."

"But the water bears are too big to be nanomachines."

"Right," Tom said. "But we're talking about the stuff they secrete. Those are the nanomachines."

"But how can they build anything that small?" Barbara asked. "If the technology existed we would have seen it in the civilian sector, or at least parts of it! The applications in medicine…can you imagine? Little robots in your body fixing things, killing cancer cells?"

"I've heard of bacteria that eat oil," Yael said. "It's not that farfetched. Nanomachines can be organic. They don't have to be actual metal robots."

"But that doesn't make sense," Alex said. "The whole waste disposal thing. Why did they dissolve people then?"

"Organic waste?" Barbara suggested.

Alex shook his head. "It seems to have only targeted people, not other animals. The jungles around us are full of life."

"Well," Tom said. "Like I said, there's data. There is data on a version of these things that targets human DNA. No patent notes, no legal stuff, just research. Overcoming body chemistry, getting them to target the brain first, distribution patterns, and activation."

"No patent notes," Yael said. "That means they made them in secret."

"If there were body chemistry issues," Barbara said. "Then that would explain why some people are completely or partially immune."

"Wait," Alex said. "You mean like…these transport things can't survive in some people's body chemistry, and they tried to overcome that? That's important. That speaks to their motive."

"I can't tell you that for sure," Tom said. "I only have research notes about the degrees of resistance of various body chemistries. Test procedures, results, that sort of thing."

"It's still not adding up," Yael said. "It seems like Fonseca made these things for waste disposal. That makes sense, because, that's a huge industry. Billions in potential profits, not to mention environment issues. And maybe they lost control of them and they spread everywhere, and being water bears, they were impossible to kill. But…why would they make ones that target people? Deliberately?"

"Let's wait until we have more pieces of the puzzle," Alex said. "Then maybe we can make it add up. Tom? What else? You mentioned something about distribution patterns?"

"Yeah. There are detailed plans on their servers for distributing these things all over the world. There's a lot of emphasis on making sure they get absolutely everywhere."

"Who are they, exactly?" Alex asked.

"About what you'd expect," Tom said glumly. "There are fancy ways to put it, but in the paradise they built in Marin County it's rich old bastards and their families, and whatever politicians they had in their pockets."

"Figures," Alex said. He could picture road blocks and park rangers telling people "this section of the park is closed, sir, please take the detour over there," while helicopters ferried in supplies and work crews. Crews that wouldn't have had a clue they were engineering their own deaths, and those of their families.

"What about Fonseca?" Yael said. "When did their involvement cease? Or did it? The nutrient power canisters, the enzyme detergent…is that a coincidence?"

"It doesn't appear to be. From what I can tell, they were involved the whole time. It was the others that came into it sometime after the WasteAway transports were created."

"Back to the distribution thing," Alex said. "You're saying these people, Fonseca and…what do we call them? The government?"

"Seems accurate," Tom said. "I have access to personnel data. There are a lot of politicians in that facility."

"Okay, the government. So Fonseca and the government distributed these things all over the world on purpose?"

"Yes."

"How? Wouldn't someone have noticed? I mean…how do they drop them on Russia without starting a world war?"

"They didn't drop them, Chief. The servers are full of information on network theory. They're self replicating, remember?"

"Network theory?" Yael said. "You mean like Vespignani and Barabási's work?"

"That's right," Tom said, brightening. "You're a mathematician. Maybe you'd better explain this part?"

"Like…right now?"

"Why not?"

"I'll give it a shot," she said. "You ever heard of six degrees of separation?"

"The Kevin Bacon thing?" Alex asked.

She smiled. "Yes, the Kevin Bacon thing. The idea is that everyone in the world is connected to everyone else by six steps or less. So like if you pick a random guy somewhere in the world, then pick another guy, the first guy will know someone who knows someone else, who knows someone else, et cetera, until we get to someone that knows the second one you picked. You could pick a random guy in some jungle in Africa and a Wall Street Lawyer and there are still only six people between them."

"Is that really true?" Barbara asked.

"It was," Yael said grimly, then frowned and shook her head, as though to clear it of unpleasant thoughts. "It didn't always work, but it worked almost all the time, like over ninety nine percent."

"That's interesting and all," Alex said. "But what does it have to do with these things?"

"It has to do with distribution points," she said. "Imagine a football field full of people, standing shoulder width apart. You are on one end, and Tom is on the other, and you want to get a message to him. How do you do that?"

"Um," Alex said, thinking. "Assuming it's too loud to yell, I can ask the dude next to me to ask the dude next to him, and so on, until it gets to Tom. But that's not six steps."

"Right," she said. "It's a lot of steps, takes a long time, and the message will get garbled going through that many hops. That's what each step is called…a hop. Now say you have a cell phone, and another guy at the other end has a cell phone too."

"I can call him," Alex said. "And he can pass the message to Tom, and it will take fewer steps…I mean hops."

"Very good. Not only can you talk to Tom quicker, but all the people on opposite ends of the field can talk to each other faster by going through you and the other guy with the phone. In network theory, the people with the phones would be called hubs."

"Like a network hub?" Barbara asked.

"Exactly," Yael said. "A hub is a point in a network where lines of connection intersect or cross. Hubs exist everywhere, even in nature and human social networks. The popular guy that everyone knows, he's a hub. If you want to find someone in school, you go to the popular guy, and he'll get you connected to the person you want much faster than if you ask people in series. And when hubs connect to other hubs, the number of connections increases exponentially."

"An airport," Alex said. "That would be like a hub, right? And they connect to other airports, which are also hubs." His mind protested the conversation—the things they were talking about no longer existed and that should make him withdraw and shut down while he processed the grief he should be feeling. It wasn't difficult, however, to put that knowledge aside and ignore it. People were, after all, creatures of habit.

"Yes," she said. "If you wanted to infect people with a virus that spreads through contact, you would infect one person in an airport. That airport links millions of people with thousands of places, either directly or through other airports, other hubs."

"So that's how they spread them," Alex said, finally understanding. "They put them in one or two airports, and in a short period of time people carry them everywhere in the world."

"More like several hundred airports," Tom said. "But yeah."

"And no one noticed these things?"

"How could they?" Tom said. "If you see one of these things by accident, you'll think it's a water bear, which are more harmless and inconsequential than dust mites. In any case, we know no one noticed, because it worked."

"So why were some things untouched? I don't mean natural substances, I mean like the boat we used. Glass, plastic, aluminum…it has all of these things."

"Easy," Tom said. "It's because—"

"Wait," Alex said. "Because they hadn't been used for a long time, right? That boat was covered up and put away…no one went on it in months, so no way to spread them. Right?"

"You got it, Chief."

"And the two who attacked us in Honolulu? Body chemistry?"

Tom shrugged. "That, or they might not have interacted with anyone. Hermits, survivalists. Two of them together…odds are both were not immune."

"So then we can count on more survivors," Alex said.

"Sure, plenty. Hundreds, maybe thousands. Spread across the world, I mean."

"That's why they gave us the weapons," Alex said. "To protect ourselves from them. If they found out what happened, they'd be really pissed, and I doubt they'd wait long enough before trying to kill us to hear our side of it. To them, we'd be part of it. That must also be why they gave us the barrier."

"Not so fast, Chief," Tom said. "The barrier was never designed as a barrier, at least not for people."

"What then?"

"It was designed to kill *them*. The transports. Destroys their nervous systems, even on low intensity The nausea and death thing was just a fringe benefit. That's why they gave the terminals the ability to adjust its intensity, but not to turn it off completely."

"They must have brought us through the barrier on its low setting," Alex said. "Like decontamination. We must have been covered in those things."

"Yeah."

"Okay," Alex said. "So now we know that Fonseca made a nanotech waste disposal system that ended up as a weapon. We know our government got involved and came up with a plan to distribute these things all over the world, and at some point, created a version that targets human DNA, presumably working with Fonseca. And we know they set up this facility to save a bunch of people based on their stupid IQ tests and who the fuck knows what else...wait a minute!"

"What is it, Chief?"

"NTF103-B," Alex said.

"What?" Yael asked.

"It's what they called my current assignment in my general orders," Alex explained. "NTF103-B. One hundred and three. That means there are at least one hundred and two others out there."

"Let's find out!" Tom said. He turned to the terminal and started pressing keys. "Interesting." The screen was reflected in his eyes as they moved back and forth, taking it in. His fingers moved with incredible speed and precision. "You're right chief. There's a shit ton of data on this."

"How much time do you need?"

"Hang on."

Yael and Patrick leaned over Tom's shoulders and stared at the screen as he worked.

"Okay," Tom said. "Lots of shit here. Project New Tomorrow, it's called."

"NTF," Alex said. "New Tomorrow Facility. Also, the program I use...NTCN. New Tomorrow Communication Network, probably."

"Yep," Tom said. "You got it."

"I wonder what or where 103-A is," Sandi muttered. She noticed the others looking at her and quickly added. "I mean...we're 103-B. So...where's A? Maybe it's nearby."

"Good question," Barbara agreed.

"Nowhere," Tom said, still typing and scanning the screen. "The A and B are facility types. There's no 103-A...but 102 can be either A or B. Does that make sense?"

"Sure," she said. "But what are the types?"

"B refers to a coastal facility meant to rely mainly on fishing, like this one, while A is an inland facility. Farming, that sort of stuff." He pushed some more keys and moved the mouse around. "We seem to be the only facility in Hawaii. The nearest one is on the mainland."

"Okay," Alex said. "So now we know something else that's important. They not only spread these things all over the world, but they created a bunch of these little colonies and populated them with handpicked people."

"Right," Tom said.

"And the barrier keeps the weapon from destroying the colonies."

"Yep."

"I was ready to go with Yael's idea that Fonseca lost control and these things spread all over the world," Alex said. "But with all the info we have now, it's starting to look like deliberate genocide," Alex said.

"No," Yael said. "Much more than that. Not only genocide, but the complete destruction of all human civilization, except for whatever they chose to protect. Who—" Her voice cracked, but she swallowed and regained her composure. "Who would do such a thing? It's evil on an unimaginable scale."

"Well," Tom said. "Let's be careful about jumping to conclusions. We don't know everything."

"Don't we?" Alex said. "We know that Fonseca made a waste disposal technology that was used to wipe out human civilization.

We know it was bolstered to go after people, and we know who is responsible, because they are the ones sitting in Marin County."

"But we don't know why," Yael said. "I can't even begin to imagine why. No sane mind can conceive of a reason to do such a thing."

"Who says they're sane?" Alex said. "Aren't all politicians and billionaires sociopaths and maybe even psychopaths, to one degree or another? Does it really matter why?"

"It might," Tom said. "If there were a compelling reason. Just because we can't figure it out, doesn't mean there isn't one."

Alex shook his head. "No. It doesn't matter. They murdered our families. They destroyed our world, and they stuck us in these colonies and they continue to pull our strings, telling us how to live. We know what we need to know."

A resolution was forming in the back of his mind, fragments of semi-conscious thought coalescing into a plan of action. He tried to put it from his mind, because as it became clear, so did its price. And it was too high.

Chapter 32

Yael was difficult. They fought by day, made fierce love by night. She alternated between demanding that he stay and insisting that she come along, which was out of the question. He would not let her throw her life away along with his. In the end, he knew that she understood, and that she would not stop him. She had her shiva, he would have his vengeance.

More than once, he almost called the whole thing off. It would be so easy to convince himself that this was bigger than him, that there was nothing that one man could do, and that a futile gesture was not worth his life. The worst part was that all those things were true, and yet when it came down to it, he couldn't stop himself. He knew that he had to go, had to try to make things right. When he thought Yael had been killed, he had acted on pure instinct, fulfilling the need for justice, or revenge or whatever label best applied to what he had done. This was his essential nature, and he could not resist it, not then, and not now. He tried his best not to think about how much he wanted to stay and be with her, but to change his mind would be to become someone else, and that was the one thing he could not do, not even for her.

It took nearly four days to get the boat ready. He had thought to take the big trawler, but Barbara did the calculations and the two hundred gallons of stale diesel in its tanks wouldn't be nearly enough to get him the twenty five hundred miles to California. The old sailboat was a completely different matter. Its small twenty seven horsepower Volvo burned half a gallon an hour compared to the trawler's four or five, and it's maximum speed, seven knots, was only three knots slower than the larger vessel's.

Transporting the extra fuel posed a problem—the sailboat had a thirty gallon tank—until they re-tasked some nutrient powder canisters for the job. The powder was easily stored in other containers, such as equipment bags from the arms room. Once they got the mast up and repaired the rigging, the boat offered the added advantage of being able to rely on the wind should the diesel fail.

Alex was no sailor, but he learned the essentials by sailing along the coast while getting ready.

"I want you to tell them," he said to Tom on the evening of the second day. He had just finished fighting with Yael, and she had stormed off to wait for him in his cabin.

"Tell who what?" Tom asked.

"The other colonies. Get word to them. You can do that, can't you?"

"Are you sure, Chief? It could cause big problems for those people. Maybe they're better off not knowing." It was a good point, but Alex couldn't bring himself to deny to others what he and his team had worked so hard to learn.

"Yeah, I'm sure," he said, and Tom sent the message out to every facility he could reach.

"Godspeed, Chief," he said when it was done.

The time to depart came too soon, in what seemed like a blur of agonizing indecision and rushed preparation. He had already said his goodbyes to the others, sharing tearful embraces, and faced Yael, alone. She had ferried him to the moored vessel on their powerboat.

"How do I say goodbye?" he asked, holding her tightly.

"Don't," she pleaded, eyes full of tears. "You can still change your mind. This is a crazy idea. Or at least take me with you."

"We've been through this, Yael. So many times."

"Well not enough, dammit! You're still going!"

"Take care of the team," he said. "Work with Barbara. Don't be like I was with Max. Remember, if you two don't agree and Tom sides with her, you have to go along." It was the way he'd set things up—Yael in charge of the "military," Barbara filling Max's role, with Tom as a tie breaker if they ever disagreed. It wasn't a perfect system, but with the three of them it would work, and work well. The only hitch was that not even Tom could reprogram the arms room without being in the arms room itself, and Alex proved impossible when Tom tried to teach him what to do. They had contented themselves with taking a bunch of rifles, ammunition and other supplies and storing them in one of the vacant cabins keyed to Yael's DNA.

"I will," she said. "Until you come back. Then you will take charge. Got it?"

"I love you," he said. "More than I know how to say."

"And I love you. More than I know how to live without."

"I'm not going there to die, Yael. That thing can reach almost a mile out, and I've been practicing." He eyed the big Barrett that they had set in the boat's cockpit on top of his Dragon Skin vest. "Besides, depending on what I find, this will most likely just be a recon mission. Maybe I'll scout the facility, decide that there is nothing I can do, and come back to get the rest of you." He wasn't lying just to make her feel better, but there was something about what he had told her that didn't feel right. It was the truth, as far as he understood it. In all likeliness, there wouldn't be much he would be able to do alone. And yet, in the pit of his stomach he harbored the certainty that he would never come back for any of them, that he would complete the mission on his own or die trying. And he wasn't sure why.

"I know," she said. "It's all I have left. I'll wait for you. As long as it takes."

"Give me two months," he said. "Then move on. Live your life."

She grimaced. "My life. I've already lost everything—everyone—I've ever loved, except you. And now…"

"I'll come back, Yael," he said. "If there's any way, no matter what, I'll come back."

He kissed her, fiercely, tasting the salt of her tears, then climbed over the side and onto the sailboat, his new home for the estimated fourteen day trip to California. She gave him one last long look and gunned the throttle, leaving the sailboat rolling in her wake.

* * *

At first he spent his time worrying that the diesel would give out and he would have to put to use what little he'd learned about sailing. Eventually he decided to raise the sails despite the motor, when the wind was right, to help it along and save fuel. After a day of that, he felt brave enough to kill the diesel while the sailing was good, which firmed up his confidence in the craft to the point where he stopped worrying. He had about forty gallons more than the trip was supposed to take, and if he cut his consumption by sailing as much as possible he might even have enough for the trip back.

Living on board the boat wasn't terrible, once he got past his seasickness and the fear that came with knowing there was nothing but a hostile empty ocean for an ever increasing number of miles all around him. When he first lost sight of the coast he had to fight panic and the urge to turn around for what seemed like hours, but eventually he adapted.

The thirty two foot cruiser had once been nicely appointed, and though it was neglected and run down, it was still comfortable. His greatest challenge was loneliness and boredom. Once he figured out how to use the windvane—a type of mechanical autopilot that maintained a constant angle to the wind—the boat practically sailed itself with occasional minor adjustments. The boat's GPS still worked, making navigation a breeze, and keeping an eye out was pointless as he had the ocean pretty much to himself. He occupied his time with fishing, though even that proved a poor distraction. It seemed as though the moment he cast out a lure, something bit.

The weather was fair for the first few days, but towards the evening of the fourth, the wind picked up and the sea became choppy, then violent. The wind howled and rain beat against the fiberglass deck. Nervously watching the flashes of lightning all around him, he remembered what Barbara had said to him.

Sailboats can't sink unless the hull breaks on a rock. If they flip over they'll pop right back up unless you're dumb enough to leave the hatch open in a storm. The worst that can happen is the rigging will fail and you'll lose your mast.

"That sounds pretty fucking bad right now," he said to himself. "Especially if it falls on my head." At that moment, a particularly bright flash off the left side—the port side—made him fearful of touching the stainless steel wheel.

"She never mentioned lightning strikes," he grumbled, wondering what would happen if the mast were hit—it was pretty high up there, at least fifty feet. Not daring to leave the helm until the storm subsided, he spent a terrifying night fighting the wind and waves. In the morning the storm blew over, and after setting the windvane, he enjoyed the first uninterrupted sleep he'd had since he set foot aboard the boat.

The days passed slowly, and he spent most of his time looking back instead of forward. The hardest part was resisting the impulse to go home. Panic was replaced by doubt. What sort of fool's errand had he set for himself? What was he trying to accomplish? He could picture Yael standing on the beach, looking out for the boat, hoping he would turn it around. Fighting the urge to do so became almost unbearable. Every time he came close to giving in, he reminded himself that the people in that facility had killed his family, and Yael's family. Everyone's family. That gave him the resolve he needed.

His only truly pleasurable pastime, and one he indulged in at least once a day, was target practice with the Barrett 50. Alex was no sniper. The greatest range at which he had been trained was three hundred meters, which was the standard distance that an infantryman was expected to be able to hit a man sized target without the aid of telescopic sights. He had never been much for hunting, but he had owned a bolt action rifle before joining the army and enjoyed long range target shooting with a scope. In Upstate New York, long range meant a couple of hundred meters at best, though his targets were usually small, sometimes as small as bottle caps.

Without the slightest trace of environmental guilt, he would toss a piece of junk he'd packed for this purpose over the side, and then use a laser range finder to gauge its distance. Once it was far enough away, he would put the fifty caliber rifle on its bipod, aim, adjust for the wind and elevation, and fire. At first, his shots were way off. Fortunately, the big splashes the rifle made allowed him to see exactly where he had hit—provided it was within the scope's field of view—and by the tenth day, he was able to hit a drifting target the size of a man's torso at over a thousand meters off of a moving boat. He knew he should be adjusting for the Coriolis effect—the difference between the Earth's rotation and the bullet's flight path—but he didn't know how to do that and it didn't seem to make much of a difference. All in all, not too bad, and it would do just fine for what he was planning.

According to the GPS, he was progressing slower than he had

estimated, mostly due to his fuel saving measures. By his rough calculations he would make landfall in California in a total of sixteen rather than fourteen days. On the flipside, he was consuming more fuel than the half gallon per hour the engine was supposed to burn. Not much more, but it was enough to mean he would have to sail most of the way back. The engine was old, and he was fortunate that it worked as reliably as it did.

On day eleven, an alarm buzzed. He had no idea where it was coming from until a quick check of his instrument panel revealed that the engine was overheating. He had the sails up, so he reduced the throttle to idle and got the checklist that Barbara had made for him.

"*Exhaust water*," he read, then looked over the transom to see if there was water spurting out of the exhaust pipe. The diesel was raw water cooled—an impeller pump sucked sea water through heat exchange passages in the engine and pumped it back out to sea with the exhaust. As long as there was water coming out of the exhaust pipe, the system was operating normally. There was, so that was one item out of the way.

"*Oil pressure*," he continued. Looking at the gauge, he noticed that it was in fact very low. He killed the engine, then went below to check the oil level. Almost empty! He had found his culprit. Checking the bilge, he found it full of oil. He had a leak!

After waiting an hour for it to cool completely, he started the engine again, then went below with a flashlight. He found the source of the leak—oil was dripping from the air filter cones. He removed the cones and watched the engine at work at various throttle speeds. It was spitting oil, probably from combustion pressure leaking through scored piston walls or worn rings.

He killed the engine again, then searched all the numerous storage compartments for spare oil. This was something he should have checked for before setting out, but he had been too preoccupied.

He finally found four one quart bottles in a small nook under the alcohol burning stove. The motor took two bottles to bring it back to an acceptable level, which solved his overheating problem. Experimenting with various throttle levels, he found that if he kept the motor below 1500 RPM it didn't spit any oil, at least that he could notice, which was good enough. This close to his destination, the resulting decrease in speed would add less than a day to his trip, and he still had his engine. Not too shabby for someone who didn't know anything about boats.

On the morning of the seventeenth day, he spotted the coast. It was cold and foggy, reducing visibility to under a mile, which didn't give him much time to figure out how to get to shore. There was no way to beach the sailboat, its keel was four and a half feet under the water, which meant he had to find a safe place to anchor and take the folding rowboat he had found on the trawler ashore. The boat was small, which meant several trips to bring his gear, and he only had the one oar.

Just as he was about to start looking for a sheltered anchorage on the GPS map, he heard the growl of an outboard motor and saw a boat headed towards him. He didn't have binoculars, so he took the Barrett and looked through its scope. A powerboat was rapidly approaching with two men on board, both wearing camouflage fatigues and carrying M4 carbines. Soldiers, and they were headed right for him.

Chapter 33

Their boat was a rigid inflatable with two powerful outboards, the kind used by the Coast Guard for intercepting drug runners. It was pretty big, about twenty five feet long with a wide beam and an enclosed pilothouse. One of the soldiers was in the enclosure, driving, while the other was out on deck near the bow, looking at Alex through a pair of binoculars. The soldier noticed he was watching him and reached for his carbine.

"Not like this," Alex pleaded. "At least give me a fucking chance!" Why would they patrol the coast? They thought they had killed everyone who was a real threat to them.

The boat was cutting through the water at an impressive speed and would be in rifle range in seconds—Alex had no time to lose. He reached for a magazine, stuck it in the Barrett, then chambered a round and looked into the scope, trying to sight in on the outboards. One hit from a .50 caliber bullet would easily disable one of the motors, perhaps even both if he got the angle right. Then he could deal with the men on board at his leisure. But the boat was moving very fast, and making the shot would be extremely difficult.

When he panned across the front of the boat, he noticed something odd. The soldier on the bow was holding his rifle over his head, pointing at the sky. There was something white tied to the barrel, flapping violently in the wind generated by the boat's movement.

A white flag?

The soldier was waving the rifle side to side. Alex hesitated, not sure about what to do. Prudence dictated he fire anyway, but he couldn't bring himself to pull the trigger. He was a killer, that much was certain, but he didn't think of himself as a murderer, and killing men who were trying to signal a truce would be murder. He tried not to think about what he had done to Max and his goons, and what that meant for that particular aspect of his self image.

He set the big rifle down and picked up his M4, holding it at the ready as the approaching vessel slowed and pulled up alongside. As their boat got closer, Alex noticed the captain's rank insignia on the man in the vessel's bow, along with the "US MARINES" on his pocket. He had Asian features and a small black goatee, which was against regulations. Or rather, it used to be.

"Captain Meyer?" the man called out over the diminishing gurgle of the outboards as the boat slowed to keep pace. Alex throttled back his own engine, reducing the ambient noise even further.

"Yeah," Alex said testily. "Who's asking?"

"Captain Takahashi," the man said. "Formerly Sergeant, United States Marine Corps, currently New Tomorrow Facility 079-A, in Southern Cali. Not quite Hawaii, but it has its charms."

Alex wrinkled his brow, confused. "You mean you're not from the…um…government?" He felt stupid saying it, but he didn't know what else to call them.

"If I were," the man said with a grin. "You'd be dead." He looked down at the Barrett. "Or I'd be dead. And since no one is dead…"

"Right," Alex agreed. He exhaled slowly, relieved.

"My friend," Takahashi said, pointing to the pilothouse. "Is Captain Linnard, formerly Corporal Linnard, US Army. Now he's with 089-B in Washington state." Linnard was a tall dark haired man with bright blue eyes. He waved at Alex from the pilothouse, then came out and walked over to stand next to the much shorter Takahashi.

"How do you know who I am?" Alex asked. "You couldn't have read my name tag, my rifle was blocking it."

"We were expecting you," he said.

"Expecting me? How?"

"Your friend, Tom, we've been in contact with him. Ever since he sent out word about what's happened."

"Tom?" Alex asked incredulously. "That fucking guy blows my mind sometimes. You said 'we,' did you mean you and Linnard? Or are there more?"

"I think it's best if you just anchored this thing, grabbed your gear and came with us. It's easier to show you."

"Not until I know what's going on."

"Tom said to call you 'Chief' and to tell you that you could trust us," Takahashi explained with a shrug. He was of average height, but looked tiny standing next to his companion. Linnard wasn't overly muscular, but neither was he particularly slender. He towered over Takahashi like a bear standing next to a wolf.

"Fine," Alex agreed. "I'll go with you, as long as you don't expect me to disarm." If Tom believed that these men were trustworthy, then odds are they were trustworthy—or very good liars. Tom should be able to spot the difference, considering what he used to do for a living.

"Not at all. You'll need your weapons." That last bit could have been construed as a threat, except that Takahashi's tone suggested nothing of the kind.

It took the better part of an hour to find a good place to anchor, secure the boat and transfer his gear to the other vessel, but less than five minutes at full throttle to get the three of them to their destination, a tiny beach around the tip of a narrow peninsula. It was a very secluded area. Stark stone cliffs towered over the sand on all sides, standing thirty, forty feet high. Several tents were haphazardly pitched just above the tide line, and there were four power boats beached nearby. A steep trail rose to a narrow plateau on the east side, providing a quick escape from what was either a sheltered hideaway or a bottlenecked death trap.

"We've been here for several days waiting for you," Takahashi explained.

"Waiting for me?" Alex asked. "Why?" As the boat approached, several men and women in various fatigue patterns—army, marines, navy and air force—emerged from the tents and approached the beach. A group of them gathered there and stood ready to greet the boat. They were all armed, but they wore their weapons casually, and none seemed hostile.

"I'll let the major explain," Takahashi said. "He was a captain before all this, so we all agreed to promote him and put him in charge."

"In charge of what?" Alex asked.

"You'll know soon enough."

Takahashi jumped off as soon as the boat touched the sand, and offered Alex a hand. He shrugged it off and jumped down. It felt strange to be on land again after so long at sea. Everything was moving, swaying, as though he were still on a boat. He knew it wasn't real, but sure felt like it was. His legs were wobbly and he was slightly nauseous, as though his sea sickness would return now that he was back on dry land.

"Captain Meyer," one of the gathered servicemen said. "Pleased to finally meet you." He had tiny slit eyes above a hawkish nose. That was about as much of a distinction as Alex was capable of noticing from among a crowd dressed in pattern disrupting combat uniforms.

Alex looked at the man, then down at his rank insignia. "Captain," he said, nodding a greeting, then looked at the next man, the woman after him, and the man after her. "Captain, captain, captain…I'd keep saying captain but you guys might think water bears got into my brain."

A few of them laughed. No one tried to take his weapon, or seemed the least bit concerned with it, which put Alex at ease.

"Winters is a lieutenant," one of the men said, indicating a man with blond stubble around a reddening bald spot. "But he's Navy."

"Right," Alex said. "O-3, same as captain."

"And Bundy is a woman," Winters said. "In case you couldn't tell." More laughs. Alex turned to look where Winters pointed. He could tell quite easily, despite her tight bun, lack of makeup and form disguising fatigues.

"This woman is about to knock you on your ass, Squid," she said, grinning at Winters like a wolf sizing up its prey.

"We're all like you," Takahashi explained. "From the nearby colonies. The farthest one after yours is about six hundred miles away, near Seattle. That's Linnard's facility. No one's come from quite as far away as Hawaii, though."

"I think I'd better see this major of yours," Alex said. "I need to know what's going on here."

"I'm Major Terkeurst," one of the men in the crowd said, stepping forward. He was wearing captain's bars, just like the others. "Not much opportunity to get new insignia," he explained. "Come, we'll take a walk, stretch those legs, and talk." Terkeurst was an unassuming man with an easy smile and friendly eyes. His hair was cropped too short to be sure of its color, but much of it looked gray. He carried his cover in his right hand and switched it to his left temporarily to shake Alex's hand.

"After you, sir," Alex said, feeling strange to be in the presence of a real officer, as though he were an impostor playing dress up. The major led him up the trail and onto the flat area above, which was covered in a thick blanket of green grass. It was beautiful, so much open space, no trees or mountains to limit visibility. The peninsula curved around to the northeast before fading into the slowly receding mist, and Alex could see more sheltered beaches across the water, similar to the one they had come from. Dark shapes moved on the sand.

"Seals," Terkeurst explained. "The real ones, I mean, not the Navy kind. A lot more of them here now, as though they know that man isn't around to bother them anymore."

"So what's going on here?" Alex said. "Why are you guys camping out on a beach, away from your colonies? Why are you waiting for me?"

"Last question first. For one, we need all the men we can get. Also, you're the one responsible for all this, so it wouldn't feel right to go without you."

"I am? Because I..." He was about to say that he killed his governor, but he held back. It felt wrong, somehow, as though he would get into trouble. Of course these men had to know what he did, if they had spoken to Tom. Unless he had lied.

"Some of us suspected," the major explained. "That what the president was telling us wasn't kosher, but all we could do was grudgingly accept it and move on, working for our bright new tomorrows." He said the last bit with obvious scorn. "But when your man Tom sent us all that data, and then stuck around to verify it and how he got it, well, that changed everything."

"I can imagine," Alex said, looking back across the water from whence he came. "I wish I never found out."

"A part of me does too," the major said. "But the rest of me wants to kill the bastards that killed my family. They murdered them, Meyer. Plain and simple. My mother, my sister, my aunt, my brother, all of them. Murdered. And that can't stand."

"No," he said. "It can't."

"Every man and woman here feels the same way. They're not

all prior-military, some of us are ex-civilians like your guy Tom."

"Hackers?" Alex asked dubiously.

The major chuckled. "That's a big negative. No hackers. You're the only one so blessed. I mean people like your team back home, that you recruited to help you, people with prior service, people that knew their way around weapons, whatever. People that can fight. We're not much on labels here."

"So what are you guys planning? An attack on the facility?" Asking the question thrilled him. He wouldn't be alone. All these soldiers, on his side!

The major nodded. "Not just an attack. We plan to take it over."

"Take it over? Is that even possible? Tom told me there are over fifty soldiers stationed there, if the personnel records can be trusted. I was just planning to do some recon, figure out what I was dealing with. If I could peg the president from a mile out, that would be nice, but I wasn't betting on it. How many men do you have?"

The major smiled. "That's a lot of questions. Yes, yes and twenty two, including you. Not all of them are here. We have two recon parties watching the facility. It's about twenty miles northeast of here."

"Those aren't good odds…twenty two against fifty. The personnel records, did Tom tell you about them? Most of those guys are Green Berets, SEALs, Delta Force, you name it. They didn't exactly pick guys like me to guard them, they picked the best."

"As I said," the major explained. "We're not much for labels. I was with Delta, before I injured out. I'd rather have a guy like you on my team, a known quantity, than someone with a fancy patch on their arm that I don't know from Adam."

"Me?" Alex asked incredulously. "I'm just a regular grunt!"

"That's a label, Alex," the major chastised. "What you are is a man who survived for half an hour in the barrier—"

"At only seventy one percent!" he protested.

"The normal operating parameters for lethal defense call for seventy to ninety five percent. Tom didn't tell you that part, did he?"

"No," Alex admitted, a little shaken. "But still…"

"Then you took on four armed hostiles, alone, before even giving yourself a chance to recover."

"But they were just buffoons, they didn't even know how to use their weapons properly! Besides, you Delta guys deal with more bad guys than that, don't you?"

"We try not to," Terkeurst said. "If we can help it. But yes, we did, as a team. You did this solo. I'm not saying there's not ten guys in our group that couldn't have done the same. There probably are, but what I am saying is that I bet there's guys in that complex, special ops guys, that couldn't do what you did. The point is, labels are just labels. Special Forces means you train more, get better gear and spend more time learning how to use it. You did just fine on your own."

"Are you trying to butter me up, sir?"

The major grinned. "Yes son, I am. It won't do for any of us to fear our enemy. They are nothing more than men with guns, just like us. We have a difficult task ahead of us, and most of us are probably going to die, though I'll do everything in my power to make sure that doesn't happen."

"I came here knowing I'd probably die," Alex said morosely, turning away to stare over the southwestern horizon. "You don't need to motivate me, I'm good to go. I don't care what patches those guys are wearing on their shoulders, they're going down. They chose the wrong side." He hesitated. "Unless they're dupes like us?"

"They could be," the major said. "But it doesn't matter. We don't have the luxury of asking them. We have a mission, and they're in the way. At the very least, they're not asking themselves too many questions. In their situation, they have access to a lot more information than we did."

"True. So does everyone get a pep talk like this, or am I special somehow?"

The major chuckled. "Yes, everyone gets a pep talk. There's not that many of us, and we have lots of time. But you're also special, because I have a particular task in mind for you."

"Me?" Alex asked. "I mean sure, I'll help any way I can, but what can I do?"

"Let's talk about your governor first."

Alex was suddenly very nervous. "What about him?"

"Tell me why you killed him." Terkeurst's expression and tone were difficult to read, but didn't seem to be accusatory or reproachful.

Alex looked away. "He had one of his goons put a gun to my girl's head."

"That's it?"

"That's it. I tried to take him down peacefully, but he didn't go for it. Once he threatened her life, he was dead. It's that simple. I also thought…" He hesitated, fighting back pain. She was so far away, out of his reach, it was almost as though he did lose her that day after all. "I thought that they'd killed her. Turned out she was just hurt, not dead."

"You didn't find it difficult," Terkeurst asked. "To depose your lawful governor? And later to kill him, even though he was surrendering?"

Alex felt a little exposed. Tom must have really trusted these people to give them so many details.

"No," he admitted. "I didn't. Deposing him was a no brainer. He was a giant douche bag and he had to go. He was trying to run the colony like a chain gang. I regret it took me as long as it did to see that, but what's done is done. Killing him…I regret that, sometimes. He could have been a normal person, if they hadn't put him in charge. He had some good ideas, and he was taking us in the right direction, just in the wrong way. But he did what he did, and I did what I did, and that's that. Are we going to have a problem because of it?"

"No," the major said, shaking his head. "I agree with your decision to depose him, given the facts, and I can understand why you killed him, even if I don't think I would have done the same."

Alex nodded, relieved, though he was still curious why Terkeurst was so interested.

"So am I the only one?" Alex asked. "That had a problem with his governor?"

"No," the major admitted. "A few of the others did also, but they removed them peacefully, or semi peacefully. Like you did originally, but without the ensuing complications. Most of us, though, have had a lot of luck with our governors. Mine, for instance, was very gung ho about this mission, and she had people working night and day to fix up one of those boats you saw on the beach to get me and two of my men here. None of us were unfortunate enough to land the type of despot that your facility got stuck with."

"Aren't you worried that your governor was just playing along and that he—sorry, she—would warn the government as soon as you left?"

"No, she's a good woman and I trust her. But even if I didn't, Tom made that impossible."

"He's handy that way," Alex said. Tom was more than a stroke of good fortune, he was probably the single most important human being alive. If not for him, none of this would be possible.

"Yes he is."

"Major," Alex said, growing impatient. "I appreciate the pep talk, but what's really going on here? You asked a lot of questions, yet you seemed to already have formed an opinion about what I did. What gives?"

The major nodded. "Fair enough. It's like this. We're going in there to exact vengeance, justice, whatever you want to call it. That means we have to stand face to face with the president of the United States, the commander-in-Chief, and blow his brains out. And the others responsible also…senators, and so on. I'm in command, so that's my job, but I'm not sure I have what it takes."

"Sir?" Alex said, confused. Terkeurst was former Delta. If he didn't have what it was going to take to accomplish the mission, who did?

"I picture it in my head, how badly I want him dead, and then I see him saying 'stand down, soldier, that's an order,' and like some brain washed Manchurian candidate asshole, I'm fucking scared to death that I'll lower my weapon and stand at attention. I'm an officer in the United States Army…the old one. Before that, I was enlisted, for many years. I follow orders. It's what I do, and if the president gives an order, I'm not sure I am capable of ignoring it."

Alex blanched, piecing it together. "You want me to kill the president?"

"Not exactly," Terkeurst said quickly. "It's my responsibility. I just need someone behind me that I can trust to give me a shove if

I falter. And only failing that, someone who can do the job if I can't. I know how fucked up it sounds, but you're my best bet because of what you did. We're all soldiers, conditioned to obey orders, to respond to authority. You're different. You didn't face a moral crisis when you deposed your lawful commander as I would have, you only wondered why it took you so long. I'm betting my life, all of our lives, that if the President of the United States of America, such as they are, gives you a lawful order, you will tell him to die on a dick and shoot him in the face. Can I count on you, son?"

Alex thought about it before answering. Could he kill the president? Not too long ago he had been a college student, hitting on girls and studying for exams, and then a soldier, following orders, just like every other soldier. When had he become such a killer that a former Delta operator needed him to do his dirty work?

"Yeah, you can count on me." If there was no one else, then it fell on him. It was just that simple. His parents deserved no less than the death of their executioners.

"Thank you, son."

"Can I have a few minutes up here?" Alex asked. "It was a long trip."

"Certainly, take your time."

When he was alone on the plateau, Alex started walking along the northern edge and eventually spotted his sailboat, anchored in the crook of the peninsula. For the first time since Tom had told him the truth, he knew there was a real chance that he would make it home, make it back to her. It filled him with hope, and with fear. If there was a good chance of making it back, then he had a lot more to lose than he'd thought he would. Terkeurst was right, he was capable of killing the president. But was he capable of making it that far against such formidable odds?

Walking slowly to the other side of the narrow rise, he saw the soldiers milling about, talking, preparing equipment. Those people were giving up comfortable lives, risking it all for the sake of justice. He knew that many of them would pay for it with their lives. He was suddenly so choked with pride that it was almost hard to breathe. He had joined the army looking for honor, the warrior spirit, and had found mostly fools, thugs and gangsters. Yet down there, on the beach, *there* was honor. *There* was valor. For the first time in his life, he was proud of his uniform. Not just of how he looked in it, or of how much attention he got wearing it, but for what it stood for. What it stood for *now*.

Chapter 34

They had drilled for days, spent hours looking over sketches and listening to reports from the recon teams, but when Alex saw the complex for the first time, he was afraid. He realized, once he understood the nature of the facility, how completely ridiculous his original plan had been.

The facility was underground, with an entrance carved into the side of a mountain and protected by massive titanium doors. At first he wondered how such a thing could have been constructed without drawing a lot of attention. Perhaps the same things that had dissolved the cities of the world had hollowed out a vast complex in a manner of days or even hours. Simpler explanations abounded—covert funding, re-tasking of an existing facility and so on—but Alex preferred the more elaborate answer. It seemed more fitting.

The most he could have hoped for on his own with the 50 cal sniper rifle was to take out one or two of the four sentries that manned two M134 electric mini guns and two XM307 belt fed grenade launchers. The six thousand round per minute mechanized Gatling guns could shred their entire assault team in seconds if they were caught out in the open, but those weapons paled in comparison to the grenade launchers.

The 307s were essentially grenade firing machine guns with smart ammunition capable of air busting at a programmed range. If Alex's assault team were pinned down behind a big boulder that could stop the mini guns, then the sentries could fire grenades over the rock. Grenades that were programmed to detonate in the air over the team's head. This essentially gave the defenders the ability to reach around corners and over obstacles.

The weapons were mounted behind clear ballistic shields that would stop pretty much all small arms fire, and the guards were equipped with FLIR—forward looking infrared optics that made advancing at night more dangerous than during the day. Approach from behind, over the mountain, was impractical without equipment they did not have, and the sides were just as open as the front. The closest they could get was one hundred meters away, straight on, approaching behind some rock formations at the base of a steep cliff. The cliff itself had been considered, but there was no practical way down and no cover at the summit.

The attackers had two things going for them. The first advantage was the relaxed attitude of the guards, who thought the only thing they had to fear were a few scattered survivors. They spent most of their time talking amongst themselves, smoking cigarettes and occasionally scanning the surroundings with binoculars. The second advantage was that there was effectively no barrier. The facility had one, but Tom confirmed that it was always kept on the lowest setting. That made perfect sense. Considering the formidable defenses, running the barrier at full strength was an unnecessary power drain.

Alex watched the guards from behind a rock, afraid to stick his head out too far. One of them laughed and swiped at another's head. The second one ducked and poked the first one's belly with a finger. All four chuckled, and Alex knew that he would never sleep peacefully again. These were American soldiers, and he and his team were about to murder them. He couldn't know how complicit they were in what happened to the world, but knowing how the people on top operated, it was almost certain that they were ignorant and innocent. They were most likely just like him, soldiers, plucked from their lives and deposited there, making the most of it. Maybe some of them had found love, and were waiting to get off shift to see their girl. Or their guy. One of them was a woman.

They were victims, but whether due to ignorance or a willful decision, they were working for the enemy, and they would give their lives to protect that enemy. They had to die, and a part of Alex and the others would die with them.

Surviving a war doesn't make you stronger. It makes you weaker. So weak, that you can barely stand to be alive sometimes. Medlock had told him that in a rare moment of humanity when he had run into him in a bar in Barstow, the shithole town closest to Fort Irwin. He'd been alone until Alex showed up. They drank together, and then never spoke of it again. Alex hadn't seen much in Afghanistan, but it had been enough to understand that people can never erase their memories, no matter how much they may want to.

"Sir?" Bundy said. She had mistaken his introspection for radio communication.

Alex turned and looked at her. She had a stern face and worn eyes, with about ten more years on them than he had. She and seven others had been assigned to his team, which was tasked with approaching from the west side of the clearing. Eleven others, led by Terkeurst, would approach from the east side. If their snipers couldn't get the job done in time, at least there would be a chance for one of the teams to get through. That was the idea, anyway. Looking at the defenders' weapons, Alex wasn't so sure.

"Stand by," he said. "We'll be on our way soon."

"I just wanted to say," Bundy said. "Whatever happens, thank you for what you did. Getting us the truth." Her hard eyes glistened for the briefest of moments, then dulled once more. "I wanted to tell you that now, in case I don't make it."

The others murmured assents. He didn't even try to remember their names. In fact, he tried not to, and succeeded. Bundy was the exception because she was the only woman on his team. He had assigned them call signs based on his first impression of their faces. Smiley, Baby Face, Pirate, Hero, Hardass, Moustache and Pimp. Bundy was just Bundy. He hoped that she didn't feel left out.

"We're all going to make it," Alex said. "The plan is sound."

The plan was desperate. He was scared, because he knew the likelihood of failure was high, but he was determined. One way or another, it would all be over in a matter of hours, maybe less. Then he would either be dead, or on his way home.

"Alex," the major's voice said through his radio earpiece. "Ready?" He was about to answer, but hesitated, momentarily balked by a sudden wave of panic. *Someone who can do the job if I can't.* Could he actually fire on the president? He had been sure before, but now he was anything but.

"Meyer?" the major asked.

Alex turned to the others and said, "Ready?" They all nodded, almost together.

"Ready," Alex said. Only one way to find out.

"Go!" the major said.

"Go!" Alex echoed.

They jumped to their feet and circled the edge of the cliff, then started running across the relatively flat clearing right at the sentry posts and their mounted, unbelievably lethal weapons. Alex felt exposed, vulnerable. He cringed, foolishly trying to hide his face behind the brim of his Kevlar helmet. His equipment weighed him down—Dragon Skin, twenty spare magazines, sidearm, grenades and more—but he moved quickly, fuelled by desperation. They could have opened fire first, or fired as they moved, but either of those would slow them down, and they had to close the gap before those guns opened up on them.

The sentries saw them almost immediately. Eighty meters to go. They stared at the rushing attackers stupidly for several seconds before one of them started screaming. Seventy meters.

They scrambled for their mounted death machines. Fifty five meters. Alex felt a slight twinge in his stomach as they passed through the facility's barrier.

The first man made it to a mini gun and Alex watched with horror as the weapon's six barrels oriented on his team.

The aluminum oxynitride shields protecting the tripod mounted guns buckled as 50 caliber sabot rounds struck them. The distant cracks of the Barrett rifles echoed across the hollows between craggy cliff sides. The transparent ALON shields were capable of stopping a standard 50 caliber armor piercing round, but one of the men had been smart enough to bring sabots, smaller, denser projectiles enclosed in plastic shells that fell away as the bullet left the barrel. That man, Captain Meloy, was their only trained sniper. The other shooter was doing well, but not well enough.

The M134's barrel began to spin and belch fire. A buzzing noise like giant angry wasps passed over them and Bundy's torso came apart as she ran. Her blood splattered all over Alex's exposed face. The buzzing stopped. The snipers had done their job, but not in time to save her. Alex looked back. Not just her. Smiley, with his ginger beard, was gone as well.

"Keep moving!" Alex shouted, not daring to spare even a moment. He had told her that they would all make it. He had lied.

They were now thirty meters from the big titanium doors, which were starting to close, sliding slowly. The two teams split into four as some of them took control of the mounted weapons, which they started turning around to face the doorway as the remaining attackers fell into two columns on either side of the approach, clearing a direct firing line into the facility.

Muzzle flashes burst to life in the blackness beyond the slowly moving doors as the pop of small arms fire accompanied the rumble of supersonic rounds flying inches from the approaching team. A man next to Alex screamed and fell, spraying warm blood across his cheeks. Baby Face, hit in his namesake.

Another one on the opposite column collapsed as the men in the lead returned fire with their M4s, though they couldn't see what they were shooting at. Something hit Alex dead center in the chest hard enough to knock all the wind out of him, then again in his stomach, even harder. He continued running. His lucky armor had saved him again.

He fired a few token shots before the roar of mini gun fire drowned out all sound as a fireworks display of sparks erupted inside the entrance tunnel. The thump of the 307s and the resulting thunder of the 25mm air burst grenades soon joined in a cacophony of carnage. Nothing inside could survive such devastation.

The team made it to the entrance before the doors closed half way, and as their supporting fire cut off they rushed inside, weapon lights painting a grim picture of men torn to shreds. Blood was everywhere, forming crisscrossing patterns on the dimpled walls. Alex stepped on something squishy as he ran and felt so queasy that he momentarily wondered if Tom had been wrong about the barrier before remembering that they had already passed through it.

Taking up positions behind what little cover they could find in the large entrance bay, they waited while the four outside abandoned the mounted weapons and raced to join them.There was no time for the snipers to make it. They would remain outside to cover the team's retreat, if it came to that. Ideally, their task would be to take care of anyone who tried to escape.

"Fourteen dead," the major announced. Alex wasn't sure how he could count the shredded corpses accurately, but he wasn't about to ask. "Let's move out." As far as Alex could tell, they had lost five of theirs. If he was right, there were now fifteen of them to thirty six of the enemy, not counting the snipers, which were now out of play.

Fourteen American soldiers. Dead by their hand. Fourteen of a precious few survivors of the greatest catastrophe in history. How would he be able to cope with what they had just done? At least he hadn't seen any of their faces. That would help.

Past this point, none of them had any idea what lay within the complex. There had been no floor plans on the servers, and getting inside was possible only after the type of direct assault they had just completed. From here on in, it was all snap judgments and seat of the pants flying.

They were in a large bay with fifty foot high ceilings and a massive cargo elevator on the far end. An elevated catwalk circled the upper half of the chamber and led to two doorways, but there was no access from the floor below. The lights were out, but fifteen high powered weapon lights provided sufficient illumination to make out most details. They shared the bay with two M3 Bradley fighting vehicles, sitting menacingly still, 25mm cannons pointed straight at the closed outer door.

"There are personnel elevators there!" someone shouted, and the major motioned them onwards. They fanned out into two elements, circling the Bradleys.

Out of the corner of his eye Alex caught movement on the catwalk and raised his weapon in time to see two men taking aim. He fired quickly, no time to acquire a target, and the men ducked inside one of the doorways. The thump of an M203 made him cringe as he anticipated the blast of the grenade in enclosed quarters. An impossibly loud crack sent sharp pain shooting up his ear canals, but his helmet provided some measure of shielding. Dust and smoke drifted from the doorway, and nothing moved beyond.

The team split in two and advanced to the passenger elevators, one on each side of the cargo lift.

"One man in each lift, hit the button then get the hell out," Terkeurst said. He turned to Alex. "You were OPFOR, right? Mechanized infantry?"

"Yes sir." He wondered how the major knew that. Had Tom accessed his service record?

"Good. Get in one of those Bradleys and start that fucker up. We're taking it down the cargo lift. Winters, Collins, watch his six."

A part of Alex wanted to correct the major, since OPFOR did not use Bradleys, but he had driven one in Afghanistan during a brief stint as mechanized infantry and so he kept silent. He also didn't appreciate Terkeurst overriding his call signs. Collins was Hardass, not Collins. He didn't need the confusion, but he kept silent about that too. He climbed inside and got into the driver's seat. The diesel engine started right away, and Alex turned to the others.

"Anyone else know how to drive this thing?"

"I drove one once," Collins said.

"Good, you drive," Alex said as Major Terkeurst and three others climbed into the back of the vehicle. "I was the gunner, and that's where I need to be right now."

"Got it," Collins said, and replaced Alex in the driver's seat.

"What kind of armament do we have?" Terkeurst asked.

"Full load in the main gun," Alex said, taking a quick inventory. "Including HE." High explosive ammunition would be devastating at close range indoors, but only against dismounted hostiles and lightly armored vehicles. "We've got TOW missiles too, but they won't be any good in here."

"Excellent," the major said, then turned to the men outside. "Stay behind this thing until we're done shooting. Okay, let's move!"

The driver turned the vehicle around and moved it onto the cargo lift platform. One of the men taking cover behind ran out and activated the lift controls. Nothing happened.

"They've locked out the lift," Terkeurst said. "Bastards! Linnard, get out there!"

"Yes sir!" Linnard jumped out of the vehicle and headed towards the lift's control panel.

"He's a tech guy," the major explained. "Electrical engineer. Maybe he can jury rig the panel." They waited nervously for several minutes until Linnard returned to the Bradley.

"I've got control of the panel, but they've cut power to the lift," he explained. "There's no way to activate it."

"Fuck!" the major cursed. "We'll have to blow it and rappel down, or use the elevator shafts. Alright, back this thing off." The engine thrummed as the Bradley slowly moved backwards off of the lift. Alex was disappointed. He had hoped to be able to use the vehicle's cannon.

"Sir!" Someone shouted. "The lift!"

Alex heard it almost immediately, the lift was moving.

"Get us back on it!" the major shouted.

"Too late!" one of the men outside screamed. "Stop! Stop! You'll fall in!"

"Fuck!" the major cursed again. "Okay, get those elevator doors open, let me know where the cars are. Winters, get the C4 ready to blow the cables."

"Yes sir!"

"We'll wait in here," Terkeurst said. "Alex, keep that gun ready in case they try to come in from above." He ducked his head outside the vehicle. "Anyone not working, get in the other Bradley."

Several minutes passed slowly as Alex turned the turret from one catwalk doorway to the other, using FLIR to try to spot any sign of enemy movement.

"The lift is moving again!" Winters shouted from the elevator doorway. "It's coming back up!"

"What the hell?" the major demanded. "Take a look. Be careful!"

"Holy shit!" Winters shouted. "It's an Abrams! There's an Abrams on its way up! One hundred meters down and rising fast!"

Alex swallowed nervously. An M1 Abrams main battle tank was just about the nastiest thing on the ground. It could turn the Bradley into a smoldering pile of garbage with a single shot from its 120mm cannon.

Terkeurst stuck his head into the gunner's capsule. He glared at Alex for a moment, looked him up and down as though sizing him up, then said, "Meyer, you miserable towel headed opposing force bastard…there's an evil capitalist American tank on its way up here to reign fire and death down upon us. Can you take out that tank for me, son?"

Alex thought about it. "I don't think so, sir. The TOW missile could take it out, but its minimum range is sixty five meters, we don't have that here so it probably won't even arm itself. All I've got is the 25mm cannon, and that won't take out a tank."

"That's not good enough, son. When I had the misfortune of being in that hell hole Ft. Irwin, you god damned OPFOR camel jockeys took out our Abrams tanks like flies in July. Think, god damn you!"

"Those were just war games," Alex protested. And *war games don't make you a real soldier*. The marine sergeant's face was clear in his mind's eye, as was Haag's bloody stump. Alex could almost hear him scream. The he remembered something Lieutenant Campbell had said in the hospital.

I saw a guy burn his leg to shit trying to get a missile simulator out of a bent launch tube.

"Out of the way, sir!" Alex yelled as he climbed out of the gunner's capsule.

Terkeurst moved. "What are you doing, son?"

"No time!" Alex cried as he practically pulled Captain Collins out of the driver's seat. "Make way! Someone man the gun!"

"I got it," one of the men said and Alex heard him climbing into the gunner's roost.

"I need someone out there!" Alex shouted through the open hatch. "Tell me when that fucking tank is ten seconds from the top. Then get the hell out of there and get in one of the Bradleys if you can make it! Everyone else, get inside! Now!"

"On it!" Winters shouted as he crawled to the edge of the lift cavity to look down at the approaching tank. "Thirty seconds! It's got the turret pointed right at you! They must be able to see us. Cameras, probably." The few men left outside climbed into the APCs.

"Fuck them," Alex shouted. "Remember, ten seconds, then get the hell out of there." Alex backed the Bradley up as far as he could and adjusted its position, then reached up and closed the driver's hatch. "Everyone, shut the hatches! Leave one open for Winters in the other Bradley…he'll have time to make it."

"What are you planning?" Terkeurst demanded.

"If I tell you, I won't have the balls to do it."

"Twenty!" Winters shouted. The last of the hatches closed shut, and Alex felt trapped in what was about to become a burning aluminum coffin, unless his insane plan worked.

"Fifteen!" Almost time. He could see Winters getting ready to climb to his feet through the small view hole. If he messed the angle up, even a little…

"Ten!" Winters shouted and jumped up, running towards the second Bradley.

Alex's heart beat so fast and hard that he swore its motion was causing his hands to shake. He counted to three, then gunned the throttle as hard as he could. He remembered fooling around in the motor pool parking lot after the NCOs left. Bradley racing had been a popular pastime. He knew how the vehicle performed, he just hoped this one was not too far out of spec. Or damaged. Or any number of things that could hose his plan and kill them all.

The Bradley surged forward, accelerating steadily. It was capable of forty miles per hour, though it would take much more space than he had here to reach that. It wouldn't matter, whatever speed it could reach would do.

The top of the tank crested the edge of the lift cavity just as Alex lost sight of it, the angle too great to see through his hatch's tiny view port. He felt more than he saw that menacing 120mm cannon rise above the lift wall, ready to fire.

The thirty ton Bradley fighting vehicle, moving at a good fifteen miles per hour, crashed into the front of the M1 Abrams tank. The tank's protruding cannon crumpled under the force of the impact.

The tank gunner fired, unaware of what had happened. A flash of brilliance, then blackness.

Chapter 35

"Wake up!" someone shouted, and Alex felt a sting as a hand swept across his face. He looked around, unsure of where he was. It looked like the inside of a Bradley, but it was undamaged. It had to be the one he hadn't crashed into a tank. There was also the sensation of downward movement.

"What happened?" Alex asked as he sat up. He held his hands in front of his face to make sure they were still there, then checked the rest of him. He seemed to be in one piece.

"You crazy son of a bitch!" the major shouted, grinning wildly. "You did it! I thought I lost you for a second, but the piece of shit aluminum armor held. The tank took the worst of it. I've never seen such a ballsy fucking move."

"We're moving down?" Alex asked. "How?" The back of the hatch was open and several men stood outside. He could see the walls of the lift cavity rolling slowly upwards. Very slowly, much more so than he expected.

"Gravity," Terkeurst explained. "The bastards powered down the lift again, but we crammed two Bradleys on it with what's left of the tank, and it's too much weight. Without power, they can't activate the brake, and if they power it up, Linnard will take control."

"Cool," Alex said, not sure of what else to say.

"If we survive this," the major said. "I'm going to pin a medal on your chest."

"Thank you sir," Alex said. "But I don't think we will. The second we get down there they're going to open up on us with whatever other tanks they have down there."

"I know, son, I know. Now get your ass behind that cannon. We're going to go down shooting."

"Yes sir." Alex climbed into the gunner's seat. It was identical to that of the other Bradley, but someone had left a picture of a pretty young woman stuck behind the edge of a control panel. Alex wondered if she was alive down there, or if she'd been killed outside with the rest of humanity.

The radio headset crackled to life. Surprised, Alex reached for it and put it on.

"I repeat," a voice said. "Unidentified hostile forces, this is General Roberts, United States Army."

"What the fuck?" Alex said. "Sir, there's someone on the radio!" He didn't expect this, and it wasn't good. It was easy to kill men whose faces they couldn't see. Alex hadn't seen enough in Afghanistan to break him, but he had known people who had. If they put faces and names to these American soldiers, it would be the same as taking a bullet to the brain, only slower.

"Give me that," the major said quickly to one of the others, then grabbed and hastily donned the offered headset.

"This is Major Ron Terkeurst," he said. "To whom am I speaking?"

"Lieutenant General Christopher Roberts," the man on the other end said. "Commander of the United States Army. I order you to stand down immediately, major, and surrender."

Christopher Roberts? Kristoff, Bob? A bad omen, if anything. But still, a voice, a name, but no face.

"We have no intention of surrendering," the major said.

"What the hell do you think you're doing?" the general demanded. "The President is in this complex! The President of the United States!"

"We're aware of that," the major continued. "That's why we're here. We know who is responsible for all this, and I'm sure you do too, so cut the shit. They have to pay for what they've done."

"What the hell is he talking about?" a background voice asked. It sounded familiar.

"Nothing," the general said sternly. "Cut the connection."

On a sudden impulse, Alex pressed the transmit button and said, "Who said that? Do I know you?"

"I said cut the connection, colonel!" the general barked.

"Sir I know that voice," the other man said, and the familiarity struck Alex almost as hard as he had hit the tank.

"Lieutenant Campbell?" Alex asked. "Bill? Is that you?"

"Alex?" Nothing more. The connection was severed.

"Who is Lieutenant Campbell?" Terkeurst demanded.

"Holy shit!" Alex said. "It was him! He was my platoon commander in OPFOR! What the hell are the odds?" And that was that. Alex had killed Campbell's men. Campbell used to be his platoon leader, so Campbell's men were Alex's men. He could already start to feel that fragile part of his mind letting go. It manifested as a tension, a tightening deep in his chest, while his mind flailed like a drowning child, desperate to grab hold of something. But there was nothing to latch onto. It was making it hard to concentrate, hard for his eyes to focus. A fog settled over the world, swirling in rhythm to the flailing of his mind. He was slipping. What if they were wrong? What if Tom made a mistake? What if these people were not the ones responsible? That last question called a sense of dread out of the abyss of Alex's subconscious, a monster that clawed its way to the surface of his mind, ripping him apart on the way up.

The lift continued to descend slowly, buying them time. If only he could talk to Bill, convince him. Alex was sure he would listen. Then no one else had to die. But his grasp on sanity was dropping faster than the lift was. He had massacred his own brothers and sisters. How much longer would he be able to hold it together? A part of him didn't want to talk to Bill, and he didn't understand why.

"Was he smart, this Lieutenant of yours?" the major asked, thankfully breaking Alex's chain of thought.

"Campbell? Yeah, he was a lazy genius. I guess that explains why they picked him…he must have aced their test." It was strange, hearing himself speak. He sounded normal. Not at all like a man who eagerly awaited the thunder of 120mm tank cannons to end his pain.

The radio crackled to life. "This is Colonel Campbell. Alex, is that you?"

"Bill! It's good to hear your voice!" Only it wasn't. Why wasn't it?

"You too, Alex. We've…detained the general. You've got two minutes to explain why the hell you're attacking my facility, Alex, and it better be good, because a lot of my men are dead."

Alex looked at the major questioningly. He couldn't explain. He wasn't up to it. He didn't want to. Why didn't he want to?

"It's your show, son," Terkeurst said. "You started this, now finish it."

"I—" Alex started to protest, tried to find the words to explain what he was feeling, and suddenly, everything became clear. Since he had set out on his mission of vengeance, his emotions had undulated like a roller coaster. Peaks of fear and hope paired with deep valleys of self pity or bone weary resignation. He wanted to live, he was ready to die, then he wanted to live again. But now he realized that all of that led to a single truth. And with that realization, the maelstrom in his mind calmed, and all was still. He saw the face of the monster that had risen from the depths of his soul. It was his own face. He was the monster. How could he not have known, all this time?

He didn't want to talk to Bill, didn't want to explain, and he understood why. He understood why he had gone off alone on a fool's errand, a hopeless mission that everyone with any sense had tried to talk him out of, that Yael had tried reason, extortion, manipulation and finally begging to keep him from undertaking. It all made sense.

Alex wanted to die.

He had kept telling himself that he hadn't seen enough in Afghanistan, not like others. Not like the broken men and women who feared the night, because it meant they would be alone with their demons. Alone with themselves. No, he had told himself, he wasn't like them. But he had lied. He told himself that he had only killed people at a distance, not seeing their faces, but he saw them. Eventually, he saw them. Distorted, bloated, collapsed, hollow, ragged faces. Entrails and severed limbs. And not just those of the enemy.

When he killed Max and his goons, when he caved in Bob's skull with the butt of his rifle, he hadn't lost his soul, because it had already been lost. All he had done was drive the proverbial last nail into the coffin of his shattered humanity. He hadn't come to this place to get revenge, except maybe upon himself. He had come to end the suffering. To end his life.

"Alex?" Terkeurst said, narrowing his eyes.

"I—" The perspective shift was startling. Just a few seconds ago he was a brash young soldier, a superstar, someone who had all the answers, someone who always did the right thing, looked out for others, handled problems. Now he was a broken thing, a fool, and a coward. He wanted death, because he had nothing left to live for, no strength left to go on. And with that realization came something unexpected. Anger. Anger at the world for being such shit. Anger at himself for volunteering for military service at a time when his country didn't need him, didn't need the wars it was fighting. Anger at his failure to deal with what he had seen, what he had felt, failure to seek help, to accept himself as he was instead of lamenting the loss of who he had been. Anger at his betrayal of the woman who cared for him more than he deserved.

I don't know about you, but when I told you I loved you I meant that I'm with you, always, no matter what.

Yael had pledged her life to him, and he had left her. If there was anything in this world still worth living for, she was it. And he had just walked away.

"What's wrong, son?" Terkeurst said.

"Nothing," Alex said. "Not anymore." His fists trembled with barely suppressed rage. He would not die today, even if he had to kill every last motherfucker in this complex. President, general, everyone. He had spent years fucking up, and it was time to make everything right. He would live, and he would come back to her, no matter what.

He took a deep breath to calm himself, then spoke into the radio. "Bill. What did they tell you? About what happened."

"It was a Chinese attack," Campbell said. "Nanorobotic weapon. Destroyed most of the world, we nuked the rest in retaliation."

"You buy that?" he asked. There was a pause.

"It has its problems," Campbell admitted.

"Like how they managed to set up hundreds of colonies across the world, just in time?"

"That does stretch their credibility a tad, yes."

"It's bullshit, Bill," Alex continued. "It was them, they did it. They released the weapon, spread it through the airports. And it's not even a fucking weapon, it's a god damned waste disposal system."

"I'd like to believe you Alex," Campbell said. "But you're asking too much. How can you possibly know any of this?"

"It's all on your computers," Alex said. "We have a hacker, he got into the servers. You can find it there."

"We don't have access to most of the data on those servers, Alex. And I'm sorry, I can't just take your word for it. Not this time."

Alex was about to say something, try to reason with his friend, then reconsidered. He had an idea. It was desperate, and it probably wouldn't work, but it was their best bet. If it worked, it would give him validation. If he was going to make a life for himself with Yael, he needed to make peace with what had happened here. What was still happening. He needed to know that he had done the right thing. Maybe if he had that much, that certainty that there had been no other choice, then just maybe he would find a way to live with himself. But if he couldn't get Bill to believe him, to accept what he had done, then it wouldn't matter what happened next.

"Can you communicate with the colonies?"

"I don't know," Campbell said. "Give me a sec."

Agonizing seconds passed before he returned. "Yes we can. Why?"

"Send a message to the 103-B governor's terminal. Ask for someone named Tom. Tell him that Alex wants him to give you access to the data you need to learn the truth."

"There isn't time!" Terkeurst protested. "If Tom isn't at that computer right now, at this very moment, then there's no way the message will reach him in time!"

"It's our only chance," Alex said. It's my only chance.

"Message sent," Campbell said. "But it's a text thing, like email. It could take him hours, or days to get…what the fuck? Hold on, Alex."

Alex exchanged nervous glances with the major.

"Apparently," Campbell said. "Your guy is sitting at the terminal right now."

Alex closed his eyes, but not soon enough to keep the warm sticky tears from sliding down his dust covered face.

"We just got a reply," Campbell continued. "He said to hold on. Alex, I don't know what—"

The radio died.

"Bill? Are you there?"

"He's gone," the major said. "They either cut power to the radio or the general got 'un-detained.'"

"We were so close!" Alex said. "So fucking close!"

"Get ready. We're going to be down soon. Take out as many of those guys as you can."

"Yes sir," Alex said, and looked at the photo of the young woman. He didn't see her face. He saw Yael instead. "I'm sorry," he whispered. "I never should have left." He could have skipped the mission and been happy, lived with the woman he loved and never looked back. He had been such a fool.

The lift lowered itself out of its shaft and sank toward the floor of a humongous chamber filled with tanks and APCs standing in neat rows. An area had been cleared near the lift and three Abrams tanks, engines idling, stood with their turrets tracking the sinking platform.

"Fire!" the major ordered. "Let's take them out!" An impossible task, but he might as well try.

Alex grabbed the turret controls and brought the Bradley's gun as close to the active tanks as the angle would allow, preparing to fire the TOW missile. He doubted he had the sixty five meters he needed, but maybe it would work anyway. In any case, he had nothing to lose. Men jumped out the back of the Bradley, their weapons barking as they laid down suppressive fire and moved into position at the rim of the lift.

Small arms fire peppered the APC like torrential hail as Alex swept the turret across the inactive tanks in the background. The 25mm gun thundered and bright spots of light flashed in his vision as the lift platform shook with the force of detonating HE rounds. The 25mm gun wouldn't hurt the tanks, but if there were dismounts taking cover among them, the exploding rounds would tear them apart. Alex could tell that just a few more seconds would bring them low enough to intersect the arc of the lead Abrams' main guns, and then it would be over. He didn't know why they hadn't armed the more distant tanks, as those would have already been able to fire, but he suspected it had something to do with the infrastructure that would be behind them at this angle.

The pounding of the small arms fire against the Bradley's armor cut out suddenly and Campbell's voice roared through their headsets.

"Cease fire!" he shouted. "Cease fire! The tanks have been ordered to hold their fire, my men are pulling back. Hold your fire!"

"Hold your fire!" Terkeurst screamed back as loud as he could. "Hold your fire! Stop shooting goddammit!"

Alex saw Campbell and a group of soldiers armed with rifles but not wearing body armor run out into the open area of the hangar. Campbell was waving his rifle with a white t-shirt tied to the muzzle like a flag.

When the platform came to a stop, Alex and the major climbed out of the Bradley and walked up to meet Campbell. The rest of the assault team spread out behind them, their weapons at the ready.

"Alex," Campbell said, and stepped forward to embrace him. Alex clasped his arms around his friend and hugged him tightly.

"It's good to see you, Bill!"

"What's going on here?" the major demanded.

"I've got control of this area," Campbell explained. "Your guy came through. He gave us access to the specs for the weapon. That's all we really needed to see. I can't believe they did this. I just fucking can't."

"They did it," Alex said.

"Yeah, I know. That' why I'm with you. I have nine men here, they're yours. Four more in the personnel quarters on their way here, if they can make it. The rest won't play ball. They didn't see the evidence and I guess they don't trust me enough to believe me."

"That leaves eighteen," the major said.

"Sixteen," Campbell corrected. "I didn't count myself, and you didn't count the general. He's indisposed." He looked over his shoulder and shouted, "Forget the tanks, fall in on me." The tank motors cut off as soldiers began to climb out, three from each one.

"You're in command of the op, major," Campbell said. "I have no idea what's going on here." He turned to Alex. "Let's go make them pay."

"Colonel," one of the soldiers came forward with a radio. "It's over, sir."

"What the hell do you mean, it's over?" Campbell demanded.

"The president, he shot himself."

"Coward!" the major growled, and spat over his shoulder.

"The rest of the men have surrendered," the soldier continued.

"Just like that?" Alex asked. He had been prepared to die, then ready for a bitter fight, and now that it was over, he was left shaking, unprepared for the sudden change in reality.

"Where are the others?" the major demanded. "The people in charge?"

"They're in a safe room at the bottommost level," Campbell explained. "With their families."

The major nodded. "Secure everyone who just surrendered. I want them locked up until we sort all this out."

"Got it," Campbell said, then turned to his men. "Watkins, make it happen. The rest of you, you're with him." Campbell's men ran off towards the back of the chamber where two sets of double doors led to well lit corridors.

"Take us to this safe room," Terkeurst ordered. Campbell led them through the same double doors and a series of corridors. There were people there, staring out of open doorways, whispering quietly. Alex caught a glimpse inside one of the rooms. Personnel quarters, eerily similar to the cabins back in the colony, at least on the inside.

"Who are these people?" the major asked.

"Soldiers' families," Campbell explained. "Technicians, engineers. That sort of thing."

"Your families?" the major demanded. "They survived? They're here?"

Campbell nodded. "Some of us, yeah. Wives and kids only, though. They claimed they didn't have time to save the others."

Terkeurst said nothing, but Alex could tell what he was thinking.

Eventually they came to a set of heavy metal doors, presumably titanium.

"How do we get them open?" the major asked.

Campbell raised his radio. "XO to command center, open safe room doors."

"XO, this is command center, opening doors."

Alex briefly heard a mechanical whine before it was drowned out by the rumbling of the big doors sliding open. He braced himself. He was about to come face to face with the greatest mass murderers in the history of the human race.

"There are two soldiers inside," Campbell warned. "But they acknowledged the surrender."

"Get ready," Terkeurst ordered, and Alex and the others raised their weapons.

As the door slid open, Alex saw something he didn't expect, though of course his expectations were foolish. He saw faces, ordinary faces, scared, huddled together. The two soldiers stood in the front, their unloaded weapons on the floor by their feet. A white haired corpse lay in a pool of dark blood, a pistol lying near his head. The President of the United States. Had he really killed himself? Or were these two responsible?

"Secure those men," the major ordered, and four of the assault team stepped forward and used zip ties to tie the soldier's hands behind their backs.

Alex looked around at the huddled leaders of the new world order and their families. Most of them were women and children, some as young as three or four, some in their teens, both boys and girls. The remainder were men, ranging in age from late thirties or forties to old men with white hair. Some looked familiar, others didn't. He had probably seen them on television—politicians, captains of industry, whatever. They stared at Alex and his team with undisguised terror.

"What does one say to things like you?" Terkeurst said coldly. "Murderer doesn't even begin to describe what you are." He waited, but no one said anything. "I want you to try to deny it, or even better, try to explain it to me. Tell me why you murdered my family! My niece was two years old!" He was screaming, trembling with rage. Finally, he turned around and faced his men.

"Waste them all," he ordered in the coldest voice Alex had ever heard a human being use. The men hesitated, then raised their weapons. A young girl screamed, and others followed. There was movement as they scrambled to protect themselves behind chairs and tables, hands in front of faces, mothers shielding children.

Can I count on you, son?

"Hold your fire!" Alex shouted, then moved in front of the men and turned to face them. "Don't any of you dare fire!"

Terkeurst whirled on him. "What the hell do you think—"

"You asked me to do what you couldn't do," Alex said to him. "You asked me to kill the ones responsible if you couldn't pull the trigger. And now you want to murder women and children? Yes, I'm a killer, and yes, I can kill every rotten old bastard in this room. But not their god damned families! Not their children! And I won't let you do it either. If you want to kill them, you're going to have to kill me first."

"And me," Campbell said, and stood next to Alex. "I didn't surrender the complex to you so you could do this. These people are guilty, I understand that now. But not their families."

The soldiers looked at each other and lowered their weapons, some of them with ashen faces. They looked at Alex with gratitude. What they would have done here, none of them could have lived with.

"They had to have known!" Terkeurst shouted, still furious. "They had to have known what they did! They had to have gone along!"

"I don't know what you're talking about!" A woman shouted. "What did they do?" She turned to the man next to her. "What did you do?"

"Shut that bitch up!" the major growled. "Or I'll shoot it myself!" He was enraged, not thinking clearly.

"You want revenge," Alex said. "I understand that. But we didn't come here for revenge, we came here for justice. If you can't tell the difference anymore, then you need to stand down, major."

Terkeurst glared at him, his eyes flaring in enraged indignity. "I..." he started to say, then looked around, blinking, as though surprised. He looked at the people he had ordered shot, then at the faces of his men, and seemed to deflate.

"Captain Meyer," he said softly. "Take command of the operation. You know what has to be done."

"Yes sir," Alex said, and Terkeurst turned around and walked out of the room. He had left Alex with a heavy burden, maybe too heavy, but it had to be done.

"Get the women and children out of here," Alex said to the others. "At least those women who weren't in charge. Bill, you know who they are, help sort them out."

Winters and a few of the others began herding the family members out of the room. When they were done, thirty two men and two women stood near the far wall, staring about in fear and disbelief.

Alex opened his mouth to give the order, then stopped. "I can't do this," he said. "God help me, but I can't do it." He looked at Campbell, then at the members of his team, looking for help, support, whatever. No one could meet his gaze. It seemed he wasn't quite the killer Terkeurst had thought.

"I had a daughter," someone whispered. Alex looked for the speaker and saw Takahashi. He was weeping. "She was three years old. She made pictures for me, and they weren't just stick figures either, she was good. 'I made this for you, chichi', she would say." He looked up at Alex, almost apologetically. "That means dad in Japanese."

"I thought they weren't supposed to pick people with children," one of the others said.

"Her mother died," Takahashi explained. "Legally, my grandmother was her guardian. I was away all the time."

"Looks like they fucked up," Winters said. "I'm real sorry, man."

"Let me do this," Takahashi pleaded, looking at Alex. "Please, let me do this. For her."

"Everyone, clear the room," Alex ordered, and followed them out.

Chapter 36

Just as they turned into the corridor, they heard someone shout, "Wait! We didn't do this! Please! Let us explain, please!"

Alex hesitated. Maybe something they said would mean they wouldn't have to kill them. He wasn't sure how he felt about that, but he knew relief was a major candidate.

"Hold on, Takahashi, hold your fire." He walked back into room, avoiding the eyes of the people he was about to murder. Campbell and the others followed him.

"Alex…" Takahashi said in a voice that was almost a growl.

"If we're going to kill them, the least we can do is hear them out. Who was that talking before?"

A woman stepped forward. She was in her fifties, perhaps sixties, slender, still clinging on to youthful beauty despite steel gray hair and hard lines.

"Who are you?" Alex demanded.

"Chambers," she said timidly. "Madeline. Formerly the Deputy Director of the CDC." The others were silent, all staring at the floor. A few looked up every now and then but quickly turned away when he or one of the other soldiers made eye contact.

"The only thing I want to hear from you," Alex said. "Is what kind of idiot you think I am." He was angry, partly at her, but mostly at himself. She looked so pleasant, so normal, so human, that he didn't want to see her shot. But she was a monster, a destroyer of worlds on a scale Oppenheimer never imagined. She had to die. They all did.

"I don't understand."

"You expect me to believe that you didn't do this? That you didn't engineer those…those *things*…and use them to wipe out most of humanity? We have the evidence. We hacked your servers, we know all about it."

She seemed to deflate, but then her body tensed and relaxed, and she returned his gaze, suddenly resolved.

"Then you know," she said. "That Fonseca made them. They were supposed to be a waste disposal system."

"Yes," he said. "That's in your data."

She nodded. "Do you also know that they lost control of them? That they started showing up outside of containment?"

Alex nodded, though there were few details about that part of it in the servers.

"Hang on," he said, then turned to Bill. "Can you get Tom on video conference? Like a laptop or something? He's the one who read their files, he should be here to shoot down whatever bullshit excuses she tries to feed me."

"On it," Campbell said and left the room.

"You just shut the fuck up until he gets back," Alex told Chambers. She nodded and wiped at her eyes.

Bill returned in a few minutes carrying a laptop with Tom's grinning face on the screen.

"Chief!" Tom said. "You did it!"

"It's not done yet, Tom. Did Campbell tell you why I want you here?"

"Yep. I'm ready to listen."

"May I speak now?" Chambers asked.

"Go ahead," Alex said as Campbell set the laptop down on a nearby table with the camera pointing at Alex and the woman.

"You have to understand," Chambers began. "They were supposed to be an industrial waste disposal system. The need for such a system was more immediate than most people ever knew. Our oceans were choking, we were drowning in waste. Fonseca offered us salvation. They tested them for years in containment, and they worked perfectly. No one knows how they got out. No one knows what went wrong. It could have been a mutation, sabotage or just bad design. But they were out there, and they spread."

"How did they spread?" Tom said. Alex could see him working the laptop's keyboard and touchpad, probably looking for the data on selective breeding and network theory that he had mentioned earlier. He was giving Chambers enough rope to hang herself, which was just fine by Alex. He wanted there to be no doubt when he gave Takahashi the go ahead.

Chambers frowned, and tears began to roll down her cheeks. "Please, you have to understand. We had no choice! You have to let me explain!"

Alex narrowed his eyes. "You will be allowed to speak. Take your time."

She nodded, swiping at her eyes and dripping nose. "They were spreading everywhere, slowly. Starting in the Midwest and working their way out. By the time Fonseca realized that they couldn't handle it and called in the CDC, they were making their way into Canada and Mexico, and there were incursions into Europe, China, the Middle East, everywhere."

"Was this before or after you people stepped in and helped them spread even faster?" Alex demanded.

"Before," she said. "Of course we tried to find a way to eradicate them, but it was impossible. We can't eradicate lice and these things are a fraction of the size. We couldn't even figure out a way to detect them."

"There was no way to detect them? And you were about to approve them for commercial use? Are you fucking insane?"

"They weren't supposed to breed outside of a specific environment! There were all manner of safeguards, but they—"

"Well obviously not fucking enough!"

"It wasn't my job to approve them, or not to. I'm just telling you what I know."

"Great," Alex hissed. "Pass the buck." He knew he was berating her, and that he should stop and let her talk before he broke her resolve, but he couldn't help himself.

She looked like she was about to speak, but faltered under his glare. "I can't!" She began to sob, covering her face with her hands. Too late. The damage was done.

A man coughed and stepped forward. "May I?"

"Go ahead," Alex said.

The man, short and plump with thinning white hair, said, "Andrew Hughes, Deputy Secretary of State. Former, that is." He had narrow eyes that moved a lot, back and forth. Alex didn't like his face.

"I don't give a shit who you are," he said. "Just explain what she wants you to explain." He was angry, and getting angrier by the second. Knowing that he was mostly angry at himself made it worse. Was he doing the right thing, letting them try to weasel their way out of it? If so, he knew he was going about it poorly. He had to get his emotions under control.

"Of course..." Hughes hesitated, as though unsure where to start. "After they got out, they spread by..."

"I know how they spread. I also know you helped spread them."

Hughes nodded. "Yes, we did. We also had Fonseca create a version that targeted human DNA."

Alex blinked. "You...you're just going to admit that?"

Hughes nodded. "There is no sense in denying it. We did what we had to do. And if you didn't know most of it, you wouldn't be here."

"Alex," Takahashi growled. "I've heard enough."

"No," Alex said. "Let him finish." His curiosity was eclipsing his anger. Why would he just admit that? Didn't he realize he was sealing his fate?

"They were spreading everywhere. They were triggered randomly. They would be all over a building and just sit there, eating, shitting, reproducing. Then a few would trigger, and that triggered all the ones near them. Within range, that is. They were networked, you see. A simple biological implementation of a digital technology, but effective enough. We had building collapses, bridge collapses and worse. We did our best to keep as much of it out of the news as possible. Towards the end we had the military occupying entire towns and keeping them under martial law. Stuff still leaked out on social media, but people dismissed it as the usual conspiracy theory nonsense. Jade Helm and such. The more of them there were in an area, the more densely packed they were, the more the trigger effect would spread. Once they reached sufficient density, then a single triggering event would set off all of them, across the entire world. Or at least a continent. And then it wouldn't take long before the others were triggered."

"Why help them spread? Why build ones that target humans?"

Hughes looked at Alex. No, he *glared* at him. "Because we had to! Can you imagine, son, what would happen if one day, all of our buildings, all of our infrastructure, all of our technology, just disappeared? Down to the last screwdriver? Seven billion people just standing around, no way to feed themselves, nowhere to take shelter? No tools, no technology, nothing!"

Alex couldn't believe what he had heard. He took a step toward Hughes, fists clenched. "You…you thought life would be too hard so your answer was to fucking kill everyone?" He wanted to reach for his rifle. Takahashi could have the rest, but this bastard was his.

"No," Hughes said, looking at Alex with an expression that was almost pitying. "Of course not, son. We tried everything we knew how, and some things we didn't. We came up with the disruption field, the one we ended up using in the barriers. We started sweeping vast areas of the country with it. It worked, to a degree, but not enough. Power was the issue. A small area, a few thousand feet, no problem. More than that and the field was too weak to be effective. Either way, we'd miss a spot. And they'd come back. We tried it for months, tried increasing the power. We even developed fusion power to make it happen. " He smiled wistfully. "Too little too late. It's amazing what you can achieve though, when you're trying to save the world. But it wasn't enough, and we all have to live with that." He swallowed, then hastily added, "For as long as you let us."

Alex stared at him, unsure of what to say. Hughes had preempted his question about using the barrier technology. "I still don't understand how you could have allowed Fonseca to develop a self replicating organism capable of wiping out human civilization."

"Fonseca was a mega corp, son. Nobody *let* them do anything. They did most of their early work overseas. By the time they had enough invested in these things, they had an army of PR people and lawyers convincing every congressman and senator that the WasteAway system would solve all of our problems and was completely safe. And to their credit, they put in a lot of work to make it safe. I'm not gonna bore you with the details unless you want me to, but they had a lot of safeguards built in. What happened…it wasn't supposed to be able to happen. Every contingency was planned for. But…it just happened. Like any fuckup. No one saw it coming. And we never did figure out how. Suffice it to say that the transports that…that ended up…out there…they were not like the ones that Fonseca initially produced." He was faltering, finding it hard to speak, which Alex found surprising. The man had been so sure of himself.

"Mutations?" Tom asked.

Hughes shrugged. "I suppose. As I said, no one was able to figure it out in time. There were people who warned us that this could happen, but come on. Destroy the world? It sounded crazy at the time. Then it started happening."

"Okay," Alex said. "I get it. But for fuck's sake, you tried one thing then said, 'Oh well, that didn't work, let's kill everyone instead'?"

"No, son, of course not. We tried a lot of things. Fonseca tried to engineer a predator species to wipe them out, but there wasn't time. We tried to develop counter measures, same problem."

"The barrier," Alex said. "You could have created safe zones. Places with supplies, places people could hide until it was over."

"We did," Hughes said. "Your facilities."

That stung. A lot more than Alex was prepared to deal with. These people had saved them all at the expense of the rest of humanity, and so he, Alex, and the others, shared in their guilt.

"No, bigger, with room for more people."

"You mean, without killing everyone on the outside," Hughes said.

Alex showed his teeth. "Yes. That would have been nice."

Hughes nodded. "We thought of that. We did the math. We didn't have the time to put away enough to save even a tiny fraction of the population. Can you imagine the entire population of Hawaii showing up, naked and starving, outside of your facility?"

Alex opened his mouth, ready to make an angry retort, but closed it. "No."

"We're not talking about our technology no longer working," Hughes said. "We're talking about it disappearing. These people, these seven billion, wouldn't have so much as a nail or a hammer. No roofs over their heads. Do you understand that? They would be naked, out in the cold or heat, with nothing. *Nothing*! And if they tried to build anything, it would be destroyed all over again. Because if we didn't trigger all of those things at once, if we didn't spread them out to every corner of the world, every nook and cranny, then some wouldn't trigger. And they would reproduce. Can you imagine what that would be like?"

Alex held up a hand to silence him as he tried to picture it, to process the possibilities. It was mind boggling.

"I can't imagine it," he said finally. "I don't want to."

Hughes nodded. "Most of those people, seven billion, would die horribly. Starvation, cannibalism, exposure. Our experts told us there was a fifty-fifty chance humanity would not survive the event. At all. Not a single person. Our tools, our greatest strength, would have been taken from us had we not acted. Not temporarily, but forever."

"You don't know that," Alex said, realizing that he was repeating himself. "You could have given them a chance. Given us…" He stopped. He knew what Hughes would say next.

"We did, son. We gave *you* a chance! We built the facilities. We worked around the clock, as quickly as we could. Did as much as we could. Yes, we saved our own asses too! We did that! But we also saved as many regular folks as we could. We saved *you*! You're not politicians, you're not rich, you're just regular people. The best and the brightest, people of all races, all over the world. Our best hope for the future. What chance would you have had if all those people were still around? They would have stormed your facility and ripped you to pieces! Mobs of millions."

Alex took a step back as it all sunk in. "But..spreading them…you don't get to play God!"

"Someone had to," Chambers muttered. "The real one was a no show."

"They reproduce, son," Hughes explained. "As long as a few are left, they'll make more. Always. I already told you, there was only one way to get rid of them, and that was to make sure they got everywhere. *Everywhere*. Had to be. Not a single spot left uncovered. And then set them all off at once."

Takahashi took a step forward.

"Yes, we set them off!" Hughes shouted, a little spittle flying from his mouth. "What if we hadn't? They'd spread on their own, and eventually trigger. Maybe a few days later, maybe a week, maybe even a month, tops. But before then? What? What would China do if the western world disappeared and all that was left behind were a few settlements? What about Syria or Iran? All we did was make sure they went off at the same time, everywhere. All we changed was when, not what! We had to make sure that our plan worked. That the New Tomorrow facilities wouldn't be attacked! We didn't kill anyone who wasn't going to die within a day or a week anyway! And we did them a favor! Can you imagine how they would have died if we hadn't?"

Alex looked at Tom though the laptop screen. Could what they were saying actually be true?

"You killed my daughter!" Takahashi growled. "My little girl."

Hughes looked at him and his gaze almost dropped, but he held it. He spoke softly. "And if we hadn't? What would have happened to her? She felt no pain, son. Nothing more than a headache, and maybe not even that. She just went to sleep. And then, she was in heaven. And I'm sorry, so sorry, that we had to make that decision. But would you have wanted us to make a different one?"

Takahashi's body trembled, but he said nothing. Alex knew what he was thinking. What if they hadn't killed her? And in that moment, he couldn't deny the reality. If she survived the building collapse, her death would have been brutal and agonizing. These people, they had spared her that fate. And they had spared Takahashi from having to imagine his little girl calling out for her chichi as she suffered and died.

Hughes kept talking. "We had to move fast, to build the Seed colonies. Once we accepted that we couldn't stop these things, we had to ensure the survival of our species. Of humanity. This was the only thing we could do, and nothing, nothing in the history of human civilization, has ever been more important. Do you understand that? We had to save the human race."

Alex nodded.

"We barely managed to do it in time. Even as we rushed to populate the colonies, we started to get headaches, and not all of us made it." He shuddered, looking away. "They were inside our heads, eating our brains. The things we made to save us!"

"Headaches…" Alex said, remembering.

"We both had them," Campbell said. "That night in the hospital."

"Are there any left?" Alex asked. "Are they all gone?"

Hughes slumped and the fight went out of him. "There

shouldn't be. What we did…spread them, fire them all off…that should have taken care of them. We are constantly broadcasting the activation signal, even now. But we can't be sure. We can never be sure. As long as you maintain the barriers, they shouldn't pose a threat. It takes them a long time to build to sufficient quantities to kill a human being, even the ones we bred. But you have to stay in the colonies, indefinitely, or at least until we know they are all gone. You can venture out for days, maybe weeks, but you have to return, always. And if the fusion generators fail and we can't fix them…"

"Indefinitely?" Alex asked. "As in forever?"

"Not forever. But for now. For a long time. Until we're sure. This must never happen again." He paused, looked at Alex, then at Takahashi, and finally at Tom on the little laptop screen. "We did what we could. Believe me, if we could have done more, we would have. We knew some peoples' body chemistry was resistant, and we tried to replicate it, thinking we could spread it all over like a vaccine, but all our attempts failed. It wouldn't have been enough anyway, not nearly."

"Yeah," Tom said. "I did read that in your files, though at the time I thought you were trying to overcome the resistance. In retrospect, I can see where I read into your data."

"So all of this," Alex said, turning to Tom. "The whole world, all of human civilization, gone, destroyed, because some fucking biotech company played around with nanotechnology?" It was unbelievable. The worst disaster in human history—no, in the history of world, akin to the Permian extinction—decided in a board room by old rich bastards looking to make a fast buck.

Chambers, who had stopped sobbing, nodded. "Terrifying."

"Terrifying doesn't even begin to cover it, lady," Tom said. "That little invention killed seven billion people."

"What about the rest of the world?" Alex demanded. "Other countries? Did you tell them?"

Hughes nodded. "We told our allies. We told the Russians. A few others."

"A few?"

"We couldn't take the chance," Hughes said. "We told whoever we could trust to cooperate with our plans. We acted on our own in some countries, to save as many as we could. Do you understand that? We did what we could!"

"I understand," Alex admitted. It was a difficult admission, but it was true.

"Hold on," Campbell said. "Are you guys buying this? "

"I don't know," Alex admitted. "But even if I do, that doesn't change the fact that these people spread the transports to places where there weren't any."

"No, they were everywhere, just not in sufficient—"

"I know," Alex said. "I heard you the first time. I understand what you did. And we're going to verify it, but for now let's say I believe you. You did what was necessary. I get that. But you still killed billions of people, and you can't just walk away from that."

"But if we hadn't then all of us would be—"

"Enough," Alex said, cutting him off. "You've said your piece, now shut the hell up."

Hughes turned away, his eyes dancing faster than ever. Beads of sweat rolled down his forehead, which had turned bright red.

"So what do we do with them?" Campbell asked.

"Kill them," Takahashi said. "I don't give a damn if they made these things or not. They killed my little girl!"

"No!" Chambers said. "We—"

Takahashi stepped forward and punched her in the face before Alex could stop him. Red mist exploded from her nose as she collapsed, screaming, clutching her face with both hands as thick blood oozed from between her fingers.

"Don't you speak to me, murdering bitch!" Takahashi roared as he raised his weapon. Alex put his hand on the muzzle and forced it down.

"There's been enough killing," he said.

"I agree," Campbell said. "But we can't just let them get away with it. What do we do with them?"

"Alex," Takahashi said. "We have to kill them."

"We should," Alex said, and Chambers whimpered. He looked down at her, sitting on her knees, holding her shattered nose, and felt a nausea almost as bad as that of the barrier. So much death.

"But I can't do it," he said. "There are so few of us left. We have to verify their story, make sure it's true."

"And then?" Campbell asked.

"Spread them out through the colonies," Alex said. "No more than one family per Seed. Make them work, like the rest of us." He turned to Takahashi. "That's not justice, I know. But it's all I can do. Bill, you're the colonel, if you want to do something else…"

"No, I'm with you on this. There's been enough killing."

"Good, let's get it done."

Takahashi hesitated, as though he would start shooting anyway, but Alex knew that he wouldn't. In the end, Takahashi was a soldier, and soldiers followed orders.

Campbell gave instructions to some of his men, who began escorting the former leaders of the world to their holding cells while he and Alex went to look for Terkeurst.

"If they, um," Campbell said. "If they're still out there, what can we do? Those generators won't last forever."

"I don't know," Alex said. "But what can we do about it? Besides just go on with our lives?"

Campbell nodded, and said nothing. His eyes were moist.

They found Major Terkeurst sitting against the wall, sobbing. He looked up at Alex.

"I brought you here as an executioner," he said. "But you were my conscience. I almost lost it in there. I almost killed children."

"All things considered," Alex said. "I can't blame you too much. And wait until you hear the load they just dropped on us. This is your op, so you— "

"No," he said. "I'm done. I don't want to be in command anymore, I just want to go back to 043-A and never see this place again. Captain Meyer, I'm leaving you in charge. Of this facility, of everything."

"No way," Alex said quickly. "I'm going home. There's a girl there waiting for me, and I mean to make it back to her."

"Who then?" the major asked. "There is a government to run here, Meyer. There are factories that need overseeing, hundreds of colonies that need support, someone has to do it."

Alex turned to Campbell. "How about you, Bill?"

Campbell was taken aback. "Me?"

"Can you trust him?" Terkeurst asked.

"He's a good man," Alex said. "I can't think of anyone I

would trust more."

"I'm honored," Campbell said. "I don't know if I'm up to it, but I'll do the best I can. If there's anything you need, either of you, you just let me know."

"I just want to go home," Alex said. "To 103-B." He turned to Terkeurst. "Major, if I may take my leave."

Terkeurst nodded without looking at him, once again lost in his own world. Alex didn't think he had survived the operation. He wasn't sure if he himself had either.

"Come with me," Campbell said, and Alex followed him down the corridor, trying to make sense of things as he walked. In a way, he had gotten what he needed, but it wasn't enough, and he needed to crawl into his hole and lick his wounds. As Alex had hoped, it turned out that he had done the right thing. The enemy, once they were given all of the information, had become allies. But there were doubts. The people they had just interrogated, if they had told the truth, then they had done what they thought was the right thing also. It was incomprehensible, evil, terrifying, yes. But wouldn't Alex have done more or less the same thing in their place? And didn't that mean that all the people they had killed in this facility were in fact innocents? Innocents butchered to sort out a misunderstanding?

"Bill?" Alex said. "Do you think that…I mean…could we have worked this out without attacking? Could we have gotten you the data somehow? Reasoned with your leaders?"

Campbell shook his head. "I know where you're going with this, Alex. Don't. Just don't. Sure, if you knew everything you know now, you could have done things differently. But that's not how the world works, and you know it, so cut that shit out. You did the best with what you had, the only thing you could do. The same thing I would have done."

Alex looked down at the ground. "Yeah I guess." He wasn't convinced.

Campbell put a hand on his shoulder. "Don't, Alex. These people that were just groveling before you, spilling their guts, acting all humble…they only did that because you were holding guns to their heads. Do you think for one second they would have stepped down off of their pedestals to speak to you as one human being to another under any other circumstance?"

Alex thought about it. "No, I guess not."

Campbell nodded. "You people killed some of my friends, Alex. Some of my brothers."

Alex's eyes widened. "Bill, I'm sorry…I…"

"Do you remember how we used to say that we were the bad guys? How we were fighting for oil and invading sovereign countries for bullshit reasons, killing their people, and, you know…all that other shit?"

"Yeah, and you used to tell me to suck it up because we were soldiers and soldiers follow orders, that it wasn't for us to figure out why."

"That's right," Campbell said. "We were on opposite sides of this. Not because we wanted to be, but because that's where our orders put us. This time, you were the good guys, and we were the bad guys. And once I realized that, once you helped me see that, we were able to make it right. People died. People I loved. People I may one day come to hate you for killing." He saw the look in Alex's face and put up a hand. "But I'm going to tell you right now, and you better fucking listen and you'd better fucking remember. You did the right thing. And you can take that to the grave. If twenty years from now, I'm a fat old drunk who says different, I give you permission to punch me in the face. Okay?"

Alex nodded. "Thank you Bill."

"Now how can I help you get home?"

"I need to get to my boat, it's not that far from here. Can you get somebody to give me a lift?"

"I have a better idea," Campbell said, suddenly smiling. "You're airborne qualified, aren't you?"

Chapter 37

The C-5 Galaxy transport plane came in low over the ocean, startling the colonists of NTF103-B. They scrambled outside, looking up into the sky in amazement. It was a gargantuan aircraft, with a wingspan of two hundred and twenty two feet and a cargo capacity of nearly five hundred thousand pounds.

As it passed over the colony it banked and began to turn, its massive cargo doors opening slowly. On its second pass, it dropped twelve large containers that landed on or near the beach, their descent slowed by oversized parachutes.

The colonists milled about in confusion, looking up and pointing. The plane came around yet again, this time higher.

Alex looked over his shoulder and shouted, "You guys better not break that thing!"

"We won't sir," the airman replied with a casual smile. "We're good at this."

He nodded, satisfied, then ran down the cargo ramp and out the back of the airplane. He'd never done a jump where he had to deploy his own chute, but there was a first time for everything.

His mortal fear of heights made it all the more exciting as he stepped past the edge of the ramp and the wind grabbed him and tossed him into the plane's exhaust stream where he tumbled about like a handkerchief thrown from a speeding car. As soon as he was free of the aircraft's wake and falling steadily, he pulled the cord.

The parachute unfolded and yanked him violently as it grabbed the air and slowed his descent. From this high up the beach looked impossibly small, a tiny strip of beige between a blanket of green and the vast stretch of dark blue ocean, coming up fast. He managed to guide the parachute over the sand where a small crowd had formed, barely saving himself from the embarrassment of an ocean dunking. As he touched down, he saw Tom and Barbara, and behind them Patrick, Ryan and Sandi. They were staring at him, eyes alight with wonder.

Unclipping himself from the chute, he scanned the crowd desperately, looking for Yael.

"Alex!"

He spun towards the sound of her voice, and saw her rushing towards him in a blur of motion, the little dog keeping pace at her feet.

"Yael!"

They collided with such force that she almost knocked him over. Managing to keep his balance, he scooped her up in his arms and, oblivious to onlookers, lifted her off her feet, kissing her with a desperate ferocity born of the loneliness of their long separation.

"Alex!" she cried, her face wet with tears of joy. "I can't believe you came back!"

He wanted to speak, but couldn't find the words. Holding her tightly, he rocked back and forth, overcome with emotion. The little dog yipped and ran in circles around them.

"Give the Chief a minute," he heard Tom say. "There'll be plenty of time to say hi."

"I prayed every day," Yael said, still weeping. "I hope that doesn't piss you off." She managed a smile.

"Not since it worked!" he said.

"Ever the pragmatist." She smiled at him as she ran her hand through his hair.

He kissed her again, then, still holding her, turned to the others.

"Tom," he said. "I don't know where to begin. You saved my life, man. Shit, you probably saved the world, or at least what's left of it."

Tom grinned sheepishly. "Cut it out Chief, you're embarrassing me."

Alex walked up to him, and hugged him. Then Barbara, and the others. Turning back to Yael, he took her hand and pulled her close.

"What's in the crates?" Sandi asked.

"Ah," Alex said. "Almost forgot. Food, mostly, and other supplies too. Frozen steaks, cakes, that sort of thing. One of the boxes is a big refrigerator...we can plug it right into the generator. Oh, and those big ones have a few thousand gallons of diesel and gasoline in flexible bladders. This isn't it, either. We'll be getting regular deliveries."

"Sweet!" Barbara said. "We can use the boat again! But what's the diesel for?"

"You'll see."

"The plane's coming back," Ryan said, pointing at the sky. It was approaching from the west, flying extremely low and parallel to the strip of beach beyond the barrier.

"Is the barrier still down?" Alex asked Tom.

"Sure is, Chief. We only keep it on at night now."

"What's it doing?" Yael asked, looking up at the massive aircraft with wonder.

"It's dropping something off for me," Alex explained. "It's a long story, but a buddy of mine is in charge now."

"In charge of what?" Barbara asked.

Alex shrugged. "Everything, I guess. The government, the military. He wants me to be a senator or something, told him I'd think about it. Anyway, this buddy said I could have anything I wanted, so I asked for that." He pointed at the plane. "There wasn't much else to choose from."

The C-5 rumbled almost overhead, stirring up a huge cloud of sand as it passed over the beach beyond the barrier. It ejected a massive object from its open cargo doors, followed by two smaller ones. The big one, trailing a parachute to slow it down, fell onto the sand and slid to a stop as the plane rose into the air and banked towards the ocean, heading back to the mainland.

"What the hell is that thing?" Tom asked.

"It's our M3 Bradley fighting vehicle," Alex said, grinning. "And two crates of cannon ammo and missiles."

"A what?" Yael asked, shaking her head. "Is that what I think it is?"

"Yep," Alex said. "Armored personnel carrier. It's like a light tank with room to transport soldiers. We're going to kick ass and take names!"

"We're on an island!" she said. "There's no one else here!"

Alex shrugged. "So what? They're fun. You'll see." He turned to the others. "It's really great to see you guys again, but could you give Yael and I a minute or two alone?"

Barbara smiled. "I think you'll need more than a minute."

"Okay, guys," Tom said. "Let's give the Chief some space. We need to secure those supplies before the vultures pick them clean." The two of them herded the others towards the crates while Alex led Yael away from the beach.

"He offered you anything you wanted," she said, shaking her head. "And you took an armored personnel carrier?"

"Well I wanted an Abrams tank, but they couldn't air drop one of those."

"You're incorrigible! What am I going to do with you?"

"I can think of a few things." His smile left him as he considered what he had learned at the compound. Tom had gone over the data on the servers very carefully, and everything Chambers and Hughes had told them clicked into place. Hours of intense questioning had revealed no holes in their story. It was just so utterly and incomprehensibly stupid. A fancy trash disposal system had all but wiped out human civilization. Was it lack of testing? Had they rushed to production to meet a deadline set by greedy shareholders? Was there a single decision made in a board room that set the world upon a doomed course? These questions could drive him mad, if he let them.

"Besides," he said, his smile returning. "He couldn't give me what I really wanted, so I settled for the Bradley."

"What did you really want?"

"You, dumbass. The only thing I really want is you."

"I love you, Alex," she said, reaching out to put a hand on his cheek. "And I've missed you so much." Her moist eyes sparkled in the bright Hawaiian sun.

"I'm really sorry," he said. "I should never have left you. It was a mistake." There would be a price to pay for the things that he had done, that was a certainty. But he had Yael's love, and Campbell's forgiveness, and that would have to be enough.

"The only thing I care about is that you're back now," she said, then turned away, her lips pressed together tightly. "What's going to happen to us? This place?"

"Whatever we want," he said, and he believed it. "Our lives are our own now." Maybe they would be prisoners in the colony for the rest of their lives, hiding behind the barrier from a world that would forever seek to destroy them. Or maybe the Fonseca

WasteAway ED REV 3 Transports were all gone, having simultaneously released their unprecedented destructive power and paid for it with extinction. It didn't matter. Whatever their circumstances, they would make the most of them, and they would do so in a manner of their choosing. Gone was the old world, gone were its rules and its limitations. This was their world now.

The early morning sunlight lay a warm hand on his forehead as he squinted against its brightness. A flock of small green birds took to the air at their approach, their flight shaking the branches of a nearby tree. He watched them disappear into the forest canopy.

He turned to Yael, who smiled up at him. He was home, with the woman he loved and the best friends he'd ever had. He wondered once again if he would give them up to get it all back. The world, the people.

He looked into her eyes, and she into his. He didn't want to answer, not when he thought of his parents or the small infant jumpsuits, blue ducks on yellow, drifting amongst the wreckage of Honolulu. But he was glad he didn't have to.

Author's Note

Thank you for reading! If you enjoyed this book, please consider leaving a review on Amazon, Goodreads and/or your various social media accounts. Independent authors need reviews and word of mouth in order to succeed. If you have any questions or want to leave a comment, look for Michael Edelson on facebook, or find the link to my facebook page on my website:

www.michaeledelson.net

If you want more but are disappointed that there isn't a sequel, check out one of my other books. Though varied in plot and genre, they will feel very familiar. If you liked this book, I'm confident that you'll like the rest as well.

My other titles include:

All are available at Amazon.com and other online retailers.

Audiobook versions are available at Audible.com, Amazon and iTunes.

About the Author

Michael lives in upstate New York with his wife, two kids and too many pets. He is a firefighter with the Andes Fire Department, teaches historical fencing and, when he has the time, writes books.

www.michaeledelson.net

Made in the USA
Middletown, DE
02 September 2019